Praise for *Jesse's Hideout*

Oh my gosh, I loved, loved, loved this heartwarming romance… The spell woven by Jesse's Hideout is enthralling and comforting. The byplay between Jesse and Amelia was fascinating. Kallypso Masters has given us a wonderful view into small slice of rural Kentucky and its history. Made me want to take a road trip. The recipe section at the end was such a bonus.

~ Melanie M., Amazon reviewer

~ ~ ~

Having grown up in Kentucky and loving the Bluegrass state, I must admit to homesickness after reading this book. Tillie took me back home with her history lessons and folklore. Kentuckians are bound in tradition and Tillie shared her love for Southern food, hospitality and customs. She introduced whimsy to Greg and lightened his heart. I am new to this author but love Southern stories with quirky characters. The addition of a supernatural element gave a delightful aspect. It is such fun to think of matchmaking from beyond the grave. I look forward to the next installment of this series.

~ Rebecca G., Goodreads reviewer

~ ~ ~

Once I started this story I couldn't put it down. I was intrigued from page one to the very end.

~ Karen H., Goodreads reviewer

~ ~ ~

I always enjoyed reading all of Kallypso Masters books. But I think this series will be one of my favorites. I enjoyed reading the history that was included in the story line. I can't wait until the next boom comes out.

~ Bunny, Amazon reviewer

~ ~ ~

Fantastic! Romance, excitement, suspense what more could you ask for. This story about two people who were made for each other with help from some friends from the other side is exactly what I needed. Kallypso is a fantastic author and has a flare for history and making you hungry while you read. This book is truly enjoyable and I would recommend to all my friends and have.

~ Anonymous Amazon reviewer

Books by Kallypso Masters

Bluegrass Spirits

(Contemporary Romance…with a Haunting Twist)

Jesse's Hideout

Kate's Secret

Rescue Me Saga (Erotic Romance)

Kally has no intention of ending the *Rescue Me Saga* ever, but will introducing some new series with new worlds and characters when these characters aren't talking to her. The following *Rescue Me Saga* titles are currently available in e-book and print formats:

Masters at Arms & Nobody's Angel (Combined Volume)

Nobody's Hero

Nobody's Perfect

Somebody's Angel

Nobody's Lost

Nobody's Dream

Rescue Me Saga Extras (Erotic Romance)

This will be a series of hot, fun, short-story collections featuring beloved couples from the *Rescue Me Saga*.

Western Dreams (Rescue Me Saga Extras #1)

(New scenes with Megan & Ryder and Cassie & Luke)

Roar (a *Rescue Me Saga* Erotic Romance Spin-off)

(Erotic Romance with Secondary Characters from the *Rescue Me Saga*. *Roar* provides a lead into the trilogy with Patrick, Grant, and Gunnar's stories.)

kallypsomasters.com/books

Tricia,

Find *your* treasure!

Thanks for stopping by at the Bardstown Fair!

Jesse's Hideout

Kallypso Masters

Kallypso Masters

Ka-thunk! Publishing

Jesse's Hideout
Kallypso Masters

Ka-thunk! Publishing
Print Edition
E-book ISBN: 978-1941060278
Paperback ISBN: 978-1941060285
Original e-book version: March 28, 2017
Original print version: March 28, 2017
Last revised for e-book and print: June 11, 2017

Developmental Edits by Meredith Bowery and Dana Delamar
Content Edits by Ekatarina Sayanova
Line Edits by Jacy Mackin
Proofread by Laura Combs, Annette Elens, Barb Jack, Angelique Luzader, Eva Meyers, and Christine Sullivan Mulcair
Cover design by Linda Kuhlmann of Two Trees Studio
Cover photos—Couple photo by Dreamstime; House photo by Kallypso Masters
Cover photos graphically altered by Linda Kuhlmann
Formatted by BB eBooks

To discover more about this book and others, see the *Other Books By Kallypso Masters* section at the end of this book. For more about Kallypso Masters, please go to the About the Author section.

Dedication

To my second oldest sister, known to my readers as Mary 2. You've inspired me to embrace life to the fullest and to never give up. And I firmly believe that we will never be parted, even when we aren't on the same soul plane. Just as the ethereal characters in this book come back to guide and watch over those they love, I know we will *always* be a huge part of each other's lives.

To my dad, Joseph, who inspired me to tell Jesse James' story—albeit from a fictional perspective—in his hometown of Samuels, Kentucky. All the times we drove past that beautiful Federal-style house and you said "Jesse James used to hide out there" sparked my creative juices, and here, at last, is the fruition of those flights of fancy! You've also shown me that our loved ones never leave us, even when separated by the veil between Heaven and Earth.

Acknowledgements

Bringing my ninth novel and tenth published book, ***Jesse's Hideout***, to you has ignited a passion for writing and story telling in me that has had the words pouring out again. I couldn't have done so without the help of those I consulted with for expertise or inspiration. I want to acknowledge them here.

Fellow author, **Kennedy Layne**, is largely responsible for getting me to envision myself writing something other than my signature series, the Rescue Me Saga. While I'll never stop writing those books and rescuing those characters, during a visit with Kennedy in late October, she saw that I needed a change to rekindle my passion. I'll explain more about why I chose this as my first departure series in my Author's Note. It wasn't the series I first told her about. However, I'll get to that one eventually, too. But the way the words poured out once I shifted to writing this book that has been in my head since the early 1990s made it clear that I really did need something different and to flex my writing muscles with a new genre—Contemporary Romance (Mainstream Romance). I owe her a debt of gratitude for the much-needed intervention and for helping me rediscover this story. And to her lovely mom, known as "**Gram**" to all, a huge thanks for spoiling Charlotte Oliver and me during our two visits late last year. She even inspired me to have Greg call his grandmother "Gram"!

Kelly and Elmer, the owners of the house on the cover, shared the real house with me on a private tour in December, pointing out architectural details and telling ghost stories from their encounters there. While I fictionalized their house when I turned it into Jesse's Hideout B&B, the stories Elmer and Kelly told helped make the house come to life in the pages of this book. (Please respect their privacy and do NOT go looking for the real house or bothering anyone who lives there, because it's a private residence and I don't want them to regret opening their home and hearts to me while writing this book.) More about why this house in the Author's Note.

I always enjoy asking readers in my three Facebook discussion groups to help me with my research and story questions. Before I started a group for this new series, I asked **The Rescue Me Saga Discussion Group** what would be the perfect secret ingredient Mrs. Foster (aka Gram/Amelia) would have used in her oatmeal-raisin cookies that made it impossible for Tillie to replicate the recipe until the card surfaced. The winner was **Kerri Trayah**. I'll let readers discover for themselves what that secret ingredient was when you read the story. But don't miss the special Recipes section in this book for all the details on the dishes Tillie makes in the pages of this book.

Then in my new **Bluegrass Spirits (Kallypso Masters Series)** Facebook group, I requested help with character surnames and **Vanessa Cedillos** suggested Hamilton. My fourth-great-grandmother was Mary Hamilton. Perfect! My third-great-grandmother was Margaret Foster, another name I used in the book.

Readers in that group also gave me suggestions for a gift Greg might give Tillie, and I chose the ideas that **Judith Hill** and **Billie Faris Helms** shared, plus one e-mailed to me from **Kelly**, the owner of the house in Samuels. I'll let you learn more about the specifics inside the book! And an honorable mention goes to **Maria Palma**. Her specific examples weren't the same as what I wrote, but she and Kelly were thinking along the same lines!

The Bluegrass Spirits group also came to my rescue in identifying the style of bed in Tillie's room as a combination spindle and pencil bed. **Connie Shingleton Miconi** was the first to suggest pencil post bed. And **Carol Capper** identified the spindle headboard. Then **Lisa Simo-Kinzer**'s theater-set friends pinpointed the probable time period as post Civil War and that it is a unique style of its own.

Thanks also to **Charlie D.**, who helped me find the perfect bicycle for Greg to replace the one destroyed in his pre-story accident. Charlie is a serious cyclist and took into consideration issues like snow and rain that Greg would have to deal with in Minnesota.

My deepest gratitude to **Meredith Bowery**, who not only had first crack at developmental edits on this book and who kept me straight as far as continuity and character development throughout, but she came back when I had some doubts in the ending and tweaked some more story issues to help me gain the confidence to know it was ready for my readers. She also is my go-to person whenever I need to find the perfect vehicle for the hero or heroine to drive. When I texted her for help on Greg's vehicle, I received an e-mail with questions about his height, build, occupation, whether he works mostly in the office or out in the field, and more. Then she went to work determining the perfect vehicle.

I brought in a new developmental editor this time, too—**Dana Delamar** of By Your Side Self-Publishing. Her feedback helped me to flesh out missing scenes and emotions before sending it on to the content editor, **Ekatarina Sayanova** of Red Quill Editing. Saya both confirmed what I'd nailed at that point and let me know what could still be improved. She also agreed to take it on at the last minute when I was in the midst of one of my anxiety attacks I seem to go through with every book. While she was a beta reader, **Barb Jack** caught numerous inconsistencies and asked questions that helped me straighten out the backstory about Jesse and Caroline, among others.

More thanks go out to my line editor, **Jacy Mackin** of Jacy's Red Ink Editing, who also did double duty by joining me on my private tour of the house that inspired this story. She took lots of photos that helped me remember details to add to the story later and to flesh it out even more. Her challenging me to get to the bottom of why Tillie was so upset with Greg in that one scene led to me dig a little further into Tillie's past and make the story even richer.

My new process in writing this book didn't involve the beta readers until I had a complete draft. **Margie Dees**, **Robin Henley**, **Barb Jack**, **Ruth Reid**, and **Lisa Simo-Kinzer** came in during the content-edit phase and gave me their honest opinions about what they thought of this book and the new series. They helped me uncover plot holes and fix unresolved character-development issues. Barb and Lisa came back again for yet another read-through before line edits to help me further nail down the story details and fill still more plot holes. And Barb was my angel of mercy yet again as she read through it one final time the night before it went to the formatter.

While I had fewer betas on this book than I usually have, I added a new one to provide local expertise. Robin made sure I was true-to-life in my characterization of Greg Buchanan, the story's hero, who hails from Minneapolis where she lives. While I was visiting the city last October, she took me on a tour of places that became part of this story (even though at the time, we were looking for back story on Adam Montague, the "patriarch" in my Rescue Me Saga series). She even took me out to see where Mary Richards had lived in the early years of the MTM show, and as a result, I chose to have Greg live in a similar Queen Anne-style Victorian along the Lake of the Isles. I guess I fell in love with Minneapolis long before I ever went there the first time in 2016, since I've now got two characters from there, probably thanks to my adoration of the late Mary Tyler Moore and her 1970s show that influenced my life so greatly, including inspiring me to pursue a writing career and journalism major (with a women's studies minor).

My awesome proofreaders—**Laura Combs**, **Annette Elens**, **Barb Jack**, **Angelique Luzader**, **Eva Meyers**, and **Christine Sullivan**

Mulcair—made sure the new typos I made at the last minute as well as any remaining inconsistencies or inaccuracies were corrected and wouldn't jar you from your enjoyment in reading this book. They also had some intriguing story questions that helped me iron out some confusion.

Of course, despite my amazing editorial, proofreading, and beta-reader teams, all errors left behind are solely mine to claim. If you see something you think needs correcting, never hesitate to let my assistant, Charlotte Oliver, know by e-mailing her at charlotte@kallypsomasters.com or messaging her on Facebook. She will share them with me, and if I agree it's a problem, I'll correct it in later versions.

This is the first book where I can identify my awesome cover artist by her full name—**Linda Kuhlmann**. She and I were colleagues in my last position before I quit to write full-time. She worked wonders with the couple in the leaves, making them closer to how I pictured my characters, and was able to make the house stand out as if on a sunny day rather than the way it looked in the gloomy-day photo I sent her from another stop I made there.

As always, I owe a debt of gratitude to **Paul Salvette**, who takes my Word files and makes them into beautiful e-books and print books for you. He adds touches I would never bother with (or know how to do), and I have never had any fear of formatting issues once I've placed a book in his capable hands.

Last, but never least, to my amazing personal and executive assistant **Charlotte Oliver**, who was there to take away much of the day-to-day stress of being a self-published author so that I can focus on the fun parts of this job—like writing and engaging with my readers and fellow authors.

Author's Note

Dear Reader, I'm so glad you have followed me or joined me with this new Bluegrass Spirits series. I've explained in my Dedication my belief that our loved ones communicate with us after they pass to the other side. This isn't *para*normal to me, but normal. I have played with matchmaking spirits before in my Rescue Me Saga (with Joni, for instance), but this will be the first time I've given the dearly departed their own point of view.

But as you read, be aware that the two worlds aren't necessarily on the same page. Amelia and Jesse know more about what's going on than Tillie and Greg do—and that sometimes carries through the entire story. But you, dear reader, will be in on everything as you experience what the hero and heroine do as well as what the spirits are up to. The disconnect between the two planes does not constitute errors—just the reality that we don't always know what's really going on. I believe that, once you pass over, you can see and know things you didn't while you were living and tried to show that happening in his book.

Now let me explain a little about how this particular story came about. As a kid, I often visited aunts, uncles, and cousins in Samuels, my dad's birthplace in Nelson County, Kentucky. Almost every time we drove by the house pictured on the cover of this book, he'd point to it and say, "Jesse James used to hide out there." Jesse's brother Frank James surrendered in 1866 very near this house (and we believe he probably was hiding out with Jesse when the authorities came for them—perhaps distracting them so his brother could make his escape).

My dad's words have been stuck in my head for fifty years. Actually, about twenty-five years ago, I penned another version of a story set in this house, including a cookie-baking grandmotherly spirit. However, I didn't keep most of the stories I wrote over the decades, so when I decided to begin a new series, this one came to mind almost immediately. But I started from scratch and think the story is so much richer this time around.

The book you hold in your hands (or on your e-reader) is my fictionalized tale involving many of the facts I discovered while researching what historians knew of Jesse's visits to this county and the house once owned by his stepfather's cousin, Dr. Samuels. Then I went off on a flight of fancy to play with a recurring legend that Jesse James didn't die in 1882 after all. I played the "what if" game and have him returning to this house half a century later.

Because this series is set in my home state of Kentucky, I included family names, favorite places, family recipes (at least in this book), and personal stories that are dear to my heart. Next in the series will be *Kate's Secret*, which will feature a totally new couple (Kate and Travis) in the setting of Midway, Kentucky (Woodford County). However, I've found a way for Tillie and Greg from *Jesse's Hideout* to cameo in Travis and Kate's book so you can see how they're doing after the epilogue.

Oh, please don't miss the special Recipes in the back of this book! Many of these are family favorites or Kentucky treats—like jam cake (probably not what you're picturing if you haven't had a Kentucky jam cake) and banana croquettes. While I don't intend to include recipes in every book in this series, Tillie practically lives in her kitchen, and whenever I needed to come up with a special dish for her to cook or bake, I realized I'd just have to include the recipes for you!

For timely updates, sneak peeks at unedited excerpts, and much more, sign up for my e-mails and/or text alerts!

kallypsomasters.com/newsletter

I hope you will enjoy this series as much as I'm enjoying writing it! Happy reading!

Prologue

"Are you sure this will work, Jesse?" For some idiotic reason, Amelia Foster tightened her grip on the red oak tree branch the two of them perched on. Even if either fell, they couldn't die again.

Well, make that a third time for the infamous outlaw seated beside her.

They were disembodied spirits, after all, stuck in this ethereal plane for far too long, hovering outside the gates of Heaven where both hoped someday to rejoin the greatest loves of their lives. Amelia was convinced the only way she would ever "slip the surly bonds of earth" and move on would be after her grandson and the girl Amelia loved like a granddaughter found happiness, preferably in one another's arms.

"This has to work." She tried to convince herself if no one else.

"Trust me," her accomplice in spirit assured her.

"Jesse Woodson James, I'm not so gullible as to fall for those words from the likes of you."

"Miss Amelia, darlin', I'm true as steel. Have I ever let you down?"

"Where shall I begin? How about the sixty-third running of the Kentucky Derby in 1937 when you stood up me and my no-good first husband?"

"Confound it, woman! How was I supposed to show up at an event like the Derby where dozens of people would have recognized me? As far as ever'body knew, by then I'd moldered in the grave nigh on half a century. Hell, if I'd stuck my face out in public, I'd have spent my remaining years in prison or been hanged outright as a bank robber. Maybe even a murderer."

Amelia asked the question she hadn't been comfortable enough to ask him in life. "*Did* you ever murder anyone, Jesse?"

"No court convicted me of nothing."

"That's not what I asked. Quit your evading the truth after all this time."

Jesse shrugged, dismissing her challenge. Instead, he focused his attention on the side yard of the brick Federal-style house from their vantage point in one of the trees Amelia and her second husband had planted just before World War II.

What did she expect? He'd been caught up in his own legend for more than a century.

Whether Jesse had murdered anyone was a moot point. Both of them had a personal stake in seeing this mission come to fruition if they ever wanted to set foot inside the Pearly Gates.

While Jesse wasn't likely to divulge any secrets to her at this stage in their relationship, her dearest friend, Caroline, *had* shared secrets about ol' Jesse that would send historians into a tailspin. No doubt those revelations were what kept Jesse earthbound, too. Guilt, perhaps?

Regardless, he'd agreed to help after she'd shown him the consequences of his actions. She might not like his methods—and had read him the riot act after what he'd done to her poor Gregory on his bicycle a few months ago—but perhaps the ends would justify the means. That so-called accident seemed to have been the wake-up call the boy needed. Besides, Gregory hadn't died.

Finally, after hovering between Heaven and Earth nigh on fifteen years, Amelia was the closest yet to achieving her dying wish. A little late, but she felt in her bones—well, she would if she still had any—that her grandson and Tillie Hamilton were destined to be together at last. If such success could only be accomplished by going into cahoots with the crafty, somewhat unscrupulous devil, er, spirit, beside her, then so be it.

Amelia wouldn't be able to complete her life's journey as long as Tillie remained lonely and enshrined in that big old house. Of course, Amelia had expected Gregory to return much sooner than this.

Oh dear. Their efforts *had* to do the trick. Those two young'uns were frittering away their most precious years and needed to be shown how to grab the brass ring while they still had breath in their bodies. Why, by Tillie's age, she'd already ditched her cheat of a first husband, entered her second marriage, begun her travels to the four corners of the map, and enjoyed a life as full as any woman of her day could have hoped.

What in tarnation were these two waiting for?

She sighed. "Gregory Buchanan doesn't see anything but what's right before him. And Tillie hides herself away in that inn as if it's Shangri La. Do you think they'll ever figure it out?"

"Most humans don't, do they?"

Sadly, no. A moment of uncertainty overtook her once more. "What if we try—"

Jesse patted her folded hands. "Miss Amelia, by the time you've finished figurin', I'm already finished doin'."

"Like the time you had Gregory knocked off his bicycle and nearly got him killed?" Admittedly, this might still be a sore spot for her.

"Stop your frettin' now, woman. Haven't we set into motion what's going to bring them together again?"

"I reckon."

"Rest is up to them."

She nibbled the inside of her lip as she watched over her young charge. "That's what I'm afraid of." She'd watched her hopes and dreams slip through her fingers with these two far too many times. When Gregory married Nancy, she'd given up. She wouldn't change a thing, though. That union had given Amelia her darling great-grandson Derek, whom she simply adored.

But her grandson's marriage hadn't worked out for reasons she worried Gregory might repeat in a relationship with sweet, innocent

Tillie.

Oh, I hope he wakes up and smells the roses before it's too late.

Tillie continued to rake leaves fallen from the oak trees near the playground below them. Amelia blew a kiss to the young lady who had won over a lonely old woman's heart at the tender age of eight and remained her utmost concern the rest of her earthly life and well into the hereafter.

Tillie cupped a gloved hand over her cheek and looked around with a quirk in her brow. She'd caught some hint of Amelia's kiss. The old woman smiled. Tillie had become more in tune with the spirit world over the past year. Unlike that grandson Amelia had practically given up on—well, not quite yet. She'd give Gregory one more chance to join the living. Amelia's daughter and her cold-hearted Yankee husband had sure done a number on him, but Gregory was beginning to show signs of life, especially around his son.

All he needed was a little nudge in the right direction.

"Here he comes, Amelia!" Jesse's excitement was contagious.

Her gaze shot up the road where she saw Gregory's vehicle approaching. Amelia glanced at Tillie again, her heart about to burst. Only time would tell whether their matchmaking efforts would bear fruit. Now it was up to the young'uns.

Chapter One

Despite the chill in the air, Tillie Hamilton's cheek grew warm as if she'd been kissed. A sense of calm and comfort came over her. *Dear Mrs. Foster.* Her eyes stung from the wind, and she blinked rapidly until she could see clearly again.

Raising her gloved hand to her face, she relished in the unexpected visit. She turned around almost hoping to find the woman standing there, but of course she never could see her. No, Tillie was alone, at least until her new guests arrived this afternoon or evening.

The man and his young son had booked Amelia's Suite for the longest stay on record in the decade plus she'd run the inn—ten nights. He also asked to have meals here, adding to her income. That should tide her over until the holiday season started in a couple of weeks.

She resumed her raking. No doubt the little boy would want to play out here, and she hadn't cleared the leaves on this side of the yard since the neighborhood children's Halloween party over a week ago.

The Buchanans could arrive at any moment. She'd better get to work if she wanted to don one of the vintage dresses she liked to wear to greet new guests. She had chosen and laid out on the bed a soft-lace over satin, ecru long-sleeved 1920s drop waist dress—not antebellum hoop skirts like those worn at the famous Federal Hill in Bardstown. But she enjoyed making this house's long history part of her own persona and the character of her inn.

As she walked closer to the picket fence around her herb garden to start another pile, yet another oak leaf fell from the tree. Rather than plop where it landed, this one skittered in a jagged path across the yard until reaching the side of the house where it promptly disappeared.

What on earth?

Coming closer, she saw that the windowpane had been broken.

Oh no! Not now!

First making sure no shards of glass had fallen on the ground, she laid down the rake and knelt beside the hole. The cold damp earth seeped into her jeans as she inspected the damage. No glass was visible on the ground, which meant it must have fallen inside, but she didn't see any jagged edges, either.

Tillie hadn't noticed anything awry yesterday. Had it happened today while she was in Bardstown grocery shopping?

She peeked at Mrs. Foster's fob watch pinned to her flannel shirt. While she might be able to measure the window and place a call to the glass shop before her guests arrived, she couldn't run to town again and replace the pane before they arrived. Giving the impression she was lax on maintenance irked her, but without question, she had to be on hand to greet new guests. Perhaps she could divert their attention away from the playground until tomorrow.

A slow-moving SUV coming through the S-curve up the road caught her eye.

Please don't stop. Please don't stop.

The driver's head swiveled in her direction, and a small boy with wide eyes appeared to shout something to him while pointing at the playground equipment. The turn signal flashed on a second before they were obstructed by the trees.

Great. No such luck in trying to cover the window now. Or dressing appropriately. *Oh, what the heck*? She broke out in a dead run for the dining-room door off the herb gardens. She could transform herself into the proper innkeeper in a flash before they even removed their suitcases from the SUV.

As she raced up the stairs to her bedroom, she asked herself how such a beautifully planned day had gone so wrong. With any luck, she'd be able to put her best foot forward and impress her incoming guests.

* * *

The tree-lined, winding country lane swept Gregory Buchanan back to an obscure memory from his childhood. He'd been twelve and seated in the passenger seat of his mother's Volvo on his way to see his maternal grandmother for what would end up being their final visit.

The two women had never been particularly close, but Gram had doted on him those five prior summers. He'd pushed the memory of the house and even Gram to a great extent to the deep recesses of his mind over the intervening years.

Until now. Time to right a wrong. No, two of them.

His chest grew tighter as his heart pounded so loud he thought his son would be able to hear it from the backseat. "Hey, Derek," he said, glancing in the rearview mirror at his five-year-old son. "Here's the place where we're going to be staying." He hoped his son would take away some special memories to last a lifetime, too, even though he hadn't told him the significance of this house for fear of tipping off the charlatan innkeeper.

"They have a playground, Daddy! Can I go down the slide?"

Shooting a glance out his side window, Greg saw a ponytailed woman in jeans and a red flannel shirt at the side of the Federal-style house watching him approach. He turned on his blinker. Was that an expression of horror on the woman's face? The innkeeper must have hired her to rake leaves, judging by the piles in the front and side yards. Had the worker been instructed to finish before they showed up? Not that he cared about fallen leaves. It was autumn, after all.

Greg remembered building Indian forts in that very spot that first summer when he was eight and his parents had left him here before they headed off on a river tour of Europe.

Gram had given him all kinds of tips on how to construct a strong fort then joined in to play with him. Despite always seeming ancient to him, she'd engaged in kid-related activities more than his parents ever had.

Would his son want to do things like that, as long as the innkeeper approved? Derek had napped most of the way from Minnesota, so it didn't surprise him the boy had energy to spare, and he'd want to play on the swing set in the yard as early as possible. Of course, Greg didn't know what shape the playground would be in and didn't make any promises he couldn't keep. But from here, it appeared to be well-built and modern.

The house had been partially obscured by a row of golden- and red-leafed trees, but the familiar split-rail fence looked the same as it had been all those years ago.

Greg entered the now-paved circular drive at the side of Gram's house and stared at the place that had sparked his interest in pursuing a career in architecture. The two-post, black on white *Jesse's Hideout B&B* sign in the front lawn clashed with what had been in his mind's eye all these years, though.

Greg's heart pounded in anticipation of entering Gram's house once again. How would it have changed since his last visit? Would her presence still be felt there?

"Go, Daddy! I wanna slide!"

Blinking back to the present, he drove forward and found a spot in the parking area next to a blue Toyota Camry. The house had three entrances on this side, the one closest to the road entering the office where his grandfather had practiced as a country doctor. The man had been but a memory shared by Gram when Greg had visited here.

The center door would put him in the dining room of Gram's house, while the third accessed her kitchen. Gram had used the dining-room entrance most often. He noticed a welcome sign on that door, so assumed the innkeeper did as well.

Exiting the Range Rover, he stared at the side of the brick house, unable to tear his gaze away.

Warm. Inviting. Home.

He shook off the fanciful notion. Gram hadn't willed the house to him, for whatever reason. It had been out of the family since her death.

The woman who inherited it likely had coerced her into changing her will.

Two flowerbeds on either side of the dining-room door burst with fall colors of chrysanthemums and ornamental kale. He remembered helping Gram plant a riot of colorful blooms there—bachelor's buttons, zinnias, and larkspur being her favorites. Gram devoted many pages in her journals each year talking about her flowers and prize heirloom roses.

Those journals had both tormented and given him solace. Her attorney had sent them to him soon after Greg's twenty-fifth birthday, as specified in her will, along with a pocket watch dating to the 1860s or 1870s purported to have belonged to the legendary Jesse James. He kept it in his safe-deposit box to be passed on to Derek one day.

While recovering from the cycling accident, he'd soon grown tired of the introspection about how his life had fallen apart since his divorce two years earlier. He'd enlisted his assistant to retrieve Gram's journals from the attic so he could delve inside someone else's mind for a change.

He'd read each one cover to cover—devoured them, truth be told—and probably wouldn't see the world in the same way again as a result. She'd begun writing in her teen years and continued until the last entry seven years before her passing. The later ones were difficult to decipher because either her hand was shaking or her eyes not quite as sharp.

What he'd taken away from those was that Mother had lied to him about when Gram had died, much later than she'd told him. Mother had robbed him of so many more years with Gram.

Greg shook his head, not wanting to wallow in regrets or stir up anger over something he could do nothing to fix. Turning toward the shed across the driveway loop, he saw the now-spent rose bushes. Apparently, the new owner had kept Gram's roses growing or at least continued that tradition.

Glancing at the second-story window where he and his mother

stayed during that last visit, he pictured the blue pencil bed he'd seen on the inn's website. Gram said she'd had to take out the window to get it in there and had no intention of ever moving it again. Good thing the subsequent owners hadn't detested the bed and busted it up. Not that he'd booked his stay in that room; he may not be able to take a peek at it.

But Gram had bequeathed the house to a "dear friend," as she stated in her will, who'd probably since died, paving the way for it to fall into the hands of the charlatan now running it as a haunted inn. How dare this interloper tarnish the memory of his grandmother with her public claims asserting that Gram continued to linger at the place and actively shared recipes with her from beyond the grave?

Apparently, the money-grubbing innkeeper would do anything to make a buck—her latest scam a cookbook claiming to contain these ill-gotten recipes. Exploiting Gram's memory was beyond acceptable to him. He might not have been here for Gram in her final years, but he sure as hell would protect her memory now.

While the innkeeper had every right to ignore his request, Greg hoped she would do the right thing and agree to cease and desist or attribute some other fake ghost to be the one doing the so-called haunting. Greg didn't have a legal leg to stand on, though. The dead couldn't be defamed, libeled, or slandered, after all. Still, he intended to appeal to the woman's sense of decency. If that didn't work, he'd resort to publicly debunking her preposterous claims.

He'd also come here to prove Gram's outrageous but intriguing claim in several journal entries that the outlaw Jesse James lived well past his infamous 1882 murder and returned to this house—or at least the community of Samuels—long after the last known sighting of him recorded in local history books.

He'd been a history buff since, well, since Gram had instilled a love of the past into him during those five summers together. She'd talked about Jesse James as if she knew him personally, but he'd chalked it up to her play-acting and a wild imagination.

"Daddy, let me out!" Derek banged on the window, and Greg opened the rear door. In seconds, Derek had unbuckled his seatbelt, scampered from the booster seat, and scooted out the door. "Let's go play!"

Greg sighed. He'd have his work cut out for him on several fronts and only ten or eleven days to do it. But he wasn't one to give up or back down easily. He'd uncover the truth on both counts—and enjoy this vacation with his son as well.

* * *

Tillie pinned her fob watch to the bodice of the old-fashioned dress and hurried downstairs to await her guests. She'd had to skimp on some of the vintage undergarments in her haste, but had the basics covered. When no knock came to the door, she peeked outside the window to see the man staring up at her bedroom.

Her heart beat like a jackhammer. What a gorgeous man. She reminded herself to breathe. His neatly trimmed, medium brown hair offset a classically handsome face, which boasted a strong chin and jaw line, with a thin, straight nose. But those eyes! They pierced through to her very soul.

Why did they seem so familiar?

Oh, come on, Matilda. He's looking at the house, not you.

Her late mother's voice yanked her back to reality. The man no doubt had a wife at home, although it seemed odd that she wasn't here with him and his son.

None of my business.

But it *was* her business to greet her guests. What had come over her? She entertained guests of the opposite sex often. Well, usually accompanied by wives or girlfriends—sometimes even male partners. Perhaps Mr. Buchanan was gay.

Just my luck.

As if she had a chance with someone as handsome and sophisticated as Greg Buchanan. Of course, she usually put the brakes on a relationship before it went beyond seeing a play together or having a nice supper somewhere she'd rather not dine alone.

When he let his son out of the SUV, she decided it might be best if she greeted them outside. Brushing non-existent wrinkles from her dress, she stood up straighter. Taking a deep breath and plastering a smile on her face, she opened the door.

She wasn't prepared for the intensely fierce gaze he shot in her direction before quickly masking it. Or had she imagined it? Why on earth would he be angry at her? They'd never even met.

If he didn't have his son along with him, she might have been inclined to refuse to provide him a room.

Coming down the two steps onto the cobblestone walkway, she closed the gap between them, extending her hand. "You must be Mr. Buchanan. I'm Tillie Hamilton, the owner of Jesse's Hideout B&B. Welcome to my home."

His handshake was firm, but not bone crushing like some men used to intimidate women and weaker males. As she suspected, his eyes did a number on her insides.

"Call me Greg."

"Greg, it is."

A tug to the skirt of her dress brought her attention to the boy beside her. "Can I go down your slide?"

"Um, why, of course!" Thank goodness he couldn't be injured on any shards of glass if he strayed from the playground.

Tillie hunkered down in front of Derek to offer her hand. He stretched out his tiny one with a shy grin. "Hi, I'm Tillie." After shaking hands, she raised hers, palm outward to him. "High five." He smacked her hard, and both laughed. "Fist bump," she prompted next, which made the boy giggle.

"Hi, Tillie. I can spell my name. D-e-r-e-k."

"She's Miss Tillie or ma'am to you, Derek."

"Oh, please. Let's not be so formal." The man's height was even more intimidating from down here, so she stood. He gave her dress the once-over, and she realized her appearance was indeed quite formal.

"His mother and I are teaching him the importance of respect, so if you don't mind, I'd prefer he address you as Miss Tillie."

She shrugged and smiled, happy to hear he wasn't gay but envying his wife.

What made him such a stuffy man for someone so young? He seemed to be about mid-thirties. Definitely no older than forty. She detected no gray in his hair, anyway, and he had a young face.

Her focus returned to his son. She had no desire to undermine his parenting responsibilities. "We're going to have great fun while you're here, Derek."

For the next ten days, she intended to treat them as if they were her own family.

* * *

The woman's auburn hair caught his eye first—long, curly, and gathered into a half ponytail while the remainder tumbled loose over her shoulders. Her friendly, guileless smile almost took the steam out of his temper. How could such a pleasant woman be perpetrating a hoax on the public?

Before allowing her to work her way under his skin with her beauty and charm, Greg leaned his hip against the side panel of the SUV and crossed his arms.

Tillie was much younger than he'd expected given her name. She didn't appear to be thirty. To run a successful business like this, he'd expected someone more mature.

Her name seemed familiar, but he couldn't place her. Those sparkling emerald-green eyes would be impossible to forget. Tillie's accent was milder, too, than he'd expected. Had she lived here in Kentucky her whole life? Or were some areas less prone to a southern twang than others? The woman was a mass of contradictions.

She cocked her head. "Have we met before?"

Her question had him wondering the same thing again. "Not that I'm aware of."

"Hmm. You're familiar to me for some reason." She shrugged.

"Weren't you raking leaves on the other side of the house when I drove up?"

"Yes, I was." A blush crept into her cheeks. Charming. His gaze swept over her full-skirted dress and low-heeled pumps. "That was some quick change." Did her past include a stint as an actress in the theater?

She laughed. "I was running behind." As if embarrassed, she changed the subject and pointed to the cargo area. "May I carry in one of your bags?"

Greg pointed at Derek. "I'll take care of the luggage if you help me corral my son before he makes a beeline to that slide without us."

"By all means. This house is rather compartmentalized inside. It once was used as a traveler's rest. Your room is on the other side, so it might be easiest to come through the front entrance and up the stairway rather than wind your way through the house. Follow me." She took Derek's hand. "Come with me, honey."

Greg wouldn't admit he knew exactly where his room would be, not ready to reveal his identity yet, so he scrambled to retrieve their two bags from the cargo area. Derek's small, colorful one sported a sunglass-wearing Mickey Mouse. Greg's was large and basic black.

"I can do mine!" Derek broke free of Tillie and took the handle only to drag it on the wrong side.

"Here, son, remember Mickey needs to be facing up." Greg quickly flipped it over, and Derek rejoined Tillie, who led them around to the front of the house on the brick walkway. Derek struggled with his bag, but Greg had learned he liked doing things himself so let him take his time to navigate the bumps in the path.

Greg couldn't take his eyes off her as she walked, the gentle sway of her hips mesmerizing him. When she stopped and started to turn his way, he quickly shifted his gaze to the front entrance.

Thoughts of Tillie vacated his mind as, once more, the house called him back to those earlier visits. The prisms in the fanlight would cast enchanting rainbows on the foyer floor on sunny afternoons like this one. Perhaps they'd see them even now.

Tillie pushed open the wooden door and indicated for them to precede her. He imagined countless guests must have entered the home this way over the past one hundred seventy-five or so years. A sense of history overcame him. He couldn't wait to tour the house to see how she'd changed it from what he remembered.

Realizing she waited for them, he lifted both suitcases up the steps and into the foyer. Inside, the past slammed into him like a battering ram to the chest. Visceral images superimposed over a hallway that hadn't changed one iota in the almost twenty-five years he'd been away.

He set down their bags inside. The wide central hallway was much shorter than he remembered. Its bare plank floorboards hadn't been painted over, though, maintaining the checkerboard pattern he remembered. He had to respect Tillie for keeping the character of the original house.

"Rainbows in the *house*?" Derek tried to capture one of the prism reflections only to squeal with delight when the rainbow temporarily tattooed itself on his hand. Greg smiled at his son. They'd had pretty much the same effect on him as a boy.

"Follow me." She led them up the stairway and into what would be the master bedroom if this were a single-family home. While he'd been inside this room before, his memories had faded. The covered canopy bed, velvet-covered chaise, and fireplace fought to dominate the room.

"The bathroom is en suite and through there." She pointed to a door across the room. That room had been added after he'd last been here, because there had only been one bathroom when Gram lived here, off the kitchen. Well, that and the outdoor privy, which he had to admit had fascinated a city boy like him. "Derek, that will be your closest bathroom, too. Your room is right through here," she said, guiding them into the hallway again and to the small room at the front of the house. "You'll be right next to your dad."

His grandmother had used the adjoining room as her sitting room, but past owners with children probably had used it as a nursery.

She must have noticed Derek's lack of enthusiasm about sleeping alone in a strange room.

"Feel free to keep the doors open between the two rooms. Your rooms are the only ones on this side of the house, and you're my only guests during your stay."

"Can we keep them open, Daddy?" No doubt being in a strange house would make him a little nervous to be disconnected from Greg at night.

"Of course."

She met Greg's gaze. "And if there's *any*thing I can do to make your stay more enjoyable, don't hesitate to call. I'm rarely farther away than the kitchen."

"Oh," she said, pointing to the two rooms, "there are skeleton keys in each of the doors. You can lock up whenever you leave, if you'd like, but there's no real need. Now, I'll get out of your way so you can settle in." She started for the stairway before turning back. "I almost forgot. Supper will be about six. Feel free to make yourself at home up here, in the parlor, or any of the common areas."

"I wanna go outside, Daddy!" The boy jumped up and down, tugging on Greg's sleeve.

Greg chuckled. Maybe having Derek to himself without Nancy to call on to bail him out would help him build a stronger bond with his son.

Tillie's face became strained. "Yes. Of course." Why had she hesitated? "The playground is yours to enjoy, too. I built it five years ago and have added new equipment or features to it every year."

She's obviously proud of the equipment, so why do I get the feeling she's not thrilled that we want to use it? Or did she not want them to go outside? Before he could figure out what the problem was, Tillie stopped mid-step on her way to the stairs and faced him, her smile firmly in place again. "Oh, I'm baking cookies for dessert tonight. I hope you both like chocolate chip."

Greg's favorite had been oatmeal-raisin ever since Gram had made hers for him. Not that he'd ever found any since that came close to those. But Derek loved cookies of any kind.

"Who doesn't?" Greg responded. "Thanks."

Her smile lit her face even more, if that were possible. "Great. And I'm happy to work out menus to suit your preferences for any meals you'd like to have here."

When he'd booked the rooms, he'd asked to have dinners here, too, providing him with more opportunities to figure out her game. As a bonus, having a home base for two meals of the day would give Derek a routine to help things run more smoothly during this time away from his mother.

The boy would be in bed by nine o'clock, even though their days would be filled with a number of excursions, including paying his respects at his grandmother's grave. Long overdue.

"Sounds good. I should warn you Derek would survive on fast food if given his choice—pancakes, hot dogs, and chicken nuggets mainly."

Tillie laughed, a sound that came from deep in her chest. Before his attention could stray in her direction, she tossed her parting words over her shoulder. "Don't worry. I've charmed more than a few boys into falling for my goodies."

I'll bet you have.

This time she continued on her way, and he watched her go down the stairs until he could no longer see her. Mentally, he shook his head clear of the spell either Tillie or the house—or both—had cast on him. He smiled at his son. "Sure. Let's unpack real fast so you'll have time to run around the yard a while before dinner."

Twenty minutes later, Derek bounced up and down as he started toward the stairs. This was the happiest he'd seen him since they'd left his mother's yesterday morning.

"Hold on to the banister!" he called before joining him on the staircase.

"Hi, again!" Tillie greeting them as they stepped off the stairs. She came from the doorway to the L wing of the first floor where the kitchen and dining room were located. She wore an apron over her elegant dress and wiped her hands on a dishtowel as she walked toward them.

At the foot of the stairs, she hunkered down. "How do chicken strips sound, Derek?"

"Yea! With fries?"

"Of course!"

Obviously, she knew how to charm little boys.

Well, don't expect to charm me, Tillie Hamilton.

Rising, she addressed Greg. "Oh, the parlor is through this door." She pointed out the only door he could see—across from the stairs. "Unlike the typical L-shaped Federal home, there's no way to go directly from the front hallway into my office on the other side of this wall." That had been his grandfather's office. "The prior owner told me that had to do with the fact that the house had originally been built as a stagecoach inn so the Samuels family wanted to maintain private living quarters as well. They could easily lock off their bedrooms and parlor from where the overnight strangers were staying."

He'd seen many Federal-style homes before—even renovated some—but had never seen any with as unique a floor plan as the one in this house.

"Consider it your living room during your stay. I'm happy to serve you coffee, tea, milk, and snacks in the afternoons or whenever you'd like provided I have a little notice. I'll also leave snacks and fresh fruit on the table in the dining room through there." She pointed to the doorway through which she'd entered.

"Thank you, but we'll probably be off sightseeing most afternoons. I have a long list of places to take Derek."

"If you need any recommendations, let me know. On the end table in the parlor is a wicker basket filled with brochures on local attractions, too."

The house had been a maze of rooms as a kid. He smiled, remembering how he'd gotten lost in the rooms of this house in the past, sometimes on purpose. Gram encouraged him to explore, though. She often told him he'd one day live here, but that hadn't come to pass thanks to—

Wait a minute. Tillie *Hamilton*. It wasn't her face that was so familiar, but her name. Matilda Hamilton was the "dear friend" who inherited this house from Gram. *Tillie.* All he'd remembered from seeing the attorney's letter nearly fifteen years ago was the name Matilda. He'd definitely pictured someone close to his grandmother's age.

Had she been hired to take care of his grandmother on her deathbed? Did Tillie charm Gram out of her house?

He intended to find out before he left here.

Chapter Two

Who is *that man?*

Tillie couldn't shake the feeling that they'd met before, although he'd never been a guest here in the years she'd operated her bed and breakfast. She didn't know anyone from Minnesota, did she? What was it about his gray eyes that seemed so familiar?

The air had practically vibrated between them. Perhaps his classic handsomeness addled her brain. Most of her guests were older, but Greg Buchanan was in his prime. As if a sophisticated city man would be interested in a country homebody like Tillie.

She re-entered the kitchen to drop more chocolate-chip cookies on the baking sheet, trying to put that nagging thought out of her mind. With the three of them taking two meals a day here during their stay, no doubt she'd come to know them better and perhaps even pinpoint where they'd met, if indeed they had.

Looking down, Tillie noticed the tattered recipe card that must have shown up on the counter while she was showing her guests to their rooms. Oatmeal-raisin cookies! Finally!

"Thank you, thank you, Mrs. Foster!" These cookies had always been her favorites. Why had the dear woman taken so long to share it with her? Actually, she hadn't dropped a new recipe onto Tillie's kitchen counter in quite a while.

Tillie couldn't wait to bake a batch and would debut them with her new guests. She'd tried for years to replicate the woman's oatmeal-raisin cookie recipe without success. Poring over the list of ingredients, Tillie spotted the elusive one immediately—Chinese five-spice powder.

Who'd have thought a woman from rural Kentucky would have had access to such an exotic spice? Of course, Mrs. Foster had traveled in "the Orient," as she called it. She'd also served in Hawaii as an Army nurse during World War II. Perhaps she'd encountered five-spice powder there.

Regardless, Tillie doubted her local store would have any on hand, so she went to her laptop and placed an order to be overnighted. She hoped the cookies would taste as good as she remembered.

For now, the promised chocolate chip cookies would have to suffice. After placing another sheet in the oven, she returned to the counter at the same moment she heard the door to the herb-garden porch shut. Going into the dining room, she watched Derek beeline to the curved, bright yellow slide. He must have an incredible amount of pent-up energy after such a long drive.

Moving more slowly, surveying the yard as if searching for something, Greg arrived on the playground in the nick of time to catch his son at the bottom of the slide. A genuine smile broke out on the man's face—the first she'd seen since his arrival an hour ago.

The man seemed to keep himself on a tight rein—around her, at least. As Derek scrambled up the ladder again, Greg couldn't take his eyes off the house. His gaze lit first on the upper floor—the room where he was staying—before homing in on her. Trying not to appear guilty of spying on them, she made a production of arranging the perfectly placed candle on the windowsill. Tillie waved at him, as though she hadn't been totally caught in the act, before escaping back into the kitchen to keep an eye on the cookies and start supper prep.

For some reason, an inexplicable sense of loneliness overtook her. She'd long ago grown accustomed to her chosen life of solitude, but she wished so badly she could join them.

Don't be ridiculous.

Oh no! The window!

Tillie dropped the knife she was using to peel potatoes. Given the way he was scrutinizing everything, he'd probably already seen it, but she hoped to head him off if possible.

Wiping her hands on her apron, she whipped it off and rushed toward the door they'd exited a few minutes earlier. The two of them had moved to the swing where Greg was pushing his son. The man stared in her direction. At least he didn't appear to have seen the window yet.

"Beautiful day, isn't it?" she asked as a means of greeting. How was she to explain why she was out here? They'd already discussed tonight's menu.

"Miss Tillie! I'm flying!"

"Hold on, sport." He'd opted for the swing that didn't have a toddler seat, and she appreciated they were being cautious. Greg Buchanan struck her as the type to sue if an accident occurred. To her, he added, "Yes, it is. Much warmer than Minnesota."

Uncertain what to say, she pointed to the piles of leaves. "Feel free to play in the leaves here or in the front yard. I can wait and bag them after your stay is over."

Greg nodded toward the house. "I noticed you have a broken window."

Well, of course, you did.

"You shouldn't leave it open like that or you'll have all kinds of critters moving in, not to mention doing damage to the walls and floor of the cellar."

Tillie didn't appreciate being told how to run her inn, but plastered a smile on her face. He was a guest, after all.

"Yes, I only noticed it had been broken the moment you drove up. I'll take care of it after supper."

"I'd be happy to board it up for you."

"Oh, let me take care of that. You only need to worry about enjoying your stay."

"No trouble at all. I'm sure maintenance on a house this size can be a challenge for one person."

Tillie was about to tell him she had no trouble at all when she heard an alarm go off in the kitchen. A smoke alarm. The cookies!

"Excuse me!"

She rushed toward the house only to find the kitchen filling with smoke. Turning off the oven, she grabbed the oven mitt and removed the tray of charred treats. She hadn't burned anything in as long as she could remember. Why today of all days? Her guest probably thought her totally inept.

"Can I help with anything?"

No, but you can *leave my kitchen.* Her conscience warred with her desire to behave like a brat since his arrival. *Behave, Matilda.*

"No, thanks. I guess I tried to do too much at once."

Derek coughed, holding his throat. "Is your house on fire?"

"No, sweetie," Tillie assured him. "Don't you worry. I baked a whole tray already for tonight. These were extras." When the boy stared dubiously at the cloud of smoke, she added, "The excitement's over now. Why don't you go back out and play?" *And take your daddy with you.*

"Derek, go in the parlor and play with the Civil War chess set. Daddy wants to check on something in the cellar."

Apparently, he'd already checked out the parlor, but she still didn't want him to be bothered with the window.

"Where's the parlor, Daddy?"

Or perhaps not, unless the boy simply didn't remember, given the unusual name for what he might know as a living room. "I'll show you." To her, he said, "Give me a minute. Then we can check out that window together."

"Really, Greg, I can take care of it. You're on vacation."

He waved away her concerns before staring a moment at the bodice of her dress. "You might want to change into old clothes before we head down there."

"Oh, don't worry. I call it a cellar, but it's not quite that primitive. It used to have a dirt floor, but I decided to make it a more functional space."

"I see."

Puzzled why he'd care one way or another, she crossed the room to open the door to the parking area. "Let me air out the kitchen." When would anything go right today? She then opened the window near the bathroom. "The house was designed to have a cross breezes almost throughout. Quite useful during the hot, sticky summers."

"No central heat or air, I take it."

"No, but I love using fireplaces on cold days. And the house stays surprisingly cool in the summer."

"They knew how to build them in the days before air conditioning, for certain."

When he started toward the front of the house, she followed. While she wasn't thrilled that he'd be going downstairs with her, she didn't want him to go without her, either. The window was her responsibility.

"Wow, look, Daddy! Soldiers!" Derek acted as though he was seeing the chess set for the first time. How had Greg known it was there? She watched from the foyer, not wanting to intrude while the man showed his son the Civil War set.

"Derek, be very gentle with the pieces. They're antiques, just like my set. And stay in here. We're going downstairs, but we'll keep the door open if you need us. We won't be long."

"Okay." Derek focused on the set as he maneuvered two of the pieces across the chessboard squares.

Greg joined her a moment later. "After you." He indicated the cellar door across the hall.

"How did you know that's the way to the cellar?"

He averted his gaze a moment before answering. "I'm an architect."

"Oh." That would explain his knowing the layout of her house, she supposed. Her mind must still be trying to figure out where she'd seen him before. For some odd reason, she wanted to say it had been in this house, which was impossible. She never forgot a guest.

Tillie retrieved a flashlight from the center drawer in the mirrored table nearby, unbolted the cellar door, and flipped on the light switch before beginning to descend the stairs. "Even with the overhead light, it's dark down here."

"I'll bet."

"Hold on to the railing. The steps are steep."

"Do you have any cardboard we can use for a temporary fix?"

"Yes, I keep some down here."

At the bottom of the stairs, she prepared to open the door to the northern end when his hand covered hers. A tingling warmth spread up her arm, surprising her, and she released the knob. "Let me check things out first." He pulled out his phone and turned on the flashlight app.

Relinquishing control to him bothered her, but she'd learned long ago to choose her battles. "I'll grab the cardboard, box cutter, and duct tape. The light switch is to the right of the door."

She crossed the central space and opened the canning room door at the opposite end of the cellar to grab what she needed, catching up with him quickly. Upon joining him in the room, her gaze flew to the two windows at the opposite end.

Greg hunkered below the broken one before facing her. "Did you find broken glass outside the window?"

"No. It fell inside." She crossed the room to lay the supplies near-by.

He shook his head and pointed to the floor. "There's no glass here."

"How can that be? It had to go somewhere."

"Are you sure this is a new break?"

She set down the cardboard and squared her shoulders. "Yes. Quite certain." Why would he think otherwise?

"Is it possible someone came in through the window?"

"An intruder who cleaned up after himself?" A rock settled in the pit of her stomach. "Not that I'm aware of."

"Anything missing lately?"

As a matter fact, yes. My sense of security just vanished.

"N-No. Not that I'm aware of." *Calm down. You don't know that anyone actually came in here.* She took a shaky breath and waved her hand around the room. "I mostly use this part of the cellar for storage." From experience, she believed the northern end to have at least one spirit, although she'd never experienced anything malevolent. Just—paternal perhaps, if spirits possessed such human characteristics.

"I'll agree it doesn't have the pleasant vibe the rest of the house does." So he felt it, too? "Nothing out of the ordinary upstairs?"

She shook her head, facing the growing certainty that someone had broken into her house. "I keep the cellar door locked from the foyer side at all times."

"Good. That means they didn't get beyond the cellar. Look around. Tell me if you see anything amiss."

She held up her flashlight and homed in on the corners. After inspecting every inch of the floor, she shook her head. "Everything appears to be fine."

"All right. Let's check the rest of the cellar."

They reentered the central area, closing the door behind them. The mood lightened immediately. She truly never liked the vibe in there.

But now she also feared entering the canning room, even though she'd been in there a few minutes ago—alone, no less. Thankfully, Greg took the lead.

When might someone have broken in—no, more importantly, why? Perhaps they'd been scared off when she returned from the store. God, if she'd been any later…

What if she'd caught someone in the act? While she kept a loaded revolver in the gun safe upstairs, she didn't carry it around with her. She still wasn't convinced anyone had broken in, but what would explain the windowpane's complete disappearance? It hadn't walked away.

A pulse throbbed in her temples. "Should I call the sheriff's office?"

"First, let's see if anything's missing or disturbed. If not, I doubt they can do more than dust for prints, but we've already disturbed the scene by walking around. A detective friend of mine once said fingerprints are extremely difficult to lift from wood anyway, and I would guess the windowsill and frame would have had the most evidence."

Without any proof of an intruder, she'd only appear silly to the deputy.

They crossed the cellar to the canning room, and Greg searched the outer walls, shining the beam from his phone's LED app into the darkened corners. How would he know if anything was missing? He'd never been down here before.

To help, she did the same with her own flashlight. The windows on this side were intact, and everything appeared to be the way she'd left it when the canning season ended last month. Turning around, she found Greg focused on one of the stones in the wall that had loose mortar around it. "See anything?"

"What?" He lowered his phone. "Sorry, no. I'm fascinated with the construction of the house."

"Oh, I still owe you the nickel tour." Of course, an architect would want to see how the foundation of the old house was built. "I had this room converted to a summer kitchen of sorts. Mostly I used it for canning and sorting and ironing laundry, but on truly hot days and nights, I often escape down here. I've even set up a twin bed over there to sleep on hot nights when I don't have guests."

She shined her light into the nook. "I'm not quite sure what they used that area for."

He focused on the beam on the walls and ceiling, coming to a block of stone that appeared to have new mortar placed around it. "When was this done?"

"No clue. There's a similar one in the room on the other end of the cellar. I assumed the mortar had weakened over time. It's not as though anyone could move a stone that huge."

"Perhaps." He spent the next couple minutes studying the area more closely then moved on. At least he wasn't focusing on the boxes of jars, lids, and canning supplies she stored down here. When she gave a tour of the house, it never included the cellar—until today.

"The stone masonry held up well over the decades," he noted, pointing to the walls.

"It reminds me of the original stone walls at the Old Talbott Tavern, but that building is at least fifty years older than this one."

"You don't mess with what works. Perhaps a local father and son stonemason specialized in that style, and the younger built this house. Or an apprentice of the older mason." He shrugged. "Who knows?"

Greg continued to take an inordinate interest in that one odd stone. Most likely, he already figured out more about the structure for himself than she could divulge.

"Why don't we return to the center room?" she asked, hoping to go upstairs again. Expecting him to follow, she started toward the door, but when she glanced over her shoulder, his gaze had remained riveted to that stone. What fascinated him so much? Perhaps he'd enlighten her, given his expertise, and she'd learn more about the house.

As if he finally heard her words from a few moments ago, he looked in her direction and shrugged sheepishly. "Sorry. I'm like a kid in a candy store down here."

He joined her, and she continued with her impromptu tour. "This is where I store my canned goods, keep an extra freezer, and do the laundry."

"Busy area." He focused on the three shelves filled with slightly dusty jars.

"That's where…" *Wait!* One of the shelves that held dozens of filled quart, pint, and half-pint jars had been moved away from the wall on one end. A jar of her blackberry preserves lay broken on the floor. She'd picked those berries herself and probably still had the scratch marks and healed mosquito bites to prove it. "What on earth?" Approaching the area, she tried to ascertain how anyone could have moved it. "How'd this shelf get moved?"

"You didn't do it?"

Why would he think she'd leave a sticky mess on her cellar floor? "Of course not." She hoped her annoyance came through loud and clear.

"Don't touch anything. This brings us back to a possible intruder."

Her heart pounded painfully as she surveyed the area to see if anything else was out of place. "Why would someone want to break into my cellar?"

Greg moved closer, his arm brushing hers, sending an alert of a different kind coursing through her. His aftershave wafted to her, spicy but light, which calmed her jangled nerves for some reason.

She stepped away to allow him space to shine his phone's light behind the shelf.

After a moment, he turned it off and faced her. "If it was an intruder, what might they be looking for down here?"

She shrugged. "I haven't the foggiest."

"There's lots of lore about Jesse James attached to this house. Could fortune hunters be searching for souvenirs? You wouldn't believe the number of stories circulating about hidden treasure here." As he spoke, a spark of excitement flashed in his eyes.

Oh no. Not another one.

She'd better lay those notions to rest once and for all. "This area has undergone extensive renovations. If anything had been stashed here, don't you think it would have been discovered by now?" She stared at the mess again. "Should we call the sheriff now?"

"Whoever was here, they're gone now. But you might want to have the authorities check things out."

Her chest tightened at the thought of a prowler breaking into her house. "You're scaring me."

He stroked her upper arm. If he'd intended for the motion to calm her, well, no such luck. She took a step away to put more distance between them, immediately missing the warmth of his hand.

"Do you have an alarm system?"

She shook her head. "I never had one installed. My guests and I are in and out so much that it would be a nuisance to mess with."

"Well, I'd like you to mess with it, especially with you being out here alone for the most part." That he cared about her safety ought to reassure her, but how much would this equipment and service cost? She had more important things on her priority list, like the new roof she'd put off until after next spring's violent weather season was over, just in case. "I'll check into it. Maybe after the holiday rush is over."

"If you'd like, I can check the national and local registries and suggest a good contractor. You could probably have one installed within the week."

She needed to remind him who ran things around here. "Money doesn't grow on trees, unfortunately. I had to repair major hail damage in the spring, and my car took a hit at the mechanic's in September, which pretty much ate into this year's maintenance budget. But I'll be happy to provide a list of names for future reference. Thanks."

"No worries, but keep in mind that vandalism, if that's all that happened here, can escalate. Someone might be testing you to see how far they can go or whether you have a working security system. Could be local kids up to no good, but until you know, it's a good idea to do what you can to protect yourself and your property."

"This is Samuels, Kentucky, not the big city."

Tillie's hand shook, and she placed her hands behind her to hide the fact that he truly was frightening her. She'd always prided herself in living within her budget. The money she'd earn from his ten-day stay would cover expenses until her guests flocked to the inn again during the upcoming holidays.

Who was she kidding? The Christmas season's guests' money had to pay her utilities until next September's Bourbon Festival visitors poured in, so to speak. The rest of the year was intermittent. She shook her head. "I really don't think—"

"Look, why don't I run into town and pick up a few motion detectors and nanny cams? They won't be a big hit on the budget and will do in a pinch."

Tillie cocked her head. The man was tenacious. "Isn't it a little late for that? Besides, my guests won't like being spied upon, and neither would I."

"I'd only install them in the cellar near the windows and around the perimeter of the house. They work on wi-fi, so no one will even be aware of them."

"I suppose." She ought to be grateful for the offer. She already needed to go to town for the replacement pane. The cameras might restore her peace of mind. She had her guests to think of, too.

Tillie loved everything about running her inn on her own, but purchasing and installing security equipment wasn't on the list of duties she had any expertise with. At least Greg was offering to help.

To be honest, the thought of having him here for the next week and a half already made her feel safer.

"I guess that would be a good idea. If you work for meals, I can throw in your suppers for free."

"I didn't ask to be paid, did I?"

"No, but I still don't want you spending your vacation working as a handy man for me. If someone comes back, I want them caught before anyone else checks in. I'd rather not have you deal with this during your stay."

"I'm not used to vacations. Besides, having the chance to do anything on this beautiful old house would be an honor." He met her gaze with those steely blues, and her stomach somersaulted. When he smiled, the corners of his eyes scrunched in a disarming way.

Don't become too attached, Tillie. You can't keep him.

Now she was letting her imagination run away with her. *Get a grip, Tillie.* "I think we ought to get back upstairs to Derek." Her voice sounded a little breathless.

Before she could make her retreat and open some space between them, he pointed at the heavy-laden shelves. "You canned all these?"

Her chest swelled a bit, no lie, and she smiled. "Every single one. Some of the fruits were canned earlier in the summer. By early August, the veggies from my garden are coming in faster than I can use them, so I can straight through mid-October."

He read some of the labels aloud. "Pie cherries. Peaches. Tomatoes. Green beans. Jalapeno jelly?" He turned toward her and quirked his eyebrow.

She chuckled. "It's an acquired taste, but Mrs. Foster, the woman who raised me in this house, loved that stuff, so I still make a dozen jars each year. It's popular with guests around *Cinco de Mayo* and available upon request when I have an adventurous guest wanting to try some."

He stood a little taller, tipping his chin up a bit. "I'd like to try it."

"Really?" She smiled. "You like food that spicy?"

"Sure." She wasn't convinced given his lack of enthusiasm.

"Hand me a jar, please." He did so. "I mix the hot pepper jelly with cream cheese, which takes out some of the bite. I'll need to pick up some along with some savory crackers, and we can enjoy them before you leave."

"You put a lot of effort into the little things for your guests. I can see why this is such a popular place. Why do you feel the need to promote the hocus-pocus stuff?"

His question blindsided her. *Hocus-pocus?* "I beg your pardon?"

"All the talk about Jesse James and some old lady haunting the place to attract the ghost-hunting crowd. Is that really necessary?"

She squared her shoulders, fighting hard to control her breathing—and her temper. "I haven't made up anything. Mrs. Foster, the woman who owned this house before me and left it in my care, visits me here. In fact, she left something for me this very afternoon."

"What?"

"A recipe card."

"You could have taken that from her collection. I don't buy it."

He didn't have to *buy* anything. "I don't inflict her spirit on anyone. She doesn't come here for anyone but me. And I've *never* purported that Jesse James still shows up in any way, shape, or form. But there's no denying he's been inside the house in the flesh. That he hid out here from authorities. It's documented. I love the history that's unfolded in this house and community. I simply give credit where it's due."

"I don't object to your telling the story of the house's colorful past. Let's just say I'm skeptical about the ghost tales."

"What difference could it make to you? If you don't believe in her, I'm sure she'll steer clear of you." As if she'd appeared to him outright. She'd never even done so with Tillie.

"I'm merely curious."

More like dubious.

If he didn't believe in spirits, why on earth had he chosen to stay at her inn?

Chapter Three

Why in the hell had he chosen this moment to challenge her on Gram's behalf? He regretted his accusation almost immediately, but she hadn't wavered. Without any proof, it was merely a believer in ghosts versus a non-believer. Still, he shouldn't have blown his cool by blurting it out that way.

Greg raked his fingers through his hair. He needed to fix this and get back on a good footing with her. "Do you have a tape measure? I'd like to get that window replaced tonight, rather than wait." If someone had broken in, a new window wasn't going to stop them from trying again, but he'd make sure he did what he could to put things to rights. He might not have been here to take care of things like this for Gram, but in some strange way, Tillie was an extension of her and the closest connection he had to his grandmother.

Without a word, she pivoted and walked into the canning room, returning momentarily to hand him a cloth one. "My tool box is in the garden shed. This is all I have handy."

"It'll work."

"I'll go check on Derek." Without another clipped word, she started up the stairs, pausing a moment halfway up but not meeting his gaze. "Thank you. I'll give you the address of the hardware store I use with a note telling them to put the items you need on my tab." Finally, she faced him. "If you wouldn't mind picking up some window putty while you're there, I'd appreciate it. I can keep Derek, if that would be easier."

"Thanks, but I can take him with me. I'll pick up anything you need, though."

"If he decides to stay, I'll be in the kitchen preparing supper. Just bring some of his toys in, or I can let him play with some pots and pans if he'd like."

Gram used to let him pretend to cook while she made meals. The image of his son doing the same warmed some dark corner of his soul. Not that he'd taken any of the skills Gram taught him into adulthood. He rarely cooked anything, preferring to dine out instead.

Derek did choose to stay, so he took the measurements and the store's address and drove five miles to Bardstown, the county seat. He barely recognized the place from when he'd been a kid and taken this road with his mother that last time. Many of the farms had become subdivisions, and a hospital had been built.

At the store, while they were cutting the glass cut to size, he shopped for the rest of the supplies. Armed with everything he'd need, he made it back to the house in a little more than an hour. Before heading downstairs, he peeked into the kitchen where he found Derek pounding the bejeezus out of whatever was in the pot.

"Something sure smells good."

Tillie, her arm protectively around Derek's waist, looked toward Greg. Watching the smile fade from her eyes tore at his gut a little.

"Look, Daddy! I'm smashing potatoes!" He lifted the old-fashioned masher out of the pot and bits of potatoes flew through the air. Tillie giggled as she reached for a dishtowel to clean it up.

"You sure are, son. Great job!"

"Hope you like rosemary-lemon chicken." Her smile returned when she looked toward his son. "Derek's going to help with his chicken strips next. Supper should be ready in about half an hour."

How she could stay so close to her original estimated time while having Derek as her sous chef amazed him. "Perfect timing. I'll head downstairs and repair the window while there's still some daylight left."

The domestic scene left him disconcerted yet not wanting to leave the kitchen. Is this what Nancy had found lacking in him? She'd often tried to get him to join her in preparing meals or in taking care of Derek while she cooked, but he'd kept late hours and most nights didn't even make it home in time to join them for dinner.

The failure of their marriage was largely due to him, no doubt. Nancy had moved on, finding someone she said "completed her," whatever that meant. With her remarriage a few months ago, he'd given up on any hope of a second chance. He might have been relegated to ex-husband, but refused to be ousted as Derek's father.

Greg made quick work of replacing and sealing the window, the oppressiveness of this room getting to him the way it apparently did Tillie, too. Torn between snooping around down here a little and joining Tillie and Derek upstairs, his conscience won out.

His step was light as he ran up the stairs to rejoin them, careful not to hit his head on the low overhang. Entering the dining room as Tillie placed a casserole dish on the table next to a green salad and the bowl of mashed potatoes, he announced, "All fixed."

She met his gaze and smiled what appeared to be a genuine one. Maybe she'd forgotten about their earlier exchange—or had she forgiven him? Determined to keep things pleasant, he grinned back. "Looks like you've prepared a feast."

"Hope you like everything. Let me fill Derek's plate first. Have a seat. Is sweet tea okay?"

Not his favorite, but he didn't want to make her go to any extra work. "Sounds great. We'll go wash up first."

"Bathroom is right through there and to the left," she said, pointing toward the kitchen door. Gram had indoor facilities put in long before he'd made his first visit here.

When they re-entered the dining room, Derek took his seat. "Let me plate your supper. I didn't earlier so it wouldn't get cold."

"No need to wait on us. You've done enough. Let's dine family style."

She eyed the chair then him. "I don't usually—"

"Have a seat, Tillie. Join us." When she remained hesitant, he added, "Please."

She didn't seem particularly thrilled, probably because of the way he'd spoken to her in the cellar. He needed information from her, and talking over the dinner table would be the perfect place.

"Please," he repeated.

A smile lifted the corners of her mouth ever so slowly. "If you insist." She went to the sideboard behind her and retrieved another plate and some silverware.

After they'd both filled their plates, Tillie said grace—the same words Gram had used at every meal they had eaten together—and the three of them began enjoying their food. The woman had an amazing talent in the kitchen, even if she credited the source of her recipes as coming from beyond the grave.

"Everything's delicious. Thank you for going to all this trouble."

"You're welcome. No trouble at all."

He hated being the reason for her clipped tone. Gram always said you could catch more flies with honey than with vinegar. Whatever had possessed him to spoil their first meal in this house by starting so soon to chip away at the woman's preposterous claims? While Greg only had a short time here and their interactions would be limited primarily to meals, he'd attempt to be civil.

"Have you always lived locally?" he asked, hoping small talk would save the evening.

"Yes, in fact, never more than half a mile from this house." She took a few bites, but he let the silence drag out until nervousness made her fill the void. "I did attend college in Lexington, but chose to commute from here rather than live on campus. Mrs. Foster encouraged me to go to culinary school. Most of what I've learned came from her tutelage in her kitchen in the years before her death. She was an amazing cook—and an even better baker."

"Tell me more about her." He'd take any bits and pieces he could learn about Gram, even from this charming charlatan.

A sweet smile radiated across her face at whatever memory passed through her mind, and he experienced a flash of jealousy. "Mrs. Foster had a way of stimulating my mind that made it seem like an adventure whenever I stopped by. While she wasn't very mobile in her later years and had lost her eyesight, when I was younger, she was quite the instigator for all kinds of fun. We might be in search of pirates one day or Jesse James's elusive treasure the next."

Was she aware of the story Gram had told in her journals? He'd play it close to the vest for now. "There's treasure?"

She laughed, glancing toward Derek before returning her gaze to him. "As I told you earlier, if there is, I haven't found it. Mrs. Foster hinted at secret passageways even, not that I've found any of those here."

He remembered the odd stones in the cellar. Might they be entrances to some kind of passageways? But how would anyone move those massive stones out of the way without some serious equipment or some type of mechanism in place?

"Can I search for buried treasure, too? Like on *Jake and the Neverland Pirates* cartoon?" Derek asked.

Tillie sought silent permission from Greg. After he gave a nod of approval, she addressed Derek directly. This might be the break he needed to snoop without raising her suspicions. "Of course you may. Say when, and I'll try to be ready." Darn. He'd much rather do so without being watched.

"Can we start tonight?" Derek asked.

"Well, that all depends on how fond you are of dark cellars."

His eyes opened wider. "Wh-what's a cellar?"

Greg answered, "That's another word for basement. Usually, it has a dirt floor."

"Yes, although I had my cellar floor covered in concrete," Tillie continued. He hoped Tillie's covering the dirt floor hadn't obliterated any evidence. "But one room down there is dark and dank and rather scary even in daylight." She winked at Greg, but spoke to Derek. "I think we'd best wait until tomorrow afternoon—or whenever your dad says is good for you. I'm sure he has plans for your day tomorrow."

Greg didn't want to seem too anxious, but still hoped to prove Gram's claim that Jesse James had been here—not merely in the 1860s as historians pretty much have documented, but as late as the 1930s, half a century after he was supposed to have been killed in Missouri.

He'd found stories online about a man named James Frank Dalton purporting to be Jesse James. That man had lived to be more than 100 years old, dying in 1951 in Texas, although DNA tests didn't appear to substantiate the claim. But Gram insinuated in her journals that history had it all wrong. If Greg could find any evidence that Jesse was here in the '30s, it would be an earthshattering discovery.

He smiled at Tillie. "I can't think of anything that would be as exciting as hunting for lost treasure. But there are a couple places we need to go first tomorrow."

"You'll help us find the treasure, won't you, Daddy?" When invited so sweetly, how could he refuse? Was Derek a little nervous about venturing into the cellar without him? A sense of paternal pride surged through him making him anticipate sharing the hunt with his son more than going it alone.

At least he hadn't foisted himself on the two of them.

"I suppose I could, if Tillie doesn't mind."

"Daddy can go with us, right?" Derek and Greg turned toward her in unison.

Her smile wavered momentarily. "Of course." She didn't appear to be as thrilled as Derek was about the prospect. But Greg jumped at the chance to check out parts of the house he hadn't seen in decades before he resorted to outright snooping.

During his last visit with Gram, they'd been in the kitchen and parlor mostly. Even though it had been mid-November, Gram asked him to decorate her Christmas tree. She said it was too difficult for her to do it by herself anymore, and she wanted it up before they left so she could enjoy it. His mother had read a magazine while he and Gram worked on it, as he recalled. Christmas wasn't a big deal for his mother. Unlike Gram.

When Tillie stood to clear the table, he realized he'd spaced out. He started to do the same until she said, "Leave them. You're my guests. Why don't you go into the parlor? I have some games and books you can relax with and can bring in dessert after our meal settles a bit."

"I don't mind." He stacked Derek's plate on his and picked up his tea glass. Dinner had come to an end all too soon, leaving him surprisingly puzzled as to why he wanted to prolong the moment. But he did. Perhaps because he hadn't shared a meal with anyone as interesting to talk with in a long while. Definitely not since Nancy left him two years ago.

After clearing the table, she drew him aside. "Before you get your hopes up, metal detectors scoured the cellar before I had the cement floor laid and only found flatware, bits of cracked pottery, and a Civil War ammunition ball."

That answered one question. "I'm sure Derek will love the search, whether he finds anything or not."

Again, she seemed less than enthusiastic as she insisted they leave the room while she finished tidying up. He and Derek soon found themselves immersed in a battle on the Civil War chessboard. He'd been so fascinated with this set as a boy that he'd scoured online auction sites until he'd found one close to it. He'd played hours and hours of chess with his grandmother, who had skunked him royally every single time, even that last visit, despite his having been one of the best members of his middle-school chess team.

His son knew nothing about the finer points of the game, but had enjoyed playing with toy soldiers. He moved the pieces around the board with abandon trying to find ways to attack his Daddy's blue-coated army.

As Derek's knight charged up to attack Greg's king, Tillie entered the room. "Who's winning?"

When she smiled at Greg, all thoughts of defending his army flew out the window.

Knocking over Greg's king, Derek proudly proclaimed his victory. "I am, Miss Tillie!"

She carried a tray with a pitcher of milk, several glasses, and a mountain of cookies. "It appears you certainly are, Derek. After such a hard-fought battle, I thought these might hit the spot."

Despite the filling meal, he wouldn't turn them down. "I do believe those might soften my bitter defeat."

Setting the tray on the nearby coffee table, she began pouring milk into glasses. "Milk and cookies are the cure for everything."

"You sound like Gra—" He stopped himself before revealing too much. She couldn't know he'd almost said Gram or revealed who she really was, but he needed to be careful. "My grandmother used to say the same thing."

"Another gem I learned from Mrs. Foster—among so many others."

Once again, he found himself wanting to understand their relationship more. She seemed to be more than a hired caretaker. He joined her at the coffee table. "Sounds like she meant a lot to you."

"She was like a mother to me." Tillie dropped her gaze to the rug. "Anyone would have been an improvement over my own, who was messed up on prescription drugs. Some people have no business having a child."

"I'm sorry to hear that." His own mother wasn't particularly warm and affectionate, but she made sure his needs were met. His physical ones, at least.

She smiled again. "I was lucky enough to find Mrs. Foster when I was eight. She made up for my mother's negligence and my father's absence. Absentee fathers are a theme in my family dating to at least my grandmother, and probably her mother, too, although I don't know anything about her."

While his own father had been emotionally distant, he'd been present in Greg's life for the important events like graduations and such. The story she told began to affect his resolve to expose her as a charlatan. It sounded as though she'd had a tough childhood. Maybe she found comfort believing in imaginary friends—and ghosts.

No longer making eye contact with him, she set another saucer on the table for Derek. "I apologize. What on earth got into me to go on like that?"

An unexpected tenderness suffused his heart. He could imagine how the neglected girl won over his grandmother, especially since it must have been about the same time his own mother had rejected Gram.

"Never apologize for being honest, Tillie."

She muttered her thanks under her breath and handed Derek his milk. Greg worried about the fine crystal she'd chosen to serve them in. "Should I get his no-spill cup?"

Tillie turned to Derek. "Can you handle this glass without breaking it?"

Derek sobered. "I'm a big boy now. Mommy says I grow more every night while I'm sleeping."

To Greg, she smiled and said, "He'll do fine."

Greg accepted his along with a saucer holding two cookies and took a seat on the brocade sofa. Derek chose to use the coffee table and knelt on the floor. "You seem to know a lot about kids. You'd make a great mother." No sooner were the words out of his mouth, he wanted to call them back. "Pardon me. None of my business."

She laughed and pushed away his concern with a wave of her hand as she took her own seat across the sofa from him. "I've never been serious enough about anyone to even think about marriage, much less having children. I think I'm meant to be an auntie to other people's kids. I can spoil them and send them home."

The affection that shone from her eyes as she regarded Derek spoke volumes, but he detected a hint of regret, too. Did she keep herself buried in the inn to avoid romantic attachments? Most of her clients probably were couples. Not much of a chance of her meeting anyone eligible within these walls.

But he couldn't picture her anywhere else. She belonged here. His grandmother must have seen that, too.

Wait. Don't forget why you're here.

If Tillie loved Gram so much, she wouldn't be exploiting her memory. As for Tillie's love life—or the lack thereof—that was none of his concern.

Now, if he told himself that often enough, he might start to believe it.

What the hell's gotten into you? Truly the woman was a sorceress.

Chapter Four

Tillie's hands shook as she took a sip of milk, but she had difficulty swallowing and set down the glass. She hadn't thought about her mother in a long time. Perhaps with so much going wrong today, her defenses were down.

Thoughts of the children she'd probably never have pained her, too. She believed she'd do a much better job raising them than her mother had, but because she chose to avoid serious relationships with men, it was a moot point.

Her pulse quickened as she continued to avert her gaze. The urge to tell him her story nearly overwhelmed her, but she needed to remember he was her guest, not a friend.

Derek had returned to the chess table near the window, moving the Civil War styled pieces around as he made battle sounds.

"I'll begin putting up my biggest Christmas tree in here this week in that same spot." She pointed to the chess table. The enormous tree would be filled with Mrs. Foster's treasured ornaments, more than two thousand miniature lights, and dozens of strands of beaded garland. While she would have Christmas trees and other decorations in every room, the parlor tree was always Tillie's favorite, conjuring up memories of so many Christmases together with Mrs. Foster before…

"Isn't it a little early?"

She smiled at him, happy they'd found a safe topic of conversation again. "Wait until you see the size of it. I probably won't finish until a week before Thanksgiving."

"I can't wait." She searched his face for a trace of sarcasm, but he seemed genuinely interested. "And I'd love a tour of the house tomorrow, if you have time."

"I'm happy to show you the rest tonight, if you'd like. I love showing off this place to newcomers, although you seem to know a lot about this type of house already."

"I took a lot of courses in classic design."

Ah, that explained his inordinate knowledge of the place.

"Although the en suite bathroom is a nice change from the original 1820s to 1840s design that only offered an outhouse or privy," he said.

She nodded. "Agreed! I was able to renovate two bedrooms to include bathrooms. Modern-day guests aren't keen on standing in their bathrobes in the hallway or making use of privies and chamber pots as travelers once did."

"True enough." He grinned. "Having Derek's and my rooms adjoining each other is perfect. Choosing a room with a private bath was a plus, too."

Images of the man soaking in the claw-foot tub upstairs heated her cheeks.

Do not *picture your guests naked, Matilda!*

He stared down at his saucer a moment as though uncomfortable. She hoped he hadn't read her thoughts.

Shifting her mind in a different direction, she noted the lack of a wedding band on his ring finger. She wouldn't think an architect would have a particularly dangerous job requiring him to remove his rings, sparking curiosity again about his marital status.

She had no business wondering such things, but couldn't control where her mind wandered.

"So how long have you been running an inn from this house?" Greg asked, taking another bite of his cookie.

"This is my eleventh year. I opened soon after I graduated from college." His eyebrows rose in surprise. She must not look her thirty-two years. "I've loved this house since I was a little girl when Mrs. Foster took me under her wing. I think she must have seen how lost I was."

"How did you meet Mrs. Foster and become so close?"

Hoping to put to rest any discussion of the past without going into much more detail, she responded, "Mrs. Foster helped me escape poverty and neglect, giving me my first moments of joy during visits with her."

"I'm sorry to hear things were so bad for you growing up."

She waved away his concern and picked up a cookie to nibble on. Small bites. Her throat remained somewhat closed off as memories of the past bombarded her. Thank God Mrs. Foster had been there when she needed her. Tillie had been eight, living in a rundown shack nearby when the two first met.

"One of her cats strayed across my path one day." The words came out without her consciously deciding to continue, but now she'd have to go on.

"How did you know it belonged to her?"

"I roamed the neighborhood most days, preferring not to go home until as late as possible. I'd often seen the tabby on her porch and wanted to make sure he made it safely home."

"Why don't you have a cat?"

"I inherited Mrs. Foster's last two, and when they died, I didn't want to bring in more because so many of my guests are allergic to them." She would have enjoyed the companionship of one, especially during the post-holiday months when she had few guests, but Tillie opted to accommodate her guests' needs instead.

Where was she and how had she strayed to the topic of cats? "Anyway, kids in the neighborhood had dubbed this place haunted and Mrs. Foster a witch."

"That's ridiculous." The anger in his eyes seemed a bit over the top considering he hadn't known the woman, but in retrospect, she hated that people had been so hard on her benefactor.

Which only made her next words harder to express. "I'll admit I had my fears, too, so with more than a little trepidation I ventured up the then-gravel drive to knock. Mrs. Foster opened the dining-room door that day and welcomed me home along with her cat."

Most days after that, Tillie spent her days here in this grand old house, having tea parties with the octogenarian, listening to her stories of a fascinating life, and learning how to bake and cook. "Mrs. Foster had learned to bake and cook while working as a domestic in the home of a well-to-do family in Old Louisville, all the while earning money to go to nursing school. She served as a nurse in World War II at the rank of captain."

Greg nodded as if he already knew.

No matter. Tillie fell short of admitting to this stranger that this house captivated her as much as the old woman did, both of them providing a refuge from the apathy she suffered at home and giving her a sense of belonging.

To this day, Jesse's Hideout remained her sanctuary from an unpredictable, sometimes uncivil, frightening world—one she didn't belong in.

"I miss her terribly."

"Is that why you make up the stories about her haunting the place, because you can't let go of those memories?" The minute the scowl returned to Greg's face, she knew the pleasantries were over. Oh well. They'd had a slight break in the tension at least. How the man could be charming one minute and surly the next was beyond her.

His intense gaze and rude question made the pulse pound in Tillie's ears. "I beg your pardon?" What exactly did he mean by "make up"? Hadn't she already addressed this accusation in the cellar a few hours ago?

Remain civil and professional.

The man was a paying guest, after all. Drawing a deep breath and plastering her face with her most saccharine Scarlett O'Hara smile, she faced him again. "You sound as though you don't believe someone can reach beyond the grave to communicate with the living."

She hoped her choice of words wouldn't alarm the boy across the room, but a peek in his direction showed he was making shooting sounds and engaging in a mock battle, not the least bit interested in the grown-up talk across the room.

Neither am I, quite honestly.

"Mrs. Foster only wants to help me. I don't think she has any concern about any of my guests." Not completely true, though. Her presence was stronger today than it had been in a long time.

Greg set his empty glass on the coffee table. "You said she leaves you recipe cards from her private collection."

"She does. Would you like to see one?"

He glanced at Derek, and then seemingly satisfied his son wasn't paying attention to the grown-up talk, Greg faced her again. "As a matter of fact, I would."

Tillie stood. *Good! I'll show him!*

"Wait here. I'll grab the one she left me this afternoon right after you arrived." She walked into the kitchen, trying to slow down her pulse by breathing deeply and slowly. Opening the recipe box where she kept the treasured new recipes Mrs. Foster had delivered separate from the ones already published in the first cookbook, Tillie plucked out the oatmeal-raisin one and, in the parlor once again, handed it to him.

"Here." She waited as he scrutinized it. A whiff of the coveted cookies came to her. Greg sniffed the air as well, wrinkling his brow.

"You smell them, too?" she asked. No other guest had ever been able to detect Mrs. Foster's presence before.

"Smell what? Your cookies?"

Tillie shook her head. "We aren't smelling these," she said, pointing toward the few remaining ones on the plate. "You're smelling the oatmeal-raisin ones from the recipe card you're holding."

He lifted the card to his nose and sniffed again, but of course he wouldn't find the scent on the card. He met her gaze. "You have a batch of these in the oven."

"No. I can't make them until the final ingredient is delivered tomorrow."

He focused his attention to the card once again, and she thought he muttered something about "her handwriting" and "my favorite."

"I assure you that isn't my handwriting."

He met her gaze, seeming at a loss for words. "I know it's not," he whispered.

She fought the smile threatening to erupt on her face. Were they making some progress? Did he believe her now?

His eyelids narrowed. "Why won't you simply admit you found these cards in the house when you inherited it?"

Or not.

She shook her head and drew a deep breath before exhaling slowly. She spoke deliberately, as if to a child. "No. Mrs. Foster's recipes were nowhere to be found when she died. Believe me, I searched high and low, especially for this one. She hasn't given them to me all at once, either, for whatever reason. Instead, she delivers one whenever she feels like it—or perhaps when she thinks I need one. This past spring, while I worked on the cookbook, they were arriving a few each day, but since then, they've trickled off. In fact, this is the first I've received in months. As I said earlier, it was the one I wanted most of all."

He regarded at the card again. "Why that one?"

Tillie couldn't contain her smile. "Wait until you taste one. You'll never forget them." He nodded in seeming understanding. "Knowing the elusive ingredient that has plagued me for years—Chinese five-spice powder—I can't wait to bake a batch. Tomorrow, if the package arrives."

He read the recipe card some more before giving it back to her with seeming reluctance. "What difference could one ingredient make?"

"Bless your heart." Was he familiar with the southern phrase's true meaning? Well, she didn't care. "If Mrs. Foster specified it in the recipe, then it makes a difference. She also specified the manufacturer, so I didn't want to take a chance on using one that's not the exact same compound."

He shrugged. "If you say so. I can't wait to try one ag…to try one of yours."

"Thank you." While she hadn't changed his mind about how she'd come to possess this recipe card, maybe she could warm his skeptical little heart through his stomach.

Derek yawned loudly, drawing both of their gazes.

"Sport, I think we'd better be heading up to bed."

Derek plopped on the floor and folded his hands in front of his chest. "I'm not sleeping nowhere."

"I'm not sleeping anywhere," Greg corrected.

"Me, neither!"

Tillie had to bite the inside of her lower lip to keep from laughing, but didn't want to undermine his parental authority. A muscle spasmed in Greg's jaw as he struggled to keep a straight face. Unaware of the adults' response to his inadvertent joke, Derek stuck out his lower lip.

"No pouting. We have a lot to see and do while we're here. We need our rest."

The pout disappeared as quickly as it had come. "Like what?"

"Oh, all kinds of things."

Thinking his evasiveness might mean he didn't know what things a little boy might enjoy doing around here, she spoke up, hoping he wouldn't think her interfering.

"When I was growing up around here, I loved to walk on the railroad tracks, play baseball, and wander around in the cemetery."

"You have a graveyard?" Derek asked, wide-eyed.

Perhaps this wasn't the best thing to be talking about right before Derek went bed, but pride in her community's history kept her talking. "Of course we do! The earliest burials date to almost two centuries ago."

"I know what happens in graveyards."

She cocked her head to the side, surprised a five-year-old would have given such places any thought. "You do?"

He nodded with great assuredness. "When you die, you get buried there. Then your hand pokes up out of the dirt, and you turn into a zombie."

Tillie was at a loss for what to say and sought Greg's help, only to find him fighting back another grin. This kid could be a stand-up comic. She'd have to tackle this one on her own and said to Derek, "I'm afraid you aren't going to find any zombies in our old church cemetery."

The disappointment on his face left her wondering if he'd find anything here the least bit entertaining if zombies were his benchmark for excitement.

"Do you have any ghosts here?" Derek asked.

"Well, now, that's another matter. We've had a few ghosts in the neighborhood over the centuries. Some even say the notorious Jesse James hides out here on occasion."

Derek came over to sit on her lap. "Daddy said he robbed lots of trains. Have you seen him?"

After reassuring herself with a curt nod from Greg to make sure he had no objections, she went on, beginning with one foot firmly planted in reality.

"I was alone in this house one night about a year after the previous owner passed away, asleep in the room where your daddy is staying now. The house had a number of renovation projects going on, and I was exhausted. After locking all of the doors and windows, I went to bed as soon as it grew dark and drifted off to sleep."

She lowered her voice to a whisper and leaned closer to the boy. "Suddenly, I heard footsteps on the stairs. Heavy, plodding footfalls. Someone was in the house! But who could it be? Had one of the workers stayed behind, up to no good?"

"Was it a bad guy?"

"Well, when I opened the door, holding a baseball bat in case I needed to use it—"

"All you had for protection was a bat?" Greg interrupted, pulling her out of the story.

She wouldn't tell him it was a miniature Louisville slugger or he'd be even more incredulous. If she'd jabbed the end in a vulnerable spot, she could have caused great harm.

Choosing to ignore him, she focused on Derek. "Deciding that the element of surprise was on my side, I swung open the door—but no one was there. However, I still heard the heavy footsteps. They continued to come up and down the stairs for another half an hour after I went back to my bed. Finally, I called out to the spirit that I was tired and needed some sleep so please stop."

"Did it?" Derek's eyes were as wide as saucers now.

"Yes, it did. I've heard those steps again on occasion, especially when I'm making renovations or moving the furniture around. Spirits don't like change."

"Will I hear steps tonight?" His eyes showed a mixture of excitement and fear.

"Oh no! I'm not doing anything that would stir up the spirit right now."

The boy relaxed his shoulders and rested against her chest, eliciting every maternal instinct she possessed. "I see a ghost in my room at home, but Mommy says nobody's there." He shook his head. "She sure looks real to me."

"Son, sometimes we can let our imaginations run wild and conjure up all kinds of scary things when all we need to do is take a moment to analyze things and figure them out."

Apparently, Greg didn't think much of her ghostly footsteps story, either. Regardless of what this exasperating man thought, her experience was the God's honest truth.

Greg's disbelief still firmly in place, he said, "That must disappoint the guests coming to have an otherworldly encounter."

She met Greg's gaze, fighting to rein in her temper as, once again, he called her a fraud and a liar.

If he'd done any research on the local tourism sites, he'd know that ghosts abounded in this county. Still, her inn wasn't so much haunted as visited by Mrs. Foster. She preferred to call her a spirit, since she'd known her in life.

But the night she'd heard those heavy footsteps had been as real as the sound of his own steps on the stairs. Could she convince him by sharing one more story? Why she bothered, she didn't know, but she didn't like being called a liar.

"While construction men were wiring the cellar, they reported hearing otherworldly sounds in the northern room of the cellar. And something kept playing games with the electricity."

"How can 'lectricity play games?"

"Well, the workers would plug their electric drills into the same outlets as the overhead lights were connected to, but the tools would suddenly lose power. However, the lights continued to shine even though both were plugged into the same outlet."

"Sounds like they needed a better electrician."

Why did she bother?

Ignoring Greg, she spoke to Derek instead. "The workers became so frightened they quit for the day, but came back the next day and found all the outlets working fine."

To this day, Tillie hadn't figured out which spirit had been responsible for that prank, but Mrs. Foster wouldn't do anything so silly.

Greg rose from the sofa, setting his empty saucer on the table and putting an end to her storytelling. "Come on, Derek. Let's put the chess pieces away and straighten up our mess."

"Don't worry about anything," Tillie assured him. "I'm sure he'll want to play with them again. Leave them as they are until then."

"You're sure?"

"Positive." Fatigue suddenly weighed Tillie down, unlike she'd experienced in forever. She stood and gathered the empty saucers and glasses placing them on the tray. "When would you like breakfast?"

"Our bodies are on Central, so let's say nine."

Thank you! She could sleep in a bit.

"Nine, it is. If you need anything overnight in the kitchen or anywhere, help yourself. Good night, Derek. Sleep well. Oh, and Greg, I promise to finish your tour tomorrow."

"Sounds good. Night, Tillie."

She lifted the tray and started out of the room before turning back. "Good night, Greg."

She met his gaze, and he added, "Thanks. For everything." He smiled, but the corners of his eyes didn't scrunch this time.

Day one down. Nine to go. She'd so anticipated having them here, but the roller coaster of emotions she'd ridden today made her wonder what lay ahead.

Greg Buchanan, just you wait. I'm going to charm your skepticism away before you leave here.

Chapter Five

Sleep didn't come to Greg that night as quickly as it did Derek. The boy was out before Greg finished his second five-minute bedtime story. Greg left him snug under the covers and appliqued quilt. He walked into his adjoining room, checked e-mails, read a while, but still couldn't get his mind to stop rehashing the day's events.

The handwriting on that recipe card was Gram's beyond a doubt—the same cursive used in her journals. There could be no other logical explanation than that Tillie had found the recipes here in the house or had been given them by his grandmother. Tillie had inherited the house and most of its contents after all.

He recognized enough of Gram's furniture throughout the house to know it was from her estate. Where else would the recipe cards have been all these years if not inside some drawer, dresser, or cabinet?

Why lie about it?

Because ghosts are popular now, and she had rooms available awaiting unsuspecting travelers.

He wouldn't mind running into the ghost of Jesse James. The first question he'd ask was where in the hell was this hidden proof of his delayed departure from this world? Why hadn't Gram been more forthcoming in her journals?

Of course, he'd love to have a chance to talk with her, too, and apologize for what she must have perceived as a rejection during her final years without any contact from him? When he'd discovered the truth about when Gram died, he'd confronted his mother, but she seemed to have no remorse over her actions. How could she be so callous toward her own mother—not to mention what her actions had cost her son.

Greg spent the next few hours poring over two key volumes of Gram's "personal ramblings," as Mother categorized them, trying to see if he could uncover any new clues. When Gram's journals had arrived initially from the attorney, he'd been working for Nancy's father's firm—fresh out of architecture school and keeping extremely long hours in addition to carving out time to date his future bride. The journals had been tucked away and promptly forgotten.

Until his accident. Gram poured out her heart and soul on every page. She'd bucked the norm for women of her day and age. What on earth had his mother disliked so much about her? Maybe he'd come right out and ask her someday.

Or not. Neither he nor his mother engaged in deep conversation about anything that mattered. And ever since he'd learned the truth about the devastating way his family had deserted Gram in her final years, the last thing he wanted to do was have a heart-to-heart with his mother. His anger toward her was still too raw three months later. Oh, he had demanded to know why she would do something so horrific, but she'd only said she'd changed since then.

There would never be an excuse good enough to appease Greg.

He set down the journal and closed his eyes. As he began to doze off, he thought he heard a rocking chair down the hall. Was it coming from Tillie's room? Was she unable to sleep, too? Served her right, only she was probably staying up late to concoct some new ruse to make her ghost stories plausible.

But how could he hear her all the way on the other side of the house without a connecting hallway upstairs? The walls in the center of the house were probably a foot thick.

Tossing the quilt aside, he grabbed his phone for a flashlight and opted to go downstairs for a look-see. She'd told him to make himself at home. When would he have a better opportunity to explore without being watched than in the middle of the night?

The parlor was a good place to start. He shined the LED light inside the fireplace, hoping to find some evidence of one of the secret passageways Gram had mentioned to him. Oddly, none were mentioned in her journals, though. Had she played to a boy's imagination? Tillie's, too, because she'd heard the stories as well.

Next, he shined the light on the walnut mantel. Beautiful craftsmanship, but nothing…what's that? Upon closer inspection, he saw scratching in the wood that looked like the initials J.H.

John Howard was one of Jesse James's aliases. Could it be that he left them here on one of his visits—whether in the 1860s and 1870s or the 1930s?

"Oh, it's you!"

Greg looked up to find Tillie in a long robe and gown more sheer than he'd have expected the old-fashioned innkeeper to wear, more reminiscent of the glamorous days of Hollywood in the '30s. Her loose hair was haloed by the foyer light.

"I-I hope I didn't wake you," he stammered. How to explain what he was doing in here at midnight or whatever the hour? "Couldn't sleep and thought I'd do a little…" *Snooping?* "Uh, exploring. This house fascinates me."

She smiled. "Go right ahead. I'm just glad you aren't an intruder." Her hand came out of the folds of her robe to reveal a revolver. Thankfully, she kept it pointed toward the floor.

"I see you're able to take care of yourself. I won't have to worry about Derek coming upon that, will I?"

She entered the room, set the revolver on the end table, and flipped the switch for the lamp. "Not at all. I usually keep it locked in my gun safe unless I'm alone and will return it there tonight."

"That puts my mind at ease." He'd taught his son never to touch a gun and to seek out an adult if he found one, but why tempt fate?

Pointing to the mantel, she said, "Those initials are from Mrs. Foster's last beau."

Beau? She'd been involved with someone after his grandfather passed away? Well, she'd been widowed for several decades. Why shouldn't she seek out companionship? And that was as far as Greg intended to take the relationship in his mind. This was his grandmother, after all.

While he wasn't ready to relinquish his original idea that the initials might have been etched by Jesse himself, he ought to hear her out. "What makes you say that?"

"I have some letters written by Joseph Hill—who I believe carved the J.H. there." She pointed at the mantel. "He was an important person to her later in life. On her deathbed, Mrs. Foster told me about him, describing as the last great love of her life. She didn't meet Mr. Hill until decades after she'd been widowed. I think she said she was about seventy-two years old. For whatever reason, the two of them never married."

Greg remained riveted to her words. Gram had mentioned a traveling companion in her journals, but not by name—and she hadn't indicated he was male.

When Tillie came closer to where he stood, she reached out to touch the carved initials. "Instead, the two simply traveled together to cities far from local prying eyes—places like Cincinnati, Chicago, St. Louis, and once even to New York City. Mostly to meet and spend time together in cities that had a lot to offer—plays, ballets, operas, and always fine dining." Tillie grinned impishly. "I have no idea if the relationship became physical. Mrs. Foster wouldn't have told me anyway, because I was only a senior in high school, and the old woman thought me naive when it came to boys."

He'd guessed at Tillie's naiveté with dating already. Someday, she'd make the lucky man who could win her heart very happy.

"After her death and before renovations began for the inn, I scoured the house looking for treasures of hers I wouldn't want lost or damaged. I discovered many of the letters she received from Mr. Hill, a number of them tucked between the pages of her books. The affection in the correspondence was quite formal and distant by today's standards, but Mrs. Foster cried when she told me he'd died tragically in a bus accident while on vacation in Mexico. Thank God Mrs. Foster hadn't been with him."

Greg's focus returned to the initials. Perhaps Tillie was right. The initials might not be Jesse James's alias at all, but most likely belonged to this Joseph Hill—a man who couldn't claim his grandmother at the altar, but wanted to leave his mark on her home at least. The initials provided a legacy for the man and a daily reminder to Gram of his existence. He had to have carved the initials decades after Jesse James had died—either time.

"That's an amazing story." The woman had a knack for storytelling in general. This one he believed, not only because of her tone of voice and sincere facial expressions but because he'd read about Hill in Gram's journals. The thought of the old girl seeking another companion, if not lover, late in life made him smile.

Tillie broke into his reverie. "Since you're up and I need to put this revolver back in the safe, why don't I show you the two remaining rooms on this floor?"

Greg wouldn't pass up this opportunity. "Sounds great. Lead the way."

He closed the LED app while she retrieved the revolver. "Follow me. Let me put this away first," she said as she crossed the first room he'd cut through to the dining room a few times. She turned on lamps as she made her way to what he remembered to be his grandfather's office. "Why don't you join me in here first?"

These two rooms combined were smaller than the parlor. The office was only seven or eight feet deep from the doorway to the birthing room and the exterior wall of the house, but its length was the same as the parlor on the opposite side of the house.

"Mrs. Foster's husband was a popular country doctor, and this was his office where he saw patients. Of course, he also made house calls. She said his patients paid him with all manner of barter from bacon and steaks to eggs and produce."

"Hard to imagine a doctor working like that today."

"More like impossible. Interestingly, Jesse James's relative who lived here in the 1860s also was a physician." She pointed to a walnut cabinet with glass-front doors. "This is my liquor cabinet. It's unlocked, so anytime you'd like to have a drink, help yourself."

He doubted many innkeepers offered guests an open bar. The cabinet boasted every type of alcohol he would imagine anyone would want, with an abundance of various types of bourbon. "Thanks. I'm not much of a liquor drinker, especially when I'm responsible for Derek, but I'll keep that in mind."

In the corner, near the driveway side of the house, he saw a gas fireplace. In front of it sat a wing chair with a crocheted afghan and throw pillow, flanked by a small table.

"My guests love that spot for reading on a cold or dreary day."

"How about you?"

She cocked her head. "Me?"

"Do you ever slow down long enough to curl up with a good book or a glass of brandy in front of the fire?"

Wistfulness flashed across her face. "On occasion."

"Lately?"

She shook her head. "I stay busy from spring planting to fall harvesting and then holidays will be here. I'll curl up in front of the fire in January," she said with a smile.

Unbidden, a fantasy popped into his head of the two of them cuddled up in front of the fire at his house, sipping hot toddies, their legs and feet intertwined.

Where the hell had that come from?

Drawing himself back to the conversation, he asked, "All work and no play?"

A spark of fire lit her eyes. "What do *you* do in your spare time?"

"I stay busy running my architecture firm."

"That's all?"

"Of course when Nancy doesn't have Derek, I spend time with

him."

"Nancy's your...wife?" She hesitated, and he realized she had no clue what his status was.

"Was. We're divorced, but share custody."

"I'm so sorry." She sounded as though she meant it.

"I usually have Derek every other weekend. This trip happens to be the longest we've been together since she left me two years ago."

"It must be hard for Derek to be apart from one or the other of you at any given point."

He shrugged. "We broke up so early in his life, all he remembers is us being in separate homes. But there are times when he clings to me when I take him home, which makes me wish we'd been able to work it out." For some reason, he opened up more than he would to someone he barely knew. "I made some poor choices, spending long hours at the office and not giving my marriage and family the attention I should have. Oh, I saw to their financial needs, not unlike my own father, but that's no excuse."

"Sounds like we both immerse ourselves in our work."

"I don't work when I have Derek." *Tell the truth.* "Not while he's awake, anyway."

"What else occupies those long Minnesota winters?"

Feeling defensive and not wanting to sound too dull, he added, "I do things like cycling, hiking, reading."

"Let me guess—*Architectural Digest.*" Her lips twitched as she had some fun at his expense, but he appreciated her lightening the conversation.

So what if he liked to stay abreast of matters concerning his career? "That, but I also read novels by Ildefonso Falcones, Ken Follett, Dan Brown, and John Berendt." He fired off the names in a clipped tone. Honestly, though, he hadn't taken time for pleasure reading in years, but didn't want her thinking he did nothing but work in between visits with his son. How pathetic did she think he was?

"I loved *Midnight in the Garden of Good and Evil,*" she said, apparently satisfied with his reading choices. "Have you been to Savannah?"

"Quite a while ago. It's an architectural treasure."

"So you don't focus solely on northern architecture."

"Not at all. I consult with several firms throughout the south, but tend to gravitate toward Federal and Georgian-style homes."

Tillie took a sudden interest in the floor. "I'll admit, I have no business calling you out for being a workaholic. I hide away here rather than date or go out socially."

"We make some pair." The words took a different meaning as soon as they left his mouth. He quickly added, "I suppose being proprietors of our own businesses has an effect on our somewhat solitary lifestyles, too."

"Indeed." Tillie moved through the pocket doorway without making eye contact again. "Next let me show you the birthing room."

He'd been waiting for this after reading Gram's journals, but chose to play ignorant. "The what?"

"That's the response I usually receive whenever I tell visitors the name," Tillie said with a grin. "This is where Dr. Foster's pregnant patients came and stayed until they had their babies. I'm sure it was used for other critically ill patients, too. The nearest hospital back then was eight miles away on the old roads. Around here, it wasn't uncommon for babies to be born at home well into the 1940s, before hospital births became a trend."

"If only these walls could talk," he said. She'd kept many of Gram's furnishings in here—overstuffed chairs in front of a primitive chest with reading lamps for each chair. The olive green chair rail and fireplace mantel gave the room a calming effect. He tried to imagine a woman on a bed in here giving birth like the one described in Gram's journal.

"Thanks to Mrs. Foster, I'm able to pass on a number of its stories. I'm even working on a new book that combines recipes along with more history of the house." She paused. "That will be one of *my* winter projects this year."

The woman had a lot of ambition. "I'd like to buy a copy when it's published."

"I appreciate that since it's primarily of local interest, but I'll be marketing it to my prior guests, so watch for an e-mail." She smiled, sweeping her arm to encompass the room. "And this concludes our tour."

"Thanks so much." While he wasn't the least bit sleepy and would give anything to do a little snooping here, especially around the fireplaces, he didn't want to raise her suspicions. "Well, I'd best be getting to bed. Thanks for the tour."

In the foyer, they stood near one another, seemingly reluctant to go their separate ways. Greg broke the stalemate.

"Good night, Tillie. See you in the morning."

"Night, Greg." She made no move to leave, so he made his way to the stairs, locking gazes with her as he ascended to his room. When she finally was out of sight, a sense of emptiness came over him.

Tillie Hamilton, I don't think your house is haunted. I think you're a witch.

She certainly had bewitched him.

* * *

"Wake up, Daddy. Let's go to the graveyard."

Greg opened his eyes to find daylight streaming in the window and Derek crawling up into his bed using the stepstool. He didn't remember sleeping a wink, and the lethargy muddying his thoughts told him he hadn't slept restfully.

"What time is it?" he asked, his voice gravelly.

"Time to wake up."

Of course Derek didn't have a watch and couldn't read one anyway. With a one-eyed peep at the clock on the nightstand, he saw it was seven thirty-eight. More like six thirty-eight at home. He wasn't normally one to sleep in late, but didn't usually arrive at work until eight, and it was only a ten-minute drive.

Coffee. He needed some strong, black coffee. Trying not to sound too grouchy, he said, "Remember, we told Tillie we'd have breakfast at nine."

"Maybe we'll see some zombies if we go now."

At least he wasn't insisting on spending the morning in the cellar treasure hunting. That would come soon enough, but Greg wanted to be more clearheaded than he was now.

"Derek, there are no zombies in real cemeteries. That's make-believe."

"Yes, there are! I'll show you." Derek tugged Greg's t-shirt sleeve. "Come on, Daddy. Get up!"

"Whoa, slow down!" He managed to open his other eye and sat up, swinging his legs over the side of the mattress. "Besides, the cemetery comes later. I need to stop at the florist to get some flowers first."

Derek cocked his head. "Flowers? Zombies don't like flowers."

Greg couldn't keep himself from grinning. "We aren't going there to visit the zombies." Okay, now he was playing into his son's fantasy. "*Not* that there will be zombies anyway." Greg stood, the rug warm on his bare feet. "Why don't you color on my bed while I'm in the shower?"

Derek's lower lip protruded half an inch from his face now. *Tough.* His mother shouldn't fill his mind with such fanciful notions. He'd have a talk with Nancy when they returned to Minneapolis.

Not ready to go to Gram's grave this early, he stalled. "If you behave today—no pouting—we're going to hunt for hidden treasure with Tillie this afternoon."

"Oh yeah!" Derek bounced up and down on his knees. "And ghosts!"

Greg shook his head. Tillie needed to stop filling his head with those stories, too, although he'd been equally fascinated by the telling of them, even if he didn't believe a single word.

"Not until we have breakfast, pick up some flowers, and stop by the cemetery. We have a busy day planned."

Derek's chin dropped to his chest, and he crossed his arms. "But the zombies will be gone by then."

"That's the chance we'll have to take."

"You're mean." The boy slid from the mattress onto the stool and went to his room. Minutes later, he returned with his coloring book and a box of crayons with practically every hue available at the Crayola Store at the Mall of America. Well, not quite, but more than Greg had ever seen. Apparently, he would get over his disappointment.

After Greg showered and gave Derek his bath, they headed downstairs to breakfast. The aromas wafting from the kitchen set his stomach to growling. In the dining room, he poured himself a mug of coffee on the sideboard and Derek a glass of milk. Rather than wait to be served, they walked into the kitchen hoping Tillie wouldn't feel it an invasion of her domain. But after dinner last night, he doubted she would stand on formality.

A fire burned on the massive hearth, filling the room with cheer and coziness. During his last visit here, Gram had shown him how early residents cooked in the fireplace. He doubted Tillie did any cooking there.

Tillie's hair was pulled into a topknot, with loose tendrils curling around her ears and neck.

"Good morning," he said to her.

She smiled up from her cast-iron skillet where she beat what his grandmother called sawmill gravy—flour, grease, and bits of sausage. He'd tried to find some like it over the years when feeling particularly nostalgic, but none ever compared.

No doubt Tillie would have Gram's original recipe. He was in for a treat.

"Have a seat at the table, and I'll bring everything right in."

He insisted on carrying in one of the platters, and she brought a plate with his biscuits and gravy.

He added sausage patties and fresh fruit. To top it all off, she poured more black coffee in his mug before serving Derek.

Tillie outdid herself with the boy's pancakes, surpassing anything

Gram had ever served Greg.

"Mickey Mouse! How'd you do that?"

"It's magic. I can't reveal my secrets."

No doubt the woman hid a lot of secrets.

But this morning, Greg wasn't interested in being her adversary. "Everything tastes great. Not that I expected anything less. Sit down and join us."

"Glad you like it. This was Mrs. Foster's favorite breakfast."

I know.

Tillie eyed the empty chair a moment then filled a plate and a mug of coffee before joining them.

"Are all these recipes in your original cookbook?" he asked. While he'd seen it online, they sold out before he could obtain a copy.

"Oh yes! There's one in the parlor if you'd like to look at it sometime." She smiled impishly. "I might have a few dozen more lying around here for guests who are interested, if you'd like one to take home."

"Would I ever."

"I didn't think you were into cooking or baking."

Busted. "I'm not, but from what I read on your website, you included the history of the house and some vintage photos, so it would make for the perfect souvenir of our visit."

"That's what I thought when I wrote it. So much rich history here I didn't want it to be lost. I'm not sure yet what I'll include in the second volume, though. I pretty much tapped myself out on history."

"Well, I'd be happy to help with architectural information if you want to go in that direction. Or you might spotlight some of the residents of the house up to Mrs. Foster or even you."

"Believe me, there's nothing to tell about me."

"Well, with the renovations you've done and your keen eye for preservation, like it or not, you've put your stamp on the place, too."

"I never thought about it that way. In fact, as best I can, I could research and discuss the changes made from one owner to the next.

There have only been about four over the past one-hundred seventy or eighty years, although the land itself was part of a land grant, so I could even mention the Revolutionary War soldier who earned it for his service."

The sparkle in her eyes lit up her entire face. She truly loved this house and its history, which didn't quite mesh with his initial assessment of her.

After everyone finished eating, the adults cleared the dishes.

"We're going to head to Bardstown," Greg announced. "Could you recommend a florist? I'd like to pay my respects to someone at the cemetery down the road."

"I didn't know you knew anyone around here."

He'd blundered into that one. "Yeah, she made a big impression on me when I was young."

Tillie seemed to be waiting for him to elaborate, but when he didn't, she grabbed a pad and paper and jotted down the name and address of a flower shop in town. After a pit stop, Greg and Derek headed toward the side door.

"Lock the doors while we're gone." He didn't like the thought of Tillie being alone in case the intruder returned.

"Oh, let me get you a key for the front door then, in case I need to run out." She went to the sideboard and opened a drawer to retrieve one on a Kentucky keychain.

Perhaps he needed to rethink his initial impression of Tillie, since nothing he'd expected had come true. But he and Derek ought to head to town now if they were going to accomplish everything he wanted to do today.

All the way to the county seat, Greg mulled over thoughts of the intriguing innkeeper.

Chapter Six

The house seemed sad and lonely after the Buchanans left, until a knock at the dining-room door a few hours later brought a smile to her face. It had to be the Chinese five-spice powder she'd had overnighted—and it was. She spent the early afternoon mixing batter and dropping the precious gems onto baking sheets.

Tillie felt the way she did at Christmas when she'd found the perfect gift for someone. She couldn't wait for Greg and Derek to return to try them. Heck, she couldn't wait to try one of these special oatmeal-raisin cookies, too. It had been too long.

While the first tray baked, she began putting away the ingredients. She picked up the bottle of homemade vanilla. The tops of the vanilla beans were exposed above the liquid, so she needed to add more vodka. But first, on a whim, she poured a bit of vanilla into a spoon and dipped her finger into it before dabbing a little behind each ear. She giggled, remembering how Mrs. Foster told her once the scent of vanilla drove men wild, much more so than expensive perfumes. Not that she usually indulged in either.

Soon the house smelled incredible, cocooning her in warmth as if she'd just been hugged by the dear woman again. These cookies, steeped in so many memories of her, made Tillie's eyes well with tears.

"I miss you so much, Mrs. Foster." She'd been mother, grandmother, and friend all rolled into one, even though Tillie had never been comfortable addressing her as anything other than her formal name.

Her mother had taught her that, much like Greg was teaching his son to respect his elders. She appreciated that Mrs. Foster had never said a disparaging word about Tillie's mother, even though she'd known what life in Tillie's home had been like. Instead, the sweet old woman had done her best to make up for her mother's shortcomings when Tillie came to visit.

And Tillie couldn't imagine what she'd have done the night she had found her mother cold and unresponsive in that bed if her benefactor hadn't been an absolute angel. Visions of that night bombarded her even now, but Tillie tamped those dark thoughts back down. Instead, she chose to recall the feel of Mrs. Foster's arms hugging her so tightly Tillie thought she'd suffocate. But she hadn't wanted to escape those loving and supportive arms for many days to come. She'd let Tillie sleep in her room those first few nights, because every time she closed her eyes…

If the dear, sweet woman hadn't come to her rescue that night by telling authorities she was her grandmother, Tillie would have become a ward of the state. No formal adoption had taken place, perhaps because she was thirteen and they assumed she would have spoken up if she wanted to be somewhere else. Or because Mrs. Foster had pulled strings behind the scenes. Tillie did a mental shrug. No matter.

Mrs. Foster promised to make everything better somehow, and she had. It wasn't until after her death that Tillie learned she'd left her house and a large stock portfolio to Tillie to pay for its upkeep and for her own education, allowing her to remain in the only place that had ever felt like home.

To this day, Tillie missed the sparkle in Mrs. Foster's eyes whenever Tillie arrived home from school. She would invariably find the dear woman preparing another of the delicious meals Mrs. Foster pressed on Tillie until the girl could hardly move. So much love had come from her hands in this kitchen.

No wonder this was Tillie's happy place. She could never leave here…

"If I didn't know better, I'd think I'd been catapulted twenty-five years back in time." She turned to find Greg standing in the doorway, a confusing mixture of annoyance and ecstasy on his face.

She blinked, reentering reality slowly. "I beg your pardon?" She hadn't even heard him drive into the parking area outside her window. Where had her mind gone? Good thing the cookies hadn't been left in the oven.

She peered behind him. "Where's Derek?"

"I think he woke up too early this morning. He's taking a nap upstairs."

Tillie'd been so lost in baking she hadn't heard them come in. Of course, their key was to the front door, and she was at the opposite end of the house.

He didn't meet her gaze as he entered the kitchen, but homed in on the tray of cookies. "Mind if I try one?"

"Please do! They're still warm." She removed one from the spatula and extended it to him. As he took a bite, the expression on his face came close to being orgasmic.

"Mmm." He devoured the rest of it and looked at her with such longing, her heart fluttered.

"Um, here. Have another." He didn't argue with her, and their fingers brushed as he accepted this one, setting off sparks.

"We'll have to try and leave a couple of these for Derek," she said as she scraped the remainder off the parchment paper and moved them to a cooling rack. Picking up another, she took a bite. "This is the closest thing to Heaven I'll ever experience on Earth."

Greg cocked his head. "I'm not sure I'd go that far, but they're awfully damned close."

The two of them didn't see eye to eye on much, but they'd found common ground on Mrs. Foster's oatmeal-raisin cookies.

"I can taste that Chinese spice, I think. And the scent of vanilla is strong."

Tillie tucked a tendril of hair behind her ear, having forgotten all about the makeshift perfume she'd applied earlier. She smiled.

"Milk?"

"Coffee, if you have it. Black. I need a little pick-me-up this afternoon, too."

"No problem. I keep a pot going all day long." After pouring each of them a mug, she carried them over to the breakfast nook, preferring to stay near the fire rather than go to the dining room. Greg brought over a plate with two more cookies each and several napkins.

"Some lunch we're having."

"Oats and raisins are good for you," he gave as an excuse.

"I like the way you think." She wanted to find out how his day had gone without prying about his visit to the cemetery and asked, "Did you find the florist okay?"

"Yes, and while they worked up a special arrangement for me, Derek and I explored the courthouse square. Do all rural counties still plunk their courthouse right in the middle of two major thoroughfares?"

"Most did away with them long ago, and a lot of our county activities take place in the courthouse annex down the street, but it used to be much more commonplace. The bypass diverts those passing by, so the square is primarily for locals and tourists. We like that throwback to our past."

"So did I. Derek probably was bored out of his gourd, but I had to go inside and see how it had been constructed."

"Who knows? You might be sparking an interest in architecture with him."

"Perhaps. Right now, he's more interested in pirates, zombies, and dinosaurs."

Tillie smiled. "He's adorable, and you know it."

Greg nodded as he took another bite. "Wouldn't trade him for anything in the world."

They ate and drank in silence a while. "There are a lot of historic buildings in this county, many of them well-preserved. I love that you aren't only interested in constructing glass and steel buildings."

"Construction is someone else's territory. But I'll admit I've drafted more than a few plans for those sterile structures. I try to add as much flair as I can, but there are definite limitations if bricks, native stone, and wood aren't incorporated into the design, in my opinion. Luckily, a number of people and corporations are willing to pay for something truly unique these days. As long as we make it function in today's world, they're more open to traditional elements."

They spoke a bit about some of the projects he was most proud of, until she looked down to see they'd eaten all of the cookies. "If I didn't think we'd spoil our supper, I'd go through a dozen cookies."

"I could as well. What's on the menu tonight?"

"Another chicken dish, but with the five-spice I used in the cookies, along with brown rice and braised asparagus. Not too bad if we want to eat light. What do you think Derek would like?"

"Hard to say. I want him to try more things, but we might be pushing it. How about a less exotic grilled or baked chicken breast?"

"Doable. What vegetables does he like besides potatoes?"

"Corn. He'll even eat broccoli as long as he can dip it in barbecue sauce or ranch."

"Seriously?"

"Nancy and I were just happy he was eating some veggies."

At least both parents made a point to be a part of their son's life. She'd always wondered about her absent father and even her mom's relatives who'd seemed nonexistent. The two of them had been quite isolated despite living in a close-knit community.

"It's wonderful that you're there for him."

Greg looked down and furrowed his brows. "I love him so much, even if I'm clueless sometimes as to how to raise him."

Her sperm-donor of a father hadn't wanted any part of her life. Not that she desired having him around if he had zero interest in her.

"I'm no great expert on parenting, Greg, but I think you're doing a wonderful job. Derek clearly adores you."

He shrugged, but when their eyes met, she thought his mood had lifted. "I haven't tried as hard as I could in the past, but I noticed a change came over him soon after we arrived."

Tillie cocked her head. "How so?"

"I don't know, but the trip down here was miserable. He was angry at me for taking him away from his mommy and didn't like being cooped up in the car for two days. Then he woke up shortly before we arrived here, and everything changed. Seeing that playground equipment made his day," he said, grinning briefly. "But it's more than that. You didn't cast some kind of spell over him, did you?"

Was he joking? Was he now accusing her of witchcraft? She started to laugh the statement off until she saw him scrutinizing her more closely as if searching for some crack in her façade.

Typical. He reverted to being a suspicious jerk just when she'd started to like him. But she wouldn't lose her cool with a guest. Actually, she didn't lose it with anyone. Hadn't since she was a child.

No wait. She'd had enough of his accusations. "First, I'm conjuring up fake ghosts. Now I'm a witch or a sorceress?" If only she could control the shaking in her voice she might hide her fear at confronting him. She stood and picked up the plate and her mug and carried them to the sink.

"That isn't what I said."

She turned around to face him and leaned against the sink. "But it's what you meant."

"Look, I can't explain why it matters, but you've come dangerously close to…" He ran his fingers through his hair and glanced away. "Maybe it's this house, not you."

What was this house? Perhaps if she could understand why he objected so fiercely to the way she marketed her inn to guests and the world—which was totally her decision to make—they could move beyond the incredible level of distrust he harbored against her.

Drawing a deep breath, she decided to question him and try to understand him better. "You believe houses have personalities of their own?"

"I've been around enough of them to know so. This one definitely has a strong persona. Perhaps remnants of its formidable former owner."

She didn't want to talk about Mrs. Foster with Greg anymore and let him besmirch her as well, but he seemed as fascinated by her as Tillie was. Maybe he was on to something. Tillie had never been able to separate this house from Mrs. Foster.

In many ways, losing her had been more devastating than losing her own mother; her mom hadn't nurtured and cared for Tillie the way Mrs. Foster had. She blinked rapidly and turned again to fill the dishpan with soapy water, not wanting him to see he'd scored a direct hit. She didn't want to think about the woman right now, either.

Tillie seized the opportunity to divert the conversation away from her friend and asked, "Were you able to find the grave you were looking for?"

"Yes. The headstone was easy to find. I'm glad she and her husband will be remembered for a long time."

He wasn't going to give her a name, but she tried to remember who had the more prominent stones, besides Mrs. Foster, anyway. She sighed. It had been a while since she'd wandered around there, she supposed.

"I always love the elaborate stones from the old days," she said. "Like buildings, tombstones haven't improved over the ages."

"Their designs have become rather mundane, haven't they? But the ones with photos of the deceased or their family on them are nice memorials."

She'd seen those, too, and one local artist etched images of the deceased's life on stones, everything from deer and mountains to their John Deere tractor. But the old-fashioned ones touched her heart in a different way, probably because she'd spent so many hours playing amongst them as a child. They'd become like friends. In many ways, her interactions with the stones weren't unlike those with her stoned mother—neither spoke back. Such a lonely point in her life.

Okay, now she was being downright maudlin. How had the mood shifted so dramatically from when they'd been eating the cookies? The crash after the high made her reluctant to try any more. She might want to stick to the memories instead.

Trying to lighten to mood again, she said, "We don't have any like this in our local cemetery, but Mrs. Foster used to tease me that she was going to have one like the weeping woman in the My Old Kentucky Home graveyard. You'll have to check that out during your stay—and tour the house, too."

"It's on my list. You know I wouldn't pass touring a house named Federal Hill."

She smiled but continued washing dishes. Maybe they needed some space between them to be civil. "Have you ever been to one of the Victorian cemeteries with the huge angels?"

"Can't say that I've visited many cemeteries."

"Well, I love those, too. Cave Hill in Louisville has some. Eerily beautiful. If you venture up that way, you should check them out. I think Derek would be fascinated by that place. It's more like a park, so he can visit the peacock near the cave, and there are ducks, geese, and maybe even swans on the lake. Colonel Sanders and Muhammad Ali are buried there."

"Interesting. I'd planned one day in Louisville to go to the downtown history and science museums Derek might like and maybe another day for the zoo. But I'm not sure I want to encourage his fascination with zombies by taking him to another cemetery."

She smiled, wiping her hands after setting the last dish in the drainer and pivoting toward him. "True. But I wouldn't worry about this phase too much. He merely has an active imagination, which is wonderful these days."

"I'll say he does. You should have seen him searching them out when we were up the road. He's been obsessed with them ever since Halloween when some older kids scared him while out trick-or-treating. Now he expects them to show up at every corner. When we hit a patch of fog before arriving at our overnight stop in Indiana, he asked me if zombies were going to come out of the fog and eat our brains."

"Well, while most kids would be fearful of them, your son seems to welcome the sight. Brave boy."

"Who's a brave boy?" They turned to see Derek standing in the doorway rubbing his eyes.

When Greg held out his arms, the subject of their conversation walked into them and was lifted onto his daddy's lap for a hug. Greg's arms were strong and protective, and the sight of them together made her chest ache so badly she almost closed her eyes.

"Why, you are, son. We were saying how brave you were chasing down zombies today."

He cocked his head. "But we didn't see any."

"I guess you were right; they prefer nighttime over day," Greg said. Had Greg experienced a change of heart about humoring his son and his obsession with zombies?

"But I'm afraid of the dark." Derek turned toward Tillie with his big blue eyes. "Have the zombies ever come down here from the graveyard?"

"Oh no. Not that *I've* seen, anyway." His mixture of fear and anticipation made her smile. "But you might be a zombie magnet, so I'll be sure to keep my eyes open for some while you're here."

His eyes opened wide. "Cool!"

She suddenly remembered the window and said to Greg, "I can't tell you how grateful I am to you for repairing that window. You'll have to give me a lesson in how to handle all the camera views on my computer. How many did you install?"

"Six."

Six?

"I'm not sure I can monitor them on a regular basis. How long will it save the video before it loops around and replaces it?"

"I chose a motion-detection system, so it only records when it detects some type of movement. And it's backing up to a Dropbox account I set up for you."

"How much is that?"

"No charge. See if you like it first. Then we can talk about you picking up the expense, but I've already ordered a year's subscription. You should be able to record for months, but as you watch them, feel free to delete and clear off space."

She wasn't sure she was ready to enter the 21st century, but if anyone broke into her house again, she'd at least be able to catch them in the act.

Tillie glanced up at the clock. Almost four. "If you don't mind eating supper at six, I think we could go"—she glanced at Derek and decided to spell out "treasure hunting" in case he had changed his mind. In truth, she simply wanted to see whether the cameras were working and how easy it would be to view the videos.

"Six is fine. We're in for the night." To Derek, he added, "Just in case any of those zombies are on the prowl."

"Daddy, they don't prowl like cats. Zombies walk with their hands out. Real slow. Like this." Scrambling off Greg's lap, Derek extended his hands in front of him and made his body and steps stiff as he took a few steps much like Frankenstein walked.

What an adorable zombie. He'd have a blast with the other kids in the neighborhood at her Halloween party. Not that he'd ever be here for that.

You can't keep them forever.

To his son, he asked, "Would you like to go on that treasure hunt?"

Derek jumped up and down. "Yes, yes, yes!"

Tillie's excitement level rose with Derek's enthusiasm, and she removed her apron and laid it over the chair at the island. Taking a flashlight from the drawer, she handed it to the boy. "Would you like to be in charge, Explorer Derek?"

The boy stood taller as he accepted the light and turned it on while nodding.

"Then follow me, boys!"

Leading the way to the cellar, she unbolted the door and started to open it when Greg placed a hand on her shoulder to stop her. A bolt of electricity charged straight to her core.

"Allow me."

Until that moment, she'd forgotten all about the threat of an intruder. She wouldn't grab her revolver, though, feeling safer with Greg around than if she'd been venturing downstairs alone.

"Wait here," he said. When he reached the bottom, Greg quickly checked all three rooms and gave them the go-ahead.

"Derek, let me go in front of you." If he lost his footing, she wanted him to fall against her and not down the stairs. "Hold on to the railing."

Unlike Greg, neither of them had to duck under the overhang.

"Where should we look first?" Greg asked.

Derek pointed to the room where the intruder had come through the window, as luck would have it. Greg opened the door, flipped on the light, and stood aside to let Derek lead the way.

"Hold my hand, Daddy." The boy's eyes were as round as saucers.

Derek stayed close to Greg with Tillie following behind. The beam of the flashlight was joined by the LED light from Greg's cell phone. She should have brought one of her own, but a red light shone in the upper outside corner, not far from the replaced window. Must be one of the new cameras. Not obtrusive at all and only she would be in here for the most part.

"What kind of treasure do you think we'll find, Derek?" she asked.

The boy remained silent as he shined the light in a corner of the room. "I don't like this room."

Could he feel what she sensed here? Hadn't Greg mentioned the coldness of the room, too?

"Run for your lives!"

Without warning, he spun around and headed for the center room.

"What the heck?" Greg asked.

She heard Derek's feet on the stairs before she and Greg ran after him, catching up with him at the top of the stairs.

"I'm never going down there again! It's scary down there!"

Greg hunkered down beside him and wrapped the boy in his arms while Tillie took the flashlight from his trembling hands. Had he seen something?

"What did you see?"

"A bad guy with a gun."

Tillie's heart skipped a beat. She and Greg hadn't seen anyone down there. Had he seen a ghost, and was that entity the one that made the room a little frightening to her at times, too? Could it be Jesse James himself?

Don't you start with that nonsense, Matilda.

"We don't have to treasure hunt anymore if you don't want to," Greg reassured the boy.

Abruptly, he separated from his father. "Good! Let's go play outside, Daddy."

"Sure." To Tillie, he added, "I'll get out of your hair now."

"I'd better go finish supper."

"Thanks." Greg hurried to keep up with Derek as he bounded toward the dining-room door.

"Have fun!" Tillie called after them. If only the father could have the joy for living his son did.

She returned to the kitchen. If she didn't have to be an adult, she'd follow them. She hadn't felt playful in a long time, usually keeping herself busy, so much so that she wasn't even aware of anything other than running her business and sticking to her routine.

But isn't this what she loved?

Being booked solid for most of the coming holiday season, her workload would only increase in the weeks ahead. Still, the urge to join them outside made her heart ache. She walked into the dining room and peeked out the window at them playing on the swing again.

Perhaps she needed to nurture her inner child a bit. Mrs. Foster had tried to infuse some playfulness in their days so she wouldn't take life so seriously. But she'd been a child then. Now she had the responsibility of making her business a success.

Tillie sighed, wishing she could stop being practical for a few minutes.

Not today, though. She had supper to make.

* * *

Greg couldn't shake the feeling of being watched, but when he turned toward the L-shaped porch and dining-room window, he didn't see anyone.

He surveyed the house as he pushed Derek on the swing, but his eyes kept straying to the window where he'd caught a glimpse of Tillie yesterday. At the same time, he hoped he *wouldn't* see her staring out at them again with what seemed like longing.

Man, you're messed up.

Being with her last night and today as they devoured those amazing cookies, he hadn't been able to keep his eyes off her. So strong yet fragile. A beautiful young woman. What was she doing all alone in that house? Did she date? Had she loved and lost like Greg had? Okay, so he rattled around his own huge house more often than not. But he must be losing his touch with the ladies if she'd interpreted his inability to tear his gaze away from her earlier as anger instead of his being speechless because she'd charmed not only him but Derek, too. Kids could cut through bull and see a person's true character.

Why was it taking Greg so long to figure her out? He couldn't blame Tillie for expecting the worst from him, the way he kept lashing out at her.

If she wanted to make up ghost stories about this place, what harm was there? Guests like him could ignore them; others could eat them up. Bottom line, if they helped her stay afloat, then why not live and let live?

Still, having Derek seeing ghosts didn't sit well with him. All this talk had put ideas into his head.

The woman worked too hard as it was, never allowing herself to have much fun. No wonder, given the way she'd been raised. The story about her mother broke his heart.

Thank you, Gram, for being there for her.

The love Tillie showed for Gram's house was unrivaled. Sure, he loved this place, too, but even he wouldn't have devoted his every waking moment to seeing that it was preserved and maintained for future generations. He could well imagine what a mess the renovations had been to live through, having worked on a few historical preservation projects himself, including his own home.

He waffled between wanting nothing to do with her and needing to get to know her better, but in truth, the two had absolutely nothing in common, except for a love of Gram's cookies and house. Of course, they lived seven hundred miles apart. When would they see each other after this stay anyway?

"Higher, Daddy!"

Regaining his focus, he complied with his son's command. Still, he glanced at that damned window a few more times, never seeing Tillie or anyone else but unable to rid himself of the feeling of being watched.

Perhaps the house is watching you. He grinned. All this talk of houses and their personalities—not to mention Tillie's ghosts now appearing before Derek, coupled with the boy's zombie obsession—had rattled his head.

Greg had to admit that Tillie rattled him, too. He hadn't expected to find someone so young—or likeable. He wanted to remain distant with her, but she kept crawling under his armor and charming the hell out of him.

When Derek grew tired of the swing, Greg extricated him, and the boy ran to the slide while Greg took his place and sat. Did Tillie ever come out to enjoy the playground she'd built? Doubtful. When would she fit it into her busy day? She never had the luxury of leaving business behind after a long day of work because it surrounded her.

The solid construction of the set indicated the woman had yet another talent—a Jill of all trades. Cooking, baking, and hospitality might be her mainstays, but she was no slouch when it came to wielding a hammer, screwdriver, or saw, either. She said she'd even managed to recreate the unique pattern of gingerbread in the privy she'd turned into a garden shed—Victorian, but a style he'd not seen before. A white picket fence surrounded her raised herb beds tucked in the area where the L shape of the house came together and within easy reach of the kitchen for her cooking. Beyond the fenced in area, toward the boundary trees in the backyard, was a large tilled area where she must grow all those vegetables she'd put up. Talk about a labor of love.

Greg made a vow not to argue about her stories of hauntings anymore. It was her truth, and if she wanted to believe them, what harm was she doing?

As for the other things bothering him, he hadn't the first clue what to do about anything. Most especially about one Miss Tillie Hamilton, who had thrown him for a loop.

Chapter Seven

"Daddy, who was that lady rocking in my room last night?"

Greg closed the storybook and rested it on his lap. He'd heard rocking last night, but thought it had come from the other side of the house—Tillie's room, to be exact.

"Here in *your* room?"

His son nodded. "She had white hair and a black dress with pink flowers on it."

Was Tillie playing some kind of game to influence his son with her claims that Gram haunted this house? *Be real.* He'd seen no evidence that she'd do anything to scare Derek.

Heart thumping, he tried to find a logical explanation for what Derek had seen, but the memory of the way Gram had looked the last time he'd seen her wouldn't let go of him. Her dress had been black with pink roses.

"Was her hair long or short?"

"Short."

Greg relaxed. Gram had waist-length hair. He'd often brushed it out at night. Couldn't be her. Maybe Derek had been dreaming.

"Well, it was bunched up on top of her head, like Tillie's was today. It's the same way the lady wears it when she comes to my room at Mommy's house."

Greg slowly set the book on the nightstand and moved to sit on the edge of the mattress. "You're saying you've seen her before?"

Derek nodded. "But Mommy said it was just my 'magi…" When he couldn't find the word, Greg offered the one he thought the boy was seeking.

"Imagination?"

"Yeah!"

"Did she wear glasses?"

Derek nodded.

No way could his five-year-old son have seen the woman who died long before he was born. Greg possessed no photos of her, thanks to his mother, so he'd never shown Derek a picture, either.

This had once been Gram's sitting room. He'd often found her up here in the summertime, reading or crocheting. She always had a stack of storybooks and a children's Bible at the ready on the end table to read to him.

Greg glanced toward the spot where her rocking chair had been on the other side of the room. He could see her clear as day.

Gazing down at his son again, he asked, "Did she say anything?"

Derek shook his head. "She smiles at me. She didn't scare me like zombies do."

To Greg, ghosts were as preposterous as zombies. There were no such things. But how had the boy seen Gram's apparition in his St. Paul bedroom? Something didn't add up. Tillie couldn't have had anything to do with what Derek saw in St. Paul. He had to believe his son when he told him he'd seen Gram up there. He'd never known the boy to lie.

No, Tillie wasn't behind this and, apparently, had nothing to hide. He'd seen how pale she'd become when he'd suggested there might have been an intruder in her cellar, and she hadn't objected to having cameras set up as long as they didn't intrude on her guests.

When Derek yawned, Greg leaned over and kissed his son on the forehead. He'd sort all of this out later. Right now, however, his son needed to get his sleep.

Greg eased out of the bedroom, not quite closing the door shut behind him. His son liked knowing his dad was close by when he awoke, although once asleep, he rarely roamed around at night, not even to go to the bathroom.

Inside Gram's former bedroom, he couldn't shake the feeling his grandmother was with him. Rather than freak him out, he found some odd comfort in imagining her nearby again. This room had been rated by reviewers on her website as being one of the most haunted. Some even stayed here with ghost-hunting equipment to see what they could detect. Had they detected the spirit of Amelia Foster all this time after her death?

The grandfather clock on the stairway outside his room chimed eleven o'clock. He began to undress, but no way would sleep come for him yet. A hot buttered rum ought to take the edge off his nerves. Tillie had probably already retired, but she'd told him to help himself to anything he wanted in the liquor cabinet.

Greg descended the stairs lightly, not wanting to wake either of the other occupants in the house. A squeaky floorboard below the landing made him pause. Then another creaked with his next step. It would be extremely difficult for anyone to sneak around this place at night. He remembered her tale of the heavy footsteps she purported to hear on these stairs.

Using stealth was ridiculous. Why bother? He wasn't doing anything illegal or out of the ordinary for a guest. No doubt, many of Tillie's patrons raided the fridge or came downstairs for a drink at some point during their stay.

Thankfully, though, the hallway floorboards weren't quite as noisy. He walked toward his grandfather's old office and retrieved the Captain Morgan's spiced rum.

Carrying the bottle into the kitchen, unexpected movement across the room stopped him in his tracks. At the island, facing away from him, Tillie stood dressed in the sheer flowing nightgown and robe she'd worn the other night, but this time was covered in a cotton apron looped around her neck and tied behind her waist, which accentuated the curve of her hips.

Greg couldn't tear his eyes away from her.

She cracked and added three eggs to the bowl, picked up the handheld mixer, and flipped the switch. The motor whirred to life, stirring up flour and other ingredients into the air from the large bowl.

She hadn't heard him approach, apparently. Why not watch her a while? Had she been unable to sleep, too? More likely, she did midnight baking frequently in order to have breakfast ready on demand for her guests early in the morning.

Tendrils spilled from her now-haphazard topknot, its wisps kissing the back of her neck. What might it be like to place a kiss against her warm skin?

Too intimate a thought to have about this prim and oh-so-proper innkeeper.

Not wanting to scare the hell out of her and before being caught red-handed, he cleared his throat when she silenced the mixer. Unfortunately, she must be wound tighter than he, because she jumped, bringing the beaters out of the bowl as she turned around.

"Oh!" She placed her hand against her breasts. *Chest. Keep it PG, Buchanan.*

"You sca—surprised me."

Was she afraid of something—or some*one*?

"Sorry. Couldn't sleep and thought I'd seek out the one person who might do the trick." He raised the Captain in full view. "Care to join me in a hot buttered rum, or should I consider making yours with bourbon?"

"Sounds wonderful—and rum would be perfect. I should be ready to put this orange-cranberry-walnut bread in the oven long before the rum kicks in."

He walked over and set the bottle on the counter near the stove. "Don't you ever sleep?"

She grinned. "I don't require much sleep. Confession time—I usually take a nap on days I've burned the candle at both ends."

"Did you take one today?" The question might be totally inappropriate, but images of her stretched out on the sofa with her hair spilling over the cushion to the floor overruled his brain.

"Hardly," she said with a laugh. "Too busy, which I suppose contradicts what I said."

Why did the thought of watching her nap stir up fantasies he ought not be feeling for the charming innkeeper?

You might be divorced, but you aren't dead.

The sudden desire to loosen her topknot and run his fingers through her hair nearly did him in. Clearly, he needed to start dating again. Minneapolis boasted lots of savvy, experienced women—far removed from this naïve, old-fashioned young lady running her rural Kentucky inn.

Tillie cocked her head when he simply stood there and pointed toward the stove. "The pans are hanging over there."

He didn't need a reminder of the obvious, but her prompting jumpstarted his brain. He crossed the room to get busy, even though he was no longer confident in the rum's abilities to quiet his mind—or body—tonight.

"The spice rack is beside the stove. I think you'll find everything you need."

"Your kitchen is much better stocked than mine." He gathered the cinnamon sticks, whole cloves, and ground nutmeg. She stopped long enough to give him a section of cheesecloth to place them in, as well as some softened butter and dark brown sugar. Apparently, she made hers about the same way he did.

Greg tried not to find too much pleasure in the way she anticipated his needs.

"Would you like some cookies?" she asked. Tillie hadn't moved from the spot where she now added dried cranberries to the bowl.

"Sounds good. I'll get them." He removed two saucers from the cupboard and went to the covered plate on the island to retrieve two cookies for each of them. After setting them on the table in the nook, he returned to the stove to add the spices to the rum simmering in the pot. The two worked side by side in relative silence, except for the occasional mixer.

About the time she placed the loaf pan into the oven, he poured the rum into two mugs emblazoned with poinsettias. The woman did like to start the season early. She removed her apron, and her holiday preparations were the furthest thing from his mind. Catching a glimpse of her silhouette in front of the fireplace—high breasts, flat stomach, and rounded hips—made him long to undo the pearl button holding the collar of her robe together so he could discover what her neck and shoulders would look like in the glow of the fireplace. A strong desire to reveal the valley where her neck and shoulders met overcame him.

Show some restraint, man.

Blissfully unaware of his lecherous musings, she lifted the mug to her face and inhaled. "Mmm. Smells delicious." She closed her eyes and took a tentative sip, her face melting into a smile. A drop of rum lingered on her lower lip. The urge to kiss it away morphed into a fantasy that would haunt his dreams of deepening the kiss.

Greg blinked, more turned on than he'd been in a long time. "I guess you don't have anyone serving you often, do you?"

She met his gaze. "No. Normally that's my preference, but I needed this tonight. Thank you."

"You're more concerned about the intruder than you've let on."

Her smile faded, and she nodded. "I am. There's a feeling of violation knowing someone's entered your home uninvited." She took another sip. "Oh, the sheriff's office came out this morning."

"I'm glad you called."

"Well, they didn't find anything to go on. No prints—finger, foot, or otherwise. I've been unable to identify a single thing missing, but that shelf didn't move itself. Given the number of jars on it, I couldn't make it budge without clearing off at least half of them first. Whoever did it was strong."

A man most likely. Greg didn't like the thought of some creep skulking around her house, especially if she was home alone.

"If you had to make an educated guess, what do you think the intruder was searching for?" Could he be after the same thing Greg was—proof of Jesse James's return here in the '30s? Who else knew about it?

"Still no clue." Tillie shrugged. "I've heard those tales of Jesse's treasure my entire life, and on occasion have wondered, what if there *is* something valuable hidden away down there? But how can there be? I've been over every inch of the place, albeit not seeking the elusive stash of gold or whatever it might be. There's nothing hidden away here."

He wouldn't reveal what Gram had written in the journals. Gram hadn't specified the location as being in the cellar, simply somewhere in the house, and he didn't want to look as though he'd lost his mind. Hoping to shift her focus away from what evidence Jesse James had or hadn't left behind, he said, "I would say your labors of love are the greatest treasures down there."

She smiled, her shoulders relaxing. "You're too kind. Around here, home-preserved food isn't quite the rarity it must be in Minneapolis."

"Where did you learn to can? Seems like a lost art these days."

"Mrs. Foster taught me. I was nine the first year we put up beans and tomatoes."

Hearing her speak about her experiences with Gram added to his guilt for not being around, although he wasn't sure canning with her would have thrilled him all that much. Still, if he had known she lived until he was about twenty-two, he would have come back to see her. Mother had sufficiently quashed any chance of his continuing a relationship with his grandmother. They'd had a falling out when he'd first discovered the truth and now barely remained civil when they saw each other. She'd done the unforgivable.

"It always had to be the hottest days of the summer and fall, when the crops came in," Tillie shrugged and took a longer sip of her toddy. "When I had the cellar redone, I made sure I could do my canning in the southern room where it's much more comfortable."

"Sounds like you enjoyed every minute with her."

Her eyes lit up. "Oh, I did! I learned so much from her. Every year, we added new things until she was teaching me to can preserves and chutneys."

Enjoying Tillie's dishes was much like being a guest at Gram's table again. Tillie kept so many of those traditions alive. Hell, she even dressed like a throwback to an earlier time. At first, he'd thought she dressed that way as part of the ambiance of the inn, but he was beginning to think it was an integral part of her persona.

"What else did you learn from her?"

"Table settings and etiquette, crocheting, tatting lace, and decorating for Christmas."

"What's there to learn about decorating a tree?"

She laughed, and her eyes sparkled. "You haven't seen the extent to which this fine old house is decked out for the holidays."

He wished he'd be here to see it now.

"Almost every room will have a tree of some kind…"

She shared her plans, but his mind reverted to that last visit again. He wondered if Tillie had also inherited Gram's ornaments. He'd probably never know. Besides, he couldn't reveal that he'd been here before. Not yet, although his desire to paint her as some nefarious charlatan no longer held any appeal for him.

"…keep my decorations up until Epiphany in early January. I always hate to take them down and pack everything away until next year. We don't get a lot of snow that sticks here, so winters can be awfully bleak."

"One good thing about Minneapolis is that the ground is covered with snow almost all winter. You should come up for a vacation sometime. We're only thirty minutes away from the Mall of America. There are some other shopping areas, too."

"I do most of my shopping locally and online. But I'm curious. Is that how Minnesotans survive cabin fever—by going shopping?"

He chuckled. "No. There are enough winter activities that no one has to feel cooped up unless they want to be."

Tillie took a nibble of her cookie, reminding him he hadn't touched his own. "I can't think of a thing the Mall would have that I couldn't as easily order online."

"Okay, so shopping isn't your thing. Come see Minnehaha Falls."

Her eyes opened wider, and she swallowed. "From *The Song of Hiawatha*?"

Greg nodded.

"*Hiawatha* has been one of my favorite poems since fifth grade."

"It's a beautiful place. There's even a statue of Hiawatha and Minnehaha above the falls."

"Maybe I should venture out in the world a bit before things get hectic again next year."

"I'll second that." He finished his second cookie and said, "God, these things are becoming my crack."

Her face blanched, and he realized how insensitive his words had been given her mother's addiction to drugs, although she'd said they were prescription pills. Before putting his foot in his mouth again, he finished the last bite of his remaining cookie, polished off his toddy, and stood. "Thanks for the cookies and the company."

She pushed her chair away from the table, stacked the dishes, and carried them to the sink as the buzzer went off. "You make a mean hot buttered rum. I'll sleep like a baby tonight." He watched her remove the bread from the oven.

Don't picture Tillie asleep in her pencil post bed.

He'd let down his guard tonight in more ways than one. Tomorrow, he needed to focus on the search for what Gram had hinted about in her journals. He kept hoping for more time alone down in the cellar because his earlier inspection revealed several places he wanted to explore further without prying eyes. But an opportunity to sit and sip toddies with Tillie was hard to pass up.

"I can't tell you how nice it's been having you here this week," she said.

The appreciation in her eyes made him feel like a heel when all he really wanted was a chance to snoop around.

Please don't make me feel any worse than I already do.

* * *

Crawling into her pencil post bed after Greg returned to his room, the only thing disturbing Tillie at the moment was the man sleeping at the other end of the house. How could a near-stranger make her feel so…much? So intensely? She'd never allowed anyone to come this close, especially within a few days of knowing each other. It wasn't that she didn't trust men. She'd had a couple of dates with Mark Peterson from the county's historic preservation society—but all they had in common was their love of old houses and local Jesse James lore.

While she preferred to let things develop slowly, Mark set her senses on edge with his grabby hands and pushiness. She couldn't help but compare him to Greg. How could she be obsessing over a man she hardly knew?

Utterly ridiculous.

Flipping off the bedside light, she rolled onto her side. *Enough already.* Greg Buchanan would be gone from her life by next week. Why was she letting him get under her skin this way?

Tillie closed her eyes. She drifted in and out of sleep throughout the night. When the six o'clock alarm went off, she groaned and slapped the snooze button. This was going to be one long day.

It's your own fault, mooning over a man that way. And a patron at your inn, no less.

Such whimsical notions needed to be squelched into oblivion or she ran the risk of setting herself up for heartache.

She was busy in the kitchen when Greg came in about an hour later, and his nearness set her heart to fluttering all over again. *So much for trying to ignore him.*

He stood a few feet away, mug in hand, watching her set the griddle on the burner for later before removing the orange-cranberry bread from the oven to slice. She rarely had anyone in the kitchen with her, but he seemed to be in here whenever she turned around. Not that she could blame him. This was her favorite room in the house.

"Good morning. The bread smells delicious."

"Thanks." He'd come down alone. "Derek's sleeping in?"

He nodded. "I think all the excitement of this trip has worn him out." Greg went to the coffee maker to help himself while she set the table.

"Pancakes okay for breakfast again?" she asked. "I have lemon curd and raspberry topping or New England maple syrup, whichever you'd prefer."

"Lemon curd sounds interesting."

"Made it myself. Let me run down to the cellar and get a jar."

"Don't go to any bother. Better yet, why don't I go down for it? I'm sure it's labeled." He walked toward the dining-room door.

She removed her apron and draped it over the bar stool at the island. "Why don't I go with you? You can show me where you installed the surveillance cameras." The pressing of his lips together told her he was less than thrilled she wanted to join him, which made no sense. Perhaps she was reading something into his expression that wasn't there.

In the foyer, she unlocked the cellar door and started to precede him down the stairs when he stayed her arm.

"Let me go first, in case there's been any more trouble."

Tillie hadn't given any thought to the possibility the intruder might have returned. Of course, she hadn't thought to check the laptop to see if any of the videos overnight had detected anything. The cameras would take some getting used to.

"Thanks." She flipped on the light and waved for him to go first. When they'd both reached the floor, he opened the door to the northern room and shined the LED light on his phone around the room. "Nothing else appears to be out of order. No more broken windows at least."

He closed the door soundly, and she crossed the space to the shelves and retrieved a half-pint jar of lemon curd.

"I still can't believe you make all this yourself." Greg had come up behind her so close she could feel the heat emanating from his body. She sidestepped before facing him, but the way he scrutinized the jars, he'd only been interested in getting closer to the shelves, not to her.

"Mind if I come down later and remove the jars to take a better look behind here since that's where the intruder had focused his attention?"

She didn't want to keep dwelling on the fact someone had been down here. "Well…I suppose not."

"I'll label where everything came from so that I can put them in the same spots later." He must have misinterpreted the reason for her reluctance.

"You don't have to worry about putting them away. I'll do that."

He cast his gaze downward a moment before facing her again. "I hate to ask, but would appreciate it if you could keep an eye on Derek while I'm down here."

Did he not want her down here with him?

"After yesterday, I'd rather not bring him down here again."

Don't be so distrustful. He had the boy to consider and was only trying to help her out.

"Of course. I'll be happy to watch him." If Greg would put his son and their vacation on hold to investigate the break-in, she'd be rude not to accept the offer. She simply wasn't used to handing over control or responsibility for the inn to anyone else. "Before you leave, you'll have to explain the equipment to me and how to work it."

He smiled and melted her heart. "Absolutely."

Together, they walked upstairs, and he left her in the kitchen while he went upstairs to prepare Derek for the day. By the time they joined her, she'd placed everything on the sideboard and had the third batch of pancakes bubbling away on the griddle.

"Pancakes! My favorite!" Derek cried as he took his place at the breakfast table, as if dining here for the first time. His hair was still wet but combed neatly. Such a sweet little man.

"I remembered. Good thing you love them, too, or I'll have way too much batter left over. I'm counting on you both to eat these up."

Once seated, Greg slathered butter on a piece of the bread while she delivered a plate with a Mickey Mouse pancake to his son.

"Tillie, you're going to spoil us rotten."

"That's what I'm here for." Somehow, spoiling these two gave her much more joy and satisfaction than she'd received from anyone else who'd ever stayed here. Okay, Greg could be a bit annoying and judgmental, but overall, he seemed to be a good person. Perhaps he had a lot of stress in his life. Clearly, he wasn't used to having to think about a five-year-old twenty-four hours a day.

Already she'd noticed he wasn't quite as harsh with her as he had been in the beginning. Perhaps she could find some activities and interests that would help them bond more and make this trip a life-changer for the two. One they'd never forget.

Despite having only known them a short while, Tillie knew the house wouldn't be the same without them. Neither would she.

Chapter Eight

"Jesse, while I have your wandering attention, how in tarnation is this going to work if you go around scaring that little boy the way you did last night?"

"I didn't do anything on purpose. How can I help it if he saw me?"

The two spirits had retreated to Elmer's office after breakfast. This had always been one of her favorite places in the house, conjuring up fond memories of her husband and the many hours they'd spent here together as physician and nurse. She could almost smell the vanilla tobacco from his pipe.

She couldn't recall when she'd fallen in love with the man, although if she ventured a guess, it was the night he'd delivered Caroline's baby in the birthing room.

Amelia forced her mind back to the present. If she intended to reunite in Heaven with her beloved husband and her dear traveling companion Joseph Hill, she had work to finish on this plane first.

"I'm not sure Tillie and Gregory are ever going to trust each other for more than a minute. How is this going to work without that foundation?"

"Darlin', don't you worry about a thing. Didn't you notice the way he stared at her when she was making that bread last night?"

"No. I went up to watch over the boy again while Gregory was down in the kitchen. Didn't want my great-grandson to wake up alone and get scared."

"Don't you think seeing another apparition might scare him more than the dark?"

"Stuff and nonsense. He's seen me plenty of times and always gives me the sweetest smile. Kids don't spook as easily as grown-ups do."

"You never spooked when I showed up."

"You're different. I'd known you for years before you passed—although a lot of folk thought you'd passed fifty-seven years earlier. I considered it a comfort when you popped in for a visit ever' now 'n' then."

"You know why I'm still here."

Amelia nodded. "I didn't flatter myself that you'd only come to see me. I understood that all along."

Each was lost in thought a moment before Jesse said, "I scared Tillie good that first night when she heard my footsteps." He sighed. "Wish she could see me, too, though." His disappointment must cut like a knife.

She shared the same regret. "Not everyone is clairvoyant." At least Tillie sensed her once in a while and remembered her daily. "However, I am happy she's finally starting to see my grandson as someone other than another guest."

"Matilda Jane reminds me of my Zee."

"What's your wife got to do with my Tillie?"

"Nothin'. Zee was dead and buried long before Tillie was a twinkle in God's eye."

"Don't you think I know that?"

"I'm just saying it took some work for me to get Zee Mimms to see me for who I was, even when I was alive. We stayed engaged for nine years. She weren't one to jump into nothing."

"How'd you finally win her over?"

"Charm and patience, I reckon."

Amelia huffed, but perhaps Zee saw a different side of him. "I'll bet she'll be none too happy to see you when you finally cross over."

Jesse shrugged. "I *had* to disappear. In the end, we were checking over our shoulders at ev'ry step. Thought my family would be better off without an outlaw putting them at risk. 'Sides, Bob Ford promised he'd make sure Zee and the kids were looked after. Bastard pocketed every penny I left for them, along with the reward money from the State of Missouri." He sighed. "Fortunately, she forgave me. About that stunt, anyhow. She's still a little miffed about Caroline."

"Well, what's done is done. No sense crying over spilt milk. Zee was long dead when you met my dear friend."

"Tell that to Zee. Now I'd like to make up for abandoning my offspring." He glanced down at Tillie.

"Well, the only unfinished business I have has to do with those two young'uns. Jesse, do you think I'm going to need to go down there and knock some sense into them?"

"You can't override their free will, Amelia, even if you do know what's best for 'em."

"I know. I know." She let out another puff of air. "Don't have to like it, but I'm fully aware of the limitations we must abide by."

Amelia watched as Tillie gathered up an arrangement of autumn flowers. Not again. "Oh dear. Tillie's getting ready to go for her weekly trip to the cemetery."

"Why do you let it bother you so much?"

"Because it's the most depressing place on Earth. I'll never understand why either of them feels the need to visit me there when usually I'm hanging around much closer to them."

"My mama was the same way, watching over what she thought was my grave—although I think she mostly wanted to keep souvenir hunters from diggin' up my bones and sellin' 'em or something."

Amelia shook her head at such a thought, but soon smiled. "Maybe I ought to have a little bit of fun if she insists on drawing me to that cold stone so often."

"Want me to join you?"

"Nah. No sense dragging you along, too, and makin' you hang out in that sorry place. I may just kill two birds with one stone."

"What do you have in mind?"

"Watch and learn, Jesse. Watch and learn."

* * *

Every Thursday morning, after feeding any guests their breakfast and sending them on their way for good or for the day, Tillie paid a visit to Mrs. Foster's gravesite to tend the flowers she planted each spring and summer. Most of the blooms were gone now, so today she brought a gold-and-burnt-orange silk flower arrangement for the Thanksgiving season. Tomorrow being Veterans Day, she also brought a flag to place there in honor of the woman's service as an Army nurse.

Tillie parked off the edge of the narrow lane and carried the bouquet toward Mrs. Foster's grave. She rounded the headstone and was surprised to find a fresh, professional flower arrangement in the pot. No one had left flowers here since Mrs. Foster's funeral. Tillie knelt on the grass to place her artificial flowers next to the beautiful bouquet.

A card fluttered among the apricot-colored roses and baby's breath, but she couldn't be nosy and remove it from its place amidst the blossoms.

A breeze kicked up, making the air feel much chillier than the fifty-two degrees she'd read on her thermometer before leaving the house. It swirled around her as if wrapping her in an embrace.

Stop anthropomorphizing the wind.

The air current increased in intensity, and the card sailed out of the arrangement and onto the ground. The words stared her in the face. How could she not read them?

With love to Gram.

Her grandson had been here? As far as Tillie knew, he'd rarely visited Mrs. Foster. She'd only seen him in Samuels once, soon after Tillie had first met Mrs. Foster.

Tillie had watched him and his mother from afar, but hadn't been brave enough to venture anywhere near the house again until after they'd left. Mrs. Foster's daughter had an air about her that left Tillie flat-out cold. Worse, their presence had caused Tillie's dear friend to be sad for weeks after they left, which didn't sit well with Tillie, either. Honestly, as Tillie became more and more attached to Mrs. Foster, she was glad they never returned. Guilt washed over her at the thought. Mrs. Foster deeply regretted not seeing her grandson again.

The boy, on the other hand, always intrigued her, even though they never spoke a single word to one another. However, there had been a brief eye-to-eye glimpse between Tillie and the grandson as he rode away. Those sad, gray eyes would haunt her forever.

Tillie blinked back to the present. The boy's eyes reminded her very much of Greg's, but that wasn't possible. Or was it?

She reached for the card, fully intending to place it inside the arrangement where it belonged, but a burst of wind flipped it over and just out of reach. More handwriting.

I'm so sorry.

Gregory

Greg? He was the grandson Tillie had seen all those years ago? Why hadn't he told her who he really was?

Heck, why hadn't she realized he had Mrs. Foster's eyes before? No wonder he seemed so familiar.

Tillie picked up the card before it could get away and tucked it inside the arrangement. Why had he included a card at all? Had he needed tangible evidence of his sentiments?

Suddenly, his occasional bursts of anger made sense. He clearly didn't like for her to refer to Mrs. Foster as being the spirit haunting her inn. Perhaps he also resented Tillie living in his ancestral home.

But he'd had no relationship with the woman in the last ten years of her life as far as Tillie could tell. Tillie had lived with Mrs. Foster during her last few years and didn't recall any phone calls or letters.

When did he plan to reveal his true identity to Tillie? If ever.

And what was he apologizing to his grandmother for? Not visiting her as an adult? Clearly, he'd broken the woman's heart by not coming back, but realistically, he was probably in college when she died. Had Mrs. Foster's daughter painted a less-than-flattering portrait of her mother?

She stood, realizing she hadn't spoken a word to her friend. "Mrs. Foster, don't you worry. I'll see that your grandson and great-grandson are treated with the same hospitality you would show them."

First, she needed to head to the grocery and liquor stores. By sharing Mrs. Foster's favorite foods, Tillie could help Greg become closer to his grandmother.

Why are you ignoring the fact that he's lied to you, by omission at least?

What her guests chose to reveal or not about themselves was none of her business. Tillie didn't make waves. She didn't make anyone uncomfortable. Maybe her years of tiptoeing around her mother—trying not to be sent off to foster care or to cause her mother any other reason to pop pills—had made her tolerant of bad behavior.

For now, she'd play along with the ruse that he was a total stranger here, mainly to see what he was hiding from her—and why.

* * *

Greg inserted the key into the lock. He'd insisted on Tillie keeping the house locked up, especially while here alone, but she had no reason to follow through with his request other than fear that the intruder would return.

The moment he opened the front door, a blast of bourbon hit him.

What the…

Tillie didn't seem the type to hit the bottle. But she did live in the county where the international bourbon festival took place each year.

"What's that smell, Daddy?"

"Um, flavoring."

"Do I have to eat it?"

"No. You're a minor."

"Like on Minecraft? I like to mine everything, but the best thing is crafting Ender crystals so I can kill Ender Dragon!"

Greg shook his head. Things sure had changed since he was a kid. "Not that kind of miner. I mean you're too young. Bourbon's a grown-up flavor."

"Oh." He seemed disappointed. Then his smile returned. "Usually, it's a bad thing to be too young, but I'm glad I don't have to try that."

They started down the hallway toward the kitchen where Christmas carols were blasting as Tillie sang slightly off-key to the music. Honestly, both the singing and the aroma were growing on him. He walked into the room to find Tillie liberally pouring bourbon from a fifth-sized bottle over several loaf-sized breads or cakes wrapped in cheesecloth.

"Mummy cakes!" Derek declared as he drew closer to inspect them. "Whoa!" He backed off when the fumes got the best of him and wrinkled his nose.

"Oh, hi, boys!" Tillie laughed at Derek's reaction.

Who are you calling a boy? Hell, he felt like anything but a boy around her.

"Sorry that it smells like a distillery in here, but it's fruitcake baking day. I need to have nine of them wrapped, soaked, and stored by tonight in order to have enough to get through the holiday parties and guests from mid-December to New Year's."

"What's the rush?"

"They'll need to mellow out and for most of this bourbon to dry up."

"I see." Judging by how much she was pouring—and the two empty fifths on the counter—a serious amount of sour mash bourbon went into the making of these cakes. Good thing he wouldn't be offered any; fruitcake was *not* his thing.

"Anything we can do to help?" Would he be corrupting a minor by having him surrounded by all this booze? At least no one was drinking it, as far as he could tell. And they would be long gone by the time she unwrapped any and took her first bite, so he'd be spared pretending to enjoy it.

"You could take the steaks out of the freezer to thaw for supper. The butcher paper is labeled. Choose whichever cut you'd like. I have rib eye, New York strip, and even a porterhouse."

He rummaged a minute before choosing a rib eye for himself and Derek to share. "Which would you like?"

"Ribeye, please."

Setting the two wrapped steaks side by side on the counter, he watched as she recapped the bottle and went to the oven to stick a toothpick in one of the next three cakes.

She'd pulled her hair into a loose bun at the nape of her neck. Her apron covered a tan sweater and skin-tight leggings of the same color that hugged her legs and—well, all the right places. The outfit was a departure from her usual vintage dresses, but his heart pounded in a way that told him he found her sexy as sin no matter what she wore.

What the hell was he doing noticing her in that way?

With only a few more days left here, he was tempted to book a return trip during the holidays for no reason other than to try a piece of fruitcake, despite his initial opinion about them. Everything Tillie made was out of this world, so why would these be any different? And with the amount of bourbon she soaked them in, how could hers be dry like the one he'd bought in the grocery years ago?

But there probably wouldn't be a single room available. The way she talked and how she went all out to give her guests an authentic Kentucky Christmas experience, people must make reservations months, or even years, in advance.

Christmas had never been celebrated much when he was growing up. His parents were busy entertaining colleagues and clients, leaving little time for him. He didn't want to pass that legacy on to his son. This year, he'd give Derek a Christmas like Gram might have done.

"Can we go outside and play, Daddy?"

Derek's request jarred him into the present. "Sure. What do you want to do?"

"Play in the leaves!"

To Tillie, he asked, "Mind if we make a mess of the piles in the front yard? We'll be happy to rake them up again afterward."

"Don't worry about that. Just enjoy yourselves." She closed the oven door. "My place is your place during your stay."

"You've certainly made us feel right at home."

"Then my work here is done." Her smile warmed his cold heart. She truly had kept this place a real home. Maybe he could figure out hers and Gram's secret and recreate it when he returned to Minneapolis. Unfortunately, a large part of the feeling was what happened in this room. Tillie poured herself into everything she cooked or baked. He wasn't particularly handy in the kitchen, so it would be a stretch for him to replicate that anytime soon.

Maybe he'd ask Tillie for some simple cooking lessons before he left. Hell, he didn't even know how to make grilled cheese, one of Derek's favorites. And how the hell did she make those Mickey Mouse pancakes the boy loved so much? Was it as simple as joining three pancakes to form the head and ears, or was there some trick to it?

Outside, they spent half an hour burying each other in the leaves and raking them up again for Derek to jump into. Greg hadn't played in leaves in…well, forever.

They crawled around in the leaves until he heard a woman shout, "Ready or not, here I come!"

Greg rolled onto his back as Tillie launched herself toward the pile squealing like, well, Derek might. Full-out abandon. Greg had placed himself in such a way as to catch her so she wouldn't hurt herself. Her eyes widened when she saw who was in her trajectory.

"I'm so sorry! I didn't mean—" she sputtered before landing on his chest and knocking the air out of him.

Her soft curves and vanilla-bourbon scent warred with his ability to remain cool and detached. She felt right in his arms, but the horror in her eyes made him grin. Was being in his arms such a horrible fate?

Well, perhaps, given the rocky start he'd made of it here.

He rolled to his side to place her gently in the bed of leaves, and they sat up simultaneously, both breathing hard. He stared at her a moment. Her rosy cheeks paled only to the redness of her lips. Natural. Not made up.

Sexy as hell.

She seemed to become aware of their nearness and pulled farther away, leaving him to wish she'd come closer once more.

"Sorry. I normally would never intrude on my guests this way. But when a bottle of bourbon was accidentally knocked over and spilled, I had to go to the office for another and saw y'all out the window having so much fun. I couldn't resist joining you. I've wanted to do this for a long time, but usually I simply rake and bag the leaves for my compost pile."

"That's how I perceived leaves until today, too. A nuisance to be discarded." Greg would never see them the same way again. Derek pretended to swim through a pile nearby. "Nothing like having a kid around to give us an excuse to act childlike."

"I think you're right," she said. He turned toward her once more. "Although if you hadn't been enjoying yourself as much as he was, I doubt I'd have gathered up the courage to make a fool of myself the way I did." She averted her gaze, her cheeks growing redder until a smile broke out, and she stared into his eyes. A knot formed in his stomach as he fought the urge to lean forward and kiss her before her widening eyes reminded him who he was. Who *she* was.

Abruptly, he stood to place more distance between them.

Jeez. What the hell's the matter with you?

Once more, his inappropriate thoughts concerning her had nearly led him astray. He worked with women on a daily basis, and none ever affected him the way this one did. He reminded himself that he needed to focus on his remaining mission here—finding evidence that Jesse James lived beyond 1882.

Focus, man.

But that merely touched the tip of the iceberg of all that Gram's journals revealed to him. He'd begun to reassess his choices in life—no longer satisfied with choosing work over family and everything else. While there was no chance for anything more with Nancy, he had a lifetime to be a dad to Derek and didn't want to screw it up any more than he already had.

He'd been doing all the same things wrong that his own father had done in raising him. In just a few days, this trip had shown him how much he enjoyed being with Derek. If no other treasure surfaced during this nostalgic trip, that knowledge would be reward enough.

Tillie stood, reminding him that once again he was about to screw up his priorities. He hadn't come here for any kind of romantic or sexual involvement with the inn's owner.

Glancing up the road to regain his composure, Greg watched a white van drive past the inn followed by a silver sedan. The driver of the van slowed down even more than one might, despite the curve. The man at the wheel turned away before Greg could get a good look at him and accelerated around the bend. His intuition told him whoever it was might be up to no good. Was he casing the place, waiting to attempt another break-in to steal whatever it was he wanted?

"Did you see that van?"

Tillie, brushing the leaves from her hair, scanned up and down the road. "No. Why?"

"Seemed suspicious."

"Describe it."

"Nondescript white full-sized van."

"Sounds like a caterer friend of mine."

"No logo on the side panel."

"She's independent. I can't see her having trouble finding the location of a party or delivery here, though. She lives less than a mile away."

"No, definitely a he, but his face was hidden. He hit the gas when he saw me watching him."

"I can report it to the sheriff's office, but it's not a crime to drive slowly by a house checking it out. All the same, I don't suppose you saw a license plate."

"No. Drove away too fast."

"Well, I'll keep an eye out, but wouldn't worry much. This is a busy road with all the subdivisions."

Derek dove into the leaf pile they'd vacated, and all thoughts about the van or potential threats to Tillie or her house were obliterated as the three of them played together another fifteen minutes before Tillie begged off to return to finish baking her fruitcakes.

Greg watched her walk, a little-girl stride with her arms swinging casually at her sides and not a care in the world.

At least she'd let herself have fun for a short while. How else could he bring out her inner child to play?

Chapter Nine

Tillie couldn't believe she'd actually spent twenty minutes of her busy day cavorting in the leaves. Whatever had possessed her? One moment, she watched out the window and wished she could be so carefree; the next, she'd pounced on Greg in the middle of the pile.

Her cheeks warmed at the memory. Dear Lord, what must he think of her? She was supposed to be running the inn, not behaving like a five-year-old.

Lighten up, Tillie.

Mrs. Foster's words eased her guilt. That had been the most fun she'd had in longer than she could remember. Maybe she should offer babysitting services in the future to give her an excuse to be silly and childlike.

She lifted the plastic bin holding the first three cheesecloth-wrapped cakes and set it on a shelf in the pantry. For the next few weeks to a month, she'd flip them over at least once a day allowing gravity to pull the bourbon evenly through the cakes. After a couple of weeks, she'd occasionally leave off the lid to let some of the remaining liquid evaporate.

The Christmas season never began for her until she had her first bite of Mrs. Foster's Kentucky bourbon fruitcake. Apparently, the woman had gifted them to many of her neighbors, too, and Tillie had continued the tradition with the remaining elderly ladies who enjoyed a good fruitcake. Tomorrow, she'd bake one more batch in small, aluminum loaf pans. Sadly, each year, her list of recipients grew smaller. But she still had eight to give to this year. She'd send the ninth cake in that batch to Greg so he could try one.

She thought Mrs. Foster would like that her grandson would be able to enjoy one of the woman's favorite things.

The front door closed, and she heard footsteps on the stairs. After she wrapped and soaked the latest three fruitcakes, she began preparing supper. She still had three more full-sized cakes to bake tonight. That last batch might not be out of the oven until midnight, but the more time they had to mellow, the better. She'd made the mistake of serving her first bourbon fruitcakes the year the inn had opened after they'd only mellowed about two weeks, and her guests had nearly gotten drunk off of the fumes alone.

For supper, she'd chosen to have a southern cookout. While it wasn't hot outside, the sun was warm, and Indian summer made it comfortable. Mrs. Foster wouldn't have passed up the chance for Greg to experience this treat, and Tillie considered herself an extension of the woman in many ways. The produce wouldn't be as fresh as in summer, but all the same, she hoped he would enjoy everything.

Tillie wrapped five ears of corn in foil, still in their husks, and set them aside. She'd made the banana croquettes this morning, a local treat she'd learned from a woman at church. Only Tillie dredged the bananas in watered-down peanut butter rather than mayo before coating them with peanuts. Mayonnaise wasn't her thing. In about thirty minutes, she'd start the charcoal, but first needed to put the finishing touches on the potato salad and German coleslaw.

Working mechanically, she let her mind wander to the current state of her burglary case. Well, it wasn't really a burglary unless they stole something, was it? Nothing seemed to be missing or damaged except for the broken jar of preserves and the window. She'd had difficulty sleeping last night, wondering if every sound she heard outside might be the culprit returning again to find whatever it was he wanted.

"What can I help you with?"

She nearly jumped, not having heard Greg approach.

"Sorry if I scared you again."

"No, no! I was just thinking too hard, I suppose." She didn't want him to view her as weak.

"Sounds serious."

She also didn't want to talk about the intruder, even though it remained on her mind a lot lately. At the moment, all she needed to focus on was tonight's meal. As her luck would have it, she didn't have to bring up the subject.

"What did you decide to do about the van?"

"Nothing. I can't jump at every shadow. With nothing to go on, I don't see any point in reporting it." Hoping to divert attention from the intruder, she changed the subject. "Usually when I start my fruitcake baking, I also start dragging out Christmas decorations from the attic above my bedroom. I like having the place fully decorated by the weekend before Thanksgiving, but I wondered if it would confuse Derek to see me putting up a tree more than six weeks before Santa is supposed to arrive?"

"By all means, go about your normal routine. I can explain to him that Santa won't come for weeks after we go home. My wife—ex—usually decorated right after Thanksgiving, so it's not all that much difference."

His divorce must have been recent for him to still accidentally refer to her as his wife. "Of course, you're both welcome to join me in decorating the Christmas tree in the parlor." She wondered if it would spark any memories of his visit to Mrs. Foster where he'd have seen so many of the decorations before, albeit on a new and taller tree. Tillie preferred to use artificial trees to prolong the season safely and liked to fill the space in the room with a tree that came closer to reaching the fourteen-foot ceiling. "I probably won't start on that one until after some of the unoccupied bedrooms have been decorated, though, in case I book any more reservations. Everyone seems to want Christmas earlier and earlier these days, and I'm happy to oblige. It's my favorite time of the year."

"I'm not sure how much help we'd be decorating."

"Oh, the parlor tree is old-fashioned and doesn't have to be precise. I actually prefer it to have the appearance of having been decorated by a family—so having you and Derek here this year will make it all that much more authentic."

He seemed undecided, making her wonder if she'd crossed a line by inviting him to participate in such a domestic scene with a near-stranger. Somehow, he didn't seem like a stranger anymore, though. They'd formed a bond, perhaps because of the intruder or maybe over a mutual love and respect for his grandmother.

"Mrs. Foster always said kids have their own special way of decorating trees." Tillie recalled her own insecurities about helping with the tree that first year. She'd soon been divested of such worries.

He smiled. "That they do. If you get to that one while we're here, then we'd love to join in."

A silly euphoria swept over her. She hadn't had anyone to share in the decorating for ages. Most of the decorations on the main tree had belonged to Mrs. Foster. Some had been handmade by Tillie when she was young and came for visits. Others had been made by Greg's mother, bringing tears to Mrs. Foster's eye every year for what might have been.

It was Tillie's favorite tree bar none, and she was excited by the prospect she wouldn't have to decorate it alone. Perhaps she'd fend off the melancholy that often overcame her as memories of Christmases past bombarded her.

* * *

Somehow Greg managed to convince Tillie to relinquish enough control to let him light the charcoal. There wasn't much else she'd allow him to do. He liked that she didn't grill with gas. Somehow, food tasted better with real smoke.

"Let me lay these on the edges of the coals," she said, bringing out some ears of corn. She also placed a long flat foil packet on top of some coals. "Derek made that for his supper."

"It's a hobo sack, Daddy!" Derek bounded down the porch stairs to the patio. "It has hamburger, potatoes, and carrots. No onions or mushrooms. I don't like those."

"He's going to be quite the chef someday," Tillie said.

Usually, Derek didn't like carrots, either, but apparently, having a hand in the process made him more adventurous. Greg didn't want Derek to grow up being picky and not knowing his way around the kitchen. Did Nancy include him in meal preparation? Were there some simple things Greg could learn to make where he could request Derek's help?

"Can I go on the slide?"

Greg smiled. His short attention span would require that it be fast. "Sure. I'll keep an eye on you from here."

The boy scampered off. "How do you like your steak, Greg?"

"Medium."

"Me, too. Be right back."

Greg scanned the nearby woods, making sure there weren't any threats. Maybe he was being overly cautious. Three small incidents—a shattered window, broken jam jar, and suspicious driver—didn't portend doom. So why did he feel the person driving by was waiting for him to leave?

And he'd need to leave in a couple of days because he'd promised Derek excursions to the zoo and Louisville science and history museums. Would Tillie go with them? If she were with them, he wouldn't be so uneasy.

He stepped up onto the porch just in time to open the door and let Tillie out with the platter of steaks. She'd already seasoned and tenderized the meat, so they were ready for the grill. He almost offered to take over the grilling, but instinct told him not to encroach on her territory. After all, he was a guest, despite how domestic this scene might be.

A tendril of hair had come loose from her bun. Her hair fascinated him for some reason. Nancy's was short, but Tillie's was long and thick. What would it feel like to bury his hands in the locks? He fought the urge to curl a loosened strand around the shell of her ear. Overwhelmed by the desire to touch her, he shoved his hands in his pockets.

He hadn't been attracted to a woman in so long, and his sex-starved mind kept telling him Tillie was the perfect one. Except for the fact she lived seven hundred miles away and in a vastly different world. Not a good recipe to ensure compatibility and happiness. Then again, Nancy had been the daughter of his former partner. She understood his career, his life—and it hadn't worked out, either.

Greg accepted a lot of the blame, though. His marriage had been more a partnership than a love match, although he'd loved Nancy in his own way. In retrospect, he'd merely followed his own parents' dysfunctional model for marriage and parenting. Both were workaholics who stayed away from home more than Greg had. While they ran their own business, they rarely took time to parent. He couldn't say that they even loved each other, but they did enjoy pursuing deals and working nonstop. Growing up, he'd never spent time doing kid things with either of them. Their clients had been more inclined to give him Christmas presents than his parents had. That had been the best part of Christmas back then.

What the hell had prompted this critique of his marriage?

"There. We'll let everything grill for a while. Last one to the swing set is a rotten egg."

Oh yeah. Tillie.

She bolted across the yard toward the playground and Derek. He'd wondered earlier if she ever indulged in the playground swings. Apparently, he had his answer. He didn't stand a chance at beating her, but managed to almost catch up before she claimed one. Her laughter was infectious.

"I wanna swing!" Derek left the slide and came over to join them.

Greg settled him into the seat, gave him a push, then took his place on the one between them. Every now and then, he'd reach out to give

Derek another boost. Tillie continued to go higher with each pass, leaning back and letting more of her hair escape from its confines.

"I love swinging. Have since I was little, so I made sure I could enjoy my playground when I designed and built it."

"You designed it yourself?"

"Well, design might be a strong word. But I did choose the components and came up with this configuration."

"You did an excellent job."

"Thanks." The corners of her eyes crinkled when she smiled. "I can get so busy that I forget to come out here for some much-needed swing therapy."

"It's easy to do." He enjoyed watching her give in to her playful side. Perhaps, like him, she focused too much on work and not enough on herself and her friends and family. He wondered if she even had much of a social life. There seemed no indication of it. "Do you ever have the house to yourself without any guests?"

"More often than my bank account would like." She shrugged.

He had no clue how many reservations were needed to make ends meet with a place like this. "I guess that's why you put so much effort into the holiday season. Sounds like you pack them in then."

"I do. Also during the annual festivals. People enjoy the experience of staying at a historic inn, rather than a modern chain hotel in the city. It's a lot quieter in the country. I've had people from as far away as Tokyo stay here."

He hadn't thought about this out-of-the-way place attracting a worldwide clientele—the entire county seemed isolated. "Do they find you on the web?"

She nodded. "On my web page, which is linked to county tourism sites, as well as on vacation home and B&B sites. Being a full-service inn has made mine a favorite among many, especially older couples who don't want to drive to and from the city for supper after dark."

Again, he found himself wishing he could book a stay during the holidays. To be in the home where his grandmother had entertained him as a boy might be just the connection he needed to make with Gram to fill the hole that had been left. But he couldn't justify another vacation right away. His team wouldn't know what to think if he gallivanted off again so soon.

Sometimes, he wished he could do as he pleased and not have to think about keeping things going for his employees and their families.

Maybe he was burning out.

"Oh, I'd better go turn the steaks." Tillie jumped off mid-swing and ran toward the patio. He watched as she tried to tame her hair on the way, finally deciding to ditch the band holding it up and letting the tresses spill over her shoulders.

Man, he needed to put an end to this fixation with her hair. But something told him he wouldn't until he'd finally had a chance to let his fingers dive in.

Chapter Ten

"Wow! That's the biggest tree *ever*!" Greg agreed with his son's enthusiastic assessment.

Tillie laughed as she turned to greet them, clearly not having heard them enter the house a few yards away with her Christmas music blaring so loudly. What if he'd been someone breaking in?

She crossed the room to the stereo and lowered the volume. "How were the museums?"

"Big," Greg answered. "We must have logged twenty-thousand steps."

"I got to dig for dinosaur bones, Miss Tillie! And climb on giant blocks!"

"Sounds like fun. Sorry I couldn't go with you."

So am I.

Derek approached the tree in utter awe, and Greg followed, picking him up to view it better.

"Why didn't you wait for me to haul down those boxes?" How had she managed to do all this alone? Not that she seemed to be one to rely on anyone's assistance. A number of bins lay empty after holding the 14-foot artificial tree she'd assembled in the parlor while he and Derek were at the history and science museums in Louisville today. Three plastic bins had been stacked near the tree filled with decorations.

"Actually, I still need to bring down more bins from the attic. These are only the lights and beaded garland."

Setting down his son, he said, "Derek, why don't you bring some toys into the dining room so you'll be closer to where we are?"

"Can't I come with you?"

"I don't think you need to be going up to the attic."

After they had him settled, Tillie opened the door leading to her bedroom. "Watch your head in the low doorway and be careful on these narrow pie steps."

He had been much shorter when he'd walked up those stairs before so heeded the warning.

"I appreciate your help. Normally, I give myself a week to finish decorating that tree, but I had a call from the historic preservation society this morning. They need a new place to hold their annual supper on Monday and chose my inn, so I need to get moving. They'll enjoy seeing the tree lit and some of the other decorations up in the common areas during their visit." She led the way upstairs. "You're welcome to join us if you're not busy Monday evening."

"Thanks. I'd love to hear about the projects they're working on." He had missed grown-up conversation while traveling with Derek. The times he and Tillie had engaged had been enjoyable—as long as they stayed away from ghosts.

"I think they'd enjoy the chance to share them, and maybe even get some expert advice on any renovation challenges the group might be struggling with. They can't afford to keep an architect on retainer. I could let them know you'll be joining them, but then they might bring over blueprints for you to study. Why don't we surprise them?" She grinned.

"I don't mind." He did *pro bono* work for one of the nonprofits in Minneapolis that rehabbed buildings for those in need of low-income housing. Maybe he wasn't burning out after all.

As he followed her up the stairs, he did his damnedest not to stare at her ass encased in tight jeans. *Epic fail.* Usually she wore flowing skirts and dresses, so how could he help but notice?

"The attic is accessed through this door."

While he didn't mean to let his gaze stray to her personal living space, this had been the last bedroom he'd stayed in while Gram was alive. At the top of the stairs, they simply landed in the bedroom.

The room equaled the size of his bedroom at the other end of the house. The unusual four-poster pencil bed still dominated one side of the room.

"This part of the house used to be for travelers on the stagecoach or train. Originally, this room as well as the dining room, kitchen, and the bathroom that once was a mudroom would be completely locked off from the birthing room, office, parlor, and the second floor rooms where you're staying. I chose to make the travelers' bedroom my own, though, so that I can maintain my privacy in a smaller space by locking off this room and the attic. It gives my guests full use of the rest of the house to relax in during their visits. The suite where you're staying is more of a moneymaker than this one could have been."

"Interesting." He knew much of the house's history already, but what he found most intriguing was that most of the furniture had been here when he and his mother had stayed during that last visit. His mind flashed to the afternoon when Mother had hurriedly packed their things while he'd begged her not to leave until he and Gram finished whatever it had been they were doing during the big blow-up between the two women.

"That rope bed frame is so massive," she continued, "that Mrs. Foster had to take out the entire window frame over there to get it in. No way would it make it around those pie stairs leading up here. Needless to say, this bed will be in this house forever."

Not wanting to appear to know more than he should, he asked, "What style is it?"

"I'm not really sure. Obviously primitive and handmade, possibly a mix of styles. It's been dated to the mid-nineteenth century—soon after the Civil War—but that's as much as anyone could tell."

He approached the foot of the bed. Well-worn federal blue paint covered the exposed pine. "Appears to be the original paint."

"I believe it is, too. I'm grateful no one refinished it. Oh, and the tops of the pencil posts have finials that can be unscrewed. No doubt so that summer and winter canopies could have been used to capture or release heat and prohibit drafts."

The foot rail reminded him of a double-ended writing instrument, more like a fountain pen than the "pencils" that made up the four corner posts. He'd been fascinated by the bed as a boy. He wondered if the bed had been commissioned for either a writer or student.

A yellow appliqued quilt and white dust ruffle gave the double bed a quaint air, fitting Tillie to a tee. At the base of the bed sat an old cedar chest with three drawers. That, too, had been there before.

A quick glance at the end table and his heart skipped a beat.

Gram.

And a sad-eyed little girl who had to be Tillie. The two appeared to be dressed in Sunday clothes. She'd died about ten years after his last visit. The backs of his eyelids stung as he fought the urge to pick up the frame for closer inspection.

"That's Mrs. Foster, the woman who owned this house, and me when I was twelve. A photographer came to do a church directory, and she asked me to join her. She was like a mother and grandmother to me, all in one."

"I'm glad you two found one another." And he truly was, because without Tillie, Gram's final years might have been lonely beyond measure.

She cleared her throat as if overcome with emotion, too. "I suppose we should head on up to the attic now that we've caught our breath."

Greg nodded, not the least bit out of breath. He supposed she wanted him out of her sanctuary. He could well imagine how his inordinate interest in her bed might come across.

Joining her near the window, he indicated for Tillie to precede him upstairs to the attic. How had he never been up here? If he remembered correctly, Gram had placed a large wardrobe that would have blocked the way, so he wouldn't have been able to explore if he wanted to. He honestly hadn't known another floor existed.

As they ascended into what he anticipated would be a tight space under the slope of the roof, he was surprised to find that the ceiling was at least eight feet tall in the center, sloping toward the walls on either side. There were two twin beds surrounded by shelves and bins along one wall filled with vintage toys.

"Do you rent out this room, too?"

"Rarely, because it requires me to move out of my own bedroom. But I do offer it as an option for larger groups or families wanting to rent the whole house."

"Then where do you sleep?" It was none of his business, but he couldn't help but be curious.

"I put a cot in the birthing room."

The woman would go to any extreme to accommodate guests, it appeared. Always the perfect hostess. Was there truly a victim here? No. Gram might even get a kick out of being immortalized in such a way. Her quirky sense of humor had brought her to life again in the pages of her journals.

One entire wall had stacks and stacks of clear plastic bins filled with red, green, gold, silver, and royal blue decorations. Some were labeled for which room they should be used in.

At the far end of the attic, he saw a long section of raw plaster framed with brown-stained wood. He wondered why the plaster hadn't been painted over. Upon closer inspection, he saw it had been etched with names and initials.

"Mrs. Foster told me those are the former children of the house spanning one-and-a-half centuries," Tillie explained. "This must have been a playroom for them. Mrs. Foster didn't want to lose that part of the house's heritage, so when she replastered the room, she framed this section of the wall so no one destroyed it. She told me she even took down a row of trees she and her husband planted in the front yard near the driveway after a devastating tornado came through here in 1974. She feared one might blow over and destroy the wall. It meant that much to her."

Seeing Matilda had been added to the wall, he said, "I see you were able to put your name here, too." Had Gram intended for him to be memorialized here if they hadn't departed so abruptly?

"I was about ten and had begun to hang out here more than at home when she invited me to do that. She'd called me Tillie almost from the moment we met, but I chose to put my real name there. It seemed like a solemn historical record to me even at the time."

Clearly, this place meant a lot to Tillie, too. When she went back to the bins again, he took a closer look at the names etched in the plaster. Effie, Ethel, Mary Alice, Iva, C.S., Vernon, and so many others. Finally, he found the one he searched for—Margaret. While childishly written, it resembled the way she wrote her "g" to this day.

"Mother," he whispered, pressing the tips of his fingers over her name. The precise cursive used showed the care she'd taken. Would she remember placing her name on this childhood wall of fame? Had she done so with Gram's permission or merely to be remembered with the other children?

He gave in to the urge to take out his cell phone and snap a picture. Someday when they were speaking to one another again, maybe he would coax her to return to the house she'd grown up in and see it through his eyes. How could she have been anything but charmed by this place?

Maybe not, but it would be worth a try.

A hand on his arm jarred him in more ways than one. Being so close to Tillie in a moment when his nerves were already frayed overwhelmed him.

"Everything okay?" she asked.

He chose to focus on the obvious and not reveal his attraction to her. "Yeah, sorry I'm not being much help. The history represented on that wall is astounding."

"It is, indeed."

Glancing around the attic for a distraction, he noticed a hatch in the ceiling. "Where does this lead to?"

"The roof. I like to think that was how Jesse escaped authorities the night his brother Frank surrendered down the road at the old store."

"How would he go undetected?"

"He'd have climbed over the peak of this roof, onto the L-wing, then into the herb garden, and out into the woods."

"Fascinating." If Jesse had indeed faked his own death and come here in the 1930s, Greg doubted he'd have been spry enough to make an escape through that hatch during that visit. Not that Gram would have sent him running. The two seemed to have been friends.

She pointed to the storage bins nearest the door. "Those four should do it—and now the fun begins. We'll see how far we can get before I stop to make supper. I can finish up tonight and tomorrow."

He'd never spent more than three hours setting up a tree and decorating it. Of course, he hadn't before attempted one of this size.

Downstairs in the parlor after each of them had carried two bins down in two trips, they set Derek up playing with the chess set that now sat on the opposite wall in the room. Meanwhile, they worked on adding what must be thousands of lights to the tree. His first instructions were to check each strand of lights to be sure they were fully functional. She'd stored each string in its own plastic grocery bag, so he at least didn't have to worry about untangling the wires.

After most of them had been deemed to be in working order, he handed each string to her and went on to test the next one.

"I appreciate your help. We'll get through this part much faster than I would on my own."

"I'm enjoying this, truth be told." And he meant it, too. After checking the last string, he joined her and watched as she laboriously wrapped the strands of lights around the greenery from the insides to the tips of each branch. "I didn't know there was such an art to putting lights on a tree."

Tillie shrugged unapologetically. "Well, I may be a little obsessed, but Mrs. Foster taught me to wrap the wires around each branch and then tuck the bulbs among the needles so only the lights are visible. It takes me hours to get them right, but the effect is stunning. They'll appear to twinkle as you walk by without me actually using twinkle lights."

"I can't wait to see." He remembered decorating a tree that seemed as tall to him as this one was to Derek. His grandmother, her gnarled fingers doing such intricate work with so much love, had worked on it for days. He hadn't thought about that in forever.

Lowering his voice so as not to attract his son's attention, he said, "Derek is going to love it—especially because you aren't using all clear lights. He insisted that his mom use multicolored lights last year on their tree with a rainbow star on top he picked out himself."

"Oh, Mrs. Foster would have nothing to do with one-color lights on her parlor tree. She wanted an explosion of color. Said it reminded her of the ones from her childhood. I guess she had it tough growing up, until she married Dr. Foster and moved in here at least, but she learned to love Christmas from her own mother and passed on many of those traditions. I think that's why I love this one so much. It may not be aesthetically beautiful to those who prefer a tree done in one or two colors, but these lights combined with the unique and sentimental ornaments bring back such fond memories for me, too. Most of the ornaments were hers, although I've added one each year from a local shop or museum gift store. Now old and new intermingle on the tree's boughs, as in life."

Not unlike Tillie herself—old-fashioned in some ways, modern in others.

He handed her the next bundle of lights after connecting them to the previous cord. Already, the lower half of the tree was vibrant with light. He'd have thought it had plenty already, but judging by the stack of lights she had yet to add, they had a long way to go.

"You really put a lot of thought into Christmas, too."

Her eyes brightened. "I'd do so even if I had no one to share it with. The season makes me happy for the most part, especially when I have guests at the inn."

Did she suffer bouts of loneliness, or did her guests provide her with what she needed? For him, Christmas tended to be a lonely, depressing time, especially these last two years after Nancy and Derek moved out.

He tried to keep busy at the office, but closed it for ten days during the holidays to allow his employees, many of whom weren't originally from Minneapolis, a chance to be with their families. As recently as last year, despite the divorce, Greg had been invited to spend Christmas Eve at Nancy's and to return in the morning to watch Derek open his gifts. Greg hadn't bothered putting up a tree either year. Nancy had always handled that, so Santa left Derek's presents there.

Would Nancy still invite him to Christmas dinner? Stephan, her new husband, probably would prefer to start family traditions of his own. What ticked him off, though, was the thought of Derek seeing Stephan as a replacement father. The boy already spent much more time with his stepfather than he did with Greg.

"Why so glum?" Tillie asked. "If you'd rather play with Derek, it's not a problem. I've got this."

"Sorry. It's not that. Just thinking about what Christmas might be like this year. My ex recently remarried." Why had he shared that with her? He wasn't seeking sympathy.

"Oh, I can imagine how that might be awkward for you all this year."

Maybe someone so steeped in the holiday season could give him some advice. "How can I make memories for Derek as special and enduring as yours are with Mrs. Foster?"

"Perhaps there are some traditions in the Buchanan family you could pass on to him." Tillie's hand reached for another bundle of lights, their fingertips brushing and setting off a spark of electricity. Her eyes widened. She must have felt it, too.

"My past Christmases weren't ones steeped in tradition," he began.

"My parents weren't much on celebrating." Not with him, anyway. They had closer relationships with their clients. "But I want to step up to the plate for Derek. Create some lasting memories." Ones that wouldn't leave the boy longing for something he'd never had when he reached thirty-six years old.

"Well, the best thing to do is find out what Derek wants. It might not be all that elaborate or difficult. Have you asked him?"

"No, but that sounds like a good idea. I will. Thanks." Was it too late for Greg to bond with his son in a way that would make a difference in both their lives? He hoped not.

One thing was certain. At least for tonight, he and Derek would have a chance to get into the spirit of Christmas together and make some memories while decorating Tillie's tree filled with many of Derek's great-grandmother's decorations, although he couldn't reveal that to his son yet.

Should he end this ruse and tell Tillie who he was and why he'd come here? The better he came to know her, the more pleased he was that she'd inherited this house. If left to Mother, Gram had known it would have been sold immediately to some stranger who never would have preserved it or Gram's memory as lovingly as Tillie had. And for all she knew, Greg had abandoned her, too. The only one she could count on to keep the house from ruin was Tillie.

"Derek, come and watch this." He lifted the boy into his arms and together they watched Tillie's long, slim fingers wrap and tuck each tiny bulb. The sight mesmerized Derek as much as it had Greg for the past hour. Seeing she was running out of bulbs on this string, he set him down. "Son, let's get more strands for Tillie." They picked up one of the many bundles strewn about the floor near the storage bin that he had tested earlier and carried them back to Tillie.

Now was as a good opportunity to start the conversation. "What's your favorite thing to do at Christmas, Derek?" she asked.

"Open presents."

She laughed. "Of course. How about before Christmas morning?"

"Eat cookies."

"Oh, the cut-out ones with icing and sprinkles?" Greg could have sworn her voice sparkled, as did the lights in the tree.

"Uh-huh. I like the frosting more than the sprinkles."

Tillie gasped. "What? Why, I can't imagine one without the other."

Derek became serious as he looked up at Tillie. "Well, I promise I'll try sprinkles this year. Maybe I'll like them now."

Greg smiled, seeing how his son had been equally charmed by the woman.

Greg hadn't been a part of the cookie-baking and wasn't aware of that. Usually, he was either coming from or going to the office. Given his ineptitude in the kitchen, he doubted he'd be able to pull off that tradition on his own.

"Perhaps we can make a batch before you leave," Tillie suggested, coming to his rescue. "You can help me get in the groove for when I'll be baking them for parties next month." Once again, Tillie to the rescue.

"Do you have a dinosaur cookie cutter?"

Tillie pursed her lips and raised her eyes. "Hmm. I'm not sure that I do, but the hardware store in town has a fabulous collection, so I'll make sure I pick up one before we bake."

Greg asked him, "Actually, Derek, would you like to go pick out some special cookie cutters and make cookies with Tillie?"

"And your daddy," Tillie added. He hoped she was aware of how useless he could be in the kitchen. He'd let her take the lead in making them.

"Yeah! I want dinosaurs and a doggie and a train…" As Derek rattled off any number of shapes he wanted, Greg hoped the hardware store was as stocked as Tillie indicated.

Greg suggested, "Since you're five, why don't you pick your five favorite shapes and we'll add a new one every year?" If the hardware store didn't have them, they'd find them somewhere else.

"Awesome! Thanks, Daddy!"

Caught up in the spirit, Greg asked, "What are some other things you like to do at Christmas?"

"Well, bemember last year, Daddy, when you took me back to Mommy's one night and we saw lots of lights on the houses?"

Derek still wasn't able to pronounce the word "remember," but Greg tried not to get hung up on it as he scanned his memory for the scene Derek described. He came up blank. Not that he'd admit it. "Which were your favorites?"

"The swirling star ones. That was cool. And bemember when we saw the Grinch stealing those lights? I think he already took most of the lights on that street. It was really dark. And bemember that green house? That's where the Grinch lives. We don't want to go there."

Tillie interjected, "But it's okay to visit after Christmas because the Grinch's heart grew big by then."

Derek considered that a moment. "Maybe. But I don't wanna go by myself." The boy turned to Greg. "Can we do it this year, Daddy? Can we? Maybe we can catch the Grinch this time before he takes them all."

How had he missed that last year? Had he been preoccupied while Derek had told him about all these things he'd seen during that drive home? Greg smiled. Tillie was right. He didn't need to overthink this. Focus on finding the things Derek liked doing.

"You betcha, sport." But he wanted a couple of surprises for Derek, too. Greg made a mental note to at least pick up a laser-light projector for the front of his house. Maybe he could find a Grinch figure, too.

"And can we get a Santa and sleigh and Rudolph for your yard?" How had the boy known what he'd been thinking? Greg added those to his list.

His neighborhood association might have some rules against such displays, but even if he had to remove them when Derek wasn't there or set them up in the backyard, he'd suffer the fines.

"I don't see why not. And we can put lights on the front of the house. We should have snow on the ground by then."

"Don't you have it all winter long?" Tillie asked.

"There's about a seventy-five percent chance, but we had a brown Christmas a couple years ago. Now, in the northern part of the state, it's all but a certainty they'll have snow."

"Must be wonderful to be so sure of having a White Christmas. Here, more often than not, it's a brown one. Sometimes it's so warm that the grass is still green. And when we do get snow, there are so many accidents that it spoils families being able to get together. So most of us hope it will remain clear without snow or rain."

Greg connected the new string of lights and handed her the bundle as she finished the last one. While no static electricity struck them, he did feel sparks between them as their fingers touched repeatedly.

"Miss Tillie, can you come see us this Christmas? You're fun!"

Derek's enthusiastic invitation had the two adults staring at one another with a mixture of indulgence and fluster. Tillie's cheeks grew red when she met his gaze, leaving Greg puzzled. Would she want to leave her perfect Christmas here and venture to the frozen north? Would she be interested in seeing his city when clearly she was a country girl at heart?

Whatever prompted Derek to ask, now that the invitation was out there, Greg wanted her to say yes in the worst way.

"I'll second the invitation."

She opened her mouth to answer before pressing her lips together and staring down at her hands. "I really couldn't impose."

"Come on. It would be no imposition. I can imagine how busy you must be at Christmas, but if you came to Minneapolis, you'd experience an old-fashioned winter holiday like none other. One of my staffers has a farm with horse-drawn sleighs, cows, and sheep. I'm sure she could extend the season a bit into January after your busy period is over, if you wouldn't mind a late Christmas."

Her eyes lit up, even though he wasn't convinced he'd won her over yet. If she did agree to visit, it would be an important step in case he wanted to pursue a relationship with her beyond this stay.

"Well, I can't make any promises." Greg waited for her to reject the idea while his son stared at her almost as expectantly as he was himself. "But I'll think about it. I do have that hand muff and furred cape I wear for Christmas caroling and the lighting up of Bardstown."

Greg pictured her, snow falling in fluffy flakes and landing on her eyelashes and cheeks as she sang like an angel. "Sounds quaint."

Fire spit from her eyes. "It is, and we love it." Her defensive tone told him she'd taken his words as a slur on the event. Not the way he'd intended at all.

"Quaint is a good thing, even to a city boy." *Now she has me calling myself a boy.*

"Sorry. Anyway, they let me sing with them even though I have a tin ear."

"I heard you singing while you were baking fruitcake and found your voice charming."

"You're too kind." Her blush charmed him even more. With a will of its own, his hand reached up to brush a stray tendril of hair behind her ear. Greg wasn't sure which of them was more surprised by the intimate gesture.

"I'm hungry," Derek announced. And the moment passed much too quickly.

Tillie squinted down at the familiar watch pinned to her shirt. The antique watch with its metallic ribbon and filigreed gold face had once belonged to Gram.

"Um, oh dear. I'm s-sorry."

When Greg met her gaze, he realized she must think she'd been staring at her breasts. Her blush was a pretty shade of pink.

"I got so wrapped up in what we were, um, doing that I forgot the time." She laid the bundle of untucked lights on a tree branch and symbolically dusted off her hands. "I'll call you for supper in about thirty minutes, but if you'd like an appetizer, I have one I can serve beforehand."

"What's a appy…appyteaser?"

Both adults laughed, the tension fully dissipating from a few moments ago. Greg did the honors. "It's something you eat at the start of the meal. Kind of like when we order wings before pizza. The wings are the *appyteaser.*"

"I like wings!"

"Well, I'm afraid I don't have wings, although I was planning on pizza tonight. How about some homemade breadsticks?"

"I like the crust best!" Derek announced as he walked over to take her hand.

"Any kind of bread is your favorite," Greg pointed out.

Derek ignored his father's comment and asked Tillie, "Can I help?"

"Absolutely!"

Greg watched the two of them head toward the hallway before he stared again at the tree. Working on it without her expert supervision wouldn't be wise.

"Hey, wait for me!" He followed them into the kitchen, fighting the urge to draw her aside and insist that she take their invitation seriously.

Please say yes, Tillie. You'll make our Christmas complete.

Chapter Eleven

Tillie's heart nearly burst with excitement all through supper. The conversation was friendly and focused mostly on Christmas—no adversarial comments from Greg. If only they could engage in pleasant moments like this more often.

Stop wishing for the impossible, Matilda.

Tillie sighed. After clearing and stacking the dishes, she couldn't wait to continue trimming the tree.

"Before I can finish with the lights, I'm going to need the ladder to work on the higher branches."

"Lead the way," Greg said. "Derek, wait for us in the parlor."

Greg followed her toward the cellar door under the foyer stairs, her rear end tingling where she imagined his gaze boring into her backside.

As if a man like Gregory Buchanan would have any interest in my backside.

Maybe not, but his seeming fascination with her hair had led to him tucking a stray tendril behind her ear, which had let loose a flock of butterflies in her stomach. And there had been those many touches in the attic and parlor that set off sparks—okay, most of them literally from static—but there had been other moments when the air sizzled between the two of them, too.

Perhaps he no longer saw her as the innkeeper out to exploit his grandmother, although she wished he'd open up to her about who he was. Seeing the color drain from his face when he saw the photograph by her bedside had left her wanting to wrap her arms around him and ease some of the pain he must feel over her loss.

Did he resent the fact Mrs. Foster left the house to her and not his family? Tillie had nothing to do with that decision, but had been incredibly honored to be entrusted with the place and the responsibilities that entailed.

On the bright side, if she hadn't been here running this inn, she'd never have met Greg and Derek. Perhaps fate had stepped in to give her a glimpse at what might be possible if only she'd allow someone into her heart...her life.

At the doorway to the cellar stairs, he insisted on preceding her. *Clearly not focused on my butt.* When he reached the floor, he peered around the middle room. Uncertain which way to go, she supposed. When she joined him, she pointed to the laundry area in a nook behind the stairs. "It's in there."

He hesitated, staring down at her. The butterflies took flight again. "Thanks, Tillie. I can't tell you how much I'm enjoying tonight here with Derek—and you."

The air suddenly vacated the small space. She licked her lips, noticing that his gaze followed the movement, leaving her even more breathless.

He's not coming on to you, Matilda, for Heaven's sake.

He'd only thanked her for sharing one of her Christmas traditions with them. His, too, to be honest, because most of it stemmed from his grandmother.

Her nearness prompted him to tuck an imaginary strand of hair behind her ear as she gave him a breathy response. "My pleasure." Good Lord, she was behaving like a gawky high-school girl crushing on the quarterback.

His head lowered toward hers, and she closed her eyes.

Kiss me, Greg.

The brush of his lips on hers sent her heart to racing. He cupped her chin and tilted her head, giving him better access. His warm lips and tongue coaxed her mouth open, and she reminded herself to breathe when her chest grew tight.

"Daddy? You didn't go in the scary room, did you?"

Derek's voice coming down the stairs broke the spell.

"No, son. We'll be up in a few minutes."

Tillie turned sideways and waved him toward the ladder again. Grinning as he passed her, he walked into the area underneath the stairs and lifted out the ladder with ease. She moved out of the way to let him go up first.

What had just happened? While she'd felt an attraction to him since the moment she saw him in the driveway, Greg must have a string of women waiting for him in Minneapolis. She'd best remember that he was out of her league. Besides, he was recently divorced. She wanted a man who chose to be with her because there was no one else he wanted by his side, not merely a dalliance to ease his loneliness or boredom.

In the parlor once more, neither mentioned that kiss, thank goodness. She increased the volume on the stereo, and Christmas carols streamed from the speakers as she and Greg worked on the top of the tree with him holding the ladder steady.

"You usually do this alone?" he asked. Was his gaze on her rear end? The heat she felt there made her wonder.

"I have to." She reached for another strand of lights.

"Isn't it dangerous for you to be this far up on the ladder? What if you fell?"

She set the bundle on a branch and retrieved her cell phone from her pocket. "Help is a phone call away. But I'm very careful."

"If I knew how to tuck those lights in half as well as you did, I would have you holding this ladder for me."

Tillie laughed, but once again became conscious of where his gaze might be focused. *Don't become flustered again.* More than likely, he was keeping an eye on Derek as he played with the strands of beaded garland, not the least bit interested in her butt.

When she'd finished with the lights at the top of the tree, she started going down the ladder. Greg's hand rested on her waist. Every touch felt as if a bolt of electricity exploded inside her.

Pulling away after her feet were once again planted on the rug, she tried to shift her focus—and his. Unable to make eye contact with him, she announced to no one in particular, "Time for the beaded garland." Her voice sounded breathless, as if she'd run a marathon.

She turned to find Derek making explosion noises as his hands let the beads spill through. They'd been carefully packed away in separate plastic grocery bags, but were now one jumbled mess. Derek looped two strands over his ears and around his neck.

"Are you decorating the tree or yourself?" Tillie asked.

Derek grinned widely. "Me!"

After untangling a few of the strands, she held one end of a garland, handing him the other. "Here, Derek, drape the beads over a branch and then let the strand droop in between until you find another branch to hook it on. Like this." She demonstrated with the first red one.

"Do we have to put them all on the tree?" he asked.

"Well, I usually do." His lower lip stuck out. "What's wrong, honey?"

"I wanna play with them. The red ones are lava from a volcano." That explained the noises he'd been making. What an imagination. Had he seen volcanoes at the museum today?

"Tell you what… Choose a red one and a gold one to play with, and we'll drape the rest on the tree in layers."

"Why don't I help?" Greg had been so quiet she'd almost forgotten he was here.

Yeah, right.

"Absolutely! After all the garland and ornaments are on, we'll add gobs of silver tinsel. You being so tall will be able to toss it high on the tree the way it was done in the movies *Christmas in Connecticut* and the original *Bishop's Wife*. Have you seen either of those movies, Greg?"

"Can't say that I have."

Did the man do anything related to Christmas? "Really? They're classics!"

"I've never been much of a movie buff."

"Well, we'll have to watch them before you leave. I have both DVDs."

"Sounds good." Greg sounded unsure about how enjoyable it would be, but the image of the two of them cuddled up on the couch with Derek between them holding a bowl of popcorn flashed in front of her eyes.

Only she doubted Derek would be interested in the romantic comedy, which morphed the vision into one with only she and Greg sitting side by side on the couch watching the screen.

Tillie tried to blink away the impossible fantasy, but the image lingered.

Caught off guard, she took a moment and a deep breath to compose herself. She'd miss having these two around. The Buchanans had thrown her for a loop. She'd never allowed herself to become so attached to visitors before, not even repeat ones.

As she haphazardly draped garland, her mind wandered. Would she accept Greg's—and Derek's—invitations to visit them? She'd half-accepted, but had he been serious? Greg had fed into her fantasy Christmas with talk of a sleigh ride. She and Mrs. Foster had watched those movies every year. Even before that, Tillie had been addicted to Hollywood classics and dreamed of a world that couldn't exist realistically. But Mrs. Foster had shown her glimpses of that life, and Tillie fought hard to recreate those vignettes every year by carrying on Mrs. Foster's holiday traditions. Granted, she couldn't take Greg up on the offer until January, but some celebrated the season until Epiphany. She could, too.

Don't get your hopes up, Matilda.

Her mother's words reminded her that those who aimed too high often had their hearts stomped on. Best to try to live in this moment.

"Greg, why don't we trade places and you can finish up the top part?" He seemed reluctant to accept. "Your height will make it easier for you to do so without climbing as high as I'd have to."

She'd never had any trouble in the past, but capitalized on his worries about her being on the ladder. And it worked. Soon, she was handing him the gold-beaded garland and staring at his butt, enjoying the view.

Once the garland was strewn about the tree with glorious abandon, Greg descended the ladder, and Tillie walked over to the first bin of ornaments. "Derek, why don't you choose which one to put on the tree first?"

Leaving his lava beads behind, Derek joined her to peer inside, perusing the vast array of ornaments on the top row. A red and green rocking horse ridden by a toy soldier captured his attention.

"That one! I wanna ride a horse someday!"

"Go ahead and pick it up."

"What if I break it?" His solemn expression broke her heart.

"I'm sure you'll be super careful." Her more delicate ones were kept in a separate bin only she handled, so there was no harm in letting him choose any of these.

She left the hooks from the previous year on them, so he was able to go straight to the tree and hook it around the tip of one of the branches.

"Why, you're a pro at this, Derek," she said.

Derek beamed up at her. With his confidence up, he returned to the bin and picked up another ornament.

Her gaze strayed to where Greg stood near the tree, a smile on his face as he stared at her. She had no idea what prompted the smile, but bestowed him with one anyway before breaking the invisible connection between them.

Best to focus on the younger Buchanan, anyway. The five-year-old wouldn't trample on her dreams. Derek placed another dozen or so ornaments on the tree, mostly in the same area. Perhaps if she moved the bin to another side, he'd spread them out. But she wouldn't rearrange anything he put on the tree. It was important that he feel a sense of accomplishment and ownership. And when she sat in here on quiet evenings, she'd sip her tea and stare at the tree and let the memories of tonight wash over her.

She needed to start working on the higher branches if this tree was going to be finished by Monday and carried another bin to the side facing the fireplace. "I'll work on this spot," she announced. "Greg, why don't you place some above Derek's head?" As he did so, she surreptitiously retrieved her cell phone from her pocket and snapped photos of father and son. She'd share them with Greg later but also intended to keep them for herself to remember this moment in the years to come.

The three of them worked side by side, occasionally mentioning one of the ornaments found in the bin as being particularly noteworthy or interesting. Snowmen, reindeer, Santas galore, and sleds commingled on the tree once more in an ever-changing configuration, especially this year with two new variables thrown into the decorating mix.

"Wow, I remember…" He cut off his words and said, "I wonder who the thumbprints belong to."

Tillie knew instantly what he'd found in the bin. He held the salt-dough ornament in the shape of a holly leaf. This one was quite familiar to her and included two thumbprints—one of which was hers. Tillie wasn't sure how much she should reveal about the origin of the ornament or whether to point out his gaffe.

Why won't you be honest with me, Greg?

She sighed. How should she tell the story he no doubt was already familiar with, at least in part? She reached out to take the ornament from him, feeling the warmth of his hand as she stared down at it. "Mrs. Foster made new ornaments annually. That one was made when I was eight. Her grandson came for a visit. He was about twelve." She met his gaze. "It would be their last time together."

He flinched at her words, but Tillie continued the sad story. Perhaps he'd reveal himself to her afterward. "She had him place his thumbprint on the left side not long before he and his mother went home." *Never to return.*

Don't judge him any more harshly than he does himself. Clearly, he carried guilt about not seeing or contacting his grandmother. How many other young people became caught up in school or jobs or even friends and put off visiting older relatives until it was too late?

Tillie cleared her throat, overcome with emotion for him. "I came over to visit right after they'd left." She wouldn't reveal that she'd made a beeline to Mrs. Foster's after seeing Greg and his mother drive over the railroad tracks. "Mrs. Foster asked me to place my thumbprint beside his in the still-soft dough." She touched the thumbprint with her finger.

"Why?"

How would he react to what she was about to tell him? Only one way to find out. "She said that these prints sitting side-by-side would tie the two of us together forever. She was sometimes rather fanciful."

Would he come clean now?

He met her gaze, and she waited several moments. "Did it?"

Obviously, not. On both counts. But she wouldn't out him. For whatever reason, he wasn't prepared to reveal his identity to her yet.

"Only time will tell, I suppose." She held the ornament toward him. "Would you like to place it on the tree?"

* * *

While Greg didn't believe in spells, fate, and such things, he'd be blind not to see that they *had* come together again. Well, together might be a strong term, but he most certainly had come back here knowing nothing about any matchmaking scheme his grandmother had dreamed up decades ago. If he were honest with Tillie about who he was, her enigmatic assessment of Gram's prophetic words might change.

He didn't accept the ornament right away, but stared into her eyes a long, uncomfortable moment. How could they be destined for one another with their personality differences and geographic challenges?

Then he remembered the unexpected kiss in the cellar. If that wasn't meant to be, why had it felt so right?

Romantic notions wouldn't serve him well. He had no intention of remarrying, and Gram would have settled for nothing short of a wedding ring for the girl who'd been like a granddaughter to her, if not a second daughter. One much more loving and deserving than her own blood.

At long last, he reached out to accept the ornament with a sad smile. "Thank you."

Their fingers brushed, and another jolt of static electricity shot through him. Tillie awakened feelings he'd thought had died long ago.

He gazed down at the heavy holly leaf in the palm of his hand. Perhaps Gram had wanted to match them up using this enchanted ornament.

"Why don't you find a good place for it, Greg?" Tillie prompted, coaxing him into the present.

He continued to hold the holly leaf between his hands, noticing it had become oddly warmer. He slid his thumb over the much smaller print he'd made at twelve. Hers was even tinier in comparison. He fought the temptation to compare her adult thumb with this one that had been frozen in time.

His fingers tingled as if the stiff, cracked dough imparted some kind of message to him.

Nonsense. He blinked and turned toward the tree. The house seemed to be trying once more to work its magic on him—and Tillie. He'd literally not thought about this thing since the moment he'd pressed his thumb into the soft dough twenty-five years ago. His mother and Gram had fought bitterly that day—as best he could recall over money of all things—prompting Mother to hastily pack their things and leave.

Apparently, not before Gram steeped this object in his hands with her fanciful notions.

But Tillie had probably remembered those prophetic words every year she handled this ornament again. If he told her who he was now, would she take it as some cosmic sign, compelling her to fabricate a relationship where none should exist?

But what about what had happened earlier tonight in the cellar? Before that, there had been some near misses—while playing in the leaves and when he'd fantasized over kissing the hot buttered rum on her lips. Sexual awareness sizzled between them on many occasions making him wonder if Gram hadn't truly set in motion some type of hocus-pocus with this silly talisman.

Man, he had it bad for this woman if he was going to start believing in stuff like this to justify his attraction to her.

He gave up trying to fight against the spell the ornament, the house, or perhaps the woman standing next to him had cast over him. He placed the hook over a high branch and watched its weight drag it down to about her eye level.

A nagging inside made him ask, "Did you ever see the boy?"

"Yes. But only from a distance. I stayed away from the house during their visit."

Had she hidden in the woods? Ridiculous. November would have been too cold for a skinny little girl like the one in the photo upstairs.

Temptation won out. He grinned. "Did you have a crush on the boy?"

"Of course not!"

A quick glimpse of her reddening cheeks said she might be protesting too much.

Suddenly, a fuzzy memory popped into his head of a girl much like the one in the photo, her long auburn hair in pigtails, wearing a baggy coat and tights or leggings. She'd teetered on the shiny rail of the tracks, her arms outstretched parallel to the ground, as she negotiated the thin line of steel. He'd caught a peek at her from the car window as his mother drove like a bat out of hell through the town on her way to the interstate. While the moment was fleeting, he could see her in his mind's eye again as clearly as that day all those years ago.

Had that been Tillie? She'd left him longing to get out of the car and stay that day to play on those tracks with her, but he hadn't given much more thought to her once she was out of sight.

"You mentioned there are railroad tracks around here."

"Yes. About half a mile away, near where the grocery and center of town used to be. They run right behind my church."

"Maybe you could show them to Derek and me." His son might enjoy playing on them.

"Trains! Will we see trains?"

Tillie smiled down at him. "Depends on the day. Not many trains run on those tracks anymore, but the My Old Kentucky Dinner Train does most Saturday evenings this time of year. You could walk on the rails without much worry any other day."

"Why don't we all ride the train tomorrow?" Greg hoped she'd say yes, but her response wasn't forthcoming. "It will give you a night off from cooking and baking." She bit the inside of her lower lip. "Come on. My treat."

"Come with us, Miss Tillie?" With Derek as his wingman, he noticed a slight smile at the corner of her mouth.

"Well, if you insist." Her warm gaze moved from Derek to Greg. "Thank you for inviting me. I haven't ridden the train all year."

"Great. I'll go online and order the tickets later."

"You'll need to order what you want to eat at the same time. I like everything, so you can surprise me." She leaned closer to whisper, "But order Derek the Choo-choo cake." The nearness of Tillie did all kinds of things to his libido, and he wasn't sure he'd remember what she said later. "Oh, and why don't we go in costume?" she asked.

He tried to wrap his head around what she had in mind. Derek was equally confused.

"But it's not Halloween, is it, Daddy?"

"No, son. That was last month."

These two needed to let their hair down as much as she did. "I meant we can dress the way people did in the olden days."

"Like in the Tom Tom movie?"

She awaited an interpretation from Greg.

"Thomas the Tank Engine Train. He loves trains."

"Ah." She turned to Derek. "Well, I'm not sure how they dress in that movie, Derek, but I was thinking maybe a century and a half ago."

Never one to dwell in the modern world or to do anything in the ordinary way, Tillie never failed to surprise him. "I'm afraid we didn't pack anything like that."

"No worries! I have a closet full of the costumes that we use on mystery weekends here. I'm sure I can find something that will fit each of you. We'll raid the closet first thing in the morning."

At least he wouldn't be the only one dressed in period costume. Making a spectacle of himself in a crowd wasn't his thing.

But having a date of sorts with Tillie would make up for it. Greg's mood lifted as he contemplated how this might work out.

* * *

True to her word, right after breakfast the next day, she called them up to one of the bedrooms and began pulling out various pieces of vintage apparel, holding it up to one or the other of them. She'd either put it back inside the wardrobe or set it on the bed for them to try on in the bathroom. They tried on clothes until they found what each wanted to wear. When they returned, she'd laid out several hats on the bed for them to choose from.

"How about this one, Daddy?"

Derek had picked up a newsboy cap and placed it on his head. Tillie adjusted it a bit. "Authentic," she proclaimed.

"What's a thentic?" Derek looked to Greg for the answer.

"It means the real deal. That hat's perfect for you."

Tillie handed him a small bundle of vintage newspapers. "Here. The perfect finishing touch. You're selling newspapers. Lots of boys did that when they were a little older than you are. Even Walt Disney did."

"He did? I want to go to Disney World someday."

"Oh, if you do, then on Main Street you can see what many American cities looked like at the turn of the last century."

"Daddy, will you take me to there?"

"I'll talk to Mommy about it." They'd talked about taking him when he was six or seven, but he didn't know who would wind up going with him now. "I'm sure one of us will make sure you get to Mickey's house someday."

Derek began jumping up and down. "Yay! Disney World!"

Greg shook his head and met Tillie's gaze. "The boy hears only what he wants to hear."

"I'm sure one of you will make his wish come true," she said, smiling before returning to the walnut wardrobe. "Now, we need to put the finishing touches on your outfit." He'd selected a three-piece suit made of homespun tweed. She assured him this is how Jesse James might have dressed, not like the stereotypical western outlaw most people expected. "He probably eluded authorities so long because he looked the part of a businessman."

He watched her rummage through a wooden box until she removed two matching metal spurs. "These should do the job."

Before he knew what she intended to do, she knelt in front of him and lifted his right pants leg to position the metal band onto the worn boots she'd found for him. Perhaps donning the persona of Jesse James was messing with his mind, but staring down at her in her long dress with her hair in a loose topknot, his thoughts were far from wholesome at the moment.

Get your mind out of the gutter.

Still, he couldn't bring himself to stop her and do the job himself.

"Help me up, kind sir?" She reached out her hand, and he lifted her to her feet. "Thank you."

The breathlessness in her voice sent all PG-rated thoughts out the window. Or was it the way she stared into his eyes at the moment? If they were alone, he'd have kissed her again, only much more deeply than he had in the cellar. He wanted to…desperately. Judging by the blush in her cheeks, she'd have welcomed it, too. Was the fantasy of being kissed by Jesse James or by sedate old Gregory Buchanan putting color in her cheeks and a sparkle in her eyes?

"You need a hat, too, Daddy."

The spell broken, the two of them blinked back to the present. She appeared to be as stunned as he felt. Had his grandmother cast them under some kind of spell? No, she was merely an eccentric old lady with a romantic heart.

"Um, I think I have the perfect one." Tillie turned away and rummaged in the wardrobe again, retrieving another hatbox. "Wait until you see this."

She lifted a western-style hat out of the box. "It's called a Boss of the Plains and is exactly like the one Jesse used to wear. And look!" She poked her finger through a hole in the crown of the hat. "There's even a hole where the sheriff or posse took a shot at ol' Jesse as he rode out of town with their money." It appeared to him more like a cigarette burn she'd put there herself to match the story, but who cared?

"Daddy! That's the hat the bad guy was wearing in the basement!" The boy's eyes had grown wider, but he seemed more intrigued than afraid. Had Derek seen ol' Jesse himself haunting the cellar?

Greg faced Tillie, who seemed equally surprised. "So Jesse haunts the place, too?"

She shrugged. "I have no firsthand knowledge of such."

Could he have broken that window? Maybe, but how could a disembodied spirit move a heavy shelf? He'd watched the movie *Ghost* with Nancy, about the extent of his knowledge of apparitions. Patrick Swayze sure needed a lot of extra energy to kinetically move any objects in Demi Moore's world.

However, Tillie accepted the idea in stride, holding the hat toward Greg. "Try it on?"

When she asked him that way, he didn't care what kind of fool he appeared to be. Saying no wasn't an option. "Why don't you do the honors?"

Tillie attempted to place the hat on his head, but fell a little short of the mark until he bowed toward her to make it easier. After she settled the hat into place, she surveyed her work, tilting her head for a moment to assess it before readjusting. "I think cocking it a little to the right will give you a more devil-may-care air."

After making sure Derek was occupied with some accessories he'd found in a nearby box, he whispered, "Is that how you see me, Miss Tillie? Devil may care?"

"No. I…um…I didn't mean to suggest—"

He pressed his finger against her soft lips before she burst his ego bubble. Once again, he had to rein in the urge to kiss her. "I've always been a solid, respectable, upstanding citizen, if you will. Stepping out as an outlaw might be a nice change of pace. Especially with someone as lovely as you on my arm."

Her cheeks grew rosier, and she cleared her throat. "I don't think I'd have been attracted to a real-life bad boy if I'd lived in those days, but it's exciting when we're playacting."

To be seen as a bad boy nearly made him laugh, but remembering his persona, he bowed and tipped his hat. "I'll do my best not to compromise your morals, little lady." He wiggled his eyebrows, and she giggled. What a sexy sound. Everything about her aroused him.

Tillie's smile faded, and she held her hands against her cheeks as she backed toward the door. "Um, if you all leave these clothes on the bed, I'll freshen them up before this afternoon. Meanwhile, I'd better go down and prepare a light lunch to tide us over."

Was she feeling the same magnetic attraction he did? Would she run away to protect her heart from being hurt? He couldn't swear he wouldn't hurt her when he returned to Minnesota. Besides, it would be impossible for them to maintain a long-term relationship, even if she had any romantic interest in him.

What happened to his firm resolution not to let her get under his skin? The future loomed bleak on the horizon in terms of their having anything beyond this brief interlude together.

Why, then, did he want to see where this attraction took them?

Chapter Twelve

Tillie tried to calm her racing pulse as she hurried up to her room for a much needed break from her guests. Well, one in particular. She took out her journal and opened to the next blank page. Mrs. Foster had taught Tillie to journal her thoughts, ostensibly to strengthen her writing abilities.

She'd never felt such a strong attraction to any man before. Not that she was a virgin. After all, she'd been young and foolish enough once to mistake lust for love. Not that others weren't exploring the opposite sex during college, but living off campus, she'd actually gone out of her way in a period of extreme depression and loneliness to find a boy to date. That decision turned out disastrously for her when the boy's condom failed, and he promptly ditched her to suffer through weeks of a pregnancy scare before her period came. She'd decided right then she wouldn't be the one left to pay such a steep price for a moment of passion.

But she hadn't met a man who made her want to rush to her doctor to go on birth control—well, until that kiss in the cellar. Of course, that might be the beginning and ending of any relationship between them.

Oh, I hope not.

Honestly, until that kiss, she didn't know what all the fuss was about. Perhaps if she'd loved the guy or even had an incredible orgasm the likes of which she read about in novels, she'd think differently afterward. But Tillie could take care of her own physical needs and didn't intend to suffer through any more awkward, mediocre sex merely to rack up notches in her pencil post bed. As if she'd have kept track. Although her bed's marked-up baseboard and the broken spindle in the headboard spoke to a livelier history than her nonexistent sex life.

Until Greg, she hadn't met anyone worth opening up to and risking the consequences that might come of their actions. None of the men she'd casually dated made her heart race and her breathing stop. Mark Peterson had asked her for a date at a particularly lonely time, but he came in here like he owned the place. He always seemed more interested in the house than her anyway, except for those awkward fumblings on their second date.

Like most women, she wanted to live the romantic dream of happily ever after one day. She'd been pursued by a few men over the years. Had even gone online to a dating site for country girls when her biological clock told her she ought to find someone, marry, and settle down, but most of the men she'd been attracted to had told her up front they wouldn't leave their family farms. No man was worth giving up her haven, her happy place.

Not even you, Greg Buchanan.

For more than a decade, she'd never permitted her body to wander in a direction that her head screamed would only lead to heartache—and a potential baby to raise alone. While today that didn't carry the stigma it had for her mother and grandmother—or her poor great-grandmother—Tillie never found any man worth rushing into anything with.

Until Greg.

No, *including* Greg.

Use your head, Matilda.

He might as well be from Siberia as from Minnesota. When he left here, chances were she'd never see him again. She was sorely tempted to go up for that sleigh ride, but given the fact he wasn't being truthful with her, that should be the deal breaker right there. At a minimum, she deserved honesty.

So why did she allow her body to override her head right now for a relationship that would be fleeting at best?

Clearly, you've been lonely too long.

Right or wrong, she wanted to explore these feelings with him, even though it might be over in the next couple of days. Greg was safe. Their interactions would be dictated by the presence of a five-year-old boy. Derek would keep things from going too far. She could flirt, safe in the knowledge that it wouldn't lead to anything more than she could handle.

Even if they did decide to keep in touch beyond his stay here, having a sexual relationship shouldn't be out of the question down the road. Thank God for safe and effective contraceptive choices!

She paused the scratching of her pen a moment.

Oh, Tillie, what are you doing here?

I have no clue, Mrs. Foster.

Had her grandmother or even her mother justified their moments of passion in the same way or had they been overcome in the heat of the moment? All these years, Tillie prided herself in remaining level-headed around the men she dated, keeping them at a safe distance. Why couldn't she do the same with Greg?

Because logic and practicality escaped her when that man came near.

How could she long for something she hadn't particularly enjoyed? Because novels she read spoke of how good it could be with the right person, leaving her to wonder what making love might be like with Greg.

Intuition told her he would make the experience good for her. His firm, gentle hand would…

Stop fantasizing about a guest who will be gone from your life in a few days.

Unless she decided to accept his invitation to join him in Minneapolis this January.

But that was two months away. No way on earth would she be making love with Greg anytime soon, if ever. So why not live out some fantasies, play dress up, flirt a little? Mrs. Foster always encouraged her to take chances, not be so serious, and to follow her heart. Judging by the way he set her heart to pounding, she already knew what *it* wanted.

With him, she would make memories that wouldn't leave her to face any regrets. She had a reputation to uphold in the community, or her business might suffer the consequences.

Oh, the memories they could make! Enough for her to be able to reflect on this period in her life much like Mrs. Foster did with her second husband and Joseph Hill.

*   *   *

Greg and Derek waited in the dining room near the stairs to Tillie's room for her to join them. He took a photo of his newsboy son and texted it to Nancy, telling her what their plans were for the evening.

The squeak of a stair step alerted him to look up. Like an image from *Little House on the Prairie*, Tillie appeared wearing a long dress made of green calico and a prim bonnet that, unfortunately, hid her hair. She carried a reticule wrapped around her wrist, something he'd learned about while consulting on an Ingalls family preservation project in South Dakota. Over her shoulders, she wore a short black satin cape.

"Amazing." The word "sexy" followed in his mind, even though almost every part of her was covered. Removing his hat, he held it over his chest and affected an elaborate bow in her direction. Standing upright once again, he extended his elbow. "Shall we go? I do believe we have a train to catch."

Tucking her hand inside his elbow, she grinned. "I'm honored to know you'll be joining us, Jesse, and not to hold up the train."

"I never mix business with pleasure, ma'am. And this evening will be pure pleasure." A tug at his coat sleeve reminded him they weren't alone. "Yes, Derek?" he said, glancing down.

"Daddy, if you and Miss Tillie are pretending to be somebody else, who can I be?"

"How about Jesse Jr., since you're my son?"

The boy beamed and nodded his approval.

Turning toward Tillie again, Greg asked, "And to whom do I owe the pleasure of traveling with?"

"Why, you may call me Miss Zerelda—or Miss Zee, for short."

"I assume after my wife, not my mother."

"Oh, most definitely your wife, Jesse."

He hoped they wouldn't confuse Derek, but the boy seemed to understand they were pretending.

Greg drove them the five miles to town, and they waited in the depot for the departure of the train. Other patrons smiled at them and took photos while Greg showed his son the displays of railroad memorabilia.

When the boarding whistle blew, they were shown to a table for four. Derek and Tillie sat across from each other at the windows, with Greg beside his son. The fourth seat could have been filled by a single passenger, but he was grateful no one was traveling alone today.

When the tuxedoed conductor arrived at their table, he smiled at Tillie. "Good to see you again, Miss Tillie."

"Good evening, Gabriel. But today, please call me Miss Zee. And I'm pleased to introduce you to Jesse James and his son, Jesse Jr. They're visiting from Minneapolis."

"How do, folks." Gabriel punched their tickets before addressing her again. "It's always a pleasure to have my favorite innkeeper on board." He met Greg's gaze. "But I don't want any trouble on here this evening, Mr. James." He winked and smiled again. "We'll begin serving dinner soon. Let me know if there's anything I can get for you folks."

Greg shook his head, grinning, as Derek watched out the window. The train rolled out of town with Tillie pointing out beef cattle farms to the boy and the various distillery buildings to Greg along the way. She seemed to be in her element. Her love of history and this community were evident. Nothing would tear her away from this place. All the more reason to leave her behind when he returned home.

But he didn't want to think about that now. He still had a few days with her and planned to make the most of them.

She'd probably ridden this train a dozen times at least and talked about the various highlights, explaining the importance of the many rickhouses they passed. "They're merely multistoried buildings where the aging process for bourbon occurs. The placement of each barrel on the ricks is crucial to how the final product will taste. The extreme heat and cold in the seasons also factor in. Each distillery has its own formula for what's best for each label they bottle, whether it takes two years or twenty to reach the bottling plant." He listened with rapt attention, but barely glanced outside the window. He couldn't take his eyes off Tillie and the way her face lit up when she spoke about this place she loved so much.

Why not entertain a discussion about Jesse's history? "Have you ever thought about the possibility Jesse James didn't die in 1882?"

She cocked her head. "Are you one of those revisionists who swear he lived to the ripe old age of a hundred and three or four?"

About what he expected her response to be. "I'll take that as a no."

"Seriously, a history buff like you should know better. And haven't that man's claims been debunked by DNA tests of his exhumed body? They might have even conducted tests on Jesse's remains by now. So no, I don't entertain the possibility at all."

Well, given her adamant refusal to even consider the possibility, no way in hell was he going to tell her the other reason he'd come here.

The meal was presented in courses by servers also dressed in tuxes. At the end of the line, the train stopped, and the engine did a runaround to take them back to the station. The conductor asked if Derek would like to watch, and Greg took his enthusiastic son to the viewing platform at the rear of the train to do so.

Returning to their table ten minutes later, Greg asked Tillie to switch seats and sit across from him so they could talk more easily. They rocked along the tracks, over the trestle again, and past her church, which sparked another lesson in local history from Tillie about the Catholic migration from Maryland.

"The county is heavily Catholic to this day," she concluded.

"You certainly know a lot about this place." Seeing the light in her eyes as she shared the history, he could have listened to her go on all night about any topic.

"Sorry. I'm rambling."

"Oh, no need to apologize. I find it fascinating, and your love for your home comes through loud and clear."

Dessert was brought to their table, interrupting their conversation momentarily. When he'd bought the tickets, he'd ordered the chocolate choo-choo for two to share with Derek at Tillie's suggestion, but the boy announced his tummy too full to try even a bite.

"Share it with me, Til…Miss Zee?"

She compared her slice of Derby Pie to his plate filled with the hollow chocolate-mold train running on tracks of caramel ties and chocolate-syrup rails, its shell filled with chocolate mousse, whipped cream, and a fat strawberry.

"Maybe a small bite. The prime rib filled me up, but I can't resist ending a meal on a sweet note."

Tillie's smile provided that for him. He sank his fork into the mousse and extended it across the table to her. Her eyes opened wider in surprise that he hadn't let her help herself, but her lips opened as well and wrapped around the fork as he slowly slid the decadent dessert into her mouth.

She closed her eyes. "Mmm. So good."

He dipped the fork into the mixture of mousse and whipped cream and took a bite from the same fork, the intimacy of the gesture not lost on him.

So why on God's green earth was he now holding the berry by the stem in front of her mouth without asking if she even wanted more? He waited, all the while imagining her lips opening and accepting his offering. He'd sink to the depths of hell tonight trying to sleep with that image imprinted on his brain, but couldn't banish it now.

Tillie smiled. "Strawberries! My favorite!" Her voice sounded huskier than before, and her eyes twinkled as her rosy lips opened again and wrapped around the plump fruit. For what seemed the longest time, she didn't move and then leaned back taking half the berry into her mouth. She continued to smile at him as she chewed deliberately, knowing full well the effect she was having on him. When some of the juice started to run toward her chin, he nearly lost it.

Don't picture yourself licking it off her.

Too late.

She laughed and swiped her chin with the napkin. *You snooze, you lose, Jesse.*

"Sorry. I'm not used to being hand fed."

He wasn't sorry in the least. The thought of another man doing what he'd just done wouldn't sit well with him, though. As if he had any claim on her or ever would.

The woman was the real deal—no false airs or guiles. She'd never have been able to carry off a hoax if she'd wanted to.

Tillie didn't close her eyes as she had when he kissed her, but maintained eye contact with him as he bit off the remainder of the berry, his lips touching where hers had been a moment before. How could this feel as pleasurable as their kiss last night?

While he couldn't answer that question, Greg shifted in his seat, trying to ignore the evidence. He had the rest of the train ride to get the lower half of his body under control. He only hoped that would give him enough time.

Somehow, he didn't think a 19th-century woman would behave so brazenly, especially in public. Thank God he lived today and not back then. "Do you think this is how Miss Zee would have acted on a train ride with Jesse?"

Her eyes opened wider as she shook her head. "This is why I could never be a docent. I wouldn't be able to stay in character! But I don't imagine Jesse as being all that sensuous, either."

Was she calling Greg sensuous by association? He smiled. If she only knew he was out of character as well. Nancy would never have described him as even romantic before.

Abruptly recalling that his son sat next to him, he realized that Derek seemed to be deep in a solo conversation as if speaking with an imaginary someone seated in the empty chair Tillie had vacated. As he played with his toy train on the table, he glanced up every now and then to answer questions only he could hear.

Pleased his son was otherwise oblivious of what he and Tillie were up to, Greg used all the self-discipline he could muster to finish the dessert within the shell of the chocolate train as he watched her finish eating her pie and drink her coffee.

Out of the blue, he asked, "What's wrong with the men around here?"

"I beg your pardon?"

"How is it a woman like you is still single?"

Watching the flush creep up the column into her neck as she averted her gaze made him grin. Composing herself, she smiled at him and said, "I'm discerning."

He liked to think she was interested in him at least a little, but perhaps it was all an act.

"It's not that I don't date at all. But some men are a little too pushy, or they are more interested in my property than in me."

Guilty as charged?

However, his interest in the house waned compared to his desire to get to know her better. Not that he still didn't want to solve the mystery Gram wrote about and find out whether Jesse had survived his murder.

Well before they neared the station, their cups and plates—his including the shell of the choo-choo dessert—had been cleared.

"What are your plans for tomorrow?" she asked.

With some difficulty, he forced himself to focus on her words. "We're heading out after breakfast to go to the Louisville Zoo."

Her attention turned to Derek who watched the stationary railroad cars in the RJ Corman rail yard as they passed by. "Oh, Derek, you are going to love our zoo. Be sure to go downstairs at the polar bear exhibit. I'm sure they will be quite active this time of year. One might even swim right up to you."

"Cool!"

While going to the zoo had been one of the things Greg had saved until closer to the end of their vacation, he regretted being away from Tillie most of the day.

"Join us?"

"I'd love to, but that parlor tree isn't going to decorate itself."

"Save it for when we get back, and we'll help again. We're almost finished, aren't we?"

"I might take you up on saving it until late afternoon, but I need to spend the morning doing prep work for the preservationists' supper Monday. I'm sorry, but I do appreciate the invitation."

He'd forgotten all about it, to be honest. Sharing Tillie with a bunch of strangers was the last thing he wanted to do.

Greg suddenly wanted Tillie all to himself.

* * *

"What does she mean I wasn't sensuous? We might not have used that term in my day, but I had plenty of style when it came to the ladies. And he clearly doesn't know anything about my Zee. That woman, well, she kept me nipping at her heels for many years before she agreed to marry me, didn't she?"

Amelia rolled her eyes. She'd taken the empty seat at the table while Jesse stood behind Gregory. "Now, Jesse, don't get your knickers in a twist. Young folks always think they invented intercourse. They don't see us old folks as ever having been young and in love."

"Ain't that the truth?" He glanced at Tillie. "You think they're in love?"

"Judging by how much Gregory squirmed in his seat while feeding her, he's at least in lust."

"And Tillie's eyes sure have a sparkle in them the likes of which I ain't never seen there."

"Can love be far behind?" Amelia smiled. Perhaps this was going to work out fine after all. "Once we got Tillie past being so staid, things started to happen."

"Yep. Taking a tumble in those leaves was the icebreaker."

"Agreed. Glad she went to the office for that bourbon after you knocked over that bottle."

"Took a lot out of me to get up that much energy, but the cause was worth it. And you were brilliant to plant the idea of that sleigh ride in Gregory's head. If they can't work it out here with that house causing them so much grief, maybe going to a neutral location will lower some barriers."

"Derek picked up on it, too. He told me he likes Tillie a lot."

"I wondered what you two were talking about. He's a good kid."

"I can't rightly say Gregory and Tillie are solid yet," Jesse said. "If they can't lower their guard and get over some of the foolishness that keeps coming between them, all our efforts are gonna be for naught."

"Give them time. At least Gregory's no longer badgering her about using my recipes and presence to sell reservations at the inn. Why he'd think I'd be bothered in the least stumps me. I knew all along Tillie would find a way to make the old house fit her needs. She's done more for the place than my Margaret would have."

"What do you suppose happened to Margaret, anyway? Was she that stuck-up and materialistic as a child?"

"No. That husband of hers ruined her."

"What'd he do?"

"Filled her head with notions of get-rich schemes. Reminds me of my first husband. Arrogant, conceited bastard, if you ask me. Privileged, entitled…"

"Okay, I get the picture."

She wasn't finished yet. "All too worried about what other people think, as well. He infected Margaret with that nonsense. Can you imagine her showing up here with my grandson in earshot demanding I hand over her inheritance early? Why, the nerve! I started from nothing and learned to live within my means."

"Didn't hurt that you married Dr. Foster."

"He was house rich, but we had our lean years, especially in the '40s. Where Margaret got the impression she was entitled to anything was beyond me. But I swear if I'd known she'd told Gregory I died years before I did…" Amelia huffed. "Right up until I laid on my death bed, I thought she'd merely poisoned him against me and that was why he had no interest in keeping in touch. I only hope we can save him from going down the same path his parents did."

"You have to admit, though, Gregory was a might arrogant, too, when he showed up, but Tillie sure whittled away at that façade fast."

Amelia giggled like a schoolgirl. "She even managed to get him to dress up as you and go out in public! He didn't appear too excited about that at first, but took to the fun right quick."

"He sure seems excited now." Jesse grinned.

"Mark my words. This is going to be a romance for the ages once those walls come tumbling down."

"Hope so. I want Tillie to find someone so I don't have to worry about her no more."

Amelia cocked her head. "One thing I can't figure out is how on earth did Caroline's granddaughter hear about her connection to you, Jesse?"

"Well, Jessica, my granddaughter, was old enough to remember Caroline when she was placed with that family in Bardstown." He glanced away before continuing. "She also was quite intuitive. I used to visit her in her dreams when she was first adopted. She missed her mama, and I wanted her to know she wasn't alone. I might have, well, told her I was her papa."

Amelia's eyes opened wide. "Seriously? No wonder she was pegged a lunatic if she shared that story. I knew Caroline wouldn't have been so foolish as to burden the child with that information."

"Hey, I didn't say I handled things the way I should have. But I thought I was doing the right thing.

"All I can say is it's a good thing we're fixing the mess we made for that sweet girl who inherited this burden in life."

"She's stronger than I've given her credit for in the past."

Amelia stood and walked over to Jesse, wrapping her arms around him. "Tillie can take care of herself. She's merely had too many disappointments and crosses to bear so young in life. They left her too scared to share her heart with anyone else fearing they wouldn't accept her if they knew the truth about her past. I want her to feel the kind of love I've known with two of the three men I gave my heart to. Only had it broken once by my no-account first husband, George Mercer."

"Don't you get going on him again. Come on, Amelia." Jesse held out his elbow and Amelia took it. "We've done all we can do here. Let's leave them be a while." Hand in hand, they walked through the side of the train.

Chapter Thirteen

Tillie lay in bed wide awake for hours, her cheeks flushed at the memory of Greg feeding her. Whatever possessed her to behave that way? And why did it seem perfectly natural at the same time?

How would something *more* in a relationship look for them? They lived several states apart.

"Oh, Mrs. Foster. I wish you were here." This reminded her of the way she felt when asked to the prom. Mrs. Foster had given her the courage and confidence to accept. It had been her first dance.

But she wasn't seventeen anymore. This was much more serious.

Stand on your own two feet, Tillie.

Mrs. Foster probably would be thrilled she was interested in Greg. Heck, hadn't she invoked some kind of cosmic wish on the holly leaf ornament all those years ago? Maybe Mrs. Foster was somehow making things happen from the other side.

Don't be ridiculous.

Dropping recipe cards was one thing, but matchmaking quite another. Besides, the thought of Mrs. Foster watching over them would make her incredibly reluctant to be intimate with him. *Oh my!* Best not to think about her mentor, his grandmother, in this regard.

And when exactly was he going to admit why he'd come here? Should she confront him? She'd never been one to dare to speak out, but how could there be anything between them with this huge lie sitting like a boulder in their midst?

Tillie punched her pillow and rolled onto her side, resolving not to succumb to the man's charms again. She needed to keep things on safer ground. He'd only be here a few more days. If she wasn't careful, he'd leave her with a broken heart.

Or was it already too late for that?

She rolled one way then the other for what seemed the entire night. When the alarm sounded, she'd probably only dozed off for an hour or so. Hoping not to give the appearance of something the cat dragged in, she showered and tried to make herself presentable before trudging downstairs to the kitchen to prepare breakfast. Greg had said they wanted an early start for the zoo today.

Perhaps he wouldn't make any mention of yesterday's train ride. If not, she'd let it go as well, although it wasn't the train itself that she wanted to forget.

Pulling the sausage-egg casserole and hash-brown casserole from the oven to the warming area, she prepared a fruit salad, putting on the finishing touches as she heard them enter the dining room.

"Coffee's hot on the sideboard," she announced. Taking a deep breath, she carried the bowl into the dining room and plastered a smile on her face. "Good morning, boys!"

"Hi, Miss Tillie! I'm going to the zoo today!"

"So I hear. Let's get that belly filled up first."

Approaching Greg at the coffee pot where he was adding sugar to his mug, she held her breath until he turned and smiled.

"Good morning." He glanced down at the salad in her hand. "Looks great! Strawberries have become my new favorite fruit."

Her stomach dropped—*literally*—as an image of him feeding her on the train yesterday flashed across her mind.

At least the bowl didn't crash to the floor. She hadn't realized she'd included strawberries in the salad or the implication of such when she'd made it. The telltale flush warmed her cheeks as she remembered what he'd done with that berry yesterday.

"About that," she began then remembered Derek was nearby playing with his cars on the table. "Would you mind helping me in the kitchen with the two casseroles?"

"Of course not."

He followed her as she tried to decide whether to say anything about his identity. His mood appeared to be much calmer than hers.

He'd probably slept like a baby. What did he have to keep him up? Obviously not a guilty conscience.

And why was she losing sleep when he was the one keeping secrets?

"Why don't you take the potatoes, and I'll handle the eggs?" Once again, she'd chickened out. Her role here was to be hospitable and feed her guests. Nothing more. He owed her no explanations as to why he'd come here under false pretenses. He was simply a patron at her inn.

"Tillie?" he asked before picking up the dish. "About yesterday…" Surprisingly, he was thinking about it, too. She turned to face him, unsure what he wanted to say. "I wanted you to know I haven't had so much fun in a long time."

Fun. Okay, once again she'd gotten her hopes up. He'd merely enjoyed the train ride with her. Maybe the dressing up part was the thrill for him.

"I'm glad. So did I." She'd have thought her clipped tones would have conveyed her mood to him clearly, but he didn't seem to pick up on it.

"I wouldn't have thought in a million years you'd catch me out in costume like that other than at Halloween."

You're making a mountain out of a molehill, Tillie.

She forced a smile. "You made a perfect Jesse James to my Miss Zee. I enjoyed myself, too." *Too much.*

"I wish you'd reconsider about joining us at the zoo."

"Oh, I can't really. There's work to be done."

"You're always working."

"I wasn't last night." *Except working at getting my hopes up, maybe.* "Besides, when you love what you do, it doesn't feel like work." The temptation to ditch her responsibilities and run off for a day at the zoo dragged heavily at her, but she drew a deep breath. "We'd better get this food in the dining room so you two can eat and be on your way to Louisville."

"We'll be back late afternoon to finish trimming the tree, so stay off that ladder."

She didn't like being told what to do when she'd managed the ladder perfectly fine all these years, but admitted it was much more fun with them helping. "Don't worry. I have enough to keep me busy."

Besides, they still had the issue of his identity between them. Deciding not to allow herself in any deeper with him until he was honest with her, she handed him two potholders before picking up the other casserole.

They placed the dishes on hot plates on the sideboard, and she prepared a plate for Derek, hoping he'd try the things she put on there. If not, she had some microwavable pancakes in a pinch, but the thought of serving him something she hadn't made herself didn't appeal to her.

Greg prepared his own plate. "Everything smells delicious. Is this the way Kentuckians eat for Sunday breakfast?"

"Not always, but it's what I like serving guests on Sunday. All of your grandmother's favorites."

"My grandmother?"

Oh no!

Her mind had been so focused on his true relationship with Mrs. Foster—and the lie—that she'd let it slip. Perhaps her lack of sleep was to blame, but she wasn't sorry in the least. She wanted this out in the open, but hadn't expected to be the one to bring it up.

How would he respond to her knowing? Refusing to pussyfoot around it any longer, she was about to find out. Too bad her breakfast was about to become a casualty.

"Greg, I know you're Mrs. Foster's grandson. I've known for a few days now."

He set the serving spoon back in the dish and sighed. "What tipped you off?"

She didn't want to admit she'd snooped at someone's gravesite. No, not really. If the wind hadn't blown the card out, she never would have peeked. "Does it matter? Why couldn't you tell me the truth in the first place?"

"My reasons were solid. At least I thought so at the time. I just didn't know how to bring it up once I'd started down that path."

"And now?"

"Not so much. Let's sit down and eat first."

She added some fruit to Derek's plate. Greg was right. This wasn't the place for this discussion, not in front of Derek. She nodded and set the plate in front of the boy. "Here you go. Lots of good things you love here. Potatoes. Eggs. Fruit."

He stared at the plate, dubious at first, then picked up a piece of the banana and popped it in his mouth. Perhaps by not offering him anything else, she could succeed in getting him to eat it. Tillie returned to the sideboard to prepare a plate of her own, but wasn't particularly hungry any longer.

The three ate to the sounds of Derek running his cars around his placemat. She didn't make eye contact with Greg, unsure what to say without further ruining their meal.

"Tillie." At his voice, she glanced across the table. "You've outdone yourself."

Clearly, he wasn't going to talk about the elephant in the room. "Thank you."

He glanced at Derek, who seemed oblivious to them both, and lowered his voice. "Let's talk after Derek goes to bed."

"But I'm not sleepy, Daddy! I want to go to the zoo!"

Both adults smiled at him, and Tillie appreciated having the tension cut somewhat.

"Tonight, not now. I'm sure you'll be worn out by the time we finish at the zoo. Eat your breakfast so we can head out."

Derek nodded and took a tentative bite of the hash browns. Then a bigger bite. "I like these!"

"I thought you might," Tillie said. She wished she could be as enthusiastic as he was, but merely took small bites with the pretense of eating. Thoughts of the confrontation she expected later this evening spoiled her appetite altogether.

Why had she ever opened her big mouth? She'd ruined any chance with him because she'd been as dishonest as he had been by not letting on she knew who he was all along.

If only she'd confronted him sooner.

Chapter Fourteen

Tillie waited as long as she could for Greg and Derek to return, but couldn't put off finishing her tree another minute. It was growing dark already. She'd prepared everything she possibly could, and her nervous energy was through the roof.

Climbing up the ladder with a handful of ornaments, she hung them among the beads at the edges of the branches. These were some of her favorites, many of them from the fifties.

"Oh, Mrs. Foster, what a mess I've gotten myself into. I never should have let down my guard."

In her mind, she could almost hear the dear woman chastising her for the pity party. Whenever she'd moped around or felt sorry for herself, Mrs. Foster always pointed out all she had to be grateful for.

"I'm sorry. I know I'm quite lucky to have what I have. Not every woman is destined to find an honorable and loving man to be a part of her life."

For the first time, she wasn't seeing herself as being unworthy of something—someone—she wanted. Why, Greg could do *far* worse than Matilda Hamilton. She smiled, her spirits lifting at last.

More than an hour passed. Still no Greg and Derek. She'd repositioned the ladder periodically as she added the remaining ornaments and saw no reason not to finish up without them. As she descended for the topper, she hoped they hadn't run into any trouble.

In the open storage bin, she removed the golden-skirted angel from its box. The auburn-haired angel had topped the tree for as long as Tillie remembered. She always reminded Tillie of her benefactor, who'd certainly been an angel to her—letting her own such a beautiful home and have a security blanket like none she'd ever imagined as a little girl. No doubt, the woman watched over her to this day, given the sudden appearance of recipes and a niggling feeling she had of being watched. She wouldn't assign that to anyone but Mrs. Foster, or she might be too creeped out to stay here alone.

Pushing those thoughts aside, she longed for a chance to sit and have a cup of tea with Mrs. Foster tonight so she could pour her heart out. The lovely woman always made everything better.

Tillie sighed. Glancing out the window nearly every time she saw headlights coming up the road, her pulse raced hoping that perhaps Greg and Derek were back, but each vehicle passed by her drive and her heartbeat slowed again. She simultaneously wanted them home and dreaded being with Greg again.

Home? It wasn't their home.

Needing to get started on their supper, assuming they'd intended to eat here and not on the road, she hurried to finish up. She'd hoped to be able to wait until Derek returned to let him watch her put the angel on top, but he'd probably have wanted to do the honors and it was far too dangerous to have two people on the ladder at the same time.

After fluffing up the angel's skirt, she climbed the ladder once more, holding onto the tree topper by its waist. Unable to reach from the height she'd been working at, she ascended an additional rung. The ladder still had several more, but she never went beyond this one.

Reaching over the top of the tree, she placed the plastic cone under the angel's skirt firmly on the treetop. *Perfect.* Just one more thing. She always left a gold-colored light untucked and waiting for this part, but it apparently wasn't lined up properly. Stretching a bit, she snagged it and settled it into the folded hands of the angel, illuminating her porcelain face.

As beautiful as ever, Mrs. Foster.

With one hand on the ladder and another still on the light, she'd almost finished when the ladder gave a slight bobble. Fear of toppling into the tree, she overcorrected, throwing off her balance.

Oh no!

The base of the ladder became unstable. Too late to right herself, she braced herself for the fall. Tillie closed her eyes. Time stood still as she fell until her right foot took the brunt of her weight upon landing, sending a sharp pain from her ankle to her knee seconds before her head hit the coffee table. The sound of breaking glass broke her heart as the room went black. Which precious ornaments had she destroyed with her clumsiness?

Minutes—or was it hours?—later, she blinked her eyes open. The room had been cast in a rosy glow from the Christmas tree lights, but it was dark outside the windows. How long had she lain here? God, her head hurt.

She should have it examined for finishing the tree decorating without waiting for Greg. But why would she? She'd decorated this tree annually for more than a decade without any mishaps.

Opening her eyes, she took stock of her situation. The ladder lay over the top of the brocade empire sofa, but she didn't see any damage to the frame. A candle had shattered after having been knocked off by the ladder. Was that the breaking glass she'd heard before blacking out? Glancing behind her at the tree, she didn't see a single ornament lying on the floor. At least none of them had broken. She could easily replace a candle.

She needed to set the room back to rights. She started to sit up when pain radiated through her ankle and up her leg.

Ow!

Tillie came to an abrupt stop as the room began spinning. When her eyesight cleared, she glowered at the source of the worst pain she'd experienced in her life. Her ankle had swollen to twice its size. It didn't appear twisted enough to be broken, but what would she know about broken bones? She'd never injured anything before.

I don't have time for this!

Blinking away tears of frustration, she reached for her phone, but these pants had no pocket. She surveyed the room to see where she'd set it down. Clearly, she needed help and most likely a visit to the emergency room. Perhaps it wasn't as bad as it seemed, but her luck seemed to be nil today.

Damn. The phone sat on the sofa cushion partially under the ladder. Using her arms and elbows, she tried dragging herself in that direction until her stomach roiled and the room spun.

Tillie slumped against the rug, burying her face in her arms as she tried to slow her panicked breathing. *Mind over matter.* As soon as the room stopped spinning, she'd drag herself over to that phone and call 911.

Could she stay here until Greg came home? *Why didn't you wait for him in the first place, and then you wouldn't be in this predicament?* Because nothing irked her more than having to rely on someone else. She helped others, not the reverse. Still, Tillie had never wanted to see Greg walk through that door more than she did right now.

The pain dulled a bit as long as she didn't move her lower body. Yeah, with thinking like that, she could lie here in pain for hours.

Suck it up, buttercup.

Using what upper-body strength she could muster, she scooted inch by agonizing inch toward the sofa, dragging her throbbing ankle behind her. Another few feet, and she'd be there.

Chapter Fifteen

Greg's Rover crossed the railroad tracks and made a left onto Tillie's road. Derek sat conked out in the back seat again, but he had every reason to be tired. The zoo had been as intense and awesome as Tillie had told them to expect, but Greg hadn't realized how big it would be or how slowly a five-year-old would navigate its many paths.

Greg oddly found himself anxious to return to the quietude of the countryside—although he'd been dreading facing Tillie again all day. He'd dragged his feet as much as Derek had, albeit for different reasons.

Why hadn't he confessed to her sooner? Because he hadn't expected this preposterous attraction to grow as strong as it had in the past day or so.

She'd kept him so sidetracked he hadn't even thought about his mission in a couple of days—finding the truth about Jesse James. As often as he could, he'd searched for false walls and hidden passageways without any success.

Tillie appeared not to have heard the stories Gram told in her journals about Jesse James's later visits to this house. While she had followed him around a while that one day, she'd helped him with Derek and had been kept busy with her many innkeeper duties the others, so he'd had free rein most of the time. Still, nothing. Whoever broke into her house had to be zeroing in on the wrong area. Eventually, he'd find the evidence he sought—and then what? Anything in the house was Tillie's property now, not his. He was no thief.

He pulled into the circular driveway. The only lights on were those from the Christmas tree in the parlor. Had Tillie gone to bed already? With Derek sound asleep, he'd try to put him straight to bed. They'd grabbed some McDonald's on the way home and had eaten lunch at the zoo, so he shouldn't be hungry. Then it would leave the evening open to finish the tree and for him to explain exactly why he'd come here.

He sighed as he opened the driver's side door. Tillie seemed genuinely kind and hospitable. Not at all the moneygrubber he'd expected to find when he set off on this journey. Greg wished she'd shift the focus of her marketing efforts from his grandmother to Jesse James.

Why couldn't she simply shift her focus to Jesse? He chuckled. She'd succeeded in charming him for sure. Hell, he'd liked her almost from the start, despite trying to convince himself otherwise. There was something about her that was so…right.

What would he do if she did express a serious interest in having a long-distance relationship with him? Reciprocate? Reject her? Would he be willing to change to make a relationship work? What would he be willing to compromise?

Everything but Derek.

Sheesh! When had he become such a hopeless romantic?

When you met Tillie, that's when.

The voice reverberating in his head sounded a lot like his grandmother.

Tillie did have a special magic about her. Even the pancakes she made Derek, for Pete's sake. He looked down at his sleeping son. Yeah, especially those damned pancakes. They'd charmed them both.

Derek wouldn't have any complaints if he decided to pursue something with Tillie. The two had hit it off from the first moment they'd met.

He lifted Derek out of the car seat and carried him around the house to the front door. A quick peek through the window showed the tree topper was already in place. Damn it, why hadn't she waited for him?

Maybe she had. Hadn't he promised to be back here hours ago?

Tillie was as focused and driven as he, not one to rely on others for help.

To imagine someone eighteen years old taking on the challenge of owning this monstrous old house and then to turn it into a profitmaking inn barely out of college was a testament to her intelligence and business acumen. But that she'd remained true to the character of the house had won him over more than anything else perhaps.

Reaching into his pants pocket, he retrieved the key and opened the door while trying not to awaken Derek.

Greg started toward the stairs.

"Greg, come quick! I need you!" Tillie's distraught voice sent him running, his heart hammering as he raced to the parlor where her voice seemed to originate. He entered the room and quickly surveyed the scene before him. Tillie lay on the floor near the couch, a fallen ladder nearby.

Going over to the wing chair, he set down the still-sleeping Derek and hurried to Tillie's side. One glance at her swollen ankle told him all he needed to know. Near the coffee table was a shattered candle jar. "Derek, be careful of the glass." To her, he asked, "What happened?"

"Fell. Stupid. Ladder." She spoke each word with great effort.

"How long have you been lying here?"

She checked the fob watch pinned to her blouse. "About forty-five minutes to an hour ago as best I remember."

"You lost consciousness?"

She nodded then grimaced. "Not for long." Her words came out in barely a whisper. She must be in a lot of pain.

"Any concussion is serious, even if only a few minutes."

He couldn't resist reaching out to stroke her forehead. Clammy. From pain or shock? Hell, what did he know? He wasn't a medical person. "We need to get you to the ER."

He grabbed an afghan and throw pillow off the nearby rocking chair and placed the pillow under her head before covering her up.

"Why didn't you call me or someone else?"

Why didn't you get back here when you said you would?

Guilt gut-punched him.

Tillie pointed to the couch. "Phone's up there. I tried to drag myself over to it. Nearly made it. So glad you're here." Her eyes glistened, and he knew that had taken a lot for her to admit.

"What's wrong with Miss Tillie, Daddy?" Derek approached, rubbing the sleep from his eyes.

"She fell and injured her foot," he answered. "We're going to take her to the hospital."

"Oh, Derek should be in bed, not spending the night in a crowded emergency department."

She must be delusional if she thought Derek's having to sleep at the hospital was worse than them abandoning her there alone. "Is there anyone you'd like me to call to stay with you instead?"

She glanced away. "No, not really."

How could someone whose middle name was hospitality be so alone? Had she isolated herself at the inn all these years?

"Then you'll have to put up with us. Let me go to the car and move Derek's booster seat to the front so you can stretch out." To Derek, he said, "Son, I want you to stay here next to Tillie and watch over her until I come back."

"Okay, Daddy." The boy knelt beside her and patted her hand. Greg smiled at the maturity his son exhibited.

He ran out of the house and moved the car to the end of the sidewalk before adjusting the seating arrangements, leaving the rear door open. Anxious to return to Tillie, he was in the parlor again in a few minutes, but it seemed like ninety.

"That was fast," she noted.

The hospital was barely five minutes away, driving normal speeds anyway. Her upper lip was drawn and tight, making him wonder why she wasn't complaining more.

Greg picked up her hand—so cold—and squeezed it. "Ready? Soon I'll have you in the hands of someone who can give you something to take away the pain. They'll have you up and running in no time."

"They'd better." She closed her eyes. "I can't be laid up long."

"You'll follow doctor's orders, Tillie, even if it means closing the inn for a few weeks or months."

Her eyelids shot open. "*Nothing* would make me close the inn, especially during the holidays."

He didn't want to upset her now. The doctor could talk some sense into her. "Where's your wallet? You'll need your insurance card, I'm sure."

"In my bedroom. On my dresser."

He ran through the house to the dining room and up the stairs to grab her purse. When he returned, he saw Derek's lower lip trembling, and Greg squeezed his shoulder. "You did a good job, son." This was a lot of responsibility for a little boy. "Now, take Miss Tillie's purse and go hold the front door for us. We're going to put Tillie in the Rover." He scrambled to his feet and disappeared into the foyer.

"Mmph!" Her attempt to stifle a scream as he lifted her into his arms tore at his gut.

Feeling more powerless than ever, he said, "Scream if you need to."

Her eyes and lips remained squeezed tight, but she shook her head. "I'm okay."

He walked cautiously so as not to jar her head or ankle any more than necessary.

"Tillie, you're going to be fine. I'll have you there in no time."

She gazed up at him, her brow furrowed in pain. "I'm sorry to be such a bother."

"Sweetheart, you'd never be a bother."

After he walked through the door, he told Derek to grab the pillow from the floor and follow him. "Are the doors at the side of the house locked?" he asked her. She attempted to nod, her head resting against his shoulder, but groaned instead. She'd have a killer headache tomorrow, if not already.

Holding her felt so right, but he hated that it had taken something like this to get her into his arms.

When his two charges were buckled in, he retraced his steps to lock the front door and, seconds later, sat behind the wheel. He checked on Tillie via the rear-view mirror all the way to the hospital. Good thing he'd noticed it on the way to Bardstown, because she lay with her head against the seatback, eyes closed.

Tillie could lose the inn because of this injury. If only he hadn't lied to her in the first place about his grandmother or had been home earlier as promised. He should have come clean from the start. Nothing good came from lies.

He'd be here a couple more days. Maybe he could help her with running the place and make amends. But what about the cooking and baking? From what she'd told him, the next eight weeks was her make-or-break season of the year. Maybe she could hire someone to do everything. But wouldn't her returning guests expect her to fulfill those roles, as she'd done for more than a decade? How forgiving would they be?

Who cared? If they couldn't see that this woman sacrificed everything for this inn, then they didn't deserve her hospitality.

* * *

Tillie drifted into a pain-filled fog. Crossing the railroad tracks sent excruciating spikes through her head as well as her leg. In the emergency department, the triage nurse explained what they planned to do—an x-ray of her ankle and a CT scan of her head.

She came back from radiology to find Greg sitting across from her in the room, his brow furrowed. Derek slept, cradled in his arms. Greg's reassuring smile warmed her heart.

The doctor came in a few minutes later. She wished she could crawl into Greg's lap right now, too. *Wait. You hardly know the man.* All she needed at the moment was a hug. His arms had been so comforting when he'd carried her to the car.

Snapping out of it, she focused her attention on the physician. "I'm sorry. What did you say?" They'd given her something in her IV to make her more comfortable, and she was becoming seriously loopy. She didn't want to stay in this euphoric state long, though. Perhaps this was how her mother had become addicted to opioids. With a genetic predisposition, she needed to be careful.

"The CT scan doesn't show any sign of a skull fracture."

She wasn't even aware that was a concern. "How about a concussion?"

"Well, the scan won't pick that up, but you aren't presenting with any symptoms that would give me great concern. Possibly a mild concussion, and as long as you don't have slurred speech, numbness, persistent vomiting, or dilated pupils, there's nothing to worry about." The doctor faced toward Greg to wait for his response.

He nodded. "Should I wake her every hour?"

She shook her head. "Every three hours overnight would suffice. Ask her some questions about current events or dates and check her pupils. Otherwise, sleep is the best thing." After making some notes in the computer in the corner of the room, she looked toward Greg again. "You'll make sure to bring her in again if those symptoms start?"

"Absolutely."

Greg was supposed to be leaving in a couple of days, so she doubted he'd follow through. No doubt she'd have to rely on others a lot to get through this mess.

Turning toward Tillie again, the doctor said, "You also have a Grade II inversion sprain of the ankle."

Sounded serious. "Could you explain that in layman's terms?"

"Sorry, it means when you fell, your ankle twisted inward, injuring the ligaments on the outside of the foot. It could have been worse, but you're still looking at a good three weeks to a month of recovery before it will heal up. We're going to stabilize your ankle with a boot tonight, and I'd like you to follow up in a few days with an orthopedic doctor. There's one in Bardstown, as well as others in Louisville or E-town. Meanwhile, stay off both feet as much as possible."

"That might be *im*possible. I have a house full of guests coming to supper tomorrow…" A quick check with the clock on the wall showed it was past midnight. "I mean, tonight." Even worse.

The woman chuckled, but shook her head. "I don't think you're going to want to be on your feet, but the orthopedic will let you know if you can bear weight during the first couple of weeks."

"Weeks?" Was she serious? That would wipe out half the holiday season—the most lucrative half. Tillie glanced over at Greg again in desperation. "I don't have time for this! The preservation society is due at my house in fewer than fourteen hours."

"The only thing you need to worry about is getting that ankle healed before it gets any worse. Let me worry about the preservationists." Greg's stern words took her by surprise.

"But you don't cook or bake."

His brows knitted together. "I didn't say I planned to do it all myself. But that ankle is your *only* priority."

She groaned, frustrated that Greg wasn't taking her concerns seriously. This calamity could effectively put her out of business or, at a minimum, deeply in debt. Why didn't anyone understand what was at stake?

"Ms. Hamilton, we're going to fit you with a boot in a few minutes, and we'll send you home with crutches so you can get around in a few days. Now, lie back and rest until then."

A tear trickled from each eye and ran down her temples into her hair. The more she thought about the prospect of being out of commission through most of the holiday season, the more difficult it became to breathe. Sweat broke out on her forehead.

Greg bent over her face, filling her field of vision. "Take a deep breath."

She tried, but her chest had grown too tight. When his unrelenting stare bore into her, something made her give it another go.

"Good. You've barely taken a breath since the doctor gave her diagnosis." He smoothed the creases from her forehead, an intimate gesture given her fragile emotional state. "You're going to be fine, Tillie. Derek and I will wait on you when we get you home until we have to leave Wednesday, and then you can make arrangements to have someone help out. Now stop worrying."

How his calm voice could reassure her when her world was falling apart, she had no clue. Unable to speak past the lump in her throat, she nodded and attempted a lopsided smile.

The fog enveloped her brain, a result of the painkiller, and she closed her eyes. When she opened them once more, Greg and Derek were dozing together in the uncomfortable chairs. Feeling safe, for some strange reason, she allowed herself to drift off again.

"How are we doing, Ms. Hamilton?"

She blinked her eyes open to find a patient-care tech taking her vitals.

"Fine. A little sleepy."

The woman laughed. "It'll take a few hours for the drugs to wear off. However, it's also two in the morning, so your body is wanting its sleep. Ready to have that boot put on so you can go home?"

"I guess as ready as I'll ever be."

Greg gripped her hand while they worked on her, all the while holding Derek who still slept. "Thanks for being here."

"I wouldn't have wanted to be anywhere else when you needed me."

After they finished, she stared down the bed at the enormous black boot on her foot. How on earth would she get around in that thing, especially the stairs?

"You'll be ready to go as soon as the doctor signs the discharge papers," the nurse said. "Tomorrow, schedule an appointment for a follow-up this week. We'll give you a prescription for a pain reliever."

"No more opioids." For decades, she'd avoided taking medications that would alter her faculties, perhaps a carryover from having watched her mother be stoned so many times from prescription pills. Whatever they'd already given her was the last she wanted.

"If you stay off that foot, you should do fine with a prescription-strength NSAID like ibuprofen—or even Tylenol, as long as you don't exceed the maximum daily dose." Tillie nodded her agreement, thankful she wouldn't be given anything that would make her too groggy—or worse, addicted to the meds.

"If you're having trouble sleeping, Tylenol PM might help. Keep the foot elevated as much as possible, and move around minimally for the first forty-eight hours."

The bombardment of instructions overwhelmed her. "Not even—"

"Nothing. I'm going to see that you follow instructions." Greg's deep, authoritative voice had her glaring at him.

His bossiness rubbed her the wrong way, but she reminded herself that because of him she hadn't had to face this alone. "I'll be fine once I get home and in bed." She stared at Derek a moment. How he could sleep through all of this, she had no clue. "I'm sorry to have inconvenienced you. Poor Derek needs to be in bed."

"Trust me, this kid can sleep anywhere. I've watched him fall asleep at the table before when he's up late and missed a nap, practically face first in his fries."

"Ms. Hamilton," the nurse said, entering the room with a folder. "We're ready to discharge you. Is this gentleman going to be responsible for taking you home?"

"Yes, he's a guest at my inn." She wasn't sure why she felt the need to explain their relationship.

"Because you were given a narcotic in your IV earlier, we'll need him to sign the papers for you, agreeing that he understands the instructions for your post-care. Are you okay with him signing your discharge papers?"

She raised an eyebrow in question as she met Greg's gaze, and he nodded. "Yes, that's fine." What would she have done if she'd fallen and Greg hadn't found her? Or been here with her to take her home?

The nurse presented him with the papers, and after explaining the instructions to him again, as if he had missed a single word, Greg scribbled his signature.

"Now, let this man take you home and get you to bed." Tillie glanced at the foot of the bed where Greg stared back at her, smiling. Heat infused her cheeks knowing he heard the words the same way Tillie had. "Unless you have a problem with that," the nurse added when she didn't respond.

Greg had become more than a guest even before tonight, but the thought of him taking care of her, including trips to the bathroom, made heat burn even hotter in her cheeks. The fact he was a handsome, sexy man didn't put her any more at ease. Not that they'd be tumbling onto her mattress and making out or anything. But how would he maneuver her around the bend in the pie stairs to her room short of tossing her over his shoulder like a sack of potatoes?

She needed to rethink this. "I don't see how this is going to work."

"You let me worry about everything."

While she had many acquaintances and even a few colleagues she could count on professionally, she had no one to depend on during a personal crisis like this. She wasn't even sure she'd be able to enlist help in keeping her inn afloat the next four weeks.

Fifteen minutes later, the nurse's assistant wheeled her to the emergency entrance where Greg waited to pick her up while Derek slept in the front seat. Greg stretched her out across the rear seat again.

"I'm sorry to put you two out."

"Stop apologizing. Besides, I bear some of the responsibility for this. If I hadn't lost track of time—"

"Please, don't be ridiculous. I'm always too impatient and strong-willed for my own good."

He chuckled, but was gentleman enough not to agree aloud.

Tillie sat up so he could lock and close the door behind her then slumped against it. The small effort of getting into the SUV exhausted her. How would she ever manage to accomplish everything she needed to do today while having to be carried around like this and staying off her feet?

Behind the wheel, Greg checked on her over the seat before driving off. "Oh, I spoke with Vera Coomes while you were in radiology."

Tillie must have dozed off a little. What did he say? "How'd you find out about Vera?" The woman ran the preservation group she was hosting this evening.

"I asked at the nurses' station. One of the benefits of being in a small community, I suppose. Everybody knows everybody else."

"One of the pitfalls, too." Soon the news would be all over two counties that their annual dinner had to be postponed or relocated yet again.

"Vera would still like to hold the meeting at your place, but only if you promise not to overdo it. Apparently, the Hideout is one of their favorite old houses in all of central Kentucky."

On one hand, she was thrilled they were coming still, but she'd thought they returned so often because of her hospitality. Apparently, any host would do.

"Why the long face?"

How could he see her back here in the dark having her pity party? She met his gaze in the rear-view mirror, which he'd positioned at an angle so he could do that very thing. Perhaps he did the same when Derek was seated here. "Nothing."

"Tillie." His voice grew stern. "What's wrong? I thought you'd be happy to know their plans wouldn't need to be changed because of the accident. You'll still have the revenue and happy guests from the event."

"Oh, I do appreciate it! And thanks for calling Vera. I'm not sure I can sit idly by without pitching in."

"Well, if you can't make me that promise, then I'll call Vera in the morning and tell her they need to meet elsewhere."

She sat up, grabbing the front seat to pull herself closer. "You'll do nothing of the sort! I'm still in charge of my inn." Her voice sounded shrill even to her ears, but she needed to make this point unequivocally.

"You are, but you've been sidelined, Tillie, at least for the next few weeks. Time for you to delegate."

She slumped against the door. While she hated to admit it, the evidence was staring her in the face. She needed to rely on others at least until she got the hang of the crutches they'd sent her home with. "All right. Let them come. I'll call Beckie Pritchard in the morning to coordinate schedules and divvy up responsibilities. Good thing I didn't go to the zoo, because I already did most of the prep for the meal yesterday." Of course, had she been at the zoo, she wouldn't have fallen off a ladder. Greg was kind enough not to point that out.

They drove the last mile in silence as she made mental notes of what she'd need to oversee in preparation for the supper. Most likely, as long as she sat with her leg propped up, she'd be able to remain fairly involved.

A yawn escaped. So sleepy…

The SUV engine stopped, and she startled awake. A quick glance out the window told her she was home. She'd left her side-door keys on the sideboard, but Greg still had one to the front. How had she fallen asleep during such a short drive? She hoped she could mentally function today after the IV pain meds. She detested the way they made her feel.

"Stay right there. Let me get Derek out to hold the door for us."

"I'll help, Daddy!" He sounded wide awake now. Poor boy was going to have a tough time of it later today. He'd need a nap, but she had too much to do to indulge in one herself.

"Thanks, sport."

With the front door unlocked and Derek holding it open, Greg returned for her. He rapped on the window, and she sat up so that she wouldn't tumble out when he opened the door. One fall a day was plenty.

His strong arms wrapped around her back and under her knees as he extracted her from the vehicle. A whiff of his spicy aftershave—something sinfully delicious—assaulted her senses. Coupled with being pressed against his chest, his nearness sent her mind into a tailspin.

Afraid she'd forget because she didn't have anything to write it down on, not to mention needing to get her mind off the man carrying her, she said, "Oh, in the morning, would you mind bringing up from the cellar a couple quarts of my homemade cherry bounce? This group always appreciates it."

Greg met her gaze with a wry grin. "Cherry what?"

"Bounce. It's an old-fashioned liqueur from colonial days. I first learned about it while touring the home of Ephraim McDowell in Danville a couple of counties away. It's made using cherries, sugar, and bourbon and has to set for a couple of months before drinking. Mine's well-aged and ready to be enjoyed." She closed her eyes in embarrassment. Why did she feel as though she'd imbibed a healthy glassful at this moment? Must be the painkillers they'd given at the hospital. How long would they mess with her head and her ability to stay awake?

When she opened her eyes again, though, he merely gave her a smile along with a shake of his head. "You and your bourbon."

Feeling her spirits lift for the first time since her accident, she grinned back. "I'll tell you a little secret. I detest the taste of straight bourbon, but when I put it into my fruitcake, bourbon balls, or cherry bounce, it's quite tasty."

"I'll bet it is." He ascended the front steps and entered the house, and she heard Derek close the door behind them.

"You'll miss out on the other two bourbon treats this early in the season, but be sure to try the cherry bounce. I'd like to know what you think of it."

"I'd be delighted to." He sounded less than thrilled. "First, though, we need to get you to bed. I'm not going to attempt the stairs to your room, though. I'd probably bang your foot against the wall. So I'll put you in mine."

She glanced around and saw that they were upstairs already, but not on her side of the house. Had she nodded off again, or was her memory suddenly like a sieve?

Wait! His bed?

Oh my Lord.

Chapter Sixteen

"Derek, would you open the door for us?" Greg could hold Tillie all night like this, not that she probably wanted him around after he'd practically abandoned her yesterday. If he'd come home on time… Well, so much water under the bridge. He'd make it up to her now by taking care of her.

The scent of vanilla and citrus wafted to him from her, driving his body insane. His attraction to her was stronger tonight than before possibly because a sense of protectiveness had been added to the mix.

Don't kid yourself. You've been acutely aware of her for days.

"Greg, where are you going to sleep?"

"Derek's room, with both doors open so I'll hear you if you need anything."

He asked Derek to flip on the light switch and carried her inside, crossing the room to the side of the bed. "Derek, pull the quilt down for me." He realized his voice sounded a little gruff. "Please." The boy did the best he could with the heavy fabric on the high mattress and earned a "good job" from Greg, who set Tillie gently on the mattress and covered her. He hoped she didn't want him to undress her and put her to bed properly. She might need to hire someone to see to her personal needs after all.

"What can I get you? Glass of water?"

"Oh no! Getting to the bathroom is going to be enough of a nightmare. I'm not going to drink a thing."

"You do realize that becoming dehydrated isn't going to make you heal any faster. I should have asked before I put you in bed, but do you need to go now?" *Please, no*, he silently prayed.

"No, I went at the hospital. I'm fine."

He must have shown visible relief because she grinned.

"Do you have your cell phone?"

"Right here." She retrieved it from her purse and brandished it at him. At least she had it on her this time. He hoped she'd learned a lesson there.

"Let me program in my number in case you need me tonight. I know I'm only a room away, but I don't want to miss hearing you call for me."

She unlocked the phone and handed it to him. After programming in his contact info, he handed it back to her. "Are you sure there isn't anything you need?"

She wouldn't meet his gaze, and he waited for her to answer. Her meek voice said, "Well, I'd sleep more comfortably if I was out of these slacks."

Yeah, maybe you will, but I *sure won't.*

When he hesitated, she added, "If they won't come off over the boot, just cut the rest of them away."

He lifted her blouse and reached for the waistband. Her skin was warm against his fingers. He'd undressed Nancy before, but usually as a prelude to something carnal. He couldn't remember being in the position of caretaker before.

Levering herself on the good foot, she raised her hips. Careful not to take her panties with him, he felt for the other waistband but couldn't find it. Cautiously, he lowered the band and breathed a sigh of relief when her bikini panties came into view. Normally, undressing a beautiful woman would be exciting, but the last thing he needed right now was to make her think he was turned-on.

With the pant leg cut nearly to the hip, he had no trouble with the removal of the rest of it and looked around for what to do with them, avoiding any further view of her panties.

As if the sight wasn't indelibly stamped on his brain.

"You can lay them over the bed rail."

"Anything else I can do? Need anything from your room?"

She tried to stifle a yawn. "Not a thing I can think of."

"Well, we'll get out of your hair. When do you need to be up to-morrow?"

"About seven."

He glanced at his watch. "That's hardly three hours of sleep."

"I have a feeling I'm going to have lots of time to sleep, but I have to call Beckie at a decent hour and prepare some things before she arrives."

"Is that like cleaning in advance for a visit from the maid?"

"Not at all!" She cast her gaze aside, sheepishly. "Okay, maybe a little."

"I'll be in here to wake you and help you get ready so you can be downstairs in the kitchen by eight."

"Seven-thirty."

"Seven-forty-five. And you can expect me to stay in the kitchen with you at least until the caterer arrives."

"You're here as my guest. You will not be working in my kitchen."

"Try and stop me. Now, get some sleep." He left while he still had the last word.

* * *

Tillie wanted to stay awake and wallow in self-pity again, but her eyelids began drooping immediately. Images of Greg bringing her breakfast in bed wearing nothing but his plaid boxers lulled her to sleep.

"Wake up, sleepyhead." Greg's low voice melted her to the core. Would he kiss her awake? Wait. Why was he asking her to wake up? She was deliciously wide awake and ogling his lightly furred chest.

A gentle shake of her shoulder brought a smile to her face.

"Tillie." His whisper filtered through the fuzziness in her brain. "Open your eyes, or I'm going to let you sleep in."

She blinked awake in an instant. This was no dream. She noticed he wore a robe. Well, that bare chest had been part of a dream.

"There you are." He smiled. "I was about to let you sleep a little longer."

The preservation supper was tonight! She tossed the quilt and sheet off her legs. "I'd have never forgiven you for that." When she moved to swing her legs over the side of the bed, an excruciating pain shot up her right leg, nearly doubling her over.

"Oh my God!"

"Whoa! Here." He picked up the bottle of prescription ibuprofen from the nightstand and handed it to her. "Take one of these before you attempt to get up. I'm sure what they gave you at the hospital has worn off by now. You should try to stay on the maximum-dosage schedule at least for the first twenty-four hours."

While she didn't intend to follow Dr. Greg's instructions all day long, she removed a pill from the bottle and accepted a glass of water, downing both before handing him the bottle and empty glass. He then covered her legs again with the quilt and returned to the chair.

At least he hadn't watched her sleep. The mere thought of him being in here all night sent the butterflies in her stomach into a tizzy, especially after her dream, which must have been triggered by his scent on the pillow.

After fifteen minutes of him waiting in the wingback near the window, he stood. "How do you feel now?"

If she was going to be honest with him, she'd never get out of this bed today. He wasn't the only one who could be less than truthful. "I'm fine."

"Okay, but if you feel any pain, tell me to stop. Ready for the bathroom?"

His pained expression told her she was more ready than he was, and she grinned. "I'm sorry you're having to take care of me. Why don't you hand me the crutches and let me do this alone?"

"Have you ever walked on crutches before?"

"I've never so much as stubbed my toe before."

"For the first two days, when you don't want any weight on it, I'll carry you around."

"You will this morning. I'll call about hiring a home health aide for a couple of days so you and Derek can finish your vacation."

"Stop worrying about us. Now, I'm going to carry you in there so you can…" Greg stared down at her lap, still covered by the quilt. "…and get you seated." He cleared his throat. "This is no time for modesty. While you're in there, tell me what you'd like to wear today. I'll gather up everything from your room."

After she described the dress she planned to wear, she instructed him to stop near her dresser and retrieve a new pair of panties and a bra from the basket of laundry she hadn't put away yet. No way was she going to send him rummaging through her underwear drawer.

After she was seated, having lowered her panties while he held her by her torso, he left the room. *I'm not going to survive the humiliation.* About ten minutes later, he knocked on the door.

"I'm back. No rush. Let me know when you're ready."

"Come in. I'm as decent as I'm going to get."

He entered with her dress and draped it over the tub, laying the undergarments on top of it as though eager to rid himself of them. She suffered more indignities before he lowered the seat and sat her down again. She wouldn't tell him her ankle was throbbing unless it became unbearable. The pill ought to kick in soon.

"You'll need to stick to a sponge bath, per doctor's orders. Where's a basin for your rinse water?"

Not only her cheeks burned, but her neck and forehead as well. She pointed toward the linen closet and waited for him to set everything within reach. When he left the room again, she removed her blouse. She'd already ditched the bra under the covers last night. Nothing worse than sleeping in one of those contraptions.

She bathed as thoroughly as she could without standing up and donned the dress. It was a heavy fabric, and she decided to forego the panties. The less maneuvering during bathroom breaks the better. She tucked them into her pocket. No one would be the wiser.

Heat crept up her neck to her face. No way would Greg know she was pantyless, so why was she blushing?

Oh, Tillie. What a mess you are.

"About ready?" he asked through the closed door.

Glancing at her fob watch, she saw it was already half past eight. "Ready!"

The door opened and an all-too-perky Greg entered carrying the bottle of ibuprofen. "I don't want you to forget these." He handed it to her, and she slipped the pills hastily into her pocket.

He lifted her into his arms again, cocooning her in comfort and safety. "Next stop, the kitchen?"

She nodded. "Thanks for all your help this morning." Her voice sounded breathy.

"Don't mention it."

"No, I really do appreciate it." He walked down the stairs, careful not to hit her protruding leg and foot on either the walls or balusters. The fear of falling again caused her to wrap her arms around his neck a little too tightly. She loosened her grip somewhat. "Sorry."

"Hold on as tightly as you wish. But I'm not going to drop you. You're light as a feather."

As soon as they reached the foot of the stairs, she loosened her hold some more.

"Will Derek be all right upstairs?"

"He'll probably sleep until noon at least. Once your caterer arrives, I'll take him out for lunch."

"Will you be here for the dinner meeting? Several members want to meet and talk with an architect who understands historic preservation."

"Today is not one of those days I need to push him to try new things. I doubt tonight's menu will cater to a five-year-old's picky tastes, so I planned to stop at the pizza place next to the gas station."

"I planned on pigs in a blanket for him, if he likes those."

"Oh, he does. I'm sure he won't go hungry then. And he did try what you put on his plate yesterday at breakfast."

The reminder of where they'd left things unsaid yesterday morning slammed back to the forefront of her mind. They still hadn't had a chance to talk about why he'd withheld his identity from her. Today would be filled with meal preparation, though, so she decided not to bring it up now.

He walked through the dining room and into the kitchen. "Oh, and I'd love to stick around for dinner, if for no other reason than to carry you around some more."

His smile warmed her deep inside. He hadn't taken time to shave this morning, and an errant thought wondering what it might feel like to have his scratchy whiskers scrape her sensitive skin infused her face with heat again.

"You can put me down now," she whispered. The breathless quality in her voice gave away her arousal, but also snapped her out of this trance or whatever it was. She pointed to the bar stools at the island, "Either of those would be perfect."

Instead, he took her to the table near the window and kicked out the chair with his foot. "I'd rather have you closer to the ground and in a more stable chair, if you don't mind. I'm sure you can oversee operations as well from right here as up there—and I can prop your foot up on this other chair." He did so, and the pressure that had been building in her foot dissipated. "How's that?"

"Much better. Thanks." She'd be grateful no matter how much his bossiness crept under her skin. "Could you hand me my apron?"

Rather than hand it to her, he insisted on placing it on her and tying it before situating her in the chair.

Before making her phone calls, she told him where to find a number of the ingredients she'd need to begin working. Beckie, a middle-aged black woman Tillie first met at an event in Bardstown, told her Vera had already called, and she'd be over within the hour. That she'd drop everything to help her made Tillie's eyes sting. While she always enjoyed the woman's company, both were so consumed by their businesses that they rarely socialized.

While waiting on Beckie's arrival, she and Greg cut up veggies for a relish tray. He set up his workstation on the butcher-block island, and they worked mostly in silence. Again, not the place for a deep discussion about yesterday that would be interrupted momentarily.

Beckie arrived as scheduled, and the two women went over the menu, divvied up the remaining tasks, and caught up on their lives while working. They hadn't seen each other since the Bourbon Festival.

"If you ladies will excuse me, I'm going to shower and shave to get ready for the meeting, but I'll be back down shortly."

When he was out of earshot, Beckie whistled under her breath. "He's some looker."

"Really? I hadn't noticed."

Beckie chuckled. "Oh, you noticed all right. You barely took your eyes off him."

"I did not!" But she knew her words revealed she was in agreement with the astute woman. "Okay, maybe a little." The two laughed as they worked side by side and talked about what they'd been busy with since September.

Pleased with how well they meshed, Tillie made the woman an offer. "Beckie, I'm going to need some help to get through the holiday season here. Would you have time in your schedule to work the parties I have lined up and perhaps prepare and serve breakfasts until the doctor lets me be on my foot again? I'll find someone else to take care of the overnight guests and housekeeping, but you're so wonderful in the kitchen."

"Of course! I have a few events planned, but mostly luncheons and dinners, so nothing that would overload me."

"Great. You're a godsend. Perhaps we can go over the calendar once we finish up with today's event."

"Okay, put me to work." Both women looked up to find Greg standing in the doorway wearing khakis and a light blue, button-down, long-sleeved shirt he filled out in ways she shouldn't be noticing.

Beckie whispered under her breath, "See what I mean?"

Caught red-handed, Tillie cleared her throat. "Why don't you finish setting out the dishes and flatware on the buffet, Greg?" At least that would get him out of the kitchen momentarily. "The gold-trimmed plates in the china cabinet go at the far end of the sideboard. And the silverware chest is on the left-hand side of the china cabinet, underneath."

"I think I can manage that. Everything smells delicious, by the way." He smiled as he went into the adjoining room. Tillie's gaze remained locked on him as he walked away. He filled out the pants well, too.

"Mm-mm-mm," Beckie said, whether in appreciation of the sight or to bust Tillie's chops yet again, she didn't know.

"Would you hand me the veggies, Beckie, and I'll place them on the relish tray."

Beckie flashed a knowing smile, but brought over the bags of broccoli, peppers, and cauliflower she and Greg had cut earlier along with a bag of carrots. While Beckie worked on the dip, Tillie arranged in silence.

Fifteen minutes passed before Greg returned. "Where can I find the napkins?"

"In the sideboard, top right drawer," Tillie answered. Determined not to be caught looking again, she focused intently on placing baby carrots on the tray. "How's the chicken doing, Beckie?"

"Marinating. The au gratin potatoes are set to go in the oven. And I've sliced the sugar-cured ham, for those preferring that instead of poultry. You want me to tuck the pigs in their blankets?" Tillie nodded. "I'll put those in just before everyone gets in the buffet line."

"Beckie, I don't know how to thank you for doing this on such short notice."

"No thanks needed. We're neighbors. That's what we do for each other."

Tillie hadn't been particularly neighborly up to now, trying to go it alone here. She'd never had friends over while in school and had no close attachments except to people who flitted in and out of her inn. Was that part of the attraction to Greg? He wouldn't be sticking around either if things didn't work out for them. Tillie brought her mind back from its wanderings. "I've enjoyed having someone to work with in here today, Beckie."

"I hear you. Gets kinda lonely doing prep and seeing to every detail without anyone to help."

Greg walked into the kitchen. "Finish what you're working on then it's off to bed with you," he announced.

She held up her hands to ward him off. "I don't have time to nap!"

"You're going to make time. Beckie, you have everything under control here, right?"

"Sure do!" Beckie laughed and winked at Tillie. "You go on and let this nice man tuck you in, honey."

Tillie hadn't the energy to fight them both probably due to her lack of sleep the last two nights. "Okay, you win. But I'm setting my alarm for three so I can be back in here for the last-minute prep." They made a pit stop on the way to the bed, so at least her bladder wouldn't burst.

Three hours later, she woke from the nap, called Greg on the cell phone, and managed to be in the kitchen when the doorbell rang at four, an hour before she'd expected anyone.

Greg called out from the dining room, "I'll get it!"

Vera was the first through the kitchen door. "How are you doing, you poor thing? Oh my!" She stared at Tillie's boot. "That must be awfully painful." The matronly president bent over Tillie to give her a hug.

"It's not so bad. I'm sure when the swelling goes down in a few days, I'll be good as new."

"Only if you keep it elevated and put no pressure on it," Greg cautioned.

Tillie shot him a scathing look, but Vera must have missed it in her haste to meet Greg. "Mr. Buchanan," Vera said, shaking his hand, "I can't tell you how pleased we are that you found our dear Tillie last night. Why, she might have lain on that floor until we arrived, which would have been simply dreadful."

Vera's words reminded Tillie to be grateful to him, even if she didn't like having him dictate what she would and wouldn't be doing. Of course, she'd follow doctor's orders, because she wanted the ankle to heal as quickly as possible, but she didn't need him reminding her every step of the way.

When the doorbell rang again, Greg left to provide further host duties while Vera hugged Beckie and thanked her, too. Tillie had never felt like such a fifth wheel. Totally useless.

"Miss Tillie!" Derek stood in the doorway staring at the two strangers cautiously as if deciding whether he wanted to come into the room.

"Come over here, Derek!" His face lit up, and he ran to her side, giving her a big hug, which she reciprocated. "I've missed you. Where have you been all day?"

"I sleeped all morning and then played with the toy soldiers. Daddy won't let me go outside." His lower lip ventured out in a pout.

"I'm sorry to be keeping your daddy so busy, but I think I can spare him for the next hour or so if he wants to let you play outside a while."

"You heard Tillie, sport." She found Greg standing in the doorway, having overheard her. "Let's go outside and play a while." He was doing a fantastic job of juggling the needs of both his charges. "Then you can eat here in the kitchen with me."

"Nonsense," Vera said. Tillie hadn't even known the woman had been listening. She came from a big family, though, and could probably participate in three conversations simultaneously. "You'll both join us for dinner. We promise not to talk too much shop, at least not until after we eat."

Tillie enjoyed hearing about their projects and plans, but could see how Derek might be bored by such. "Derek, why don't you sit by me when we eat?" She'd try to keep him entertained while keeping an ear on the adult conversations.

Greg smacked his forehead. "The cherry bounce! I nearly forgot!"

"Let me get them. I know right where she keeps them." Mark Peterson stood in the doorway. "Hi, Tillie. Sorry to hear about your accident." He didn't come over to hug or greet her in any way, thank goodness.

Greg sized Mark up, gave her a smile as he shook his head, and took Derek by the hand. "Let's go, son. Twenty minutes, then I need to come inside to help Miss Tillie."

True to his word, he was back right on time. "Ready to go in?" Greg towered over her.

"Almost." She turned toward the door. "Could you check on Mark? He hasn't come up from the cellar."

"Here I am!" Mark said from the doorway, holding up two dusty quart jars. She thanked him, all but certain he'd been snooping around downstairs. What was everyone's fascination with her cellar?

"Thanks. I'll take those," Beckie said.

Tillie loosened the tie on her apron and lifted it over her head before setting it on the table beside her. "Beckie, are you sure I can't help with anything else?"

"Nothing at all. Go enjoy your guests. I'll bring in the dishes as they're ready. Let me know when everyone's here, Greg."

Tillie held up her arms, and Greg bent to pick her up. She was getting way too used to this. In the dining room, she directed him, "Let me sit at that corner and put Derek next to me. I'll see that he's entertained so you can talk with the preservationists."

"I'm sitting next to you, so I can make sure you eat everything I put on your plate. You can rest your leg across my lap, if you'd like."

His lap? This was going to be the longest supper she'd ever endured.

Chapter Seventeen

Tillie's narrowed eyelids and flattened lips didn't bode well for Greg's efforts at being her caregiver today. Clearly, the woman didn't like having to rely on anyone for anything. *Tough.* He intended to wait on her regardless, and she'd better get used to the idea. Besides, she deserved to be taken care of.

After settling her into her seat and taking Derek to the bathroom to wash up, he returned to the kitchen to help Beckie carry dishes to the dining room. Tables had been set up in both the dining room and birthing room, but both shared the same buffet on the sideboard.

He went through the buffet line, filling her plate with a little bit of everything, including both meats and the jalapeno jelly and cream cheese spread he wanted to try with crackers. His stomach growled. He'd skipped breakfast this morning. So had Tillie, he realized too late. He hoped Beckie made sure she ate while they were working in the kitchen earlier. The fries he'd eaten from Derek's leftover kids' meal had long since worn off.

The feast spread out before him was grander than anything he'd enjoyed in a long time.

"I can't possibly eat all that!" Tillie complained when he set an overloaded plate in front of her.

"Nonsense. A chef should always sample a little bit of everything. Now I'll go fill a much smaller plate for that picky little boy seated next to you."

Derek took one peek at the varied dishes on Tillie's plate and scrambled off his chair. "I'll show you what I like, Daddy." Apparently, he didn't trust his dad and probably wouldn't eat most of it. But the boy surprised him by trying a few things he hadn't eaten before.

On his third trip through the line, Greg filled a plate for himself while chatting about a church preservation project with a woman who said she lived in Bloomfield, wherever that was.

There must have been half a dozen separate conversations going on at the table once he settled into his seat, but he tuned all of them out and leaned toward Tillie. "I'm going to lift your leg onto my lap now. Are you ready?"

"There's no need, really, Greg. It's only going to be a short while."

"Are. You. Ready?" he repeated slowly. This point was non-negotiable. "Doctor said to keep it elevated whenever possible to keep the swelling down." She sighed and nodded. "Good. Now, brace yourself. I'll be as gentle as possible."

When he took hold of her leg, he noticed she was holding her breath. "Take a deep breath for me, and let it out when I say so." He waited for her to draw a breath and told her to release it as he lifted her leg in one fluid motion and settled the boot on his lap.

"Thank you. That does feel better. The binding had been feeling a little tight."

Pleased with himself, he waited for her to begin eating and then took a few bites of Gram's jalapeno jelly spread. His mouth soon became flaming hot. "That jelly packs a punch."

Tillie laughed. "Mrs. Foster and I loved it."

He drank some of the too-sweet iced tea. "Everything's wonderful."

Tillie's smile faded. "Beckie did most of the cooking."

"But they were your recipes, and you did much of the prep, too."

"These are all recipes your grandmother communicated to me over the past year."

At the moment, he didn't care how she came into possession of them. Having an opportunity to enjoy them again—or for the first time, in the case of the jalapeno jelly—was all that mattered.

Drawn into a conversation about preservation of an antebellum home in Bardstown, it was half an hour later before he turned his focus to Tillie once more, only to find her eyes scrunched and half closed with her brows furrowed.

His watch told him they'd gone past when she was due another pill, unless she'd taken one in the kitchen, which he doubted. Her aversion to painkillers, even non-addicting ones, must stem from what had happened with her mother, but he couldn't stand seeing her in pain, either.

"When did you take your last pill?"

She tried to mask the pain, apparently not realizing anyone else had noticed. "Before I took my nap."

Damn. "Where's the bottle?"

She seemed to think a moment. "Oh!" Tillie retrieved them from her pocket and extended her hand around the table leg toward him. Whatever she handed him was not simply a pill bottle. He glanced down to find the bottle wrapped in a satiny scrap of peach-colored—panties?

"Oh, God!" she whispered as she followed the direction of his gaze. Snatching the panties out of his hand, her gaze darted around the table at the other guests, no doubt making sure no one else had noticed. She studiously avoided making eye contact with Greg afterward.

These definitely were the same ones he'd brought to her this morning. So did that mean she wasn't wearing any? He fought to stifle a grin, but lost the battle.

Tillie leaned toward him and hissed, "Not a word, Buchanan. Just give me the blasted pill."

* * *

He knew. The infuriating man *knew* she was sitting here at this prim and proper supper without underwear. She'd managed to hide the fact she'd gone commando up in the bathroom from him only to hand him the damned undies at the dining-room table. At least none of the others at the table appeared to suspect. In her mortification, her pain was forgotten momentarily, but the diversion didn't last long enough to provide real relief. Her ankle throbbed. Why had she put the pills in the same pocket as the panties? Or why hadn't she taken the pill herself at the beginning of the meal and avoided this predicament?

As people finished their meals, Beckie cleared the dishes, and Tillie made sure everyone in both rooms knew to thank her again for such a wonderful meal and for coming to Tillie's aid on such short notice. Then she added in a voice only for Beckie, "Would you mind serving the cherry bounce for us in the parlor?"

Normally, Tillie wouldn't have joined her guests, but after the panty incident, she could use something stronger than sweet tea.

Beckie must have already poured the Mason jars into Tillie's cobalt blue and gold Venetian decanter. The bohemian-looking set didn't really go with anything in the house, but she'd found it in an antique store and loved the vibrant colors. Sometimes she served herself a glass of sherry or spiced rum in one late at night when her guests had gone to bed.

Beckie set the decanter on a tray with the stemware and carried it through the dining room and off toward the parlor.

"Shall we?" Greg asked. "Deep breath." He lowered her right foot to the floor and stood beside her to lift her into his arms and carry her into the parlor with the other guests following behind them.

Once everyone had been served, Greg lifted his glass toward Tillie. "To our supreme hostess, who has proven to us all that preserving the old with a flair for the modern provides the best of both worlds."

Did he just glance down at the pocket where he now knew her thoroughly modern panties were hidden? To find an excuse for the heat creeping up her neck, she clicked her glass with Derek's filled with cran-cherry juice before drinking half the contents of hers in one gulp. Greg chuckled. No doubt the rat had already detected her blushing.

How would she ever live this down? At least Greg would be leaving in two days, and she'd probably never see him again.

God willing.

Still, that thought made her a little sad. The conversations in the room filtered in again, and she accepted the praise from others for the cherry bounce but truly only wanted to know what Greg thought and regarded him with raised eyebrows.

"Excellent. I could become addicted to this elixir." His lips slightly wet from the drink, she licked her own as she imagined doing the same to his.

Tillie smiled, inordinately happy he liked it. Mark and Vera joined them.

"I don't believe we've formally met," Mark said, extending his hand to Greg. "I'm Mark Peterson, vice president of the preservation society. Tillie and I have known each other for years. Even date occasionally."

Why on earth he brought that up as though she still dated him, Tillie didn't know, but Greg sized him up and smiled back. "Nice to meet you, Peterson." Greg didn't get into a pissing match, which she appreciated. The two spoke of one project or another, and she zoned out until Mark brought up Jesse James.

"My grandfather said Jesse James left his most valuable treasure here in this house."

"That so?" Greg asked noncommittally.

Tillie sighed. That old rumor again. Most of the old-timers around here believed it. She held no faith in legends about treasure or anything Jesse supposedly left behind the various places he lived or hid out.

Uninterested in the conversation, her eyelids soon drooped again. Full stomach and still being behind on her sleep wasn't a good combination, but she wasn't about to leave the party.

"Brace yourself, dear."

Her eyelids flew open as Greg scooped her into his arms. *Dear?* Then she saw Mark's face become a mottled red and figured Greg was being territorial. *As if.* Perhaps he simply didn't care for Mark and wanted to get a rise out of him.

"Time for me to take you to bed before you fall over in your chair. Say goodnight to your guests."

"No, I'm fine, Greg." Who was he to treat her like a child? "I'd like to stay for the meeting."

"I'll give you a full report tomorrow at breakfast." He started toward the door, not waiting for further discussion. She wanted to maintain her independence, but simply had become too tired to fight.

She turned her head and shouted hastily over his shoulder, "Thank you, everyone, for being here. I'm sorry I have to leave so abruptly, but *someone* thinks I should be in bed."

To a chorus of "goodbyes," "thank yous," and "he's right," Greg carried her out of the room. But instead of going up the stairs, he headed toward the kitchen. Derek followed.

She appreciated Greg for giving her an opportunity to say goodnight to the woman who had saved this event. "Beckie, everything was wonderful. I can't thank you enough, and I'll be in touch tomorrow about my schedule for the next few weeks."

"You worry about healing that ankle. Would you like me to come prepare breakfast for you and the Buchanans in the morning?"

Before Tillie could answer, Greg said, "I'm going to take care of us tomorrow, Beckie. But thanks."

Beckie chuckled. "Sounds good." And to Tillie, she said, pulling something out of her pocket, "Oh, in case you don't have it, here's my card. I wrote my personal number on there, too. Call me whenever you need me, or even if you'd just like somebody to provide some company when things get too quiet 'round here."

The two women hugged awkwardly, mainly because of the position of Greg's arm around Tillie's back, and he started toward the door.

"Derek, why don't you stay here with Miss Beckie? I'm going to take Miss Tillie up to bed. I'll be right down in a few minutes."

The boy scrambled into the seat where Tillie had propped her leg earlier, and Beckie fussed over him, making sure he'd had enough to eat.

Soon, Tillie was being tucked into her bed—well, technically, it was his—having visited the bathroom already to change into her nightgown. The sheer thing left nothing to the imagination so she kept her robe on as well.

He tucked the quilt under her chin and bent down as he might with Derek to place a kiss on her forehead. "Sleep tight, dear."

Forehead kisses were special, leaving one feeling safe and protected. Somehow she didn't think he used those words simply because she slept on a rope bed from which the expression "sleep tight" had originated. Her skin tingled where his lips had touched her. Mark hadn't been around this time to overhear the endearment, which only confused her more.

But he didn't linger, and the effects of a lack of sleep on top of the cherry bounce soon took over again. He flipped off the overhead fixture and closed the door. It was lights out for her, too.

* * *

Why the hell had he done that? Greg hadn't given a thought to kissing her all day, but tucking her in the way he did Derek, instinct seemed to take over.

Oh right. You knew what you were doing, Buchanan.

That definitely wasn't a Derek kiss. The expression on her face told him she was as shocked as he was, but damn, it felt nice. She needed him, too, which left him with a good feeling. Nancy hadn't needed him in…forever. Not that he'd been there for her when she had. His work had always taken precedence. He'd made some stupid choices that had cost him his marriage.

After checking in the kitchen to find Derek coloring at the table, Greg returned to the parlor to find the society group members in a heated debate over when it was acceptable to use modern techniques and fixtures over restored ones. He'd fought many a historic preservation board over some common-sense adjustments necessary if a family was going to live comfortably in their historic home.

"Isn't the ultimate goal to make these homes habitable again, bringing life back inside their walls?" Greg asked. Discussion stopped, and everyone faced him as he resumed his seat in one of the wing chairs. "As an example, I doubt any of us would want to return to the days of chamber pots—at least not if we have to clean them out ourselves."

Several of the women tittered, and Vera grinned in his direction. "Excellent point, Mr. Buchanan."

"It's Greg. And thank you. There are plenty of ways of preserving the original without sacrificing comfort."

Discussion into wall treatments ensued, and he told them about an antebellum L-shaped house in Wisconsin he'd worked on in which contractors stripped away layer after layer of wallpaper to the original and had been lucky enough to find a manufacturer in France still producing that pattern.

"Can you imagine?" Vera said. "A hundred and fifty years later. We really have no concept here in the States of what constitutes old. That was merely a blip in the life of that company, I'm sure."

"Indeed," he said.

"If you can fit it in while you're here, Greg," an elderly gentleman began—Mr. Spencer, if he remembered correctly, "we would love for you to see the property we acquired at a courthouse auction. It's going to be a challenge to save, but has been standing since the early 1800s."

While not his period of expertise, the chance to have a look at the place intrigued him. "I'd love to, but am not sure it will be possible. Tillie needs me right now."

"Yes, of course," Peterson chimed in. "I'll be sure to check in on her when you're gone."

Greg had taken an instant dislike to the man from the moment he'd tried to make more out of those couple of dates than existed given Tillie's recollection of them. But the thought of him hanging around Tillie while Greg was back in Minneapolis didn't sit well with him, either.

"I'm having such a delightful time here, I'm thinking about extending my visit—after returning home to drop off my son with his mother." The words were out before he realized he'd even been considering doing that. He knew Tillie had a strong community behind her, but when it came down to it the other night, she hadn't wanted to call anyone. Stubborn and independent, she'd probably not ask for the assistance she needed. Besides, he owed her for abandoning her yesterday. He also wanted to get to know her better. He could probably have Beckie stay with Tillie overnight to allow him to take Derek home, gather up enough work to keep him busy and delegate more to his team, and fly back down here.

"Oh, Greg," Vera said, clasping her hands together with glee. "That would be wonderful! We'd love to have your expertise for some of the projects we have going on while you're here."

"Yes, of course. I'd be happy to. Of course, I'll have my own projects to do as well. But in my line of work, I don't have to stay put at the office in Minneapolis."

Peterson said goodnight and excused himself. Greg hoped he wouldn't have to spend a lot of time with the man. He gave off a negative vibe.

"Perhaps we could hire you as a consultant on the courthouse square project, once you see it," Mr. Spencer suggested.

Already he was finding work to do while down here.

He couldn't wait to tell Tillie about his decision.

And find out how she'd receive the news.

Chapter Eighteen

"You plan to what?" Tillie set down her fork at breakfast the next morning, unable to eat another bite of the leftovers he'd served from last night's supper. Apparently, Greg's cooking super power was microwaving. But she'd found the pigs in blankets and au gratin potatoes a delicious breakfast and enjoyed being waited on. Until Greg announced he was coming straight back the day after he went home.

"The society hired me to consult with them on a new project, so it gives me a great excuse to be here where I can keep an eye on you and get some work done as well."

"I'm sure they could work with you long distance, and I don't need a babysitter."

"Good, because I didn't intend to babysit."

She didn't care if he went on the defensive. "I've got Beckie to help with the inn and plan to hire a couple other people to help out. Stop feeling obligated to take care of me. The fall had nothing to do with you."

"You wouldn't have fallen if I'd returned when you needed me, as promised."

Tillie wanted to scream and did. *Infuriating man!*

"I wanna stay, too, Daddy."

She'd forgotten all about the boy in her frustration with his father.

"No, son. This could take a couple of weeks—maybe even a couple of months—"

Months!?!?

"—and your mommy won't want you gone that long."

Derek poked out his lower lip and hung his head. "I'm mad at you, Daddy. You're mean."

The boy's sulking transferred some of the tension away from Tillie. He behaved the way she would if she didn't have to be an adult.

Perhaps taking another tack would work. "Look, Greg, I appreciate your offer to help, but I have a houseful of guests arriving next weekend. I don't even have a place for you to sleep."

"Not a problem. I can put up a cot in the birthing room."

"Absolutely out of the question. I can't give the appearance that I overbooked."

"You've slept there before yourself, you said, when the house is packed. If it's good enough for you, I'm sure I can manage." Apparently, he couldn't resist proverbially tweaking her nose a bit. "I could even put it in your bedroom, if you think you might need me during the night. Just for the weekend nights when you're booked solid."

Was he serious? Didn't he realize how it would look to her guests with him sleeping in her room? Tillie's regulars were older and more conservative. They knew she wasn't married or even in a committed relationship with him or anyone else, because they were always trying to suggest men who would make the perfect husband—usually their sons or grandsons.

No way could she explain going off to her bedroom with him in tow each evening, even if he was sleeping in the attic above her. Of course, they'd understand him carrying her up there, but what if he never came downstairs that night?

Lordy, Lordy, she was going to be out of her element for a long while—and her budget wouldn't allow her to pay additional staff indefinitely. Probably not more than a couple of weeks.

"I hate being helpless or having to depend on others to take care of me." She sounded whiny and grudging, but didn't care.

Greg leaned forward, resting his forearm on the edge of the table. "Tillie, you've been taking care of everyone else for a very long time.

Let someone return the favor every now and then."

His gaze penetrated her armor. Leaning back in her chair, she closed her eyes and took a deep breath to regroup. Unable to afford to cancel guest reservations because she'd already done so much expensive preparation for the holiday crowds, perhaps she *could* let him sleep in the birthing room. He'd be downstairs if she needed him. And Beckie sounded as though she could help out with almost everything, including preparing the suppers for any guests wanting them. At peak times, she'd probably have to join him there, too.

Tillie opened her eyes and fixed her gaze on his. "I'm not relinquishing control of everything to you, Beckie, or anyone else. Only the aspects that involve me being on my feet."

The twinkle in his eye told her he knew she would relent on other points. "You can appoint me sous chef to Beckie's chef."

She glanced down at the leftovers from last night. "Can you cook?"

"Passably, but I take instruction well." He grinned. "Anything that requires you being on your feet, you'll delegate to Beckie or me."

She had no choice, and it still made her blood boil to be told how to run her inn. "Okay." Still, the word nearly stuck in her throat. "But what about Thanksgiving weekend? Won't you want to be with Derek?"

Her words doused the light in his eyes. "His mom is taking him to the north woods to meet her new in-laws that weekend."

"I wanna be here with you, Daddy."

"Derek, you're going to love going up there. Think of the woods and the adventures you'll have there."

"Will I see animals?"

"Oh sure. Lots of deer. Maybe even a moose."

"Really? I never saw a moose before."

"Neither have I," Tillie said. "You won't want to miss that chance, would you?"

Derek seemed to think about it a moment then smiled. "Okay. I'll go with Mommy."

Tillie's heart ached for him having to choose which parent to be with, but at least he had two who loved him enough to want him to be with them.

She turned her attention to his father once more. "Sounds like you'd be alone for Thanksgiving." The thought bothered her. No one should spend that day alone.

He shrugged. "I'll have plenty of work to keep me busy."

For the first time since he'd proposed his ridiculous idea of coming back here to take care of her, she smiled. She might regret this, but knew Mrs. Foster would want her to offer hospitality to her grandson. "I accept your offer to help."

"You do?"

She nodded. "On one condition."

"What's that?"

"Get caught up on your architectural work beforehand, because come Thanksgiving, I intend to keep you busy helping me fix dinner. You're in for a new tradition—a thoroughly southern Thanksgiving the way your grandmother always made."

"I'd love to help in any way I can. How many guests do you expect that day?"

She did a mental tally. "Only one couple the day of, but they have relatives in the area and will be dining with them. But I'm at full capacity—six people that Friday and Saturday night. Come to think of it, we may need two cots in the birthing room."

"I don't want you sleeping on a cot."

"I've done it before on many occasions. I'm a big girl. I won't fall out."

Apparently, he didn't realize yet that he'd be having Thanksgiving dinner alone with her. The thought that she, too, would have been alone occurred to her. She'd spent any number of holidays that way since Mrs. Foster's passing.

Excitement filled her as she thought about sharing the day with

Greg. They'd have to cook for the weekend guests who would expect at least one turkey leftover meal. But they'd also be able to enjoy turkey and all of the fixings—just the two of them.

"When do you fly into Louisville?"

"Thursday morning."

"Perfect. I could use some help getting to my doctor's appointment Thursday afternoon. And that gives us time to do some things I promised to do with Derek before he leaves."

* * *

Greg wasn't sure how he got roped into this on Tuesday afternoon, but Tillie had promised to make sugar cookies with Derek before they returned to Minnesota, and with her sprained ankle, the only chance it could happen was if he did it. When he'd said he was passable in the kitchen, he'd meant he could operate the microwave with expert skill. Being dressed in an apron with powdered sugar coating his hands as he rolled out cookie dough was more advanced than he'd anticipated.

He'd followed the recipe and her verbal instructions to the letter while she sat at the table again with her leg propped on a chair. Derek was perched on a bar stool as he slowly got the hang of it all.

Well, maybe not.

"Look at my dinosaur, Miss Tillie!" Greg smiled at Derek's joy over the five cookie cutters the boy had picked out at the hardware store—an airplane, train, unicorn, rocking horse, and the dinosaur he was so excited about at the moment. His enthusiasm reminded Greg why he was doing this. He'd have to suck up his misgivings and at least try. When else would he have a proficient instructor guiding him every step of the way? *Never.*

"That's it, Greg. Any flatter and we'd have pie dough. But that's the perfect thickness for cookies." To Derek, she said, "Are you ready to start cutting them out?"

She taught them to make every bit of dough count as they wedged the cutters into every available space, and they spent the afternoon repeating the process until all of the dough was cut and baked.

When they iced and decorated them, Tillie was able to participate. Hers were much more professional looking than either of the males', although Derek ate most of his as quickly as the icing hardened. Greg would box some of the remaining cookies for Derek to give Nancy and Stephan to enjoy. He pushed thoughts of returning to Minneapolis away, not wanting to ruin the moment worrying about Tillie, but he'd be back before she knew it.

Greg excused himself to do his online check-ins. He'd leave the Rover at the Louisville airport in overnight parking and should be back in Samuels in time for a quick lunch and to take her to the orthopedic's office.

He walked into the kitchen and saw the two of them working hard on the cookies.

"Try this, Derek." She showed him how to use the icing as boundaries and to fill each part with a different type of sprinkle. It worked best on the snowmen.

"That's cool! Look, Daddy!"

He entered the room and joined them. "Great job, Derek. Why don't we save that one for Mommy?"

"She's going to love it!" he said.

Greg realized how much he was going to miss being with his son. They'd had such a great visit here with Tillie in the home that had once belonged to Derek's great-grandmother.

While he hadn't talked with Tillie yet, he knew that would come as soon as they were alone. But it was important to him suddenly that Derek know the importance of their being here.

"Son, there's something I didn't tell you about why we came here."

"What, Daddy?"

He continued to ice cookies, which was fine with Greg, but Tillie's hand movements had stopped. "This house is special to our family history."

"Why?"

"Because it once belonged to my grandmother."

Derek stopped and set the cookie on his plate filled with splashes of every color icing and sprinkles. "Who's your gramma?"

"Amelia Montgomery Foster. I spent five summers here and then came back again the November after my twelfth birthday, but Miss Tillie knew her really well in the years after that. Gram, my grandmother, wanted her to continue living here."

"What was she like?"

"A lot of fun. She was great with kids. We built forts, went on lots of adventures, and had a lot of good times. She was also a great cook, like Miss Tillie. In fact, Tillie knew her a lot better than I did."

Tillie's eyes lit up, and she smiled. "Mrs. Foster taught me most of what I use in cooking for my guests, even though I did go to college to learn some fancier techniques. She was the most amazing woman I've ever met. Adventurous. Courageous. And she loved Christmas almost as much as I do. You know, most of the ornaments on the tree in the parlor belonged to her. If you'd like to take any favorite ones home for your tree, you may."

His eyes opened wide. "Can I have the one with the soldier on the rocking horse?"

"Absolutely! I know how much you love playing with the soldiers on the chess set."

"And it reminds me of the lady who rocks in my room upstairs and at my house."

"The lady?"

"Yeah. She comes in my room at home, too."

Greg leaned toward her and whispered. "He's described her to me. I'm convinced he's talking about Gram."

The smile left Tillie's face as she asked Derek, "You mean you've seen her?"

He nodded. "A bunch of times."

Tillie smiled up at Greg, blinking away tears. Her chin shook with emotion. "Please be sure and pack it before you go. I want him to have it. It was the first one he put on the tree."

"I remember it well, but are you sure?"

"Mrs. Foster would want him to have it. I'm certain of it."

"Thank you." He cleared his throat. "That means a lot to me, too." Greg appreciated her willingness to share something of Gram's with Derek.

But his mind once again became preoccupied with the upcoming confrontation over why he'd lied about what had really brought him here. How did he intend to explain it without looking like a total jerk? Or a nut job?

Chapter Nineteen

After a whirlwind of activity on his overnight return to Minneapolis, Greg was back in Louisville picking up his SUV at the airport Thursday morning and heading south on the freeway. A sense of excitement he hadn't experienced in ages made it difficult for him to keep the speedometer under eighty miles per hour.

He placed a call to Tillie before taking the Clermont exit.

"Hello." Her voice sounded a little breathless. Was she overdoing it?

"Hey, I wanted to let you know I should be at your place by eleven. Save the hard work for when I arrive. And eat a light lunch. We're going out tonight."

"Already bossing me around?"

"You need someone to keep an eye on you right now. I'll let myself in." He'd kept the key, with her permission, knowing answering doors wouldn't be something she'd be up to doing for a while, and he didn't want to add to Beckie's burden, either.

"See you in twenty minutes, Greg." The wariness left her voice when she added, "Hope the traffic isn't too bad."

"It was a mess heading north yesterday, but I should be okay going in your direction, barring any accidents or construction."

Greg disconnected the call using the steering wheel control pad and the stereo resumed the jazz number he'd been humming to before calling Tillie.

He grinned from ear to ear, excited to see her again, even though it had only been a day since he'd left.

His spirits soared even higher as he parked at the side of the house. He entered through the front door, calling out to her.

"In the kitchen!"

Where else would she be? He found Tillie seated at the table snapping green beans while Beckie washed dishes. "You ladies sure are busy."

"Welcome back." Beckie greeted him with a smile; Tillie focused on the task at hand. "Tillie said you'd be returning, but I didn't expect you so soon."

"I wanted to be here for Tillie's appointment this afternoon." Being with her since the night of the accident made him want to stay with her until she was healed. He also wanted to hear straight from the orthopedic's mouth what restrictions Tillie would have placed on her so he could make sure she followed doctor's orders.

Having dispensed with the pleasantries, his full attention returned to Tillie. The top and sides of her hair had been gathered into a gold barrette at the back of her head. Her rosy cheeks glowed from exertion, he supposed. Was she perhaps a little nervous—or upset that he'd returned? Why? All he wanted to do was help.

"How are you feeling?" he asked.

"Fit as a fiddle. Hope the doctor agrees and lets me put more weight on my ankle."

Whatever the doctor said, Greg intended to enforce the doctor's orders. At long last, she turned toward him and grinned. "Welcome back." Her eyes twinkled.

"Glad to be here."

Two hours later, Greg watched as Tillie left the doctor's office maneuvering on crutches. He'd like to get her a knee scooter, but it wouldn't be all that practical at her place because of the stairs and high thresholds between the rooms.

"Remember, you still aren't supposed to put weight on the foot, so if you need to move to a different room or position, let me know."

"Don't remind me." Tillie had argued with the doctor. The doctor won.

She probably wouldn't call on Greg frequently, although the learning curve for crutches and the time it took to build up necessary upper-body strength might take longer than the time she'd be hobbling around on crutches. He'd miss carrying her around as often as he had been.

"It's best that I learn how to get around on my own. After all, you aren't going to be with me every minute of the day. You have work to do, too."

"True. But I'm flexible in my hours. After we identify when you'll need me most, I'll sort out a schedule for the preservationists."

Once she had scooted into the front passenger seat, which he'd pushed as far to the rear as possible so she could stretch out her leg, he stowed the crutches behind her. When he turned right instead of left out of the parking lot, she asked why.

"I made reservations for dinner in Bardstown near the courthouse."

"Oh right. Which place?"

"Old Talbott Tavern." Always the architect, when he'd read in the binder at Tillie's that the Tavern boasted rare sections of Flemish bond patterns in the building's stone—something usually found only in brickwork—he had to see it for himself.

"Fantastic! That's one of my very favorite places." Her mood seemed to be improving already.

At least he'd scored with her there. This might be a good, neutral place to come clean with her.

After parking at the side of the building, he helped Tillie out and onto her crutches before escorting her inside the front door of the rustic tavern and inn. The sign outside dated the building to 1779. He checked out the structure as they walked.

Once seated inside, Tillie launched into her natural bent for sharing local history. He loved her passion for the stories about where she lived. "A fire here in the late 1990s destroyed much of the tavern, so renovations were made that may not be in keeping with the original, but at least they were able to save most of the building."

The 18th-century costumed hostess had seated them in a quiet corner near one of the two fireplaces. Greg helped prop Tillie's foot in the chair beside him and sat down to survey the room. Reminiscent of an old English inn with its stone hearths and dark wooden floors and beams, he admired the attention to detail to preserve that period atmosphere centuries later.

Without picking up her menu, she continued. "While the fire was contained to the upstairs, the first floor was heavily damaged with smoke and water, including this area. A member of the Beam family—famous for Jim Beam bourbon—was friends with the owner and donated wood from an old building owned by the distillery." She pointed downward. "So the floors were replaced with these planks, and unsuspecting guests would never guess they're not original to the place because they're so authentic."

He surveyed the planks. "I'm glad they took the time to rebuild and restore it to its former glory. Impressive workmanship."

"Too bad you weren't around here then. I'm sure you'd have had a lot of fun consulting on a project like this."

"You betcha. Special projects like this don't come around often. While I love renovating and restoring private homes, having your work seen by tens of thousands of people over the years is its own reward."

Greg appreciated not having to delve immediately into the conversation about his motives for keeping his identity a secret from Tillie. But the moment was coming when he'd have to discuss it if he wanted there to be anything more between them.

After ordering drinks, they opened their menus. "What Kentucky delicacy should I try?"

"The bourbon-walnut encrusted chicken or the pork chop are excellent. And be sure to try a cup of Kentucky Burgoo."

He read the descriptions on the menu, including this unusual stew made with a variety of meats including lamb, beef, and chicken. Sounded interesting. "What are you having?"

"The bourbon BBQ pork, fried pickles, and a cup of burgoo."

"Everything sounds good, but I'll take your advice and go with the chicken—and burgoo. 'Stranger in a strange land,' and all."

The server took their orders, but Greg asked to hold onto his menu to read a little about the tavern's history. "There's a Jesse James room upstairs," he noted. "Have you ever stayed in it?"

She shook her head. "I wish I'd seen the room before the fire, but I was too young to appreciate it then. The renovated room wouldn't be the same, though. It reopened to patrons in Summer 2015. I've been too busy to take time out to spend the night there. Maybe someday."

"You need to take a night off and just do it."

"Trying to tell me what to do again, Greg?" She grinned, but he'd heard an edge to her words.

"No. Just thought it might be an experience you'd enjoy."

"Not to worry. I didn't mean to snap at you. I haven't been sleeping well."

Greg reached across the table and squeezed her hand. "Hang in there. It'll get better in a couple of weeks."

She groaned, but gave him another smile, this one lighting up her eyes. "I've missed having meals with you, Greg."

He'd missed everything about her, even though they'd only been apart about twenty-four hours. All he'd been able to think about on the flight back was confessing, but the fear that she'd send him packing before her ankle had a chance to heal left him wondering how much he should reveal. Regardless, he wouldn't squander what little time they did have together. He refused to live with regrets later on.

* * *

"I missed you." The words came out before she thought about the implications of how much she was divulging about her feelings. Two more unlikely friends she couldn't imagine, but she enjoyed being with him. Perhaps this was a little like Mrs. Foster and Joseph Hill. "I'm looking forward to spending the next few weeks with you."

He stroked the knuckles of her hand, sending delicious shivers up her arm. "What happens after that?" Greg broached one of the subjects that had kept her mind busy all afternoon.

Yet she wasn't prepared to answer him. "After?" Tillie's throat grew tight, and the word came out like a croak. Oh, how she wished there could be something more between them, but fear of being hurt held her back. What she needed to do was confront him about why he'd hidden his identity from her after they'd clearly started to show interest in one another.

I hate confronting anyone, much less someone I like!

Their burgoo was served, providing the breather she needed. Neither began eating right away, though. His unanswered question hung in the air.

When she didn't respond, he added, "Surely you've felt the attraction, too."

She nodded, still unable to speak—or eat. For some reason, she launched into more of the tavern's history as being a stagecoach stop, avoiding what she needed to address. Yes, she knew exactly why she was dancing around the real issue here. Dodging conflict had seen her through her first thirty-two years of life quite well.

After continued silence on her part, Greg took a bite of his stew, and she seized the opportunity of his full mouth to tackle the subject.

"Before we decide on pursuing a relationship, Greg, I think we should discuss why you kept your connection to Mrs. Foster a secret for so long after you came to Samuels."

He set down his spoon, not meeting her gaze at first, then pierced her with those intense gray eyes. He drew a deep breath, obviously as pained by the topic as she was. "I've been trying to decide how to explain my actions, but nothing sounded logical. True, when I first came down, I had a good reason for keeping my relationship to Gram a secret. I was hell-bent on calling you out as a fraud." She opened her mouth to speak, and he held up his hand. "Believe me, it didn't take long for me to realize you truly believed what you were touting as her presence there. I'm convinced that Gram is still active in the house given what Derek says he's seen."

She'd have liked for him to believe her outright, but it was a start. "That doesn't explain why you didn't tell me later. Truthfully, I discovered your identity within the first few days of your visit—"

He cocked his head. "What tipped you off?"

She was embarrassed to admit that to him. "That's beside the point." Her heart pounded as she held her ground. Hadn't she made it clear she still wanted to get to know him better despite the subterfuge? Why wouldn't he simply come clean?

He ran his fingers through his hair, and she regretted that she'd distracted him from the meal.

No! Stop doing that! You deserve an answer!

"Tillie, there's no defense for why. I screwed up. Honestly, I didn't expect to ever have deep feelings for you, never mind to develop them so quickly. I couldn't find a way to tell you that wouldn't make me look rather petty. I hope you'll accept my apology and that we can move on."

His explanation was rather anticlimactic. *But it is what it is.* As long as he wasn't keeping any other secrets from her… Was he?

"I'll accept your apology, as long as there isn't anything else you're hiding from me." He glanced away for only a moment, leaving her to wonder if there might be something more.

When he met her gaze again, he smiled. "Confession time. I'm a huge Jesse James enthusiast from way back." Was this supposed to be a revelation to her? "He's fascinated me since Gram told me stories about him as a kid. So I'll admit to having a secret wish to learn more about him and his visits to that house."

She shook her head and grinned. Why he'd think she'd have a problem with that was beyond her. "Ask me anything you'd like to know. I think I've shown you the hatch where he escaped capture. Honestly, I'm not sure what other physical evidence exists."

He remained silent a moment before nodding. "Walking the same floors he once did, given that you haven't replaced the floorboards or even repainted them, has helped satisfy my secret obsession."

At least he didn't bring up the notion of Jesse living beyond his assassination again. In periods of confusion, her mother often claimed to be the granddaughter of Jesse James. Her delusions had caused them both so much grief and remained a hot-button issue for Tillie. She didn't intend to share that part of her past with Greg. He'd want to have nothing more to do with her.

Their entrees were served, distracting her a moment, and she tried to remember where they were before her mind had wandered. She didn't want to think about what would happen after her ankle healed and he went home for good.

She leaned toward him. "I enjoy being with you, and I'd like to see if anything more can develop between us over the next few weeks."

Again, he reached across the table, stroking the back of her hand. "I'd like that, too."

A sudden and overwhelming fear weighed heavy on her heart. What if they became involved only to be unable to sustain a relationship because of their differences and the geographical challenge? Did every woman have such insecurities when starting a new relationship, or was she merely a pathetic case? But Mrs. Foster had maintained a long-distance relationship with Joseph Hill. Why couldn't Tillie reach for a little adventure? She wasn't getting any younger, and staying holed up in the inn as she tended to do, her chances of meeting anyone were slim and none.

Be honest with yourself, Tillie.

Okay, she didn't care about meeting anyone else. She wanted to get to know *this* man better. She'd avoided opening up her heart to him far too long.

"Earlier, you asked what happens after my ankle heals. You have significant obligations back in Minnesota—your son and business, especially—and I'm firmly entrenched at my inn in Kentucky. Would you be happy having a long-distance relationship, if it came to that?"

"If that's all we could have, then, yes, I could." He leaned closer. "But I'm not ready to assume that's all there can be between us."

This didn't seem real. If she pinched herself, would she wake up in bed with a throbbing ankle and none of this would have happened at all?

He set his napkin beside his plate. "Let's get to know each other better over the next few weeks and see how we feel then. Of course, I'll need to visit Derek at least once, but there's still plenty of time for us to explore whatever it is we have or want to have before your next guests arrive for Thanksgiving weekend."

Tillie licked her lips, realizing too late she'd unintentionally drawn his attention when his gaze zoomed in on them. She didn't have a clue how to entice a man she was interested in, but apparently, her body had some ideas. Still, what exactly would he be expecting? As much as she found him attractive, casual sex wasn't happening. A man like Greg must have to fight off women with a stick. Would he be disappointed if she didn't fall into bed with him?

Wanting to be sure they were on the same page, she asked, "Explain what you mean by us getting better acquainted?"

As if he'd read where her mind had gone, he grinned in such a way as to melt her to the core. "Going on dates like this. Nothing involving a lot of walking"—he pointed to her foot—"so meals like this that you don't have to labor over, short drives to show me more of this state you love, and quiet moments alone when the inn isn't otherwise occupied." He became serious again. "I don't want you worrying about taking care of me. This is your time to be waited on."

"But my happiest moments are when I'm serving others. It's not a bother at all."

"Tillie, I want to be more to you than one of your guests."

A flutter in her chest almost caused the words to catch in her throat, but she forced them out in a whisper. "You already are." *Oh God!* Making herself vulnerable to him like this scared her to death.

His smile lit up his eyes and promised something she hadn't

dreamed could become a possibility for her.

It's now or never. "I have to prepare for the guests checking in next Friday afternoon, but the rest of the week, you will have my undivided attention."

He pointed to her bowl. "You barely touched your burgoo."

She pointed to his nearly full bowl as well. But how could she eat when they were making plans that could affect the rest of her life?

Don't put the cart before the horse, Tillie.

Why did Mrs. Foster's wise words always calm her down? Of course she was jumping ahead of herself. Again. One day at a time.

* * *

"What *ails* that boy?" Amelia couldn't hide her exasperation as she paced in front of the fireplace near Gregory and Tillie's table. If Tillie could hear her—and even her own mother at times, although Amelia tried to stay more positive—why couldn't her grandson? She'd practically been yelling at him ever since he'd spouted that non-answer about his enthusiasm for Jesse James lore. *Poppycock!* "He told her a half-truth. Why didn't he tell her the real reason he came to the inn, Jesse?"

The equally perplexed outlaw shook his head. "Damned if I know. Pardon my language, Miss Amelia. But who wants to lay bets that omission is gonna come back to haunt him?"

"If I don't haunt his days and nights first. Tillie deserves total honesty. If he breaks her heart..."

"Thought you wanted them together no matter what?"

Harumph! "Not if he intends to break her sweet, vulnerable heart. She already wears it on her sleeve." Amelia shook her head. "I should never have left her that house. Maybe if she'd ventured out into the world, she'd have weathered a few more bad relationships and be able to hold her own when things came to a head, as they surely will."

Amelia couldn't stand to watch this slow train wreck. If only she could let go of some of the pent-up emotions that kept her stuck in this place just outside the Pearly Gates.

Jesse wrapped his arm around her shoulders. "Come on. Let's go up to the mural room. I want to see how bad that fire was and if I can still see those damned birds that kept me up all night more than a century ago."

Amelia sighed and let him lead her to the staircase. Would she be able to find a way to convince Gregory to be up front with Tillie?

"Why couldn't they simply cooperate with what we're trying to do for them?"

At the top of the stairs, they veered to the hallway on the right. "Free will, plain and simple. Sure got me into a heap of trouble more than a few times."

Jesse's words did nothing to lift her spirits. Her hope was waning.

Chapter Twenty

"Cram as much in as you can, and I'll lace it up."

Greg had never had his hand up the ass of a turkey before in his life, but didn't realize stuffing a turkey was such a strenuous activity. Tillie insisted that all twenty pounds of this bird would be devoured by Sunday, and her guests would be clamoring for more stuffing than she could provide if he didn't fill every crevice. He didn't want to let Tillie or her guests down, so he shoved in another handful.

Could Tillie possibly find anything else for him to do this week that would keep them from having any quality time together? He'd hoped having the house to themselves for the past week would have given them lots of moments alone, but she'd kept him so busy, except for dinners and drives, they'd had little time to breathe.

On this Thanksgiving morning, he'd hoped to at least cuddle up and watch one of her sappy classic Christmas movies, but instead, she had him preparing a feast. While the two of them would enjoy their dinner alone later, he couldn't help but think this was more for her paying guests.

Since last week, she'd asked him to assemble and decorate a tree in every room in the house, even small ones in the bathrooms. He and Beckie had then seen to the needs of the elderly couple staying here last weekend because Tillie wasn't quite able to navigate the stairs well on her crutches yet. She'd become a pro at tooling around the lower floor, though, and practically lived in the kitchen, her favorite place to be anyway. Last night, after her guests had gone to their rooms, she worked on quick breads for their breakfast, something she called pumpkin-chess pie, and a large bowl of fresh cranberry relish.

Was she intentionally avoiding any chance of their coming to know each other better before he went home? Maybe he'd misread her interest in him. Or had she been dissatisfied with his reason for lying about his relationship to Gram? Most of their kisses and electrifying touches had taken place before her accident. Hadn't she indicated she wanted more when they'd had dinner at the Tavern?

Wariness came into her eyes in unguarded moments. Tillie kept her emotions under a tight rein, but when she did let loose, he loved it. What was she afraid would happen if she expressed her feelings for him? Time was running out. He'd promised a visit with Derek after the Thanksgiving crowd left. Besides, she became stronger every day. She wouldn't need him around much longer. Beckie could handle most of the housekeeping chores, although she'd been busy baking enough pies for an army this week and hadn't been here but a few hours—only on the days Tillie had guests overnight.

This morning, Beckie took care of breakfast for her guests and sent them off to their holiday meals with family while he tended to Tillie.

Twenty minutes later, the last of the stuffing—consisting of bread crumbs combined with a mixture of celery, onion, fresh sage, herbs from Tillie's garden, and sprinkles of water—had been depleted, and she 'd trussed up the bird.

He lifted the hefty roasting pan and placed it inside the oven. "Could you have *found* a heavier bird?"

Tillie laughed, a sound he'd grown to love hearing. "Well, yes, but then it wouldn't have fit inside my pan."

Closing the oven door, he turned to where she sat at the table applying hand sanitizer. "What's next?" he asked.

"That'll be roasting for hours. Let's clean up and relax in the parlor by the tree a while. I'm exhausted."

You and me both. Scrubbing his hands at the sink, he worried that she might have overdone it. "What else can I do to lighten the workload this weekend?"

"Oh, not a thing! You're already practically running the place, except for Beckie's meal prep. I never would have made it without the two of you."

That had to be a tough thing for her to admit. He leaned against the sink and smiled. "I'm proud of you, Tillie. It can't be easy to go from running everything to having to delegate and have others do so much." He could have sworn her eyes became brighter, uncertain why his words would affect her so. "I broke my collarbone a few months back, so I know that feeling of helplessness and of having others do what you used to be able to do easily yourself."

"You what? Why have you been lifting me so much?"

Greg waved away her concern. "It's fully healed. Besides, I like carrying you around." He grinned as her cheeks grew flushed. Man, he loved watching her blush.

"Doctor's orders are for me to move under my own steam more now that I can put weight on my ankle." Her appointment this week had lifted her spirits and selfishly lowered his. "I doubt it's going to help me sleep better, though."

"Why not?" He doubted he could do anything in that regard, but adequate rest was important to her healing.

"Every time I move, my ankle zings and awakens me."

"Ah. I remember those, too." Why then was he thinking about a different kind of zing now? Probably because she had him picturing her in bed. Looking for a diversion, he glanced around the kitchen for something to munch on. They'd agreed to have dinner around six—just the two of them. He couldn't wait, but wasn't going to last that long without a bite. A half-dozen pies sat on the sideboard in the dining room, and more pumpkin pies waited in the fridge. He wanted something with a little less sugar.

No, what I want is Tillie.

Dream on. "Would you like me to fix a platter of veggies and dip to tide us over?" he asked.

"Oh! Why didn't I think of it myself? Some hostess I am."

"Because you have a lot on your mind." He opened the fridge and removed several bags and containers. "Go into the parlor and make yourself comfortable while I get these ready. I'll join you in ten minutes or so."

After setting everything on the island, he crossed the room and helped her onto her feet and handed her the crutches. She was perfectly capable of doing that herself, but touching her, being close to her, well, never got old. She kept him at an emotional distance, so he welcomed any chance he could to narrow the gap a little bit.

"Thanks for your help." She smiled up at him. "For this, the turkey, and everything else you've done."

"You've tapped into skill sets I've never explored before, Miss Tillie." On the spur of the moment, he gave in to desire and leaned down to kiss her. Expecting her to come to her senses and retreat, she surprised him by closing her eyes and tilting her head back.

Taking that as an invitation, he changed from delivering a chaste kiss at the corner of her mouth to pressing his lips firmly against hers. When they parted, he delved inside. Warm, sweet.

Before going too far, he retreated. "If you don't want me to kiss you the way I want to, you might want to hobble into the parlor."

Her eyelids fluttered open. Finally, one of them would put an end to this. At least he thought so until he heard her crutches fall to the floor seconds before she wrapped her hand around his neck and closed the gap between them again.

The time for restraint was over.

Thank God.

Greg wasn't going to be here much longer and had no intention of doing anything to hurt her. So what if they both grabbed a little gusto while they could? All too soon, Greg forced himself to pull away again.

Greg positioned himself beside her and scooped her into his arms.

"My crutches! Put me down! Where are we going?"

"Why, the parlor, of course."

"Oh." Her breathy tone and perhaps a hint of disappointment in her voice conveyed the message she might be ready for something more, too. But she'd slept on a cot in the birthing room last night while he took that uncomfortable parlor couch. No matter how arcane, she'd insisted they not sleep in the same room. Would that change soon?

Slow down. This woman deserved a leisurely wooing, not a rushed one. He chuckled to himself at the choice of such an archaic word. Gram's house once again had cast its spell on him.

They entered the parlor, and he set her gently on the brocade couch, adjusting the throw pillows behind her back. Moving the coffee table closer, he lifted her booted foot onto it. "Comfortable?"

"My foot is."

He grinned. "Good enough. But I'll warn you my intention is to make the rest of you quite *un*comfortable momentarily."

Her nostrils flared, and her well-kissed lips lifted in a smile. He sat beside her and leaned forward. The pulse in her neck had tempted him unmercifully far too long.

* * *

Tillie's heart pounded as his lips brushed the column of her neck where he focused on her pulse, only making it beat faster. She'd never made out with anyone in this house before and hoped Mrs. Foster wasn't watching. A giggle bubbled up.

Greg sat up to stare at her, taking her chin and tilting her face toward his. "I must not be doing this right."

"Oh no! You're doing everything absolutely right. I just…" She waved her hand in the air. "Don't mind me. Carry on."

He shook his head and commenced kissing her again, skimming the tip of his tongue between her lips until she parted them. His hand grabbed her hair and pulled backward until her mouth opened wider.

Her stomach dropped, and parts of her that had long been dormant throbbed to life. She didn't want him to stop. They were alone. No one would be interrupting them until late tonight. Emboldened, she unbuttoned the top buttons of his shirt and reached inside. An undershirt. *Darn.* She supposed he was used to dressing in layers at home, but having her progress impeded by more clothing made her groan.

When his hand moved across her belly and inched upward, though, all thoughts of his undershirt evaporated. She grabbed his head and leaned back a little to give him better access without releasing his lips from hers. He cupped her breast robbing her of any remaining rational thought.

This! I want this! With Greg.

Her lungs tightened until she had to retreat, gasping for air. His breathing grew erratic as well, and they stared at one another a long moment. His pupils dilated, and she guessed it was from more than the low lighting in the room.

To have that kind of effect on a man like Greg empowered her. "No need to stop on my account," she said. "Breathing is overrated."

He chuckled and lowered his hand between her knees before moving it upward, igniting an inferno of passion. She regretted nothing about delaying love until this man returned to her life, even if she had no idea she'd been waiting since the day that lonely girl had gotten her first glimpse of him while walking on the railroad tracks. No, she hadn't realized she'd been doing that until she found out who he was and remembered where she'd seen him.

Now to catch up on what she'd been missing.

Tugging his shirt from his pants and then the undershirt, she stripped both off of him and admired his chest a moment. He may not be muscle-bound like men on the covers of Romance novels, but what he had was well-toned as she discovered when she stroked his pec.

"Equal time, milady?"

"By all means." Her voice sounded breathless to her ears.

He opened her blouse and stared at her bra. She'd chosen one of the Victoria's Secret ones that had been her little secret all these years, too. He was the first man who had ever seen one on her. She'd not been quite so extravagant in college.

"Beautiful." Somehow, she didn't think he was talking about the expensive scrap of satin and lace. He made her feel beautiful, too. His fingers skimmed the tops of the lace and blazed a trail over one peak, his knuckles brushing over her nipple.

Tillie gasped. Such torture! "Don't stop."

He grinned and slipped his hand between the cloth and her skin to tweak the engorged nub, setting other parts of her body to tingling in direct response.

Everything was so…connected.

"I want you anticipating, begging, unable to hold anything back."

Wait. Am I ready for that?

She pushed away, suddenly aware of how she'd thrown caution out the window. How easy it was to be caught up in a moment of passion in the hands of the right man. One minute she watched him stuff her bird, and the next she wanted to help him…

What am I doing?

"I'm sorry." She sat up and tugged her blouse together, hurriedly filling buttonholes, whether the right ones or not.

Greg sat up, too, and sighed as he put his dress shirt on again without the undershirt this time. His chest heaved as he tried to regain control of his own breathing.

Then he chuckled. That was the last thing she'd expected. He wasn't upset with her?

"That moved a little faster than I'd intended, especially here in the parlor." He grew serious as he stared into her eyes. "I don't want us to have any regrets, and we still have some things to work out."

They did? Oh right. Her mind eased back to reality.

"Let's take this more slowly, Tillie, and make sure the timing is right. We could have the rest of our lives to make love, but if we jump in too soon and aren't able to sustain the relationship, we're both going to be sorry. I don't want to lose you because I couldn't exert a little self-control."

Why did he have to be so damned honorable about this? Well, she'd been the one to apply the brakes, hadn't she? Her chest rose and fell rapidly as she thought about what he'd said.

"How long will you need?" she asked.

"Me? Oh, I'll be ready whenever you know the time is right. Just say the word."

"What word?"

"To be safe, something you wouldn't say in normal conversation."

She bit the inside of her lip, mulling over what word to use, then smiled. "Two words, actually. Ravish me." She giggled, but at least she'd regained control.

He grinned sardonically. "Woman, you're going to drive me insane."

She wiggled her eyebrows. "Then my plan is working."

He brushed a curl from her cheek and simply stared into her eyes several moments before speaking, once again robbing her of the ability to breathe. "I enjoy being with you like this, Tillie."

"And I, you." Again, her voice seemed to be wispy. The man kept her off-guard.

He shifted his gaze in the direction of the tree. "You don't think there's anything to that spell Gram put on that ornament, do you?"

The abrupt change of subject caught her by surprise. Was he trying to analyze the unexplainable? Or backpedaling?

She tucked her finger under his chin and turned his face toward hers again. "What do you think?"

"I honestly don't know. If it wasn't that ornament, then this house—or you—has cast some kind of spell over me."

So he was on that bent again? She tried to pull away, but he tugged her back into his embrace. "Not a spell in a bad way, just definitely not what I expected when I came here."

"And what did you come here for?"

His arms stiffened. "Haven't we been through this already?"

Perhaps it was the fact he'd lied to her long after he could have come forward and told her who he was that made her wonder if perhaps he was hiding something else. Was he?

"I apologize again for not revealing my identity sooner. But I'm no longer the man who showed up on your doorstep a few weeks ago."

She giggled, relaxing. "Thank goodness." She grew serious again. "I doubt you expected to like me at all, given your preconceptions."

"No, I didn't. But you won me over."

"How?" It sounded as though she was fishing for compliments, but her curiosity had been piqued.

"By showing me how much you loved my grandmother and for the devotion you've given to preserving this house, for starters."

"Both were so easy to love." Would Greg ever be someone she could love unconditionally, too? She tamped down thoughts about how little time they had together, and she scooted into a more upright position. Perhaps if they could become more comfortable speaking about things that mattered... "Let's continue to get to know one another. Ask me anything."

He stared at her so long she didn't think he was curious about a single thing.

"What were Gram's final days and weeks like?"

Her eyes opened wider. What an odd thing to ask at a time like this.

* * *

Where the hell had that come from? "I guess I still harbor a lot of guilt over the way my family abandoned her." The admission pained him, as well it should. "Mother told me she'd died. I swear I'd have come down here as soon as I had a driver's license and gas money if I'd thought she was still alive."

Tillie stroked his arm. "Most of that wasn't your fault, but your parents'."

He wondered how much Tillie knew about his dysfunctional family. "My mother tends to be hostile whenever there's any mention of her mother or growing up here. I think she was ashamed of where she came from, although I can't for the life of me understand why. This place is so charming. Some of my best childhood memories were made in this house."

"Stop beating yourself up, Greg." Her eyes welled with tears. "I'm sure Mrs. Foster knows the truth now."

He hoped so. "Did she ever talk about us?"

She focused on her hands. "Occasionally. You, not so much your mother."

What had she said?

Before he had to dig for more details, she met his gaze again. "She loved you dearly. Even though she couldn't be with you after that last visit when you were twelve, the memories of your times together were so precious to her during her final years. In the end, she understood that it wasn't your fault you were kept apart. Grandparents have no legal rights. Sure, she regretted whatever had caused the falling out between her and Margaret, but she never blamed you for your absence. She lived a long, fulfilling life, and you were a part of many summers, as well as that last visit."

"No bitterness even when I was an adult and didn't contact or visit her?"

Tillie didn't meet his gaze. "I have a confession to make."

Greg sat up and leaned forward, his elbows on his knees. "About what?"

She nibbled her lower lip, distracting him from the conversation at hand.

"I lied to her." Her words were barely a whisper, and he wasn't sure he heard her correctly, but before he could ask her to repeat them, she continued. "In her final weeks when she was so sick and I didn't expect her to make it, I…I—um—told her she'd received a card from you."

"You what?"

Her eyes begged him to understand. "She was nearing the end of her life. I knew she'd never learn the truth, but wanted her to go to her grave believing you were thinking of her." A tear splashed onto her hands, and he wiped another from her cheek while blinking away a few of his own.

"What did she say?"

"Nothing at first. She smiled then asked me to read it to her." She drew a deep breath. "I pretended to go down to the foyer to pick up the card and brought back one from a friend of hers at church to read to her instead." She met his gaze again. "Believe me when I tell you I didn't put words into your mouth. I simply read the sentiment imprinted in the card and told her it was signed, 'Love, Gregory.' Oh, but the smile on her face was so worth the lie."

Greg nodded. "I'm glad you did that. Thank you. It makes me feel better." He paused to wrap his head around that selfless gesture from Tillie, which must have been difficult for someone who tried to be honest and forthright. "So you were with her when she... She wasn't alone at the end?"

"I took care of her until her last breath and stayed with her until the funeral home came to take her away. She refused to go to the hospital in those remaining weeks, preferring to die here in her own bed, in her own house." As if realizing the morbidity of that thought, she added quickly, "I assure you that the mattress upstairs is a new one, not the one she...well, you know."

"Good to know." He smiled. Leave it to Tillie to worry about his comfort. But he wanted to know more about Gram's final days. "What did she say about me, before or after the card incident?"

Tillie averted her gaze again, causing him to worry that it might not have been as pleasant as she'd indicated earlier. But she soon faced him again. "That ornament wasn't the only time she talked to me about how I was destined to be with you. On her deathbed, she urged me to write back to you."

"Why didn't you?" Would things have been different if he'd known Tillie earlier? Clearly, Gram's attorney had his address, and he doubted

Gram would have asked him to keep it a secret if she was so set on matching them up.

She nibbled her lower lip before whispering, "Fear of rejection, I suppose. But I was more worried about disappointing Mrs. Foster than anything in that moment, so I assured her I would. Her attorney took care of mailing her journals to you. I could have asked him for your address, but never did. Out of fear, plain and simple."

"Well, the important thing is that we've found each other now. If you and I are meant to be together, it will work out. If not…"

"I've always kept myself safe by simply not putting myself out there to be hurt."

He grinned. "I've noticed you use this house as a sanctuary to hide away from the world."

Tillie shrugged with a shy grin before growing dead serious. "Don't break my heart, Greg. If you don't think there can be anything between us, I can handle hearing that now. But, as you suspected when I put a halt to where we were headed a little bit ago, I'm skittish. I feel like I'm diving into the deep end of a pool with no lifeline, and I don't know how to swim. So please, Greg, don't play games with my emotions and my heart."

He cupped her cheek. "I wouldn't hurt you for anything in the world. Trust me." Even as he said the words, they almost caught in his throat. He needed to tell her about the things Gram wrote in her journals about Jesse James, but she'd made it clear where she stood on revisionist history theories. If he wanted her to respect him—maybe even come to love him someday—he didn't want to come across to her as delusional.

"I'd like to, but you've not always been completely honest and forthcoming with me." She seemed to be doing better at telling him what she thought at least.

"No, and for that I'm truly sorry. I understand I'll need to earn your trust." He nodded toward her ankle. "We have a little more time on our side now. Let's keep building on what we have in common."

"Thanks, Greg. I'd appreciate that—but *please* don't get me all worked up like this again."

He chuckled. "Believe me, it was equally hard on me...pun intended."

*   *   *

At the moment Gregory began unbuttoning Tillie's blouse, Amelia faced toward Jesse, who leaned against the mantel near where he'd etched his J.H. alias initials in 1939 to let it be known he'd been here in his John Howard persona toward the end of his life. Tillie had it all wrong, as she and Gregory did on so many things, but sometimes the truth was neither here nor there. Perception was all that mattered in the end.

"For all that's decent and holy, Jesse, stop staring at them! Let's give the young'uns some privacy." She tugged on his coat sleeve, dragging him out of the room.

"It is a mite awkward, but damn, ain't that the best sight you've ever seen? Amelia, my darlin', I think our work here is done."

"Don't jump the gun. Until I see my Tillie dressed in white on the arm of Gregory as they walk back down the aisle, I'm not resting on my laurels."

"You really think he'll botch it up at this point? Didn't you see the way they opened up to each other, touched each other?"

"Yes, but you ought not to be remembering that. Wipe it from your mind, Jesse."

"Whiskey and death wiped my mind long ago, but it's kinda hard to unsee them now." The two spirits ended up in the kitchen near the low-burning hearth. "Heed my words. Any day now, they're going to quit fighting the attraction and come together."

Amelia shook her head as she stared at the flames. "I hope you're right, Jesse, but I have a feeling they haven't resolved all their issues. And don't forget Peterson. That worthless grandson of my first husband's is up to no good, I tell you. Gregory and Tillie have been so into each other they haven't paid one bit of attention to the proof that's right in their hands. Their fancy cameras caught him red-handed in the cellar when he offered to get the cherry bounce."

"I don't know nothing about new-fangled contraptions like that, but I'll agree he's up to something. Did I ever tell you I didn't care for your first husband?"

Amelia grinned. "On more than one occasion."

"Glad you dumped him."

"As am I." Amelia sighed. "Too bad he had to procreate. The world would have been better off had he not continued his line with Mark's mother. Tillie and Gregory would be better off, too."

At least Jesse and her second husband, Elmer, enjoyed each other's company, although they didn't know one another long and mostly in a professional capacity.

Chapter Twenty-One

Three busy weekends had passed since Thanksgiving Day, with a blur of guests coming and going. Greg made two visits home to Minneapolis to see Derek. Each time he left, Tillie expected not to see him again, but he always returned as promised.

Putting the casserole dish into the oven, Tillie glanced up to find Greg standing in the doorway to the dining room. He'd disappeared when they came back from the store after helping her put away the groceries.

"You aren't overdoing it, are you?"

She smiled. He must ask her that a dozen times a day. "You can't imagine how happy I am to be rid of those crutches. I haven't even felt a twinge in my ankle for days. The physical therapy is doing the trick. I should be able to drive again in a week or so."

"You've healed remarkably well."

It was a month to the day since she'd sprained her ankle. Every day, she expected Greg to say he'd be leaving, but the project with the preservation society kept him here now. He'd been invaluable to her these past weeks, doing all the heavy lifting and carrying her up and down the stairs even when she insisted she could use her crutches or even take the stairs on her butt.

What would she do when he left? Not about running the inn. She'd been doing that for the most part again already. But she'd miss hearing the sound of his footsteps in the house, sharing meals together, and laughing about whether Mrs. Foster was hiding missing objects from them that suddenly appeared in plain sight right where they'd looked earlier.

Greg usually Skyped with Derek after supper, which seemed to be working as far as keeping them from missing each other too much. Tillie found herself longing to see the little guy again herself, but never intruded on their sessions unless Greg was in the dining room and asked her to say hi.

Afterward, they spent their evenings alone sitting by the fire—in the parlor if there were no guests or in the office if there were—reading or talking about what he'd been working on with the preservationist that day. Their times together warmed her heart.

But this domestic bliss couldn't last forever, especially now that she was doing almost everything she once did.

"Supper should be ready in about forty-five minutes," she announced.

"If you need anything, ask, but I'd probably only be in the way."

"Nonsense." She'd enjoyed working side-by-side with him in running her inn, but tried to prepare herself for the day when he wouldn't be here.

I don't want to think about that right now.

"Make yourself at home, Greg." *Forever, if you'd like!* "The dining-room table is set already, but there's a tray of veggies and dip on the sideboard if you're hungry now."

"No, I can wait until dinner with you. I'll take the paper products down to the cellar and maybe read in the parlor a while. *Cathedral by the Sea* might be Falcones' finest book yet." She'd borrowed the book for him from the library a few days ago when he'd run out of reading material.

While peeling carrots, she heard the motion-detector alarm go off on the surveillance system. Just Greg. She glanced at the monitor and smiled. He'd been a godsend the past month making all of the trips to the cellar. Those stairs would have been a challenge until the last few days, but he was sweet to take the rest of the supplies down there.

She cut the carrots and placed them in a pot to boil while preparing the glaze when the alarm went off again. This time when she glanced at the computer, a transparent form showed up on the screen. Then it moved. Tillie dropped the spoon into the pot and came closer to the monitor. If she wasn't fully awake, she'd think she was seeing an apparition.

Greg came onto the screen again. Why was he coming from the canning room? He didn't go to the stairs, instead walking over to the shelves of canning jars to shine his phone's flashlight against the wall. She watched intently as he ran his hand over the stone and mortar then shook his head. Making his way to the stairs, he walked right through the apparition, stopped a moment, and turned around. Had he sensed something? How could he not see it? She couldn't wait to show him the video after supper.

Curious as to what had drawn him to the canning room—perhaps hoping to capture more spirit activity—she switched to that room and backed up the footage to a few minutes ago. This was the first time she'd watched surveillance footage since the cameras had been installed, even though it turned out to be easier than she'd expected.

The smile faded from her face when she saw him shining his light onto the stone with the more recent mortar around it. He ran his fingers around the edge as if searching for a latch or lever then pushed against the stone as if he could make the sixteen-by-twelve-inch wide block budge.

What was he looking for? If he'd been inspecting the windows for evidence of tampering, she would have understood he was merely making sure no one had tried to break in again.

But this? Was he still hunting for Jesse's treasure? Had he lied to her again?

When he left the canning room, she went to the sink to wash and dry her shaking hands, trying unsuccessfully to calm the erratic beating of her heart.

She needed to confront him, ask what he'd been doing down there. He'd been in the cellar on numerous occasions to store or retrieve something she needed. Had he been snooping around then, too?

Because she cared for him in such a deep and personal way, she needed answers. This was a man she could very well give her heart to, but not if he continued to keep secrets from her and pursued these revisionist-history stories that had haunted Tillie since childhood.

Tillie walked slowly through the dining and birthing rooms toward the foyer as if marching to the gallows. The cellar door had been bolted again, so she proceeded to the parlor where she found Greg sitting with his book on his lap reading as though nothing had happened. No, not reading. He stared blankly at the flames.

Was he concocting some new story?

When he turned toward her, he smiled. "That was fast. Forty-five minutes already?" He closed the book and started to stand.

"What were you searching for in the canning room?" She blurted out the words before losing her nerve. He closed his eyes a moment. When he reopened them, he didn't make eye contact at first, convincing her that he was about to reveal something she didn't want to hear.

He didn't ask how she knew. Since he'd installed the cameras himself, that was obvious.

At long last, he met her gaze, imploring her for—forgiveness? Understanding? Whatever. Until she heard his explanation, she held out hope he had a good reason. But if he'd lied to her about being Mrs. Foster's grandson and hid from her his real reason for wanting to be here, did that mean everything had been a lie? He hadn't come back here for her, but for his own selfish interests in finding some nonexistent treasure everyone seemed so sure had been left behind by the famed outlaw.

Everyone but Tillie.

She'd only been a means to an end for him. Tillie blinked rapidly.

I will not give him the satisfaction of seeing me cry.

"I owe you an apology, Tillie. I've been snooping around a while now..."

The rest of his words were blocked by the sound of blood rushing through her ears. Snooping meant he'd been intentionally sneaking around without her knowledge. Why?

"When I installed the surveillance cameras and fixed the window, I tried to see what the intruder was so damned interested in."

"And did you find anything?"

He shook his head. "I didn't think it would be down there anyway. More likely it's hidden in the walls or a hidden passageway. Unfortunately, I haven't found any evidence of either."

"So you searched beyond my cellar?"

He took a sudden interest in the floor, and he nodded ever so slightly. "There and in my suite and Derek's bedroom. Well, and the fireplace here." He met her gaze again. "But all that was during the first couple days of my initial stay, before I'd gotten to know you better." Again, he wouldn't make eye contact. "Then the next morning Derek said he had seen Gram in his room that first night—and had been seeing her in his room in St. Paul, too."

What did Mrs. Foster have to do with this? Clearly, he'd been out to find Jesse James and his damned fictitious treasure.

He continued, not aware of her dubious thoughts. "I'm convinced she's been watching over Derek for a while now, even though I wasn't aware of it. Apparently, he only shared those earlier visits with his mom." When he looked her in the eye again, she saw pain. No. Obviously, she wasn't seeing clearly at the moment. "I soon came to the conclusion you weren't involved in any smoke-and-mirrors activity."

Ah, so at first he'd thought she'd conjured up an apparition for Derek to see. "I've never been a charlatan or a fraud—and would never frighten a child."

He furrowed his brows, perhaps to hide his true feelings about her. "I know that, Tillie. I've known it almost from the beginning, once I pulled my head out of my..." He raked his fingers through his hair, and his voice came out in a hoarse whisper. "I screwed up. Most of the snooping happened within the first couple days I was here. Although

I'll admit I didn't believe you one-hundred percent at first, I liked you enough not to want to do harm to you or your business."

"Then what were you doing in the cellar tonight? Find anything?"

"Nothing. I swear. That wall has intrigued me since the first time I was down there, so I decided to take another look." He grinned, almost sheepishly. "I'm convinced now that the most valuable things in the cellar are your home-canned goodies."

Flattery wasn't going to work with her…not anymore. She thanked him in a clipped tone then asked, "Why do you even care about hidden treasure? You aren't exactly hurting for money."

"It's not about the money. Never has been."

When he didn't elaborate, she asked, "Then tell me, what *is* this about?"

He came closer, and she took a step back, halting him in his tracks. "Look, Tillie, I'm a history buff. I have Gram to thank for that. Finding whatever Jesse James left behind would be incredible."

"What if you'd found something? Would you have taken it with you?"

"No! How could you think that?"

She didn't know what to think any longer. Other than that, he wasn't who she believed he was.

"Tillie, I swear to you I…" She waited for him to continue, but he seemed to be warring within himself about what more to say, probably because he'd already told enough lies and couldn't keep them straight.

She needed to make one thing clear. "I've already been over every inch of this house during renovations in preparation for opening the inn. I'd have found whatever you and others were talking about if it had existed."

"No disrespect, but I doubt it. The man hid things well. People are still searching for some of his lost gold stashes out west. His cryptic maps haven't helped at all."

"Perhaps they are still searching because there's nothing to find. This might be Jesse's grand joke on the world."

"I'm not so sure. Gram seemed convinced, and she wasn't given to pipe dreams."

He wasn't helping his case by continuing to talk about this treasure as if it truly existed. "So let me get this straight. You came back here because you think Jesse James buried stolen gold in my house?" *Not because you wanted to take care of me after my injury like you claimed.*

He nodded. "Not necessarily gold, but..."

Again, she watched his lips move while the thrumming in her ears blocked out his words. At least he was being honest with her *now.*

So why did she feel even worse? "All this time you were on some crazy hunt for lost gold."

"Again, I didn't say it was gold. Neither did Gram." As if he realized that he'd inadvertently admitted he had come back to search for some kind of treasure, he held out his hand as if to appease her. "Wait! That's not why I'm here. Hell, I don't know why I decided to look again while I was down there tonight. Maybe all the talk about Jesse James over dinner last night." He shrugged. They'd found a book in the library that neither had read before and brought it home to read, sparking a number of discussions about the outlaw.

Why couldn't he be honest and tell her he simply had no interest in pursuing anything romantic with her rather than concoct this story about hidden treasure? "Did you ever ask yourself why Mrs. Foster didn't find it herself? She lived in this house for decades."

Greg sighed. "I don't know what he left behind, where he left it, or even when, but imagine what a find like this would mean for your business."

"Why the sudden interest in my business? I thought you didn't like me exploiting your family for personal gain. If Mrs. Foster's journals sent you on this wild-goose chase, then you're no better than I am."

"As I've said repeatedly, I really only spent my first couple of days here actively searching. Tonight was more curiosity about that stone than anything else." He sighed. "Doesn't the Old Talbott Tavern capitalize on stories that good ol' Jesse shot some holes in the walls upstairs one night on a drunken binge?"

Everyone in the county knew the story about the night he'd taken pot shots in the mural room when he thought the birds on the wall were 'flying' around, keeping him awake. "No doubt they renovated Jesse's room and keep it booked solid for Jesse James buffs. You find his treasure, and you won't have to worry about a thing the rest of your life."

"I'm not worried about anything now." Well, except for how to tell Greg to leave. While it broke her heart to give up on what might be her only chance at love, she wouldn't sell herself short with someone who didn't put her ahead of everything else. She wanted nothing to do with Greg and his fictitious treasure.

"You seem to forget that I've already connected Jesse to my inn with stories of his hiding out there in the 1860s and '70s. It hasn't been all that lucrative," she pointed out. "Maybe if I shot some bullet holes in the walls, I could fabricate a story—but that's not the way I do business."

"Tillie, let's sit down over dinner and talk about this."

She shook her head. "I want you to leave." *There. I said it.* "Tonight. I'm tired." *In my heart.* "Feel free to eat supper before you go, but I'm no longer hungry. I'll take the casserole out of the oven. Then I'm heading up to bed." Her training in hospitality couldn't even let her throw him out without taking care of his needs one more time. How pathetic? "Pack your bags while I do that because this discussion is over."

She didn't care if he headed back to Minneapolis tonight or to a hotel. She simply didn't have the energy to keep an eye on his every move. Honestly, she didn't have the energy to do anything right now. A heavy weight had fallen over her, leaving her rooted to the spot.

He stared at her a long, hard moment. "Can you shoot a gun with accuracy, Tillie?"

She rolled her eyes. "I wasn't serious, Greg."

"Have you had any training with firearms?"

Apparently, he wouldn't let this harebrained idea go. Knowing he thought she'd perpetrate a hoax on her guests and that he had such a low opinion of her only hurt more. "Of course I have. I live alone and have a permit to conceal carry."

He nodded curtly. "Good. I want you to keep a gun with you at all times until the authorities find out who broke in."

So he didn't want her to shoot up the walls of her house? How had she jumped to such a wrong conclusion? *Because I'm utterly exhausted.* Even the notion that an intruder had actually broken in seemed preposterous now, given that nothing had happened since then. Did he expect her to cling to him and beg him to stay? "Why are you trying to scare me?"

"I'm not. I hate the thought of you being here alone if whoever broke in returns when I'm not around."

Tillie's nerves became unsettled at the thought, but Greg needed to go. "I'll keep my revolver with me. You can leave your key on the table in the foyer."

Without waiting for him to respond, she pivoted and went to the kitchen to do as she'd promised. The meal she'd labored on so lovingly shouldn't have to suffer from their parting ways. She crossed the dining room and opened the door to her room. She heard footsteps on the hallway stairs and started up the pie stairs, thankful she missed meeting him again in the kitchen.

Well, she'd put herself out there and trusted someone only to find heartache. This inn was her entire world. She could survive without the love, especially that of a dishonorable man. But she refused to make herself vulnerable to yet another man who was more interested in this house than in her. Greg was no better than Mark.

She wouldn't be a doormat for any man. Confronting him tonight had been one of the most difficult things she'd ever done, but she wouldn't have been able to respect herself if she'd tamped down her feelings.

She might always live with regrets for what could have been, but standing up for herself and sending Greg away before he could hurt her anymore was the right thing for her to do. Her well-being and self-respect took precedence, even if she did have to suffer a broken heart, something she'd tried to guard against her entire life. In the long run, it was in her best interest to stand up for herself. No one else was going to be around to do it.

Tillie had been taking care of herself for the most part since she was a kid, except for when she'd moved in with Mrs. Foster as a teen after her mother died. She usually stayed so busy she didn't know what to do beyond running this inn. Needing someone else to validate her ability wasn't even a consideration. She had plenty of guests who fed her need to be wanted and to serve. Perhaps not as rewarding as being loved by Greg might have been—but the trade-off to keep him in her life would be too dear. She wouldn't sacrifice herself and be walked all over by someone who gave her a false sense of belonging.

At least they hadn't gone too far in their relationship. She'd be left with few reminders of what she'd risked and lost. Still, her heart would be battered and bruised for a long time.

* * *

Amelia followed Gregory up to the room Derek had slept in where he hastily threw clothing into his suitcase. His pain and disappointment were palpable, making her regret not having a contingency plan for what to do if Tillie broke her grandson's heart. But Tillie was hurting, too, even if by her own misguided beliefs and not anything Greg had intentionally done.

"Jesse, he's leaving! What do we do now?"

"Let 'em be, Amelia. They'll have to work this out themselves. If they can't trust each other, nothin' we do can change that."

"But it's all my fault. How was I to know Gregory would choose that moment to go searching for what's been right under his nose all along? I need to fix this."

Jesse patted her hand as they stood in the corner watching Gregory go into the bathroom in Amelia's old room to retrieve his belongings there. When he came out, the pallor of his face as he stared longingly at the bed where he'd so tenderly taken care of Tillie after she hurt her ankle broke Amelia's heart. He locked his jaw as if trying not to lose it altogether. Was he remembering her lying there?

Amelia wanted to cry for him, even though he'd brought this on himself. Okay, so she'd used the journals as a means to get him back in that house. She didn't expect him to become hell-bent on proving history wrong. The boy rarely became passionate about anything. She'd hoped he'd expend his passion on Tillie.

"But what if they never figure it out, Jesse?"

"Then they'll be miserable for the rest of their lives. Not everyone's lucky enough to find and claim the one person who is their destiny. For me, it was Zee. For you, Elmer Foster and Joseph Hill. We were two of the lucky ones."

But she wanted that for Tillie and Gregory, too. "Why didn't he tell her why it's so important to him to find the treasure I wrote about—even if he's so far off base it would be a miracle if he ever figured it out."

"Pride goeth before the fall. He's so worried she'll think he's ready for the lunatic asylum that he can't tell her what she means to him."

Amelia wished spirits could cry because all she'd hoped for was falling apart before her eyes. She hated to give him the satisfaction by admitting it, but Jesse was right. They'd laid the tracks to bring the two young'uns together. If they were too blind—or too stubborn—to make those tracks meet in the middle, then what more could she and Jesse do?

Blast it, no! What was she missing? Amelia wouldn't give up yet.

"Why do they have to make things so complicated?"

Jesse shrugged, more interested in Gregory's movements returning to the smaller bedroom and carrying his valise down the stairs than he was in this conversation with her.

Love was the only thing that mattered in life—whether of family, friends, or the person meant to complete you.

Which made Amelia ask Jesse, "Did you have strong feelings for Caroline? Beyond the obvious physical ones?"

"Sure, I did. I'd been lonely a long time, and Zee had been gone thirty-odd years by then, although I had to stay away from her from the moment of the assassination ruse and wasted the remainder of her years. Caroline helped to fill a void. She took such great care of me as my nurse. Then one night, we decided we wanted more. How was I to know the experience would give me apoplexy and I'd die the next day?"

Amelia remembered when Caroline came to her to tell her she'd become pregnant. Amelia was married to George then, but talked Dr. Foster into renting a room to Caroline upstairs until the baby came. The baby had been born in the birthing room with Amelia's future husband delivering little Jessica.

Jesse broke into her thoughts. "After Zee and I lost two of our four babies at birth, I wish I'd been around to help raise mine and Caroline's little girl, Jessica, but I tried to watch over them as best I could from this side. Couldn't keep Caroline from killing herself that night. Nor could I keep little Jessica or Mary, Tillie's mother, from going down the paths they took."

"I didn't know that you and Caroline were having an affair until the night she gave birth. She wanted to explain to me why she could never marry the man who had left her pregnant."

"She was a good woman. Another regret of my life was leaving her to deal with this alone. But I wouldn't exactly call it an affair. We had just the one night."

Amelia patted his arm. "You couldn't help that it was your time to go that time, Jesse." Still, so many people had been affected by what had happened. "Elmer and I, after we married, took Caroline and Jessica in, so they were never alone until we enlisted. I was in the South Pacific when she gave the little girl up for adoption. When I came home from duty, I found Caroline a wreck of a woman. She'd lost everything and simply didn't know how to cope anymore. God knows I tried to care for her so she wouldn't wind up in an asylum, but nothing we did could alleviate her remorse over giving up her daughter."

"You were good to her, I know that."

"But damn it," Jesse declared, "I am bound and determined not to let Matilda Jane suffer for mistakes I and others made before she was even born."

"I understand your frustration and remorse over not doing enough. When Tillie showed up on my doorstep that night with my wandering tomcat, it was like looking at Caroline again. I had no idea who had adopted little Jessica. Caroline wouldn't tell me. But there wasn't a single doubt in my mind that this girl was a descendant of hers. It wasn't until later that I figured out what had happened to Jessica after the adoption."

Amelia watched Gregory scribble something quickly on a piece of paper and set the paper on the table in the hallway, placing the key on top. With one last glance of longing toward the back of the house, he sighed and walked out the front door, setting it to lock behind him. Her heart broke for him. He truly did love Tillie, but the two of them were allowing petty issues to come between them. Perhaps if they hadn't been lied to and neglected by the ones they should have trusted as children, they wouldn't be so mistrustful now.

Whether Gregory and Tillie would ever come to believe in each other, their destiny was now up to them.

Would she and Jesse be forced to linger between two worlds for all eternity if these two didn't open their eyes? More than likely.

Chapter Twenty-Two

Greg didn't plan to call the office to let them know he was in Minneapolis sooner than expected. After driving straight through from Kentucky, he crashed in bed, hoping the blessed escape of sleep would blot all thoughts from his mind. But images of Tillie—smiling, laughing, jumping into that pile of leaves and trusting him to catch her—kept flashing across his closed eyes.

But he hadn't been there for her the way he should have.

Always, over and over, that final moment when she'd told him she wanted him out of her house and her life before turning and walking away. He couldn't blame her. He'd screwed up. Big time.

Why couldn't he tell her why he'd been so interested in finding evidence Jesse lived beyond what historians believed? So what if she thought he was off his rocker? If he never found anything, they would have had something to share a long, hard laugh about for decades to come.

Instead, he'd remained silent.

All the way to Minneapolis and since he'd arrived home late last night, he'd replayed their final conversation in his mind incessantly. Suddenly, something clicked.

"You came back here because you think Jesse James buried stolen gold in my house?"

Well, I'll be damned. What if she was asking about why he'd come back to her the second time, not why he'd initially come to the house weeks before that? Could he have completely misunderstood her, which led to her sending him packing?

Of course, he'd initially headed to Kentucky to debunk her claims as well as to find proof that Jesse had lived for decades longer than believed by historians. But the only reason he'd come back after Tillie's injury was because he'd wanted to be there for her, spend time with her, take care of her. Yeah, even though that drove her independent spirit nuts, he thought she'd liked having him there after a while.

Clearly not.

As for finding any treasure in that house, he'd found something beyond anything he could have ever dreamed of.

Tillie.

Only now he'd lost her.

Lost? No, more like he'd thrown her away because he was too proud to look a little demented for pursuing some elusive nonsense Gram had written about in her diary seventy-seven years ago.

Still, Tillie's reaction didn't seem logical. Something else must be going on. What was he missing? Okay, he'd kept something from her—lied by omission. He'd grown up in a family where telling half-truths and keeping things hidden from the ones you loved was commonplace, but Tillie deserved better than that from him.

The sunrise peeking through his window cast a rosy hue on the wall. Another night without sleep. The time for wallowing in regrets was over. He needed to move on.

Dancing prisms on the wall made him think of Gram. Wait. He glanced at the window to find the source, but nothing appeared out of the ordinary.

What if…

Gram, is that you?

Until five weeks ago, he'd never thought much about spirits lingering after death, but hadn't Derek seen her himself on numerous occasions? If she could appear to his son, why not to him?

Tillie received recipe cards from her, too. He'd questioned whether that was real, but in the end, he trusted Tillie to tell him the truth.

He was the one having trouble being honest.

"Gram, if you're listening, I could use some help. I don't know how to move on without her."

Man, I'm truly losing it.

Then he realized the rainbows were in the exact same pattern he'd seen on the floor of Tillie's foyer the afternoon he and Derek had arrived last month. In his mind, Jesse's Hideout was no longer his grandmother's house. Tillie had hung onto much of Gram's influence and kept the building's character intact, but she'd made the house her own.

Greg threw off the comforter and dressed quickly. If he lay here any longer, he'd be seeing ghosts, too—not only Gram's but memories of his relationship with Tillie. He needed to expend some pent-up energy. Exhaust himself. A nice long bike ride along the Cedar Lake Trail and down the Mississippi on West River Parkway would work for starters. He'd decide from there how far out of the city he wanted to bike. Regardless, he'd make sure that tonight he'd be able to sleep again for the first time in days.

He dressed in layers to combat temps in the thirties and pulled a skull cap over his head, donned his helmet, and wheeled the Surly ECR cycle he'd bought to replace the one destroyed in the accident out the front door and down the front steps. He'd barely had a chance to break it in yet.

The brisk air was hardly noticeable, perhaps because his body had been numb since losing Tillie.

Greg had left early enough that he made it through the city before rush hour and within fifteen minutes headed south along the banks of the Mississippi. He wasn't surprised half an hour later to find himself at Minnehaha Park. He'd come here a lot in the past couple years and had spent much of his childhood roaming around the banks of the creek and exploring behind the falls each winter.

Today, he found no such comfort and clearly would need to keep going, even if it was the first time he'd biked in a long while and his legs were screaming even after such a short ride. Might as well take a break here. He dismounted at the statue of Hiawatha carrying Minnehaha, but the poignant couple that loved and lost only brought up memories of when he'd carried Tillie after she'd sprained her ankle. He could almost feel his arms around her now.

I miss you, Tillie.

A strong blast of frigid air hit him full in the face, momentarily shocking him out of his maudlin mood. His eyes watered.

Absolutely the jolt he needed. Was he going to let her go on thinking the worst of him? Even if she didn't want him in her life, he needed to set the record straight as to why he'd returned to her after the accident. He couldn't do more than apologize for his initial intentions, but he didn't give a damn anymore about proving Jesse James lived beyond his murder in 1882. He no longer cared about any of that.

All that mattered was doing everything in his power to convince Tillie she was the only treasure he wanted. He hopped on the bike and began the journey back to his place. He'd catch a few hours of sleep so he wouldn't be a danger on the road and set off again to Samuels to surprise Tillie. Might as well drive rather than wait around for a flight. If he called saying he needed to talk, she'd simply tell him not to bother and hang up—as politely as she could, no doubt.

This had to work. Life without Tillie would be so much colder, darker. He wanted her sunshine back in his life. He intended to win her over again, even if it meant sticking his neck out and looking like a damned fool.

* * *

Tillie wrapped her arms around herself as she stared out the office window at the tree under which she and Greg had romped in the leaves. The pile was long gone, but she could still feel the strength in his arms as he caught her, see his eyes gazing at her as though he, too, experienced the same incredible awakening she had.

Had that been part of the act as well? If so, he'd missed his true calling.

Her head told her he wouldn't be returning and that she should be grateful she'd dodged that bullet. But her heart hurt so badly she couldn't even gear up to greet her weekend guests who would be arriving tomorrow afternoon or evening. At least they hadn't asked her to prepare their suppers. Maybe by Saturday morning, she'd be ready to work in the kitchen again.

A chill went up her spine, and she crossed the few steps to the fire to warm her hands. But nothing would warm her heart.

Not until she got over Greg. Clearly, she'd made the right choice. She couldn't trust him, and how would the two of them be able to build a lasting relationship without trust?

None of the women in her family had been able to rely on the men in their lives. Did that mean she could never count on the men in hers? So what if Greg believed the myth that Jesse James survived his assassination? What difference did it make to her?

Because I don't want people to think I'm another crazy Hamilton woman.

Tillie blinked a few times. Where had that come from?

She remembered the taunts aimed at her mother and grandmother. In her infrequent moments of lucidity, her mother had told Tillie countless times that Tillie's grandmother claimed to be the daughter of Jesse James. The neighbors labeled both women as being touched in the head—and that stigma had spilled over to Tillie in school when children plastered the label on her as well.

She'd blocked that out of her mind until now and wished she could do so again.

Three generations of Hamilton women had been abandoned by the men who fathered them, Tillie's own father included. She didn't even know the man's name, but growing up had imagined he might be a famous movie star or someone rich—all of her imaginary fathers were handsome. Had her grandmother conjured up the legendary outlaw as her father figure after growing up on the local lore, not realizing she was off by about sixty years from his last visit here before he was killed?

Well, I used to pretend Cary Grant was my father, after falling in love with him while watching old movies, and he died a decade or more before I was born, too.

The three generations of women preceding Tillie had something else in common—three women left pregnant and unwed, each of whom at some point succumbed to mental illness. All three had committed suicide. Although her mother's death had been ruled an accidental overdose, she'd still died at her own hand.

Tillie might have been next if not for Mrs. Foster.

Had they been delusional or merely unable to take being called 'the crazy Hamilton women' whenever they were seen in public? Only sometimes the people didn't always refer to them as women, but much more derogatory terms. It didn't help that her grandmother and mother had proudly proclaimed the news. If Tillie believed them, Jesse James would have been her great-grandfather.

Preposterous.

She refused to entertain the notion that a man known to have died in the early 1880s returned to the house she lived in—albeit in the late 1930s—and impregnated her great-grandmother despite being in his eighties or nineties.

I'm not one of the crazy Hamilton women!

She dashed away the tears spilling from her eyes. Perhaps conspiracy theories and revisionist history were all the rage nowadays, but she'd had to live with the stigma of those claims her entire life. While she regretted belittling Greg when he tried to bring it up on the train, she refused to go there again.

Of course, Greg couldn't possibly know why his words had such a negative effect on her. The man was curious about any number of topics, which was part of what attracted her to him.

Oh, how her heart missed him. Perhaps it always would.

She owed him an explanation and an apology at the very least. She might never win him over again, but she could try.

Pivoting on one foot, she started toward the birthing room before heading back to the office to retrieve her revolver. She'd promised Greg to keep it with her even if she didn't expect to have to use it, but had taken to sleeping with it by her bed lately. Better safe than dead.

In the parlor, she stared up at the Christmas tree they'd worked together to decorate. She hadn't bothered to turn it on at all today. Its cheerful colors would only emphasize how bleak her world had become in the past two days.

She should have trusted her instincts from the start. Greg wasn't of her world.

No, that wasn't how he'd made her feel at all while he was here.

Why the pity party tonight? She'd never had trouble being alone in this house before. In fact, it had become her escape from a world she didn't fit into. A place she could pretend to live in a bygone era where she imagined the world to be happier, even though she knew every generation had its heartaches. No one living in this house had found utopia—including Mrs. Foster, who had her share of heartache, but didn't let it hold her back from experiencing two romantic relationships in her life.

Greg had never been unkind or hurtful to Tillie. He'd only inadvertently triggered a sad memory for her.

"Oh, Mrs. Foster. I've lost him."

The thing she feared most—being abandoned—had come to pass. Only he hadn't abandoned her; she'd *pushed* him away. All to protect her heart from being hurt—and from being labeled crazy.

How's that working for you, Tillie?

The woman's voice was as plain as if she stood right next to her.

If the pain in her chest was any indication, not so well. She'd used Mrs. Foster and this house as an excuse to hide away from reality since she was eight. Perhaps that wasn't what she needed anymore. Once her weekend guests left, she'd call Beckie and see if she wanted to go see a movie or play—or simply have a cup of coffee. She missed having someone to talk with. Guests spent only a small amount of their time with Tillie, usually at check-in and over breakfast.

Too exhausted to haul herself up the stairs, she grabbed an afghan off the seat of the rocking chair and stretched out on the sofa, but immediately flashed back to when she and Greg had made out here Thanksgiving Day.

Turning onto her side, hoping to tune out the nagging thoughts in her mind, she tried to fall asleep.

Suddenly, her eyes opened wide. What was that? What had jarred her awake? She listened for the sound again, but the house remained silent. A glance at the fob watch in the lights of the Christmas tree told her it was after two in the morning.

Thump.

There! What was that? Sounded as if it came from the cellar. She sat up and reached into her pocket and took out her phone, punching in 9-1-1, wanting to catch the burglar in the act.

She whispered, "This is Tillie Hamilton at Jesse's Hideout B&B in Samuels. Someone's broken into my house." Her whisper became shrill. "He's still here!" She started around the sofa, preparing to flee the house.

"We'll send someone right out. Can you get out of the house safely?"

"I think so." She made it to the doorway of the hall, but heard footsteps coming up the cellar stairs and darted back inside the parlor. "He's coming up the stairs. I can't get out without him seeing me." Why hadn't she escaped and *then* called for help? She wasn't thinking clearly, that's why.

"Hide and stay on the phone. Help is on the way, and I'll keep this line open."

Tillie hoped it wasn't a raccoon or another animal, but after the attempt last month, she couldn't take a chance. Thank God she had her revolver, but she didn't want to confront whoever was down there. Surveying the room, she ducked behind the wing chair in the corner to the right of the entrance. Perhaps he wouldn't come inside the room far enough to see her.

"Please don't say anything," she begged the dispatcher. "I don't want him to find me."

Why now? Greg had been here for weeks, and nothing had happened beyond that one broken window just before he first arrived. Had the person been watching the house all this time waiting for him to leave?

Who the hell was in her house? And what did they want?

The sound of footsteps nearing the cellar door set heart racing. Had she locked it? She always did, but the effort of going down there a few hours earlier had exhausted her. She simply couldn't remember! Sweat broke out on her forehead as the invader tried the doorknob.

Tillie said a prayer for angels to come and protect her. "You, too, Mrs. Foster!" she whispered. No one would have messed with her if she'd been here. He slammed his body against the door twice before breaking the bolt.

Oh no! He's right outside the room!

She had no proof it was a man, but also no doubt. Apparently, he wasn't concerned about stealth. Had he seen her through the window? Did he know which room she was in?

Tillie's chest constricted to the point she could barely breathe. If he only glanced inside the room, he wouldn't see her. She disconnected the phone, turned off the ringer, and lay as still as possible, holding her breath—and her revolver.

The footsteps came to the parlor entrance. She squeezed her eyes shut and held her breath. When the intruder moved toward the stairs, she released her breath quietly. Now what? She couldn't make a dash to the front door without being seen.

How long would it take the sheriff or his deputies to make the five-mile drive if they weren't already cruising around this part of the county?

Tillie decided her best bet would be to try and escape before he came back downstairs. She waited for him to open one of the bedroom doors and darted from behind the chair. By the time she reached the hallway, she heard a squeak on the stairs. He was on the landing!

Run!

Hoping to make it to the dining-room door unseen, she ran through the birthing room, but had barely made it to the dining room when a male voice shouted at her to stop or he'd shoot.

She recognized his voice immediately.

Keeping the Smith & Wesson hidden in the pocket of her dress, she turned to face the barrel of Mark Peterson's gun. What on earth was wrong with him? Why was he threatening her? The sneer on his face was one of triumph—but what had he succeeded at? The sheriff's department had people on the way already. God, she wished they would hurry. What was going on here?

"Where is it, Tillie?"

It? "Where's what?"

"We both know what I'm here for. You and Mrs. Foster have thwarted my family for too long. I want what Jesse James left behind."

All she could focus on was the gun pointed at her. Was she fast enough to outshoot? She barely went to the range once a month anymore. Mrs. Foster had insisted she train much more regularly. Thank God the woman had convinced her of the importance of a concealed carry permit. She'd never needed to use it until tonight, but was glad she was armed.

Was it better to keep him talking until someone came?

Deciding to stall, her first thought was what his family had to do with anything in this house. "If I knew what *it* was, I'd give it to you to get you out of here. But honest to God, I have no clue. Greg searched for some elusive treasure, too, and couldn't find a thing, either. Why don't you people give up on these ridiculous claims and leave me and my inn alone?"

"You sure he didn't find the treasure himself and run off with it?"

Was she? Thinking back to their last conversation, she didn't have the impression he'd left because his mission had been completed. No, because she'd thrown him out. But he seemed to have given up on uncovering whatever Mrs. Foster had written about even before he'd come out of the cellar that night.

"No, but he'll be here any minute." She wasn't above lying if her life depended on it. "You don't want him to find you here threatening me." Once more, her focus went to the gun, which wavered in his hands. *Dear God, don't let him accidentally squeeze the trigger.*

He grinned—snarled, more like. "I saw him load his suitcases. Don't lie to me again, Tillie. I'm smarter than all you crazy Hamilton women."

Don't let him goad you, Tillie.

But he *had* been watching the house. Her gaze returned to his eyes. There was a wildness there she hadn't seen before. All this time, she'd thought he was merely grabby, but having his hands all over her had only been a distraction for getting his hands on whatever he thought was hidden in this house.

The last thing she wanted to do was piss him off. Or let him see she herself was armed until she needed to. "I've heard the same stories you have. But I've lived here more than fifteen years without so much as finding a single thing that belonged to either of the James brothers." She moved behind the table.

"Don't move," he hissed.

What on earth was he thinking of doing? Clearly, he had no intention of letting her go until she told him where this so-called treasure could be found. If he was thinking rationally, he'd realize she'd have put it in safekeeping herself. Would he kill her when she couldn't produce what he wanted? Of course he would. Otherwise, he had to know she'd go to the authorities and have him arrested. Her hand tightened on the grip of the revolver.

"Amelia Foster told my grandfather Jesse James left behind something more precious than any other treasure he'd hidden anywhere else in the country. Then that greedy bitch dumped him and dug her claws into Dr. Foster so she could have it all to herself."

Dumped him? Greedy bitch? How dare he skew reality that way?

Wait a minute. "Your grandfather was Mrs. Foster's first husband?"

He nodded. "She bilked him out of everything."

How could that be? They'd both been penniless, according to Mrs. Foster. She'd left him because he'd cheated on her. While she'd been working for Dr. Foster at the time, and the two married within a year of the divorce, Mrs. Foster was too honorable to have had an affair outside of marriage. Still, it had been quite a scandal in the community from what the woman told her—and she relished every minute of it.

But Tillie had no intention of setting the record straight with someone truly delusional or stirring up any more hatred or anger in Mark.

Was that a siren? Might he assume it was an ambulance on the way to the hospital? The sound ended abruptly, still far in the distance. She glanced toward the door, but wouldn't be able to dash across the room, open it, and escape before being shot.

He followed her gaze before casting an accusatory look at her. "Tillie, tell me you didn't call the sheriff."

She could lie, but perhaps knowing the authorities were minutes away might make him run.

She nodded, hoping he would see that there was no escape now.

Instead, he shook his head before a bone-chilling, sinister smile came over his face. "You shouldn't have done that, Tillie. I'll be long gone by the time they find your body."

He intended to kill her. Mark raised the gun toward her head. In one fluid motion, she lifted her revolver, hidden in the skirt pocket of her dress, and dodged to the side as she squeezed the trigger.

A single scream of pain reverberated after the two gunshots split the night air.

Chapter Twenty-Three

Greg exited at Clermont onto the highway to Samuels, and his adrenaline began pumping, whether from the black swill he'd been mainlining since he'd left Minneapolis this afternoon or the fact that he was close to Tillie. Damned if he'd let her push him away before he had a chance to explain what he'd decided about them. He loved her, for God's sake. That should mean something.

Yes, loved. Time to prove it.

One glance at the speedometer told him he'd be pulled over or killed before he had a chance if he didn't slow down, so he eased off the accelerator. He wouldn't wake her up in the middle of the night, but would park in the drive and wait until morning to talk with her. Maybe by then he'd figure out what words to say to convince her he'd truly come back for her after her injury, not treasure or fame or whatever she thought. Yeah, he'd screwed that up his last night at Tillie's. He needed to make amends.

Would she hear the Rover's engine? It was too early for her to be in the kitchen—nearly four o'clock. Well, with Tillie's strange hours, who knew? But with her bedroom being on the same side of the house as the kitchen and dining room, she'd probably hear him.

Well, if she did, maybe she'd let him in to talk sooner than waiting until—

He left the main highway. After crossing the railroad tracks, he glanced across a field in the direction of her house and saw red and blue flashing lights illuminating the brick inn.

Tillie!

Flooring the pedal as soon as he turned onto her road, he arrived in seconds. Half a dozen sheriff's department vehicles and an ambulance filled the circular drive. He parked in the yard in case they needed to exit quickly.

The rear doors of the ambulance slammed shut, causing his heart to hammer. He exited the Rover and ran toward the ambulance but only made it as far as the deputy's car.

The deputy looked up from her notepad then stood at attention, hand on her holster. "Stop right there. Where do you think you're going?"

"Where's Tillie Hamilton? Is she all right?"

"Who are you?"

"Her fiancé." The words came out before he realized he wasn't being truthful. Her cocked eyebrow told him the deputy probably knew Tillie well enough to guess he was no such thing. Everyone knew her around here. If he'd come back here to prove his honesty to Tillie, he might as well start now.

"Well, I will be, as soon as she says yes."

"I see."

He assumed he'd be taken inside now, but the deputy didn't move. If the deputy didn't tell him where she was, he'd lose what was left of his mind. "Who's in that ambulance?"

"The sheriff's wrapping up his statement while the crime scene investigator processes the scene. As soon as I get the all clear, I'll take you in."

The minutes ticked by interminably slowly. Just when he was about to walk over to the ambulance to see if Tillie was there, it pulled out of the drive with its lights still flashing. He kept waiting for someone to open the door to the dining room, hoping Tillie was inside and safe.

A squelching on the deputy's radio was followed by her telling him to "Follow me." She led him to the dining-room door. "Wait here."

She opened the door and called, "Tillie, do you know this man?" Thank goodness she wasn't in the ambulance. She must not have been injured, but he still couldn't wait to see her. Coming around the deputy, he saw Tillie sitting at the table wrapped in a blanket, her hair loose and wild. The sheriff, he supposed, sat next to her. Upon seeing Greg, her eyes opened wide, as did her arms as she jumped up and ran toward him. "Greg! You're here!" The deputy stepped aside as Tillie launched herself from the threshold and into his arms.

She trusted me to catch her. That's a start.

He wrapped his arms tightly around her and held her shaking body against him. "Thank God you're all right!" He'd aged ten years in the last few minutes. She trembled, and he set her down to stroke her back with one hand while holding her tightly with the other. "Shh. I have you." *And I'll never leave you again.*

After an undetermined amount of time, she leaned away, forcing him to let her go. Her eyes still had a vacant look. Was she ready to talk about what happened?

"What happened?"

"M-Mark. It was Mark. He broke in, only he didn't stay in the cellar. I had no idea how easy it was to break in from down there." Her voice shook, and tears welled in her eyes from the shock or aftermath of whatever happened.

"Mark?" *Who the hell was…? Wait.* "Peterson?" *He* was the intruder? So it wasn't some kind of ghostly prank from Gram or Jesse James? While he'd firmly believed it to be a human intruder initially, after that incident with the prisms on his bedroom wall, he'd begun to think differently.

But the thought of anyone coming in here and threatening Tillie was much harder to stomach.

She nodded. "I've never been so scared in my life."

"Did he hurt you?" Greg would finish him off if he had so much as touched her.

"No." She shook her head with added emphasis, but her vacant eyes didn't convince him. She pointed with a shaky finger at the blood-stained floor near the door to the inner porch and herb garden where a crime scene investigator had labeled a bullet casing with a tented number amongst the blood.

Grabbing her by the arms, he checked to be sure she wasn't bleeding. A gaping hole in the skirt of her dress didn't appear to have any blood. How close had they been to one another when shots were fired? "He shot at you?"

She nodded again. "He hit the window frame over there when I dodged."

He looked where she pointed and saw another of the crime-scene numbered tents taped to the splintered window frame. She'd been shot at? She could have been killed? But Peterson was the one in the ambulance. The sheriff or one of the deputies had arrived just in time.

Not wanting her to have to speak about the horror any further, he glanced over her head, making eye contact with the sheriff. "Sir, thanks for taking care of that piece of—"

The man shook his head. "I'm afraid all we arrived in time for was to save Peterson from being shot again."

Taking Tillie by the shoulders, he pushed her away and waited for her to meet his gaze. "*You* shot him?"

"I-I-I thought he was going to kill me. It was self-defense!"

A grin broke out on Greg's face. "You amaze me, woman. I wasn't sure you could fire a gun with accuracy, much less shoot someone firing at you."

She tilted her chin up, some of her old defiance returning to her eyes. *Thank God.* "I told you I could."

"Yeah, well, I'm learning that I need to trust you more. From here on out, you'd better believe I will." He sobered. "And I hope you'll trust me, too. We need to talk"—he glanced around at all the commotion—"later."

She waved away his words. "You came back. That's all that counts. I thought I'd lost you forever."

Greg glanced at the sheriff who kept making notes about something. After a moment, the man stood.

"Miz Hamilton, I don't expect any more trouble here tonight. We have everything we need and know how to reach you if any further questions arise. But we'll keep a car parked outside tonight until you can cover that window in the cellar."

She smiled and pointed toward the bloodstain on the floor. "I can clean this up now?"

"Sure. We have our crime-scene evidence."

After she thanked the sheriff department's team, offering them some cookies on their way out the door—always the hostess—everyone left. Greg led Tillie into the kitchen, sat her down at the table, and grabbed the ingredients to prepare them a pot of hot buttered rum—with extra rum this time. They both needed one tonight.

He poured her the first one. "Drink this while I clean up the mess in the dining room and cover that window."

"Let me help." She started to rise from the chair to join him, but he pressed her shoulder until she resumed her seat.

"No, you sit tight. You've been through enough tonight. I've got this. I remember where everything is from the last repair. Just relax by the fire and sip your drink."

He rejoined her in the kitchen half an hour later after dismissing the deputy and setting things back to rights. Tillie looked shell-shocked, staring at the glowing log in the fireplace. He lifted her mug from her hands and refilled it before pouring one for himself.

Without a word, she accepted the second toddy and drained the mug like it was milk. He grinned, sitting down across from her at the table.

Her voice grew raspy as she said, "I can't believe Mark would do this."

"Did he say why?" Did Tillie give the guy a chance to talk before she shot him? *Damn, I'm so proud of her.* He hadn't been sure she could shoot as well as she said, but she had proven his doubts had been all wrong.

"Turns out he's the grandson of Mrs. Foster's first husband."

Greg couldn't wrap his head around the possibility he was related to the man. He didn't even remember Gram's first husband's name, but Peterson rang no bells.

No way was he related to Peterson. "Gram made no mention of any child of hers other than my mother, and Dr. Foster was her father."

She nodded. "Mark's mother was the daughter from that man's second marriage." That would explain why Peterson hadn't sounded familiar.

Thank God that dirtbag wasn't related to him by blood. "The names Gram used for her first husband in her journals hadn't been at all flattering. Clearly, she hadn't thought much of him. Judging by the epithets she labeled him with, he'd cheated on her."

"Mrs. Foster kicked him to the curb after a couple of years."

Tillie remained quiet a long while, staring blankly at the hearth, until her hand began to shake again. He stood and closed the space between them, picking her up.

She grabbed him around the neck to hold on. "What are you doing? My ankle's fine!"

Without saying a word, he carried her into the parlor where he sat down with her on the sofa and pulled the afghan around her trembling body. Adrenaline drop was a bitch, and he knew the best remedy was simply to hold her tight and let her body recover slowly. "Let's just sit and cuddle until the shock of the night wears off."

Tillie remained rigid a moment before resting her head on his shoulder. He held her tighter, and she sighed. Greg stroked her temple and into her hair, making shushing noises. His hand traveled down her arm, under the afghan, skin on skin. So soft. Her body shook less as he brushed his hand along her thigh.

"That's it. Just relax. You're safe now."

He'd thought she'd fallen asleep when she said, "I've never been so scared before in my life. When he broke the bolt and came to the doorway here, I was hiding behind the chair in the corner over there."

She pointed. "If he'd come in to search the room, he'd have found me."

"Shh. Don't think about that anymore. It's over." But if Peterson ever came near her again, the bastard wouldn't survive. Greg would pound him to within an inch of his life *then* shoot him. He'd never been a violent man, but his own rage simmered below the surface.

Tillie's hand slipped from the afghan and stroked his cheek, repeating, "Shh. It's over now for you, too."

He grinned as he searched her smiling face, wanting to kiss her more than ever before, but knowing she needed nothing more than to be held and cared for after her ordeal. She was no longer trembling, though.

Before he took advantage of the situation, he said, "Time to get you into bed."

"I couldn't sleep a wink. Whenever I closed my eyes, I have to relive the fact that he forced me to *shoot* him."

"Then we'll have to do something to distract you from worrying about it anymore tonight."

"Like what?"

He had a number of ideas, but still didn't want to take advantage of her in a vulnerable moment. "Why don't we go upstairs?"

She scrambled off his lap, taking the afghan with her, and he stood, taking her hand in his before starting toward the front stairway.

"No. Let's go to my room. I've already made up Amelia's Suite for my guests arriving Friday—er, this afternoon, actually." They wouldn't be here for hours but if she wanted him to take her to her own bedroom, so be it. Without warning, he halted her steps and pivoted her around to face him.

Just this one.

He started to lower his face to her upturned one, but she placed her finger on his lips. "Kisses aren't allowed."

Seriously?

Okay, she was right. What was the matter with him? Being so close to her made him crazy.

She grinned. "At least stolen ones aren't, unless you pay the price."

He'd pay anything for another kiss with Tillie. "And what price might that be?"

Tillie pointed up, smiling. "Before you kiss me under the mistletoe, tradition says you have to remove one of the berries."

Greg glanced up to find a ball of the seasonal greenery with white berries dangling from a ribbon from the ceiling light fixture. A slow grin spread across his face. She appeared to be more aware of her surroundings than he.

About two dozen white berries remained on the kissing ball. He reached up and plucked one off. Then another.

"Hey, only one kiss per ber—"

His lips ground against hers, cutting off her words. They had a lot to discuss, but damn it, he'd almost lost her tonight. He needed this as much as she did. He held the back of her head and deepened the kiss. She tasted of rum, and the kiss went straight to his head.

When he pulled away, releasing her lips momentarily, he found he wasn't ready to end this. He kissed her again, and she wrapped her arms around him, letting the afghan fall to the floor. When she broke the kiss, she was gasping to fill her lungs.

He stripped the decoration of a few more berries before lifting her into his arms. He'd steal a few more kisses upstairs. While he'd have to let her walk up the narrow pie stairs herself, he needed to keep his arms around her in the worst way.

He carried her through the birthing room and to the stairway in the dining room. "After you," he said as he set her down again, climbing the stairs after her. At the top, he placed a hand on her shoulder and spun her around gently, cupping her chin as he tilted her head upward. Her eyelids drooped as if expecting another kiss, but he'd better cool it this close to her bed. She needed to be pampered tonight after her ordeal, and his libido was already running at top speed.

"Would you like me to run you a bath?"

She shook her head. "I'm just going to change and crawl into bed." A blush crept up her neck into her cheeks. "Thanks for everything, Greg. Good night."

Oh, sweetheart, you aren't getting rid of me that easily.

He yanked down the quilt, blanket, and top sheet and faced her. "Which side do you want?"

Her eyes opened wide in surprise. "I beg your pardon?"

"You heard me correctly."

She cocked her head. "I, um, usually sleep in the center of the bed."

Greg grinned. If she thought that would deter him… "Sounds cozy, but you might want to keep a little more space between us." He cupped her cheek, brushing the pad of his thumb over her warm skin. "After being on the road twelve hours straight, I'm not in the mood to sleep in a chair or on the floor."

"But—"

"Which. Side?"

She glanced at the bed and then at him. "Left," she whispered.

"Perfect. Do whatever you need to do in the bathroom while I grab my bag from the Rover. I'll join you in bed shortly and then don't intend to let you out of my sight." Perhaps, if she heard him say it enough, she'd get over her shock.

Tillie opened her mouth, no doubt to argue, but no words spilled out.

That's my girl.

* * *

Greg planned to sleep with her? Or was he hoping for much more? She had mixed feelings, especially given the fact her emotions were so raw. But one thing was certain—she didn't want to be alone tonight.

Tillie made her way to the bathroom to prepare for bed. She wasn't in control of her emotions at the moment and didn't want to do or say anything she might regret later. They hadn't talked about what happened two nights ago yet, although she'd never been happier in her life than when she saw Greg standing outside the door, worry lines on his forehead and his eyes full of concern.

When she came out of the bathroom again, she wore her semi-sheer 1930s smocked and pleated negligee under her robe. Why she didn't have a flannel granny gown for such a night she didn't know, but she'd always enjoyed sexy vintage lingerie. It wasn't as though he hadn't seen it before—at least twice. She'd been wearing it that night in the kitchen while baking bread, though she'd kept herself hidden under an apron or her robe. Then there was the time after she'd injured her foot.

Somehow, tonight it seemed much more intimate, though. They'd reached a new understanding. He'd come back despite her having literally pushed him away out of fear or insecurity or whatever it was.

Her head hurt trying to analyze it now.

Footsteps on the stairs sent her in a beeline for the bed, shedding the robe as she ran. Before she could jump in and cover up, though, Greg entered the room, and she watched him set his bag on the floor. He gave her the slowest once-over ever. Her nipples hardened under his scrutiny, and a grin broke out on his face.

"I appreciate the choice of gowns."

"It's what I usually sleep in."

"I remember." His grin widened and something lascivious glinted in his eyes. "Now, slide between the sheets, Tillie."

Squaring her shoulders, she laid some ground rules. "I'm not on birth control and in no shape to make love tonight anyway." Not that she would.

He grinned. "Good, because we both need sleep more than anything else right now."

A flush crept up her neck into her cheeks. Why hadn't she kept her mouth shut? Her knowledge of intimate relationships with men would fit in a teacup. Without another awkward pronouncement to broadcast his awareness of her inexperience, she crawled between the sheets.

Greg tucked her in, reminiscent of the night he'd done so after she'd sprained her ankle. Would he kiss her goodnight on the forehead again?

I hope so.

Instead, he reached for the lamp on the nightstand and turned it off. Hiding her disappointment, she closed her eyes when he went into the bathroom. Couldn't see anything anyway. Trying to predict the man's actions was an impossible task. He kept her on her toes, well, at the moment, her back.

The doorknob squeaked, and she opened her eyes again to light from the bathroom spilling into the bedroom until he flipped the switch. Greg rounded the canopy bed to enter it on the other side. Feigning sleep, she closed her eyes, uncertain what was expected of her in such a foreign situation.

"Roll onto your side."

Which way—toward him or away?

A gentle nudge indicated he wanted her to face away from him. Good. Less intimidating—not that she could see much of his face in the dim light. She'd let him continue to call the shots.

His hand stroked her bare arm softly, raising thrill bumps in the wake of his fingertips rather than calming her nerves. If he expected her to sleep, he could think again. This was no way to make that happen.

"Relax. Close your eyes." His soothing voice lulled her into following his instructions. "That's it. Let everything go. You're safe now. No one is going to hurt you."

She drew a deep breath and released it slowly. Until Greg, she hadn't had anyone take care of her since before Mrs. Foster passed. He'd been there for her from the night she'd fallen from the ladder and throughout the many weeks of recuperation that followed. Maybe she wasn't the only reason he'd returned to the inn, but Tillie had to admit he'd been very attentive to her needs the entire time.

"I want you to picture yourself on a warm summer morning out in your herb garden snipping off a few sprigs of rosemary or thyme for the delicious meal you're preparing for us later."

But you won't be here in the summer.

"What has you tensing up?"

"Um, the weeds in my garden."

He chuckled as if he knew she wasn't being honest. "Okay, let's move to another image. How about flying high in your swing, not a care in the world? The wind is blowing your loosened hair." He lifted her hair from the pillow, sending tingles across her scalp, and released it to slip through his fingers and fall over her shoulder and back until she shivered from the delicious sensation. She loved having her hair played with, not that anyone had since Mrs. Foster had fixed it before taking her to church on Saturdays or Sundays as a child.

"Mmm."

At her moan of encouragement—bordering on ecstasy—he buried his fingers in her hair and massaged her scalp. Stress ebbed from her body, and she sighed. Greg's hand focused more on her hair, so why had he set off a throbbing at the apex of her thighs?

Wanting to face him, she started to flip onto her back, but he stopped her with a hand to her shoulder. "I'm going to take care of you, Tillie. After what you've been through tonight, it's understandable you'd be tense, but I know something that will totally relax you. Let me do this for you. I don't expect or want anything in return. Tonight is all about you—restoring your body and mind—and giving you pleasure."

Certain that they could work out whatever needed fixing in their relationship, she nodded. She wanted to surrender fully, trusting him not to take more than she wanted to give.

His hand stroked up and down her bare arm before moving around her waist and pulling her against the hard planes of his body. Did he want to relieve mental stress or the physical kind building between her legs? An answer of sorts came when he cupped her breast, only making her tense up in surprise.

Her chest burned before she remembered to take a breath. He

kneaded her flesh and rolled a nipple between his finger and thumb. The already erect peak swelled even more in his hand.

Unfamiliar sensations built up, electrical impulses zinging between her breasts and her—"Greg!" she begged, unsure if she wanted him to stop or to do much, much more.

"Yes, sweetheart?" How could he sound so calm and matter-of-fact?

"Are you trying to drive me crazy or help me fall sleep?"

"I'm trying to relax you."

"It's not working."

He chuckled, a sound coming from deep in his chest because she felt the vibration to her core. "Give it time." He continued to touch her with only one hand, running it in a sweeping motion from her waist to her hip. When he began tugging at the gown, moving it upward in slow, methodical motions, she lifted her hips to aid him. He might think her wanton, but she didn't care. She wanted whatever stress relief he intended to dish out.

Her heart beat so loudly the sound of blood whooshed in her ears; she didn't know if he spoke any other words. She ought to stop him now, but what if she never experienced this with him?

When the hem reached her hips, his hand stroked her bare thigh, upward to—

"Are we missing something again, Miss Tillie?"

She groaned with embarrassment. "I don't wear panties to bed. Too confining."

"For an old-fashioned woman, you're full of surprises, aren't you?"

She heard the suppressed laughter in his voice, which made her a little giddy. "I guess you'll have to find out." Where had that teasing tone come from? She'd been laid bare tonight. What else could she possibly have to hide? She'd always been an open book.

"I've always enjoyed a challenge." He pressed a kiss to her shoulder blade. "First, tell me if any places on your body are off-limits to my hand."

She shook her head, although it seemed a little late to ask.

"Answer me out loud so there aren't any misunderstandings."

"No. Nothing is off-limits to you, although I reserve the right to change my mind."

"Fair enough." She heard the smile in his voice.

His hand swept up under the gown and across her belly, bypassing the place she'd expected him to home in on. Wanting to give him better access to her throbbing core, she rolled onto her back. Her eyes had adjusted to the lighting, and she could make out his eyes and the smile she'd known was there. His head rested in the palm of his free hand while he leaned on his elbow as though gazing down at her on a picnic blanket.

"Any place off-limits to my lips?"

Her heart thudded to a stop momentarily then raced away. "No." The word stuck in her throat, and she repeated it to make sure he didn't stop what he was doing.

His head lowered to her face, and he took her lips with his, tenderly, tentatively at first. Tension mounted as his hand moved to her thigh again, spreading her legs open for him. Her hips bucked upward involuntarily, and her cheeks flushed in embarrassment. Her body had a mind of its own—and knew exactly what it wanted.

Was she ready for this? Whatever *this* was. She had no clue, but intended to see how far he'd go with his unorthodox relaxation technique. So far, she was wound tighter now than when he started, but the promise of release convinced her to see if this could work.

She giggled against his lips, and he pulled away.

"What's so funny? I'm trying to be serious here."

"Sorry. Please, don't let me stop you. I'm sure it's only a case of nerves."

His lips nuzzled the valley between her neck and shoulder, and the smile left her face. *Oh dear God! That feels so good!* Turning her head more to give him better access, she moaned. He knew all the places that set her body on fire for him.

He separated the fabric at the vee neckline, her breasts remaining covered by the tight-fitting, sheer panels. His lips trailed over her shoulder and breast as though she wore nothing at all, licking and kissing along the way. He cupped her breast and took the chiffon-covered nipple into his mouth. Tillie arched her back and gasped.

His hand moved from her pelvis to her other shoulder as he pressed her down on the mattress. His delicious mouth released her. "Lie still. Hold onto the spindles in the headboard." He sounded like a drill sergeant.

She responded appropriately. "Yes, sir."

The vibration of his chuckle reverberated against her breast as he gently bit her swollen peak. She groaned as sparks of electricity shot through her breast, up her neck, and into her jaw, but she tried her damnedest not to move. Had some other woman been instructed to hold onto the spindles like this in the past, resulting in the one being broken?

His hand crept downward over her gown to her bare thigh and between her legs. It took every ounce of willpower she could muster to keep from positioning her hips closer to his hand. Instead, she waited for him to touch her while her stomach twisted into knots of anticipation. His fingertips drew circles on her inner thigh, mimicking the motion she wanted him to do to another part of her body—and soon. Between his mouth, teeth, and his magic hand, she was losing the ability to think rationally.

Ever so slowly, his fingertips inched closer…closer…until at last he brushed them lightly over her curls.

Don't you dare move! She didn't want him to stop until she exploded, which wouldn't take long at this point.

But rational thought did break into her thoughts. She wouldn't repeat the mistakes of`the other women in her family. She stayed his hand with her own. "I'm not on anything."

He pulled away from her breast, not immediately letting go of her nipple, which stretched until he released it with a plop. "I thought we'd already established that that's not a problem. Tonight isn't about me coming inside you. It's about me taking care of your needs."

"Oh." She couldn't hide her disappointment, despite the fact that's what she said she wanted. Her mind was in turmoil and her body under siege.

"Not that I won't want to make love with you one day, but for now, my only intention is to give you a screaming orgasm—or two. So stop worrying."

"Okay." She couldn't string two words together to save her soul at the moment. Wait, yes, she could. "Thank you." No man had ever made her feel so cherished before in her life.

"Scream for me when you come. Don't leave me guessing."

He was so certain she'd be able to reach that point. Tillie didn't want to doubt his abilities, but decided to prepare him for certain failure. "I'm sorry, but I don't think I'm able to—"

Her words became muffled as he pressed his lips against hers, his tongue delving inside forcefully, mimicking the lovemaking she hoped they would be able to enjoy one day. She no longer dreaded sex as she once had. Not with Greg, anyway. His fingers parted her folds before one dove between her cleft and brought moisture up to her throbbing core.

Yes!

He continued kissing her as his finger made infuriatingly slow circles around and around the bundle of nerves until she reached up to grab the sides of his head to let her tongue explore his mouth, not wanting him to stop too soon. Her next moan buried itself in his mouth as she tasted him—minty. More sexiness than one man deserved.

All mine.

The thought caught her off guard, but in this moment, she truly felt that he belonged to her. She'd fight to keep him.

Their tongues tangoed until he pulled away. "I appreciate your enthusiasm, but where are your hands supposed to be?"

Every time he ordered her to do this or that, she only became more turned on. She didn't like his bossiness outside the bedroom, but could definitely get used to it in here.

She released his head and clasped her hands on the spindles above her head, away from temptation. *For now.*

Once more, his mouth and hand moved to bring her to the peak of excitement, her entire body thrumming, begging for release. Not being in control of when she would come only heightened her desire that much more. She'd never have prolonged the gratification with her own hand—but that waned in comparison.

Her mind receded as he bombarded her senses. When he stopped putting pressure against her pulsating nubbin, she screamed in frustration. He only chuckled before his finger slid downward and entered her as his thumb worked its magic on her sex.

"Yes! Don't stop! Oh God!"

Thank God her hands were occupied or she'd give in and pull him on top of her and take this where she wanted to go. The tension mounted until her hips rose off the mattress as she screamed her release.

Chapter Twenty-Four

Greg watched her face as his finger entered her. Her eyes closed as her teeth latched onto her lower lip, as if biting back words. She'd kept her hands where he'd told her to, giving her the chance to fully experience the orgasm without worrying about pleasing him.

Not that he wasn't rock-hard for her.

She was so tight around his finger. He tried not to think about how she'd feel around his…

Her eyes opened wide as she locked her gaze on his.

"Let yourself go, sweetheart."

She stared at him as he coaxed the climax from her, but in the final moments, her eyes closed, and she screamed.

He must be grinning like a Cheshire cat for bringing her off. He'd been uncertain as to whether he could after what she'd been through tonight, but her responsiveness and trust made him feel like a hero.

Maybe he hadn't been here to protect her when she needed him, but he sure as hell could take care of her afterward.

Damn, Tillie was the sexiest woman he'd ever been with, perhaps because she wasn't aware how much her naiveté mixed with a touch of sex kitten turned him on. Her seeming inexperience left the promise of many more nights discovering what her body responded to.

"That was…amazing…" Her eyes opened. "Thank you."

He bent his head toward her and kissed her on the lips, not wanting to ignite another firestorm in her—or him—nor wanting to analyze what just happened. A chaste goodnight kiss. "Get some sleep now."

Her forehead wrinkled with worry.

"Being able to do that for you and to spend the night with you in my arms is all I need right now."

"But I—"

He pressed his finger to her lips. "Shh. Close your eyes and lie on your side so I can spoon up against you."

She didn't move until he gave her a nudge. "I feel selfish for leaving you—"

"Tillie. Go to sleep." *Before I change my mind.*

He placed a kiss on her shoulder through the sheer fabric, her skin beneath his lips warm and sweet. Yanking the hem down over her knees, he closed the space between them, grabbing a pillow and tucking it in front of his arousal rather than against her round… *Don't go there.* He wrapped his arm around her waist and pulled her to him, knowing sleep would be elusive for him tonight.

After a while, her breathing slowed. At least one of them could catch a few winks. He'd hoped to take her mind off what had happened downstairs and apparently had succeeded.

What would happen tomorrow? Where did they go from here? He closed his eyes, relaxing for the first time in days.

Sunlight streamed into the bedroom from the window across the room, and Greg blinked his eyes. How had he managed to fall asleep? He glanced at his watch. Eight-twelve. Tillie probably hadn't slept this late in ages, but she'd not fallen asleep until nearly five-thirty. He'd continue to hold her to let her catch a few more hours of sleep; then he'd take her out to breakfast.

"Greg?" she whispered.

So much for letting her sleep in. "Yes?"

She scooted onto her back and smiled up at him. "I've been lying here for ages waiting for you to wake up. But I didn't want to disturb your sleep."

Too late for that.

He shook his head with a grin. Always worrying about everyone else. "You should be sleeping."

She reached up and stroked the stubble on his cheek. "I slept more soundly than I have in ages, thanks to…you." Her cheeks grew rosy. "I thought I'd be up all night reliving that horrific moment in my dining room, but I didn't even dream about it." She grinned. "Your relaxation methods were wonderfully distracting."

"Good. There's more where that came from."

Tillie smiled and glanced away. "I should get up and start breakfast." When she moved to rise, he pressed her shoulder against the mattress.

He brushed the hair from her forehead and captured her attention once more. "We're going out. I'm taking care of you today, but you know I can't cook."

"I don't mind at all. It's what I do best."

"Tillie, where's the best place to eat around here—after your kitchen?"

"Mammy's in Bardstown, but it's not necessary. I could have it ready in thirty minutes, faster than it would take us to drive there and wait for our food."

"Humor me on this—but before we get dressed, there's something I want to talk with you about." She furrowed her brows and cocked her head. Might as well blurt it out. "I think you need a change of scenery for a while."

"Okay, okay," she said, grinning. "I'll go out with you to breakfast if it's that important to you."

Time to say what he'd come here to tell her.

* * *

Tillie followed the hostess to a booth near the fireplace. After ordering, Tillie met Greg's gaze over her coffee mug. Her heart pounded as if she was in mile twenty-six of a marathon. The trauma of last night was over. This morning, she wanted to know why he'd returned.

"Thank you again for everything, Greg. You can't begin to know how much it meant for me to have you with me last night."

He took a sip of his black coffee. The lines around his eyes were evidence of all the sleep he'd lost. And soon she'd have four guests staying at the inn.

"About why I came back."

"I was going to ask that next." She grinned before growing serious again. "You couldn't have known Mark would break in last night."

He shook his head. "I've been miserable without you, Tillie. And knowing that it was all my fault only made matters worse. If I'd come out and told you what I'd been looking for, I might not have lost you."

She wasn't so sure she'd have accepted his explanation given her own fears, but after the way he'd taken care of her last night, not only that incredible orgasm but the tenderness with which he'd taken care of her and held her in his arms for hours, she needed to make her own confession to him.

"I wasn't honest with you." Greg said the words before she was able to formulate her own. He took another sip, his gaze never leaving hers, and set the mug down again. "In retrospect, the reason's ridiculous. Let me start in the beginning. While laid up after a cycling accident, I finally began to read Gram's journals. They'd sat around for more than a decade for whatever reason. With her chronicling every little detail, I don't understand why she didn't write about you."

"Her eyesight was very poor later in life. I don't even recall seeing her journaling after I moved in."

"Makes sense. But I digress. In the '30s, before she met and married my grandfather, she had an obsession with Jesse James."

"Not surprising, given his connection to her home."

He shook his head slightly. "Not Jesse James the historic outlaw. I'm saying she spoke about him as though she knew him personally."

Tillie furrowed her brows as her heart pounded harder. She knew what was coming, but couldn't get the words out beyond the knot in her throat. "How can that be? He was killed in the 1880s. She wasn't born until 1911."

"That expression you're giving me is part and parcel of why I didn't tell you this earlier. Because you'd think I'd lost my marbles. Hell, I wanted to impress you and get to know you better."

Tell him, Tillie.

"Greg, I've always loved Jesse James lore myself. I read the claims of the man in Texas saying he'd been the real Jesse James and lived to be more than a century old. But I also saw where his claims had pretty well been debunked."

"What if someone else who kept a lower profile all those decades was the real Jesse James? What if, as Gram claimed, he was in your house in the 1930s and did leave some valuable treasure behind?" He grinned, sheepishly. "Okay, yeah, I knew this wasn't going to come out right. But hear me out."

Hear him out this time, Tillie.

She drew a deep breath, trying not to filter his words through the prism of her childhood as one of the crazy Hamilton women.

Greg continued, seemingly unaware of her discomfort. "Finding out that he survived being murdered by Bob Ford and that my grandmother might have known him—even that a friend of hers had become his nurse at the end of his life—has fascinated me for months." When she opened her mouth, he held up his hand to stay her words. "Before you shoot me down on this theory again, hear me out."

"I think I've done enough shooting for one day."

He bent over to kiss her, then both grew serious once more.

In this day and age, someone spouting ridiculous claims wouldn't be deemed crazy—merely eccentric. Could she let go of a lifetime of shame?

Honestly, the only person's opinion that mattered to her anymore was Greg's.

"Gram went on and on about his leaving behind something that would prove once and for all that he didn't die in 1882."

Could Mrs. Foster be referring to her grandmother? "What do you think it might be?"

He ran his fingers through his hair, but he smiled, perhaps encouraged that she wasn't calling *him* crazy this time. "Not a clue. She mentioned being gifted a Smith and Wesson that had once belonged to him in payment for medical care by my grandfather. But yours was manufactured long after his official death, so there's no provenance that would tie it to Jesse before or after his assassination."

"How old would he have been in the 1930s?"

"He was born in 1847, so eighties or nineties. I doubt Jesse continued to rob banks and trains later in life, assuming he didn't die at the hands of Ford. My guess would be he led an exemplary and solitary life to elude discovery, incarceration, or even being shot for real by someone going after another reward."

Tillie's heart pounded as she tried to respond with the words she needed to say, but struggled to get them beyond the knot in her throat.

"Greg, I am so sorry. I didn't want to hear talk about Jesse James being here long after he was killed because it fed into the crazy tales my mother told me when she was at her most delusional. Everyone in town labeled her and my grandmother insane for believing they descended from Jesse James without being able to prove it. I've spent a lifetime trying to distance myself from those claims, so you just opened up old wounds."

"I'm sorry, Tillie. If I'd known, I'd never have—"

She pressed her hand against his lips. "I want you to know that I don't care anymore. If you feel compelled to keep searching the house for clues, then do. It won't change who I am or the person I'll continue to be."

"The night you caught me snooping in the basement, I had some time to spare, and"—he held up his hand as if taking an oath—"I swear that I'd already decided that night would be the end of it. Hell, I'd searched everywhere, and as I sit here today, I'm convinced it was all some amusing joke to my grandmother. Clearly, she had a lot of fun with it over the years."

"You mean that you aren't curious anymore?"

"Cross my heart." He reinforced his words by doing so over the center of his chest with his pointer finger.

Maybe she truly could put Jesse James and her mother and grandmother to rest.

Greg's face sobered as he reached across the table to take her hand. "Tillie, I failed to realize the night you sent me packing. You asked if I'd come back here to search for treasure. Yes, that was one of the reasons." The old hurt returned, but he held her hand and didn't let her retreat. "In retrospect, I realized that I misunderstood which time you were referring to. Yes, initially, that's why I came to Kentucky, but as I replayed that scene over and over in my head in the days that followed, I think you probably were talking about why I returned after taking Derek home. After you injured your ankle."

How could he interpret her words any other way? Regardless, he had. "So you came back for me, not fame and fortune?"

"Tillie, my search was over. I'd already found the only treasure I wanted in the entire world."

Her heart skipped a beat.

"I found it in a pile of leaves in your front yard. In the kitchen one night wearing the sexiest nightgown I'd ever seen. In bites from a plump, ripe strawberry on the Dinner Train." He smiled, lifting her left hand to his mouth and gently kissing her ring finger, leaving her misty eyed. "You're the only treasure I found, Tillie, and the only one I'll ever want."

To be called his one and only treasure melted her heart. She wanted so badly to tell him how much he meant to her, but the old fears of being rejected reared their head. Only he hadn't rejected her, she'd sent him away. This man was worth risking her heart and soul for, even if it meant she'd have to make herself vulnerable to him.

Trust him.

He hadn't said the words, but she took a leap of faith. "I love you, Greg." The whispered sentiment spilled out before she could rein it in, followed by more heartfelt expressions of her feelings. "I don't know when I started loving you—but, like you, a good bet would be the time you caught me when I tumbled into the pile of leaves with you. Or the night you found me baking bread and we shared our first toddy together. And, no, I can't rule out the train ride when you shared your strawberry with me."

She smiled, her fingers holding onto his. "It doesn't matter when love started to grow inside me. All I know is that, when you were gone, a part of me was missing."

Greg stood, not letting her go, and came around to her side of the booth, prompting her to scoot over to make room. He stared into her eyes and brushed the hair from her forehead and temples. "You don't know how long I've wanted to hear you say that. I guess I had my own reasons for holding back. But when I'm with you, it's as if I'm on the precipice of some grand adventure—and as if I've found what's been missing from my life." He kissed her with such tenderness the welling tears spilled from her eyes.

When their lips parted, he surprised her again. "Spend Christmas with me back in Minneapolis."

While his abrupt invitation caught her off guard, Tillie mulled over the pros and cons. Could she abandon the inn and her guests to travel so far away for a few days of happiness? Could she be that irresponsible? She sighed. "I appreciate the invitation. Really, I do. I'm tempted to drop everything and go home with you, but the week after New Year's would be so much better." She all but shut down the inn the first of the year for months, except for Valentine's weekend.

The light left his eyes, and he released her hand, leaving the cool air to touch her now. "I understand how important your business is. January would be nice, too. I just wanted to give you that special Christmas with snow and all the trimmings nature can offer."

Oh, she'd love to experience a Christmas like that, especially with Greg.

"Come on, Tillie," he coaxed. "I'll even give you that *Christmas in Connecticut* sleigh ride."

She punched his arm lightly. "You aren't playing fair!" Doing so at Christmas would be magical. But hadn't he said earlier he could arrange for it in January, too? Still, she couldn't get the image of the horse-drawn sleigh out of her mind. She and Greg cuddled together under a lap robe with her hands warm in her muff. No, now she pictured her hands wrapped in his larger hands, tucked under the blanket, until his hand strayed lower…

She pushed that thought away, but not before her body tingled with awareness.

Was the inn more important than pursuing this relationship? Was she putting her guests—many of whom she barely knew—ahead of someone she might potentially want to spend the rest of her life with?

But not everyone could take their work on the road like he could. This could spell the end for her inn if people complained. What if things didn't work out with Greg? Well, she'd always landed on her feet, and if she had to start again from scratch, she could do it.

Did she follow her heart or her head?

She knew what Mrs. Foster would want as clearly as if she heard her speaking at this very moment.

Simultaneously, they came up with the same idea, "I could ask Beckie to help fill in."

"Why don't you let Beckie fill in as hostess?"

Apparently, the two of them were on the same wavelength as far as finding a solution to this problem.

Greg grinned. "She loves the inn as much as you do—well, almost." His eyes twinkled again at the prospect of her accepting his invitation. "Do you have any guests staying over the actual Christmas weekend?"

She brought up her calendar in her mind. "Actually, no, but I have some leaving the morning of the twenty-third."

"If Beckie can run things that one morning, you could still be there to greet them when they check in. We could leave the morning of the twenty-third and be in Minneapolis by early afternoon Christmas Eve.

I don't want you sitting in the car for a straight-through drive so soon after your ankle sprain."

Always putting her needs first. Everything hinged on Beckie, but it was a possibility.

Embarking on this trip was completely out of character, but oh-so-tempting. She met his gaze. "I never thought I'd admit this to anyone, Greg, but the inn has begun to feel more like a prison to me than the haven it once was, especially when you were gone. I've merely gone through the motions of running the place." Watching him drive away again without her would kill her.

"I'm not asking you to leave for good. We're talking about a few days tops. Minneapolis will definitely be a change of pace from Samuels and even Bardstown, but the city isn't so large that it's lost the unique character in each of its neighborhoods."

An adventure like this might allow her to spread her wings and stop hiding away from the world—and Greg. Of course, she had no intention of ever leaving her inn for good. However, after last night's trauma, escaping for a while might give her the perspective and distance she needed to make some decisions about what she wanted out of life when she returned.

"Your grandmother often told me she learned so much in her travels that could be incorporated into her daily life when she came home. Memories of those adventures stayed with her to the very end as she shared some of them with me."

Tillie wanted to reminisce like that for years to come—not only the places she'd visit but the memories she'd make with this man.

Staying in a single man's home seemed—well, no worse probably to prying eyes than his staying with her at the inn when no one else was around.

It's the Twenty-first Century, Tillie. Stop behaving like the lonely spinster you've painted yourself to be all these years and embrace the modern single woman you are. She intended to start living in the present instead of the rose-colored past that wasn't as perfect as she liked to portray it. The world had changed since her mother's and grandmother's days.

Thank goodness!

So would they share a bed?

"What are you grinning about?" he asked, the hint of a smile on his own lips.

Heat infused her face. "Oh, nothing." Last night, Greg showed her he'd put her needs ahead of his own, something she hadn't experienced with a man before.

It's now or never, Tillie.

"Okay, okay!" When Greg tilted his head and quirked a brow, she realized she'd spoken aloud to her benefactor, rather than in her head. Tillie grinned, shrugging. "Okay, *if* Beckie can cover for me on the twenty-third, I'd love to spend Christmas weekend with you."

He smiled, the corners of his eyes crinkling. "You'll be the best Christmas present ever." He bent to kiss her again briefly. "And if she can't and we don't make it to Minneapolis until Christmas Day"—he shrugged—"so be it. We can celebrate Christmas Eve in Illinois or Wisconsin on the way."

"As long as we're together, anywhere would be fine with me."

"Maybe you can stay a little past the weekend. When do your next guests arrive?"

Again, she pored over the calendar in her mind. "The twenty-eighth, and then I'm booked solid through the morning after New Year's." One matter needed to be discussed still. "What about Derek?"

"Nancy and I agreed that he'd have his Santa Christmas at her place and I'll see him that weekend—either the night before or the night of."

"Oh good. I don't want to come between you and Derek. I hope I'll be able to spend time with him, too. I've missed him."

"Do you think he'd forgive me if I had you that close and didn't let you see each other?"

"Well, we can't have him disappointed." Tillie would have been equally sad. That Derek genuinely liked being with her warmed her heart.

Her mind was running a mile a minute, though. All but certain he was the man for her, she wanted to get to know more about Greg. Where better to learn than where he lived?

Their intimate moment ended all too soon when her phone buzzed in her pocket at the same moment the server brought them their food.

She cleared her throat of the emotions threatening to overwhelm her at the decision she'd made. Taking out her phone, she glanced at caller ID. "It's Beckie. Let me take this. You go ahead and start."

He shook his head, but indicated for her to answer the phone. "Hi, Beckie. I was going to call you this morning."

"Tillie, are you all right? The whole county's buzzing about the shooting."

Tillie smiled and gave her the rundown on what had happened.

"I'm coming over. I'll help you clean up the mess and do whatever you need."

"No need. Greg cleaned it up last night."

"Greg's with you?"

"Mm-hmm."

"Thank you, Jesus," Beckie prayed.

Tillie smiled at him, certain he'd been able to hear Beckie's strong voice. "Speaking of Greg, I need a huge favor." She told her friend about Greg's invitation, and before she could even finish, Beckie asked what she could do to keep things afloat while Tillie was away. They talked dates, and everything would work out as she and Greg had hoped. With her guests in Beckie's capable hands, what did she have to lose?

The only thing she *was* certain of—if she didn't go, she might not get a second chance. She wouldn't risk her chance at happiness.

Chapter Twenty-Five

Greg reached across the SUV's front seat to brush the top of her hand with his fingertips, and a tingle shot up her arm. They'd left the inn and her guests in the capable hands of Beckie yesterday morning and were now somewhere in southern Minnesota at noon on Christmas Eve.

The heightened attraction between them still raged inside her even though they hadn't had sex yet—or perhaps because of that fact. But she appreciated his taking things at a slower pace. Her gut told her she and Greg had something special together, but her fear of having her heart broken if it didn't work out was a hard thing to shake.

Trust him.

She wanted to, so desperately. The relationship had blossomed since the night of the shooting. She no longer worried that they'd merely been caught up in the emotions of the aftermath. One look or a gesture would pass between them and most of her doubts washed away. For a moment.

They'd enjoyed other intimate moments when they had the house to themselves, which had only been a couple of days. Her poor mistletoe ball was stripped bare of berries, the last one biting the dust this morning as he pulled her into his arms before they loaded up the luggage for the trip. Those long, lingering kisses they'd shared under it had been worth the loss of every single one.

Some days, he'd sense how exhausted she was from trying to prepare for and keep up with her guests and would sit her down in a chair to massage her neck and shoulders. His hands took out the knots but also left her wanting more—perhaps a continuation of what they'd done the night he'd given her an orgasm. True, they had few occasions to be alone, but when they were, she found herself touching him more boldly. A hand on his thigh while curled up together on the sofa in front of the fire, a kiss at the back of his neck as she passed by him while he was catching up on e-mails on his laptop. The more she let down her guard and inhibitions, the closer she came to wanting to take that big step and making love with him. But he'd insisted they take it slowly, which was killing her.

Last night, he'd hinted in a change in their relationship this weekend. The anticipation of whatever that meant had kept her on edge and achy between her legs all the way to Minnesota.

"I still can't get over the video you showed me of when I was in the cellar." Greg brought her thoughts back to the present. She'd debated whether to bring it out, since it had been the reason for their breakup, but was happy with her decision. "It definitely didn't feel like Gram at the time. I know you're going to think I'm still hung up on the whole Jesse James treasure thing, but if I had to place a bet, I'd say it was him."

He hadn't shared that with her as they'd watched the video. She turned toward him. "What makes you think that?"

He shrugged. "Nothing specific. Just a gut instinct."

Tillie smiled. "Well, the image of the apparition was too blurry for me to even know if it was man or woman. But I wouldn't mind it being Jesse."

He squeezed her hand. "How do you feel having so many ghosts hanging around?"

"If they don't bother me or scare away my guests, they belong there as much as I do. A house as old as that one is bound to have picked up lingering spirits along the way. I hope they aren't stuck there, though. Your grandmother, for instance. She deserves a happy afterlife."

"Agreed." He drove on a few more miles and said, "Should make it to my place soon. Let's stop at the grocery to pick up whatever we might need for the next few days, but I'd like to go out for an early dinner before places close rather than have you slaving away on Christmas Eve."

"Sounds good." She'd be content with a bowl of popcorn in front of the fire, to be honest.

"I'll be picking up Derek later tonight." They had the cargo area filled with wrapped gifts. She'd enjoyed shopping with Greg this week, especially when she needed to escape the house when the memories of that terrifying night bombarded her out of the blue. "Tomorrow, I thought we could go down to Minnehaha Falls in the afternoon as part of our Christmas Day celebration. It'll be cold but, if the sun comes out, well worth it."

She couldn't wait to see the falls. No doubt, they were solid ice now given how frigid the temperatures were at their last stop to refuel.

After they stopped at the grocery, he drove about five more minutes and parked in the drive of a Queen Anne Victorian overlooking a large frozen lake.

"What a gorgeous house! I can't wait to see the inside." Of course, he would live in a historic house, given his love of classic architecture.

"Thanks. It was my obsession during that first year after Nancy asked me to move out of our old place. I figured I'd renovate this one and flip it when we got back together, but..." He squeezed her hand. "Sorry. Why don't we unload the car?" They both exited at the same time, and he pointed behind them with his thumb. "That's the Lake of the Isles, which is famous for being in the opening credits of *The Mary Tyler Moore Show*."

"No way! I've been watching reruns of that show recently on cable."

"The house they used in the first couple seasons for where she lived is just down the street. I'll point it out to you. Happens to be for sale if you have a few million dollars to spare."

"Oh, I'm not that big a fan. More a sentimental one. It was one of my mother's favorites."

She was grateful Greg didn't ask to talk about her. Tillie had made peace with her mother long ago, although the sadness still hurt her heart. At least Tillie had a few good memories of her.

He carried her suitcase up the walkway to the porch and opened the door, waving her inside. "Why don't we warm you up with something hot first while I get the fire started?"

"Sounds heavenly! Point me to the kitchen, and I'll start a pot of coffee. I think we're going to be up late tonight."

He showed her where everything was and how the coffeepot worked before returning to the living room. The white batten-board cupboards with glass doors gave the kitchen an old-fashioned charm. His appliances were stainless, but the countertops were stained wood. An interesting mix of old and new, not unlike the man who owned this place.

When he entered the kitchen again, she was filling the two mugs. "Perfect timing."

Before picking up his, he tugged her into his arms, and she looked up at him. "Meet me under the mistletoe?"

"I'm not sure where that is." She grinned, her heart not requiring anything to drive the need for a kiss with him.

He pulled a sprig out of his pocket and held it over their heads. "I picked up some in the gas station before we hit the freeway."

"My, you think of everything," she said with a breathy whisper.

"A throwback to my Boy Scout days." He leaned down and captured her lips.

When they separated after he'd stripped the sprig of every last berry, they carried their coffee into the living room, and she gravitated to standing in front of the fire. "It's real wood!"

"Like you, I want the smell of real wood in a fireplace."

"A man after my own heart." They sat on the sofa and stared at the flames while sipping their coffee for a moment. "I can't believe I'm in Minnesota. We've been so busy at the inn this past week I've hardly had time to breathe."

Greg set his mug on the end table and wrapped his arm around her. She leaned her head against his chest. "I'm glad you came home with me, Tillie."

Being with him soothed her soul. This house had a calming effect on her, too. She hadn't thought any other house would achieve that, but maybe it didn't matter where they were as long as they were together.

She couldn't shake the feeling she had Mrs. Foster to thank for moving Heaven and Earth to reunite them as adults. While here, she hoped to have a chance to read Mrs. Foster's journals, which would be like having another visit with her dear friend. Well, as close as she would get to being with Mrs. Foster again.

But, in this moment, she wanted to focus completely on the man seated next to her.

* * *

Greg took her shopping for winter gear at the Mall of America where they ate supper. Good thing he knew his way around, or she'd have wandered aimlessly for days in the monstrously big mall without finding a single thing.

"We'll have our Christmas in the morning and focus on Derek's tonight."

"Sounds perfect." She'd managed to pick up some fun and educational things for him locally and online. She couldn't wait for Derek to open them.

"When are you picking him up?"

"About seven. I thought I'd take him for a ride to see the lights before he gets here and sees the ones I put up in the yard."

"He's going to love them. I can't wait to see him again."

"Why don't you come with me to pick him up?"

She wasn't sure she was ready to meet his ex-wife. Although if she and Greg continued to date, she supposed she would have to eventually. "Um, I was thinking I'd bake some cookies for you while you're gone. Then I can spend more time with you and Derek."

"If I didn't know how much you'd enjoy making them, I'd insist that you stay out of the kitchen. But Derek and I would love some of your homemade cookies." He smiled and pressed a kiss on her cheek.

Before he left to pick up his son, they quickly set up the small tree they'd purchased with its minimal decorations. None of the decorations held any memories, but it gave them a place to display the presents they'd bought and wrapped before leaving Kentucky.

Making her way to the kitchen, she spent a good twenty minutes searching for things. Spices were hidden in the cabinet next to the sink. Measuring cups across the room near the fridge. And cookie sheets? On top of the microwave, of course. *Why didn't I think of that sooner?* Perhaps if she'd been taller, she'd have spotted them immediately.

Clearly, the man's kitchen wasn't set up for efficiency. Regardless, she was wrist-deep in cookie dough when the front door opened.

"Miss Tillie!" Derek came barreling through the house calling her name.

"In the kitchen!"

She glanced up from the tray of oatmeal cookies and wiped her hands clean before opening her arms to receive the lovable projectile.

"Derek, it's so good to see you again! How've you been?"

"Good, but I have a new boo-boo on my knee."

"Oh dear! Do you need me to give it a kiss to make it all better?"

"Silly, you can't even see it with my pants on."

"Kisses are magic. Point me to the correct knee, and my kiss will power right through the denim."

The boy crawled onto one of the kitchen chairs and presented his knee, which she promptly kissed. "All better now!"

"That's cool! Just like magic!" He hopped down and returned to his daddy's side. "Did you see the Grinch outside, Miss Tillie? He was stealing Daddy's lights!"

"No way!" she said, her eyes wide in shock.

"I told him, 'Oh no you don't, Mr. Grinch!'"

"Well, good for you!"

Greg had worked on the light display for almost two hours. While not elaborate given his time constraints, next year, she imagined there would be thousands more lights on the house and in the yard.

Greg came over to her and wrapped his arm around her waist before bending to place a kiss on her cheek. "Mmm. You smell good. Like vanilla."

Tillie smiled, not intending to give away her secret.

"I getta kiss Miss Tillie, too!" Tillie laughed as she bent down to present her other cheek to the younger Buchanan, feeling loved by them both.

"Daddy told me he had a tree. Look what I brought for it." Derek reached into his coat pocket and ceremoniously pulled out something wrapped in a paper towel.

She wasn't sure what it was until he'd started unwrapping it, and she caught a glimpse of the hat. "The toy soldier!" She blinked away the ridiculous tears at seeing the beloved ornament again. "Let's go put him on the tree." She placed two trays of cookies in the oven and set the timer before the three went into the living room.

Derek chose the perfect spot for the ornament.

The evening flew by as Derek opened his gifts and the three of them played games, built a Spiderman set with Legos, and munched on cookies until after ten o'clock.

Greg looked at his watch. "Whoa, son! I'd better get you home before Santa skips your house tonight!"

"I'm not yawning."

"Derek, you know Santa won't come if you're awake," she reminded him. "Tonight of all nights, you'll want to be in bed before midnight."

He weighed Tillie's words a moment before hurriedly rounding up his things. Tillie rode along to Nancy's, despite her nerves. She lived on a street filled with decorated houses. Derek must love it here. "The

Grinch didn't steal the lights on my street, Miss Tillie!"

"It's almost Christmas," she said. "I don't think he'll be stealing any more lights tonight."

"I had fun playing the hippo game, Miss Tillie." He yawned.

Tillie blinked away more unexpected tears and faced toward her window. "So did I, sweetie. Maybe I'll beat you next time!" He'd changed the rules on them with every game so that he always came out on top. Clever boy.

Greg reached across the front seat to squeeze her hand. "You okay?"

She turned toward him with a smile and nodded. "Just being sentimental. Holidays do that to me." He stroked her cheek before glancing in the rear-view mirror. Indicating the rear seat with his thumb, he smiled. "He's already out."

Being together with Greg and Derek made her wistful for something she'd never had—a family of her own.

Santa, maybe you can put one under the tree for me tomorrow.

But in reality only one family would do. And they lived seven hundred miles away from the place she already called home.

Chapter Twenty-Six

Tillie awakened the next morning to some wonderful, thoughtful gifts from Greg—including one box containing Mrs. Foster's journals. She met his gaze over the box while sitting with her knees bent and legs tucked to her side. Joy lit her eyes. "I could never accept these. I'd love to read each and every one, but let's consider this a loan."

"No, I insist they go home with you. They belong back in her house, and I know you'll take excellent care of them."

She opened one of the leather-bound journals. Ironically hitting on a Christmas Day entry from 1941. Wow, that was just a few weeks after the attack on Pearl Harbor.

Elmer and I enlisted today—he in the Army and me in the WACs. We can't be sure when we will see each other again if we're separated, which we most surely will be. But with our beloved country under attack, how can I not help by serving with our brave boys in uniform?

Tillie glanced in Greg's direction again. "I may not come up for air for months."

"They really are compelling reading."

"It will be like history coming to life before my eyes."

She skimmed a few pages until he prompted, "That's not all I have for you, but the rest aren't under the tree."

She tore her gaze away and grinned. "Sorry to get so absorbed and ignore you. I have gifts for you, too. Nothing as grand as these, though." She reached onto the cloth-covered tree table and picked up the rectangular box for Greg. "Here's something for you to open."

"It's heavy." He tore the wrapping paper off with abandon. "Smells like bourbon." When he reached the shoebox and opened the lid, even she could smell it. "One of your fruitcakes!" She wouldn't have given him one if he hadn't tried it along with her guests last week and loved it, saying it wasn't like any other he'd ever tried.

"It will last a year or more if you keep it wrapped and in a dark place."

"Believe me, it won't last that long, although I'm going to weigh about three-hundred pounds by the time I finish it. Maybe we can have some tonight with our hot toddies."

Kneeling so she could reach the boxes she'd stashed toward the back of the tree table, she pulled them out and tried to decide which he should open first. Selecting the smaller of the two, she handed him the one with the first-edition book she'd found on an online auction site.

"Open this next."

"Now what can this be?"

She nearly bounced with excitement as he tore off the paper and opened it. "Be careful. It's fragile."

"Now you tell me." More gently, he took the tissue wrapped book out and glanced at the face of it.

"Frank and Jesse James?" He met her gaze. "This book's ancient. It must have cost a fortune."

She waved away his concern. "Not as much as you'd think. But it is a first edition 1880 copy of *The Life and Adventures of Frank and Jesse James*. I guess Frank got top billing in those days." She smiled as he focused his attention on the book. "It was published two years before Jesse's murder."

Almost reverently, he opened the cover to the title page and read silently. The pages had frayed at the edges, but the text hadn't faded a bit, unlike the gilding on the cover.

Smiling, he leaned over and kissed her on the lips. "Thank you. I'm going to enjoy reading this cover to cover and cherish it forever."

She loved his spontaneous kisses and had missed snuggling with him in bed. He'd given her a long speech about respecting her boundaries and not wanting her guests to think badly of her, so he'd slept on a cot in the office that first weekend together. But he had yet to return to her bed, as much as she wanted to invite him there.

When he'd given her the option of sleeping with him here or in his guest room, though, she'd chosen the latter. While the drive up had only amplified how much she wanted his touch and his lovemaking, seeing how far apart they lived and knowing they weren't going to be together very often only led to worrying about those long stretches of separation in between visits. If things didn't work out, it would kill her.

She blinked rapidly at the tears welling in her eyes, thankful his attention was on the story of the James Gang. *Turn the page.* She probably should have put the tickets before the title page rather than after. Finally, he went to the next page and lifted out the printout.

"Two tickets to the Maker's Mark tour," he read, meeting her gaze. "Their family has a connection to your inn, doesn't it?"

She nodded. "Jesse James's stepfather was a cousin to the man who owned my house at one time, another country doctor, in fact, like your grandfather. Having trusted family in the area is probably why Jesse hid out there." She wouldn't go into the history of the T.W. Samuels family distillery or that a descendant had founded the distillery with the famous wax-coated caps in the neighboring county. "I want to take you on the tour because they have on display the gun Frank James surrendered to lawmen at the Samuels general store down the road from my house."

He smiled at her again. "You've outdone yourself with the perfect gifts, Tillie. I can see you put a lot of thought into them."

"I had so much fun shopping for them." She pointed to the box of Mrs. Foster's journals. "But these aren't exactly chopped liver, you know. I'm going to dive into them later today, for sure. And I can't wait for our trip to Minnehaha Falls this afternoon. Thank you in advance."

He smiled enigmatically. "I'm looking forward to that, too." When he began to collect his gifts, she stopped him.

"Wait. I'm not finished giving you your presents yet." She picked up the long box and handed it to him. This next one would probably make her cry even harder.

*   *   *

Greg felt a little overwhelmed at the incredible gifts she'd made or found for him. He almost hated postponing his big gift until later, but it would be so much more special then.

He carefully took the paper off this one, fearing he might find another fragile gift inside. While wrapped in a shirt box, it was much heavier than one would be. Lifting the lid, he found an old photo scrapbook and carefully removed it from the box.

Even before opening the cover, he knew to whom it had belonged. Sure enough, the first page included photos from the '40s of Gram, both in her uniform and with another man in uniform. No doubt, his grandfather, as they had enlisted at the same time.

The backs of his eyelids stung, and he blinked away the discomfort as he turned the page. Realizing he hadn't said anything to her yet, he looked up, cleared his throat, and uttered a lame "Thank you."

Riveted once more to the pages, he glanced down and saw photos of a baby on a bed. The white on black script below the photo identified the infant as his mother with a simple "Margaret at three months."

"My mother." He met Tillie's expectant gaze again. "This is going to be a bittersweet journey for me, watching my mother grow up through these pages."

"I'm sure she'll love seeing it."

He shrugged. "She and Dad are on a cruise in the Mediterranean right now. I'll show it to her when they come home." He needed to mend fences with them and at least let Tillie meet them. Like it or not, once they met and got to know Tillie, they'd have to accept that the subject of Gram would come up. If they couldn't, then perhaps he'd have to sever any ongoing relationship with them.

"It's been in the office all these years," Tillie said, breaking into his thoughts. "I've pored over its pages more times than I can count, especially when I was missing her. Unfortunately, the span of years in the album is fairly limited. Mostly photos of your grandparents and mother, although there are some of a friend of hers named Caroline and her daughter. The little girl is only shown up to 1941. Of course, while Mrs. Foster was serving in the war, she wasn't keeping up her photo albums. And Caroline disappeared after Christmas 1945."

"Gram mentioned Caroline a lot in the journals." Greg looked at the photos on the page, across at Tillie, and then back at the album, furrowing his brow. *Uncanny.* "Did anyone ever tell you that you're the spitting image of Caroline Simpson?"

"No. Well, toward the end, Mrs. Foster sometimes called me Caroline by mistake, but I assumed she was thinking of her friend as she looked back on her life."

"Look at the photos again," he said, handing her the album. "Don't tell me you can't see the resemblance."

Tillie leaned closer to the page and scrutinized the images before her eyes opened wider. "It's like looking into a mirror. We even share the same chin and nose. How did I not see that before?"

"Maybe you'll figure out the connection as you read Gram's journals, but I should warn you, she didn't have a very happy life. She'd been left pregnant by a man who died before marrying her. Sadly, Caroline committed suicide shortly after Gram returned from her service in Hawaii."

"That explains why Caroline disappeared from the photo albums. I wonder..." Her face became ashen.

"Are you okay?"

She nodded rapidly, but he could tell she was upset.

"What's wrong?"

Her voice came out barely a whisper, and she didn't meet his gaze. "My great-grandmother committed suicide after the war. Do the journals say what happened to her daughter?"

"She was given up for adoption when she was between five and six years old."

"How can this be?"

He leaned closer and stroked her arm, worried about what was going on. "What is it?"

"You don't suppose…"

"Suppose what?" What the hell was the matter?

"At the risk of you thinking I'm nuts or grasping at straws, there's something I need to tell you." Drawing a deep breath, she began. "My mother told me how tragic my grandmother's life had been and that she'd been given up for adoption at the age of five to a family in Bardstown. I never knew my great-grandmother's name, but am almost certain now that it was Caroline." She didn't give him a chance to respond. "Do you suppose Mrs. Foster recognized her in me that day I showed up with her cat?" Was that the reason she'd taken to Tillie so quickly?

"I don't see how she wouldn't have seen the resemblance, but Gram had a big heart and probably would have invited you in anyway."

Tillie glanced away. "I hope so. It wouldn't change how she made me feel so special, even if she initially connected with me because I looked like her deceased friend."

"I can't wait to dive into these journals. While initially I simply wanted to learn more about Mrs. Foster's life, I have a feeling that they're going to uncover all kinds of things that explain a lot of the missing pieces in my own. For instance, the women in my family never painted a positive picture of the men in their lives. So many disappointments."

"I'm glad you didn't hold that history against me."

She smiled, and he relaxed for the first time since he'd pointed out her resemblance to Caroline. "Let's just say you surmounted my misgivings with your incredible heart—and magic hands." She winked at him before picking up the journal she'd been reading a few minutes ago. He watched her a while then turned another page in the photo album. The two of them were lost in their memories and treasures until his stomach growled.

"I forgot all about breakfast," he said.

"It's in the oven on the timer actually and"—she glanced at the watch pinned to her breast—"should be ready in about ten minutes. I brought my sourdough starter from home and made my traditional Christmas morning coffee cake. Oh, and all the fixings for jam cake that we can enjoy with Derek tonight."

"What's jam cake?"

Her eyes opened wide. "Seriously? You've never heard of jam cake?" Why did she think he was asking? "I can see I still have many, many of your grandmother's wonderful recipes to share with you. Imagine a dense spice cake with blackberry jam and black walnuts mixed in the batter before baking, topped with caramel icing."

"Sounds amazing. I'm going to need to ride my bike a hundred miles to work off all that food, but it'll be worth it."

Everything Tillie did was steeped in love and tradition, two things sorely missing from his life before now. They had a lot of interests in common, too. He flipped the pages of the album and watched his mother grow up before his eyes. She didn't have the hard edge to her that was all he could remember about her. What had made her so cold and bitter?

He couldn't wait for them to meet Tillie. Time to let go of the past and mend fences with her. Maybe she could help Mother see Gram through different eyes.

He glanced over at Tillie, who was grinning at something she read in the pages of one of the journals. He'd been won over by Tillie's sunny disposition and kind heart from the beginning, once he forgot about the preconceived notions he had about her.

When a buzzer went off in the kitchen, she jumped up. "I'll take the cake out and start another pot of coffee."

The woman never took a day off. He had no clue what life would be like if she accepted his proposal or even where they might live, although he leaned toward moving to Kentucky rather than bring her up here other than for visits. Being an innkeeper was her life. He might prefer to keep her all to himself, but that would be selfish of him.

After breakfast, he bundled her up in her new outerwear, kissed her again, and drove out of the city limits. He hadn't told her about this part of the day yet, but like most visitors, she probably expected the falls to be outside the city anyway and wouldn't suspect anything until they arrived.

* * *

The landscape surrounding them on all sides was a sea of white sprinkled with bare-limbed trees and snow-tipped evergreens. "I can't believe all this snow on the ground," Tillie said, "yet even the rural roads are cleared."

"We're more used to handling snow up here."

"I'll say. This would have me snowed in for days, if not longer, back home. Any chance of snow today? Not that you need more to call this a white Christmas!" She couldn't remember a whiter—or more special—one.

"It's overcast enough to snow." He didn't sound happy about the prospect, but snow must get old when it lingered on the ground four or five months of the year.

Greg turned into a private lane rather than the falls park. She gave him a sidelong glance and saw the smile on his face. "I have a little surprise for you."

Parking next to the barn, she saw a dark-haired woman harnessing a gorgeous black horse to a two-seated sleigh.

"Greg! You remembered!"

"How could I forget? You've made me sit through so many of your favorite movies, and I don't think a single sleigh ride passed without a sigh from you."

She unbuckled her seatbelt and leaned across the seat to plant a kiss on his cheek. "I love you. Thanks so much. Oh my gosh, I can't believe I'm going on an honest-to-goodness sleigh ride!"

Tillie exited the vehicle and waited for him to join her before they went over to the horse and its owner. They wished each other a Merry Christmas, and Greg introduced her as a partner in his architectural firm. Karen then introduced them to Betsy.

Tillie reached up to pet her. "She's a Friesian, isn't she?"

"Yes, indeed. I see you know your horseflesh."

"Well, I'm from Kentucky," she said with a shrug. "Although these aren't common there, I saw some at the Kentucky Horse Park once. Such beautiful horses."

"Greg, do you want to drive or enjoy the ride?" Karen asked.

"Oh, no way am I taking the reins. I'm trying to impress my lady here and know my limitations."

My lady. Tillie's heart soared at his words, and she smiled up at him.

"Oh, I almost forgot. Wait here." Greg hurried off and returned from the Rover with something hidden behind his back. With a courtly bow, he presented it to her.

Tillie squealed. "My muff! You thought of everything." She accepted it from him and leaned closer to whisper in his ear, "But I'd been fantasizing lately about having you keep my hands—and other parts—warm on a sleigh ride."

The mixture of torture and desire in his eyes made her giggle. Greg helped her onto the rear seat and climbed in beside her.

Karen handed them a small basket covered in a plaid cloth. "There are two containers of hot cocoa in there, plus some of my Christmas cookies."

"Wow, you don't miss a thing," Greg said. "We really appreciate you doing this on Christmas Day."

"No worries. Betsy loves any chance to romp in the snow, and with what fell overnight, she's going to have a blast."

Once the two of them were tucked under a mound of lap robes, Tillie curled against him, and he wrapped his arm around her, perhaps for added warmth, but more likely to create an intimacy between them.

The horse-drawn sleigh set off around the side of the barn and through an open gate.

"Oh, Greg. This has to be the most incredible Christmas I've ever had. And it keeps getting better."

Greg reached inside the hand muff and squeezed her hand. "The best is yet to come."

"There's more? Oh yeah. Minnehaha Falls!"

How could the day be any more magical? The soft ringing of the sleigh bells, the slicing of the sleigh's runners, and the crunch of the horse's hooves were the only sounds surrounding them. Karen kept her eyes on the horse and their path, giving them their privacy.

Tillie's right hand ventured out of the muff and onto Greg's thigh. When he didn't protest, she teased him by moving it closer to his—

"Is that what Barbara Stanwyck would be doing?" he asked her.

"I think so. Of course, they couldn't show that due to the movie censors of her day, but you'd be surprised what lives the Hollywood stars led on and off the set." She was rambling now and focused again on his face. He grew serious and closed the gap between them, his lips warming her frigid ones and melting her from the inside out.

He lifted the top quilt up to her shoulders, and she thanked him before his hand cupped her breast. Apparently, he hadn't covered them to make her warmer. She supposed turnabout was fair play, and soon he squirmed in the seat.

"Okay," she whispered, glancing toward Karen to make sure she wasn't listening to them. "Let's call a truce. Until later."

"Later, it is."

Oh my! The promise in his words assured her it would keep getting better.

And then something cold landed on her cheek. And another. "It's snowing! How did you manage that?"

Greg chuckled. "I don't think I can take credit for the snow flurries."

"Well, if you ask me, you've made this day perfect in every way."

* * *

Greg hoped he hadn't planned today's activities in the wrong order, but loved her enthusiasm during the sleigh ride. All too soon, though, they were at the barn once more. Judging by her red nose and cheeks, forty-five minutes in the cold air probably was enough. He cranked up the car's heater to warm her before their next excursion outdoors.

Halfway there, the sun came out. Crazy weather, but he'd take it as a good omen for the rest of their adventures today.

They arrived in the park a little after noon.

"What a beautiful park. I can't believe we're right in the middle of Minneapolis."

"Most visitors are surprised by that as well. I wish you could see it in the summer or fall sometimes, but what I want to show you won't wait until then." While what he planned was slightly illegal, he doubted anyone would be patrolling the falls on Christmas of all days because crowds would be thinner than usual. Which is how he wanted it. An audience would ruin the moment.

"Watch your step." Greg held on to her elbow as he guided her over the icy sidewalk toward the steep steps.

"The sign says we shouldn't go beyond this barricade."

"It's okay. I'll steer us clear of any danger."

She held onto the icy metal railing and cautiously traversed the stairs, avoiding the slick spots. He tried not to bang the backpack against the cliff walls. When they reached the landing, the two of them turned toward the falls together. He hadn't been down at this level during winter since he was a kid.

"Oh, Greg! I've never seen anything so magical!" Her awe and excitement only made the experience more special for him, too.

Greg pointed the way toward the falls. "Let's head that way, but be careful. I'd carry you, but am afraid you'd be hurt if I slipped."

"We can get closer?" she asked.

"Oh yeah. With our rubber-soled shoes, we can walk on the frozen creek right up to them. You're in for a treat."

As they meandered along the path, he was happy to see that the icicles hadn't blocked the entrance to the cave, which might have interfered with his plans. Not that he'd have let a small stumbling block deter him today.

"Greg! There's an opening in the falls over there!"

Seizing the opportunity, he took her elbow once more. "Watch your head as you go inside."

"They let you go behind the falls?"

"It's a once-in-a-lifetime experience I'm dying to show you." Tillie bent over and walked under the icy arch. "Watch your step. There's usually a dry shelf behind the ice. Aim for that."

"I see it!"

* * *

After settling onto the dry bedrock, Tillie took in the wavy wall of ice to her right with wide-eyed wonder. In some places, the ice was intense blue, while others shone a mossy green. "Unbelievable!"

Behind the falls, it felt as though they were the only two people in a prehistoric land. *Surreal.*

"Minerals account for the colors," he explained.

"I've seen seasonal ice falls on Kentucky interstates before spilling out of the rock. They have the blue and green colors, too. Of course, I couldn't go behind them and see the light shining through like this. Pure magic. I can see why it was important to you that the sun be shining."

"Special is an understatement, not unlike the lady I'm showing it to."

She smiled up at him before giving in to the intense desire to touch the ice with her gloved hand. Oh no, that wouldn't do. She shed the glove, and her right hand brushed over the water, frozen with gritty bits of rocks and dirt barely visible to the eye. When heat from her hands began melting the surface ice, she pulled away.

Greg took her hand and brought it to his lips, kissing the top and sending warmth through her. He didn't let go, though, and turned it over to place a kiss on her palm. When she expected him to release her, he continued to hold onto her hand until she met his gaze.

"Tillie, it seems impossible, but you're even more beautiful in this light."

Heat suffused her cheeks. In Greg's eyes, she truly felt beautiful.

"Before we're interrupted…" Greg wrapped both hands around hers and stared deeply into her eyes. His sudden seriousness made her heart skitter to a stop for a second. When he bent to one knee, her jaw dropped.

Oh God. He isn't!

"Tillie, you have brought light and love back into my life. Perhaps 'back' isn't the right word because I don't think I allowed myself to feel love from any woman before I met you."

When she opened her mouth to say something—although she had no idea what—he brushed a finger over her lips, leaving them tingling again. "Wait, I have more to say." He took a deep breath, released it, then reached into his pocket to take out a ring box. After retrieving the ring, he held it up to her.

She couldn't see all of the detail through the tears in her eyes, but the silver art deco pattern boasted a large diamond in the raised center surrounded by smaller ones.

"Matilda Hamilton, would you do me the great honor and privilege of becoming my wife and partner in this life?"

All of the logistical problems they faced went out of her mind. She wanted so badly to find a way to make this work. "Oh yes, Greg. It would be *my* honor."

He continued, almost as if he hadn't heard her response. "I know we need to work out logistics, including where to live, but as long as we're bound together in a solid commitment, we can make those decisions together."

Tillie smiled. Such an adorable, romantic man. She'd never have guessed it from their first meeting, but at least now they seemed to be on the same wavelength.

"This might seem sudden, but—" His eyes opened wider. "Wait...What? You said 'yes'?"

"Yes! Of course I did!"

He stood abruptly and wrapped his arms around her. "I'll make sure you won't regret this for a moment."

Catching him off guard charmed her. Now it was her turn to shush him with her free hand. "Shut up and kiss me."

His gray eyes twinkled. "First, give me your left hand." He removed her glove and placed the ring on her third finger. She brought it up for a closer view.

"With your love of all things vintage, this old-European cut platinum ring seemed perfect. While it isn't one of Gram's, somehow I can see it on her finger."

"Actually, it's quite similar to her engagement ring. Of course, she never removed that ring, and I asked that she be buried in it."

"Perhaps she led me to the jewelry store where I found it."

The asymmetrical design had two ladders, which prompted her to ask what the significance was.

"While I don't want to remind you of that nasty fall, if not for your ankle injury and allowing me to take care of you, I'm not sure we'd have been able to get close enough in such a short time. Oh, I'd have been back in the months or years to come—as a guest—but I don't want to waste another minute of my life without you in it."

"I did have a problem letting people help me, as if that was some sign of weakness." She still did perhaps, but relying on Greg and Beckie over the past five weeks had freed her up to pursue this relationship and to be here with Greg at this moment. She stared at the ring again. "But what about the other ladder?"

He grinned. "That one signifies how Gram came down the stairway from Heaven to aid in bringing us together."

"Oh, I'm so grateful she did, too." She tilted her hand, and the colors of the falls made the diamonds take on their hues. "What's this?" A masquerade mask?

"Well, that's to remind me to promise I'll never masquerade as someone I'm not. You can count on me to always be up front with you." Where would her life be now if he hadn't taken a notion to come to Kentucky and debunk her, though? "I'll always put you and family ahead of everything else and will be fully present in our relationship every single day."

Before her heart burst with too much unspent emotion, she pulled him toward her by the zipper of his coat and kissed him again. When they separated, she asked, "How on earth did you find time to shop?" They'd barely been apart.

"I was still in Kentucky. You'd think I'd have searched for hours, but it was as if I'd been drawn right to that online shop. I had it overnight delivered to Karen, and she tucked it inside the basket she gave us. I quickly pocketed it while you were marveling at the snow flurries."

He'd been planning this for at least a week, maybe longer. "You couldn't have picked a better way to propose, Gregory Buchanan. I'm going to be pinching myself for weeks to make sure I'm not in a dream."

"Maybe this will convince you this is real." He lowered his face to hers and tightened his arms around her. Despite being in a cave made of ice, her body grew warm in all the right places as their lips met and his tongue delved between her lips. His kiss set her body tingling with want and awareness.

He broke away sooner than she'd like, and they both tried to catch their breath as steamy vapors hung in the air between them.

Greg started to replace her glove before she stayed his hand. "I'm not finished looking at it. Don't worry. My hand's not too cold. It's so beautiful!"

He smiled and stepped back to remove the pack and set it on the ground. Opening it, he removed two plastic champagne glasses and handed one to her.

"Sorry, no alcohol or glassware allowed in the park," he explained.

She grinned. "You didn't seem concerned about ignoring those trespassing signs."

Greg shrugged with a grin. "I figure the penalty for breaking this rule will be stiffer than trespassing. Anyway, I brought sparkling white grape juice in a plastic bottle in the hopes we'd be celebrating today."

She giggled. How could he think she wouldn't say yes? Okay, maybe she'd let some of her insecurities bubble up, but was it this morning or last night where she'd finally admitted to herself she didn't want to be apart from him? Perhaps they hadn't known each other long, but how could one set an arbitrary gauge to measure love? "I'm not much of a champagne drinker anyway. Let me hold your glass, too." She held out her hand freeing him to pull out the bottle and ceremoniously remove the foil wrapper on the screw top as though it was the real thing before half filling each of their glasses. Some men might choose to be pretentious in a moment like this, but Greg didn't seem care. Hadn't she convinced him to play dress up in public? Maybe he was losing his need for proper decorum. If he intended to live with her in Kentucky—yet to be determined—he'd definitely need to be more relaxed.

"To our future."

They clinked glasses. "To our present, as well," she said. "I think we've worried too much about the past and things beyond our control."

"Agreed. I intend to remain firmly planted in each moment we have together."

"Me, too, wherever we are."

After they emptied their glasses and returned everything to the pack, he gathered her into his arms for one more kiss until the sound of laughter on the other side of the iced-over falls told them their privacy had come to an end. As they made their way back up the slippery stairs, she asked, "When do we tell Derek?"

"Tonight would be perfect."

"Hon, I love that boy as if he were my own." Everything was happening so fast, but all the pieces would continue to fall into place. This felt more right than anything she'd ever done before.

Greg smiled, and his love shone from his eyes. "I love you so much."

"I think that's been well established," she said, brandishing the ring on her left hand with a grin before growing serious. She touched the center of her chest. "But the real proof is right here in my heart."

"Let's go home. We still have hours before I need to pick up Derek."

She hoped his near-lecherous grin meant they were about to share his bed, because all of her doubts about whether they could be a couple for the long-haul had vanished when he'd asked her to marry him.

Chapter Twenty-Seven

She said yes!

As Greg drove to the house, he couldn't contain the sense of joy—and relief—that lingered at hearing her accept his proposal. They ditched their boots by the door, and he built a roaring fire in the living room before pulling her into his arms and tilting her chin back for a kiss. He could spend every minute for the rest of his life kissing her. Maybe they'd be lucky enough to have half a century or more to live and love together.

Trailing his lips across her jaw to her earlobe, he placed nibbles and kisses, lingering a little longer over the pulse at the side of her neck. Her tiny gasp made him hard in an instant.

"Ravish me, Greg."

He released her ear and put some space between them until he met her gaze with a grin. "I thought that's what I was doing."

"Oh! And you're doing a fine job. I only want to make sure you don't stop on account of me this time."

"Music to my ears. Let's stay in here." He spread a blanket on the floor and tossed some pillows on it, motioning for her to join him. "This will be the warmest place in the house right now."

"I'm not the least bit cold."

"Well, you might be after I remove all your clothes."

She reached for the buttons at the top of his flannel shirt. "And I yours. But don't worry. We southern girls know how to keep our men warm."

"I thought that was at night?"

"I'm improvising. Work with me."

He chuckled and let her finish unbuttoning his shirt before he reached for the hem of her sweater and nearly yanked it off of her. Beneath was a long-sleeved T-shirt, which he removed as well. She kept her arms raised, and he saw she still wore the thermal top he'd purchased for her yesterday. He shook his head.

"You told me to dress in lots of layers."

"Yes, I did. How many more layers might I expect?"

"You'll have to find out." Her impishness ramped up his excitement even more.

He made quick work of the thermal and saw the skin of her shoulders and her torso covered in a silky camisole. No bra. *Sexy as sin.* "Beautiful," he said, cupping her breasts.

Her somewhat sultry smile excited him even more, if that were possible. "I figured, with that many layers, my skipping the bra today wouldn't be noticeable."

"I'm sure noticing now."

She cocked her head. "Aren't you going to remove my top for a better look?"

He shook his head. "Not yet. Anticipation is good for us both."

He'd forced himself to take things slowly until now, but all of the touching, petting, and kissing—not to mention that orgasm he'd given her the night of the break-in—only heightened their desire for one another. Turning Tillie's passion into a raging fire made him war with himself between rushing and taking his sweet time.

Patience needed to win out. Hadn't he waited for weeks, condoms at the ready, just in case? Now that they were committed to being together long-term, he planned to savor every second.

Tillie dragged his shirtsleeves down his arms. Apparently, she wasn't on the same page. Oh hell. Neither was he.

Wait! He needed to seize control now, or this moment would end way too soon for his taste. He did unbutton his cuffs but still wore his long johns. When she reached for the fastening on his jeans, he took her hands and held them behind her.

"Slow down, Tillie." She looked up at him, furrowing her brow. "I love your enthusiasm, but I'm used to being in charge. If you keep it up, I'm afraid I'm not going to be able to hold off and give you pleasure before taking my own."

She relaxed, grinning. "Take me; I'm yours."

The damned woman had no clue how her words affected him. He released her hands, but she kept them behind her back as he bent down to capture her lips in a soul-searchingly slow kiss. His tongue explored her mouth then simulated what he intended to do with other parts of their anatomy before they finished here in front of the fire.

When his tongue retreated, her knees buckled, and he grabbed her upper arms. "Whoa!"

"Greg. Stop tormenting me!"

He chuckled. "Sweetheart, I've only begun. First, let's get you out of the rest of your clothes."

She reached for her waistband, but he brushed her hands aside. "Allow me." Kneeling before her, he hooked his thumbs into the waistband and simultaneously dragged however many layers she wore downward. When her lower belly became visible, he placed a kiss below her belly button. Her hiss encouraged him to lick her skin before revealing more of her delightful flesh to his gaze.

The auburn curls he'd had his fingers entangled in their first night in bed together sprang into sight next. Soon he would kiss and touch her there, but chose to wait until he'd rid her of the rest of her clothes. All except the camisole. God, he loved her penchant for sexy underwear.

With her hands on his shoulders for balance, she stepped out of the pants and leggings. He sat on his heels a moment, taking in her beautiful body in one sweep before he met her gaze. Her smile had faded somewhat as she nibbled on her lower lip. How could she be insecure about what he saw?

His hands took her by the bare hips, and he leaned forward to place a kiss on each one, still avoiding her mound. He couldn't wait to taste her. But with evidence of her slight insecurity a moment ago, he'd made the right decision not to be hasty, instead worshipping her body first and foremost.

He stood and kissed her. "So beautiful. I can't get enough of you." His hands stroked the skin bared above the camisole and meandered over the silky cloth to her bare hips. He tugged her to his hardness. "You can feel why I need to take this slowly."

"I never asked to be taken slowly. I want you inside me, Greg. Now." When his shaft jolted against her, she smiled, her eyes twinkling with what he interpreted to be a sense of empowerment. If she only knew.

"You are a sorceress. I should have realized I was doomed from the beginning." He bent to take one erect nipple into his mouth through the satin and nipped. She hissed, and he sucked her and the flimsy cloth into his mouth. Her hands grabbed his head, more to steady herself than to push him away. He nibbled to his heart's content before switching to the neglected breast and doing the same.

"Please, Greg. This is torture!"

His head retreated with her pebble peak before releasing it in a sudden plop. He grabbed the hem of the last article of clothing and yanked it over her head. He might have heard something tear. Tough. He'd replace it with something new later on. Dragging her onto the pillows and blanket, he drank his fill of her. The golden light cast a warm glow across her skin and the fire lit sparks in her hair—both the locks on her head and below.

"Spread your legs for me."

She brought her knees up into tents and opened wide for him. Her glistening lower lips called to him like a siren. Lowering himself between her thighs, he held onto one with each hand and brought his tongue down onto her thigh.

"Wait! I need to shower before you—"

"Relax. Your scent turns me on."

"Oh."

He could tell she was holding her muscles tight by the rigidity of her legs. He'd see what he could do about that.

* * *

No one had ever done this to her before. She wasn't sure she liked it, but when he hooked his thumbs and spread her open, his warm breath sent a riot of sensations through her. Her stomach clenched, while her knees tried to squeeze together only to meet the resistance of his head. She must be blushing furiously judging by the heat in her face.

His tongue touched her boldly, and her hips jolted up, heightening the thrill. When one finger entered her then another, she moaned. Between the swirling of his tongue on the bundle of nerves and the fullness inside, she didn't think she could hang on very long, but wanted this to last.

"Please, Greg. Don't make me wait." Tugging on his thermal-underwear top, she attempted to get him to stop and tried to pull him on top of her. He did stop, but only for a moment.

"Clasp your hands above your head and keep them there."

A thrill coursed through her at his forceful words. Much as he had in bed the night of the shooting, he took control with ease.

She felt the chuckle on his lips, probably at how quickly she'd complied. Clearly, he wasn't going to be swayed by her inhibitions. She might as well relax and enjoy it as his tongue drove her higher and higher. Panting in tiny breaths, she fought the urge to bury her fingers in his hair. She grabbed onto the edge of the blanket, twisting it in her hands. Her thighs squeezed his head—whether to keep him in place or to hang on, she couldn't say.

"Oh!" A jolt of electricity passed through her. He focused all of his attention there, and she bit her lip to keep from screaming. The pressure built higher and higher, but he didn't give her the release she now sought.

"Please, now! I can't stand it!"

A third finger entered her, and her legs began shaking as her climax built. When his tongue sent her over the edge, she screamed incoherently, the sound reverberating in her mind long after Greg joined her on the pillow.

"You're so sexy when you explode for me."

She gasped for air. "That. Was. Incredible."

"There's more where that came from if you aren't sated."

She lowered her hands and pushed herself upright. Some disappointment registered on his face before she knelt beside him and began tugging his long johns off. He grinned before helping her rid him of the rest of his clothes.

"Hold on." He reached for the jeans he'd left on the sofa earlier and reached into the pocket, retrieving a foil packet and rolling the condom onto his shaft before returning to her. "I've been carrying a few of these around for weeks."

That he cared enough to think of protecting her but didn't force her into anything she wasn't yet ready for made her heart swell with even more love for him.

His warm hand cupped her breast. "I can't keep my hands off you anymore."

"Who asked you to?"

He grinned and pinched her nipple, and she reached for his shaft. "I'd also like to find out what *this* feels like buried inside me. Deep, deep inside me." His member throbbed in her hand, and she laughed at the power she held over him.

His hand left her breast and brushed lightly over her skin to her mound. She wasn't sure she was ready yet, but the instant his fingers stroked her sensitive core, she found herself close to the brink again. Tugging him on top of her, his delicious weight left her wanting more. She waited, spreading her legs open as he settled between her thighs.

His member pressed against her cleft. He took himself in hand and brushed the tip to her bundle of nerves, nearly making her lose her mind. Bringing it back to her opening, he entered her a couple inches, pulled out, and ventured in deeper, each time a little farther, watching her face—for what, she had no clue—until he'd buried himself fully. She expected him to start pumping in and out, but he simply let her body adjust to his size.

The moment her body relaxed, he retreated and re-entered her, setting a pace that left her nerves teetering on the precipice, waiting for release. She hoped she could hold out until after he came. He wedged his hand between their bodies, but she grabbed his wrist.

"If you touch me there, I'll explode."

* * *

Music to his ears. "I love watching you come apart for me."

"But I want to experience the same pleasure watching you. Come inside me."

"I have every intention of doing so, but you're coming with me."

Her impish smile and the whispered "If you insist" heated the blood in his veins even more. His fingers stroked her gently at first, avoiding the most sensitive bundle of nerves. When the smile left her face as she concentrated on what he was doing, he began to piston in and out of her with increasing tempo.

Sex was like riding a bicycle. He was thrilled to know he could get right back in this saddle, too.

So freaking tight. He never wanted to leave the vise she gripped him in, so he delayed his orgasm as long as he could. She'd closed her eyes, passion pouring from every cell in her body, and he gave up on prolonging his pleasure. He pumped harder. Tillie's eyes flew open at the shift in momentum, and their gazes locked as he rode her hard, moving his finger on her bundle of nerves until her breathing became shallow and she closed her eyes again. Almost there.

So was he.

The tension built until the explosion ripped through him like nothing he remembered experiencing before. She screamed her release with him, which only fueled his to last longer. His heart almost burst from his chest as he came with her.

When she grimaced, he stopped touching her. She smiled. "It's a little sensitive at the moment."

"I'll bet. That was beautiful, as are you, sweetheart." Resting his upper body on his elbows, he kissed her, reluctant to leave her warmth just yet. Staring into her eyes again, he whispered, "Feels like I've come home at last after a long journey."

She blinked rapidly, but he saw the glistening tears welling in her eyes. "You complete me, Gregory Buchanan, plain and simple."

He'd stay like this all afternoon if they didn't have to pick up Derek in an hour or so. What would his son think about him marrying Tillie, especially if he decided to spend most of his time in Kentucky? Of course, he'd already given Nancy a heads-up about his proposing, because he needed assurance that his living in Kentucky wouldn't infringe upon his paternal rights. This might be an opportune moment to discuss the future with Tillie, because if she wasn't on board, that would pose a major problem.

He kissed her before rolling off and heading to the bathroom to dispose of the condom. Within minutes, he'd returned to the floor and settled her on top of him before cocooning them under the blanket. She rested her head on his chest, and he wrapped her in his arms. Could she feel his racing heart beating against her cheek?

Blissfully entwined between the blankets, he stroked her hair. "I talked to Nancy about us—and Derek."

She leaned up and searched his eyes. "What did she say?"

"She wished me well and hoped I'd found happiness at last. I told her I'd learned from the mistakes I'd made with her and didn't intend to repeat." He shrugged. "But I'm human. I may screw up at some point."

She grinned. "I'll hold your…feet to the fire if you do."

He smiled. "I have no doubt you will." He smiled before continuing. "We also discussed arrangements for joint custody of Derek."

Her eyes opened wide. "That's a big step for you. I know you questioned how good a father you were when you first came to the inn."

"That's changed now, too. I know I can love and protect him better than any other man. But I also have come to terms with the fact that I'll only have him with me for summer vacations and holiday breaks when he can be away from school. How do you feel about becoming a mother during those visits?"

Her face beamed. "I can't wait. You know, if not for him, I would have given you the boot that first day. You annoyed the hell out of me at first, you know."

He shook his head. "Put a ring on her hand and suddenly the truth comes out." Good thing he had Derek with him.

"You were my guest, so I had to be polite and bite my tongue back then, even when you accused me of terrible things like being a charlatan. Derek saved your bacon and forced me to find something likeable in you—for his sake if nothing else."

"I see. So you fell for my wingman first then."

"Most definitely. And returning to your question, I'll be the best stepmom I can be to him. But are you saying you're okay with living with me in Kentucky at least part of the year?"

"Oh, did I forget that part?" He lost a bit of his mind whenever he was with her. "Of course I am. You might enjoy visiting Minnesota occasionally—if nothing else for a snow fix—but I can't picture you thriving anywhere but in that house you love so much."

"You love it, too, right? I don't want you giving up everything for me. We could probably develop a schedule and move back and forth between our two places."

He shook his head. "I like setting down roots and don't want us to be apart from one another too much. I can start a new architecture firm anywhere. I already have some potential clients and referrals with that preservation project in Nelson County."

"What happens to your firm here?"

"Yesterday, driving over to get Derek, I talked with the senior architect who tentatively agreed to put in an offer to purchase the firm. I'll stay on as an off-site consultant when needed, but she's already been running most of the business while I was gone and doing a great job."

"Sounds like you've been fitting a lot of puzzle pieces into place before you proposed."

"If any of them hadn't dovetailed so perfectly, I'd have found a way to make it work. But I'm thrilled there won't be any major repercussions to deal with, as long as Derek will be content with me whisking him off to Kentucky a few times each year and having me for weekend visits up here throughout the long stretches between major school breaks. My focus will be on you and Derek and, if we're blessed with more kids, them, too."

"You're open to having babies?"

"Babies, toddlers, teenagers—I'm up to the challenge with you by my side."

She gently batted his nose. "Stop it. You're a wonderful dad, and I hope we have at least four more."

"Only four?"

"Well, my house might be large, but there is a limit to the number of bedrooms. I do think I might have to move into Mrs. Foster's old room so we can have Derek in the next room. Somehow I fear having him in the attic above us might cramp our style."

He kissed her. "What about your guests?"

"I can set a specific schedule for when the house will have guests, but as we fill the bedrooms with kids, I fear my days as an innkeeper might be limited."

What was she saying? "You'd give up what you love doing most of all?"

"I love taking care of others. I never had anyone of my own to do that for, but I also find I enjoy writing cookbooks. And I could host special dinners for small and large groups that wouldn't involve overnight stays whenever I need to get my fix for cooking and serving others. But I intend to block out most of the calendar for us and our family. In summertime, I'll be busy teaching Derek all about gardening, and perhaps we can sign him up for horseback riding lessons, if you're okay with that."

"He certainly seems interested in it. They wear helmets, don't they?"

"I think those equestrian hats are actually helmets and not just for looks."

"Good. Then we'll see if we can find a stable where he can take lessons in the summertime and on breaks."

"And before any more little ones come along, I'd like to go on a few adventures with you, too."

"How do you feel about a road trip—mostly by bicycle?"

"As long as you're there, I'm game. Go easy on me at first and give me until the summer to get into shape for anything too long, although my garden will keep me tied down from late July to October, so we'd better plan on early November for that. I can't remember the last time I've been on a bike."

"It'll come right back to you. Trust me." The road ahead of them might have a few bumps they hadn't considered, but nothing the two of them couldn't handle. "So how long will you need to plan the wedding?"

Epilogue

"Quit your sniveling, woman. Ain't this what you wanted all along?"

Amelia dabbed at her eyes, even though there was no real moisture to wipe away. "I always cry at weddings. Isn't Tillie the most beautiful bride you've ever seen? And Gregory—what a dashing groom."

They watched from their perch on the top of the Victorian-style privy turned storage shed as Tillie and Gregory moved among their guests on the front lawn with a tuxedoed Derek in their wake. When they arrived at Margaret's side, Amelia wondered what Gregory said to make her daughter cry. Suddenly, Margaret smiled and hugged him. *That cold Yankee she married hadn't bothered to come to his own son's wedding, but at least my Margaret was here.* Seeing her at the house again did Amelia's tired old heart a world of good.

"Let's move closer. My hearing isn't what it used to be," Amelia said.

"Neither of us are what we used to be."

She slapped his arm before floating down to lean on the picket fence surrounding Tillie's herb beds, as she listened in.

"I can't thank you both enough for bringing me down here in February and helping me see what I'd been blind to for so long."

Tillie remembered that weekend vividly. Margaret had been her most challenging guest yet, but by the time she left, Tillie and Greg had helped her to see Mrs. Foster in a new light.

"You two gave me back something I never imagined I'd have again," Margaret said. "These past few days, I've read every page of the journals Mother wrote during the years I spent growing up in this house. Why didn't I remember most of those stories? Instead, I focused on a few isolated happenings of a spoiled teenager not getting her way. When I ran off and married your father, all I wanted was to start a new life far removed from the boondocks. I wanted instant gratification and threw away any chance of reconciling with my mother because of my stubbornness."

"I'm sure she forgave you, Margaret." Tillie believed the dear woman heard her daughter's regret today as well.

"It didn't help that I was angry at the world for losing my father when only fifteen. Not that I'm making excuses, because that was no reason to reject my mother."

Amelia had been so devastated to lose Elmer she hadn't been able to comfort her own daughter.

"What's important is that you've come back," Tillie said. "I know you've made Mrs. Foster very happy by being with us today."

Indeed, you have, Margaret.

"Tillie, you've kept this such a lovely, warm home. Mother was right to bequeath it to your loving care."

"Thank you. I love this place. It's been my haven for a long time."

"Greg tells me that Caroline Simpson was your great-grandmother. I'd forgotten about her until I read Mother's journals. Actually, I didn't know her personally. I was born the year after she passed, but Mother spoke fondly of her so often."

So Mrs. Foster hadn't only told Tillie about her so she'd learn more about her. "They had a special friendship. I'm glad she had Mrs. Foster, given how tragic her life was. I had a hard time reading about her after finding out she was my great-grandmother and the sacrifice she made, but I feel as if I know her now. Before, I wasn't even aware of her name."

Greg wrapped his arm around her and pulled her closer, but addressed his mother. "Gram's other journals are equally fascinating, but I chose those particular ones so you could see how much you meant to her."

Margaret dabbed at the corners of her eyes, crying the tears Amelia never would be able to again. "I promise to read every single one before I leave." She grinned and addressed Tillie in particular. "Don't worry. I read fast and will be out of your hair before you know it."

"We love having you here. So does Derek. I hope Greg's dad will arrive soon, though. Derek wants to play Civil War with him on the chess board again."

"The blizzard shut down the airport a while, but Albert thinks he'll make it by tonight. He insisted you not postpone taking your vows. We'll watch the video with Derek tonight while you're…" She glanced away. Amelia hadn't seen Margaret at a loss for words before.

To Gregory, she added, "I can't make up for all those lost years, but you can be sure I won't hesitate to come visit y'all anytime you'll have me. Your father and I are thinking about retiring and should have more freedom without a business to run."

Amelia's heart jumped. "Did you hear that, Jesse? Margaret said 'y'all.' I haven't heard her use that expression since she left Kentucky." She dabbed at her eyes.

"I do believe you accomplished more here than joining those two in marriage, Miss Amelia."

"And you can now let go of any guilt you have over ruining Tillie's life."

"Her mother and grandmother bore the brunt of heartache over my dalliance with Caroline. But you, my dear woman, your reaching out to her was what it took for Tillie to find her core strengths and to eventually learn what was important to her."

"Tillie had such a rough start in life, but seeing the woman she's grown into makes me so proud. Caroline's taking her own life at such a young age set the stage for tragedy that would last three more generations. But that cycle has now been broken."

"Indeed, it has. Society can be so cruel to the innocents."

"It's pretty rough on the guilty, too," Jesse added.

Amelia chuckled. "That it can be. I realized who she was during that first visit when she turned up at my doorstep with my wandering tomcat," Amelia said. "I knew I had to try and right a wrong. After all, if I hadn't hooked you and Caroline up—even though I'd only intended for her to be your nurse, not your lover—Tillie wouldn't have had to live in such squalor."

"If Caroline and I hadn't…well, Tillie wouldn't be here at all."

"I never thought about it that way."

"Still, it's sad how one mistake can carry down through generation after generation."

"Nonsense. No baby is ever a mistake. Why, we waited so long to have Margaret, I didn't think motherhood would be in the cards for me. And she was well into her thirties when Gregory came along, too."

"All the same, you know how bad I felt when things got out of hand. I had no business taking advantage of a young thing like Caroline."

"Takes two to tango. She loved you in her own way—at least loved the adventure of it all. That girl was always too much of a thrill seeker."

"Not unlike her dearest friend."

Amelia laughed again. "What's the point in living if you don't have some adventures to reflect on?" She glanced back at the two. "Doesn't appear they'll ever figure it out, though. Should I have spelled it out in my journals that the man Caroline slept with was you?"

Jesse shook his head. "Nobody's business. Wouldn't make no difference in their lives one way or 'nother. What would Tillie do with the claim of being the great-granddaughter of Jesse James when she couldn't tell anyone for fear of being called a liar or a lunatic like her grandmother and mother?"

"You have a point. I just wanted to protect Caroline's memory and her daughter and granddaughter when I wrote those journal pages. Not that I knew who had adopted the baby while I was off to war. You truly left your most precious treasure in that house. Little did I know those words spoken to the wrong person would almost drive a wedge between Tillie and Gregory." At least Peterson's trial was over. Tillie had testified, and with the video footage from the basement, he'd been found guilty on all charges, including attempted murder. He wouldn't see the light of day for a long while, if ever.

Amelia had made her worst error in judgment the night Caroline gave birth when she went home to her first husband spouting her romantic nonsense about Jesse James leaving behind his greatest treasure at Dr. Foster's house. If only she'd kept her mouth shut, Mark Peterson wouldn't have broken into the house and tried to kill Tillie. She'd been right to send Mercer packing when he'd taken up with another woman while she was working long hours with Dr. Foster.

She sighed. Mercer was water under the bridge. And she'd spent more than twenty years married to Elmer Foster. She couldn't wait to see him again now that her work on Earth was done.

Glancing wistfully at the beautiful pair, she said, "I hope they remember to take time to explore new places and never let this house entomb them the way it did me in my later years."

"Don't have to convince me none. Had more than my share of adventures while here on Earth."

A strange female voice interrupted them from above. "But those days are over for you, Jesse Woodson James."

Amelia and Jesse turned their faces upward simultaneously and saw Zee Mimms James swinging her legs while sitting on a branch high above them.

"Zee! You're talkin' to me again!" he said.

"I had a long talk with Caroline, and I forgive you. Figure you can't get in any more trouble now anyway." She reached out her hand. "Let's go home, old man."

Jesse revealed a spark of excitement Amelia hadn't seen in his eyes in forever. "If you'll excuse me, Miss Amelia, now that we've finished this mission, I'm ready to move on to the next phase."

She waved him away. "Go on, you old coot. I won't be far behind. But I want to relish the moment of this special day a little while before I say my goodbyes to them."

"You'll still be able to visit them now and again."

"I know, and this is what I've been hoping for since Tillie came into my life."

"I'll see you on the other side." Jesse pecked her on the cheek before drifting toward Zee. Hand in hand, the two floated into the light.

"Just one more thing before I head up there," Amelia said out loud, in case St. Peter was about the close the gate on her yet again.

*   *   *

"Daddy, Daddy!" Derek came rushing up to the three of them. "Did you see him?"

"See who?"

"That bad man that was in the basement." She and Greg exchanged a knowing glance, but didn't enlighten his mother. "Where'd you see him?"

Derek pointed toward the picket fence near the privy. "Only he didn't look mean today. He squeezed his eye shut at me like this." Derek took his fingers to close one of his eyes in a wink. "And he smiled at me, too. He was with that lady in the rocking chair."

Tillie blinked away her tears. She'd expected Mrs. Foster to be here today, but having validation warmed her heart.

Greg clasped Tillie's hand at the same moment a gust of wind whipped her angel-cut veil into the air. She held it in place to keep the satin trim from slapping her new mother-in-law in the eyes.

"I'm so sorry, Margaret!"

"Oh, nothing to apologize for! It's springtime in Kentucky, after all." Greg's mother glanced around the yard. "I'd forgotten how beautiful the dogwoods are in bloom here."

Tillie couldn't be more pleased with the way the yard had provided the perfect scenery for their special day. Daffodils and tulips abounded in the yard and surrounded her herb beds. A piece of paper fluttered in the breeze. *Oh dear.* The wind must have blown a piece of trash in. Hoping none of their guests would notice before she could snatch it up, Tillie excused herself and walked over to the fence.

What on earth?

The card was the same one she'd seen on the flowers Greg had left at the cemetery in November—more than five months ago. How had it made its way all that distance to her place? The faded handwriting was familiar, but new words had been added. She smiled.

"Everything all right, sweetheart?"

Greg placed his hand at the small of her back. The possessive gesture always set her body to tingling from head to toe. "More than all right." She handed him the card.

"How'd that get here?"

"I'd say Mrs. Foster wants us to know she's here with us. The spell she cast on that ornament all those years ago came true."

Fate—in the shape of a holly-leafed salt-dough tree ornament—brought them together for this moment.

Silently reading the front of the card, he clenched his jaw. Earlier, tears had welled in his eyes when they exchanged their vows, and she thought he might shed a few more now. Tillie wrapped her arms around him.

"Nothing to forgive." The words had been scrawled below Greg's apology on the card.

"*Now* do you believe she never stopped loving you?"

He smiled. "I've known that for a while, but didn't want to admit I was wrong."

She shook her head with a grin. "Men!"

As he took her hand to lead her back to the reception, he glanced up. "Gram, if you don't mind, my bride and I intend to make love with wild abandon in our bedroom tonight and would appreciate a little privacy."

Tillie laughed. "Do you think she'll listen to you?"

He nodded. "Somehow, I think this card is her way of saying she's ready to move on to whatever adventures await her up in Heaven."

Tillie thought about that and nodded her agreement. She followed his gaze as well. "Thanks, Mrs. Foster, for all you've done for us!"

She couldn't wait to find out what Greg had in mind for later tonight. While Beckie had outdone herself with the reception, Tillie suddenly wanted everyone to leave. "We might have to go up in the attic to keep Derek and your mother from overhearing us if they venture into the dining room tonight."

"I think we'll fit on a twin bed for part of the night at least. Of course, we can push them together, but that would give us too much space between us."

Tillie giggled. They'd proven that they fit perfectly sharing half of her double-sized bed. "No doubt we will." He was quite adventurous in the bedroom, and she never knew what to expect. "If we do stay in our room, let's try not to damage any spindles on the pencil bed ourselves." They'd had several discussions about who had broken that spindle, but Tillie had a better idea about how it could have happened after trying some of the things Greg had introduced to their lovemaking over the months.

He stopped and turned her toward him. "I can't make any promises, but with family in the house, we may need to be more subdued than we have been while alone." Sobering, he gazed into her eyes. "I love you, Tillie Buchanan, my treasure, more than life itself."

"And I you. I can't wait to see what adventures await us. We have the rest of our lives to…"

He bent down and captured her lips in a kiss at first tender then more passionate. The pit of her stomach knotted in anticipation of what tonight and their journey together would hold.

When they parted, he took her hand, and she glanced up to where she thought her benefactor and mentor might be watching over them.

Mrs. Foster, thank you for bringing him back to me. I'll take it from here.

The End

All preorder/buy links for *Kate's Secret* (Bluegrass Spirits #2) are posted at:

kallypsomasters.com/books/kates-secret

About the Author

Kallypso Masters is a *USA Today* Bestselling Author with half-a-million copies of her books sold in paperbacks and e-books since August 2011. All of her books feature alpha males, strong women, and happy endings because those are her favorite stories to read. After dabbling at writing since high school (a very long time ago!) and hoping to become a Romance writer about as long, she's living the dream and has been since May 2011.

An eighth-generation Kentuckian, Kally has launched the new ***Bluegrass Spirits*** series, supernatural Contemporary Romances set in some of her favorite places in her home state. For behind-the-scenes revelations, to help with research and story questions, or to discuss the books in this series in a spoiler-allowed zone, join Kally's **Bluegrass Spirits (Kallypso Masters Series)** Facebook group.

Kally has been living her own happily ever after 34 years with her hubby, known to her readers as Mr. Ray. They have two adult children, a rescued dog, and a rescued cat. And, as her Facebook friends and followers know, Kally lives for visits from her adorable grandson, Erik, who was the model for the character Derek in *Jesse's Hideout* (Bluegrass Spirits #1).

Kally is also the author of the *USA Today* Bestselling ***Rescue Me Saga*** series featuring emotional, realistic erotic Romance novels with characters finding alternative methods for handling and healing from past traumas and PTSD. She also has published two Rescue Me Saga spinoff books—*Western Dreams* (Rescue Me Saga Extras #1) and *Roar*, a standalone with familiar secondary characters from the main series. (*Roar* will serve as the bridge to a future Romantic Suspense trilogy with Patrick, Grant, and Gunnar.) She has two additional Facebook discussion groups for those 18 and older who want to discuss these books. To join her secret **Rescue Me Saga Discussion Group**, send a friend request to Charlotte Oliver along with a private message asking to be added to the group. There is also a closed Facebook group for *Roar* you can join directly called the **ROAR Discussion Group**.

Kally enjoys meeting readers and is on a mission to meet with at least one reader for a meal or event in all 50 states. This year, she'll mark off her 30th state since 2012 when she attends Oregon's Passion in Portland on September 23, 2017. For additional signing events, check out the Appearances page on her web site to see if she'll be near you!

And for timely updates, sneak peeks at unedited excerpts, and much more, sign up for her e-mails (kallypsomasters.com/newsletter) and/or her text alerts (used ONLY for new releases of e-books or print books).

To contact or engage with Kally, go to:
Facebook (where almost all of her posts are public),
Facebook Author page,
Twitter (@kallypsomasters),
InstaGram (instagram.com/kallypsomasters)
Kally's Web site (KallypsoMasters.com).

And feel free to e-mail Kally at kallypsomasters@gmail.com, or write to her at
Kallypso Masters, PO Box 1183, Richmond, KY 40476-1183

Recipes for Dishes Mentioned in *Jesse's Hideout*

Cherry Bounce

1 lb. tart pie cherries (Morello, if possible), fresh

1 cup Sugar (more, as needed)

5 cups Bourbon whiskey

(Can increase recipe as needed)

If using fresh fruit, wash and pit the cherries, cut them in half, and put in a large bowl. Using a potato masher, gently mash cherries to extract as much juice as possible. Using a wooden spoon, strain juice through a large, fine-mesh strainer.

In a lidded, one-gallon, sterilized glass jar, layer the cherries and the sugar in the jar and leave to sit for about an hour. Pour bourbon over fruit and sugar, put the lid on the jar, and shake occasionally to help dissolve the sugar. If some cherries float in the beginning, don't worry. They will sink to the bottom over time.

When the sugar is dissolved, leave the jar in a cool dark place for at least four months to infuse. When ready to use, you can simply pour out what you need of the liquor, or you can strain out the cherries and decant the bounce into decorative bottles. The cherries are edible. You can eat them, use them to garnish a cocktail, or spoon some bounce and cherries over ice cream or pound cake for dessert. Or serve at room temperature in small cordial or wine glasses. Store at a moderate, even temperature. Can also be stored in the refrigerator.

NOTE: There are many variations on how you can make this, so you might want to Google it. Some include different liquors (brandy, rye, vodka), others different fruits. It was a favorite of George Washington's (so much that he carried it in a canteen on a trip he made in 1874). I first learned about it from an outdoor theatre production in Danville about the life of Ephraim McDowell, who also enjoyed his cherry bounce.

Jalapeno Jelly

1 gallon of sliced jalapeno peppers (a plastic container will be easier to handle)

5 lbs granulated sugar

cream cheese (for serving later)

Strain jalapeno peppers to remove liquid. Return peppers to jar in layers of 2-3 inches of peppers followed by 2-3 cups of sugar. Repeat until you've run out of peppers or room. If you have peppers left, put the lid on and shake the contents. You can even press the peppers down into the jar if necessary.

Store in the refrigerator. Once a day for the first ten days, shake the jar for a minute or so. You might continue to do this once a week beyond that, while you're in the fridge.

To serve, spread cream cheese on top of a cracker and then add the desired number of jellied peppers.

NOTE: This is a recipe I learned from Mary 4. She and our mom love it. But if you want to lower the flame factor, you might remove the seeds first!

Banana Croquettes (Original)

Bananas

Mayonnaise, thinned with water or milk

Spanish peanuts, crushed

Slice bananas in one- to two-inch long pieces. Dip in thinned mayonnaise. Then roll bananas in crushed peanuts.

Banana Croquettes (Peanut-Butter Version)

Bananas

Peanut butter, smooth or crunchy

Few tablespoons of water, to thin out peanut butter

Spanish peanuts, crushed

Mix peanut butter and water together until it is still thick, but will stick to the banana. Slice bananas in two-inch long pieces. Dip in peanut butter mixture. Then roll bananas in crushed peanuts.

NOTE: These are a family favorite at reunions and special dinners. My mom said she'd never had one until my dad's mother served them.

Cranberry-Nut Relish

6-ounce box black cherry gelatin

2 cups boiling water

1 cup cold water

1/2 to 1 cup sugar, to taste

1 bag of fresh cranberries

2 apples, with peeling

2 oranges, with rind

Small can Mandarin oranges

1 cup chopped walnuts or pecans

Combine sugar and dry gelatin in a bowl. Add boiling water and stir until sugar and gelatin dissolve. Add cold water. (Note that it's half the amount you normally would use in making gelatin.)

In food processor, chop cranberries, apples, and oranges together. Add fruit and nuts to gelatin. Place in desired mold or bowl and refrigerate. It will set up like gelatin. Keep chilled until ready to serve.

Hints: I sometimes use other dark gelatins, including black raspberry, cranberry, or raspberry. You don't have to exact in measuring the fruit and nuts. The more the merrier.

NOTE: This is Mary 2's contribution to every Thanksgiving and Christmas dinner.

Orange-Cranberry-Walnut Bread

2 cups all-purpose flour

1 cup granulated sugar

1-1/2 teaspoons baking powder

1 teaspoon salt

1/2 teaspoon baking soda

3/4 cup orange juice

1 tablespoon grated orange peel

2 tablespoons butter

1 egg, well beaten

1 1/2 cups fresh cranberries, coarsely chopped

1/2 cup chopped English walnuts or pecans

Preheat oven to 350 degrees Fahrenheit. (Adjust, as necessary, for altitudes.) Spray a 9 x 5-inch loaf pan with cooking spray.

Mix together flour, sugar, baking powder, salt, and baking soda in a medium mixing bowl. Stir in orange juice, orange peel, butter, and egg. Mix until well blended. Stir in cranberries and nuts. Spread evenly in loaf pan.

Bake for 55 minutes or until a toothpick inserted in the center comes out clean. Cool on a rack for 15 minutes. Remove from pan. Serve warm, OR cool, wrap, and store overnight. Makes 1 loaf (approximately 16 slices).

Hashbrown Casserole

1 package frozen hash browns, defrosted

2 cups sour cream

1 small onion, chopped

1 large package Velveeta Cheese, grated

1 stick butter, melted

1 cup crumbled Ritz crackers

Preheat oven to 350 degrees.

Mix first five ingredients together in a large bowl. Spray a 13x9x2-inch baking dish. Pour mixture into baking dish. Top with crumbled Ritz crackers.

Bake for 45 to 60 minutes until cheese is melted and top is golden brown.

NOTE: I first tried this at my church's First-Sunday potluck breakfast. Love it!

Sausage-Egg Breakfast Casserole

8 eggs, beaten

1 can mushroom soup

6 slices bread, broken

3/4 teaspoon dry mustard

1 pound sausage, browned

1 cup cheese, shredded

2 cups milk

Preheat oven to 350 degrees.

Break bread in greased 9x13-inch dish. Beat eggs, then beat in milk, mushroom soup, and dry mustard. Place browned sausage over breadcrumbs. Spread cheese over top of sausage. Pour egg mixture over all. Press down with fork to make sure everything is moist.

Bake for 45 to 55 minutes. Cover with foil if it begins to brown before baking time is complete. I usually make mine the night before, refrigerate it, then bake it the next morning. If you do that, allow extra baking time.

NOTE: Another dish from my church's First-Sunday potluck breakfast.

Kentucky Burgoo

3 tablespoons vegetable oil

3-4 pounds pork shoulder or country ribs, cut into large pieces (3-4 inches wide)*

2-3 pounds chuck roast, stew meat, or other inexpensive cut of beef, cut into large pieces (3-4 inches wide)*

3-5 chicken legs or thighs (bone-in)*

1 green bell pepper, chopped

1 large yellow onion, chopped

2 carrots, chopped

2 celery ribs, chopped

5 garlic cloves, chopped

1 quart chicken stock or broth

1 quart beef stock or broth

1 28-ounce can of crushed tomatoes

2 large potatoes (red, russet, etc.), peeled (unless new potatoes) and cut into bite-sized chunks

About 16 ounces golden kernel corn (frozen or canned)

About 14 ounces of lima beans (frozen or fresh)

Salt and black or white pepper (to taste—you may not want to use as much salt as is called for below)

4-8 tablespoons Worcestershire sauce

Tabasco, Louisiana, or other hot sauce (on the side)

* Burgoo can also be made with wild game—venison, squirrel, rabbit, pheasant. Any three or more meats with differing textures will do! This is a classic Derby Day tradition. It's a clean-out-the-fridge/pantry stew, so have fun with it!

Salt the meat on all sides. Heat vegetable oil in a soup stockpot (at least 8-quart size) to medium-high heat. When simmering, work in batches to brown the meats. Don't overcrowd the meats in the pot or they won't brown. Sear one side then turn each piece over to sear the other. Remove browned pieces to a bowl and continue until all meat is browned.

Add the onions, carrots, celery, and green pepper to the pot and brown them. (You might need to add a little more oil first.) After a few minutes of sautéing, sprinkle salt over the vegetables. Add garlic and sauté another 30 seconds.

Return the meats to the pot, then add both broths/stocks and tomatoes and stir to combine. Bring to a simmer, cover, reduce the heat, and continue to simmer gently for 2 hours.

Uncover and remove the meat pieces. Let cool. Strip the meat off any bones and discard chicken skin and other fatty parts, if you'd like. Pull the larger pieces of meat into smaller, more manageable pieces. Return meat pieces to the pot and bring up to a strong simmer.

Add bite-sized chunks of potatoes to the stew and cook until done, about 45 minutes.

Add Worcestershire sauce, mix well, and taste to see if additional salt or black/white pepper is needed. You may also add more Worcestershire sauce, if desired.

Add corn and lima beans. Mix well and cook for another 10 minutes, or longer if you'd like.

Serve with crusty bread or cornbread. Have a bottle of hot sauce on the side for those who prefer a spicier burgoo.

Serves 12-16

Source: Adapted from a recipe at
www.simplyrecipes.com/recipes/kentucky_burgoo

Brown Hotel's Legendary Kentucky Hot Brown

1-1/2 tablespoons salted butter

1-1/2 tablespoons all-purpose flour

1-1/2 cups heavy whipping cream

1/4 cup Pecorino Romano cheese, plus extra for garnish

pinch of ground nutmeg

salt and pepper, to taste

14 ounces thick-sliced roasted turkey breast, warm or at room temperature

4 slices of Texas toast, all crusts trimmed and two slices cut into triangles/points

4 slices of bacon

2 Roma tomatoes, sliced in half

paprika

parsley

In a two-quart saucepan, melt butter and slowly whisk in flour until combined to form a thick paste or roux. Continue to cook roux for 2 minutes over medium-low heat, stirring frequently.

Whisk heavy cream into the roux and cook over medium heat until the cream begins to simmer, about 2-3 minutes.

Remove sauce from heat and slowly whisk in Pecorino-Romano cheese until the Mornay sauce is smooth.

Add nutmeg, plus salt and pepper to taste.

For each of the two Hot Browns, place one whole slice of toast in an oven safe dish cover with 7 ounces turkey. Add two halves of Roma tomatoes (or wedges of Beefsteak tomatoes, per video below) to each of the two remaining toast points. Set them in the dishes on either end of the base of turkey and toast. (Can warm in oven if turkey is cold.)

Pour half of the sauce over each dish, completely covering the turkey and toast. Sprinkle with additional cheese.

Place dishes together or one at a time under a broiler until cheese begins to brown and bubble.

Remove and cross two pieces of crispy bacon on top. Sprinkle with paprika and parsley and serve immediately.

Serves 2 open-faced sandwiches

Source: www.brownhotel.com/dining-hot-brown (Currently, there is a video on this site showing how the restaurant makes the legendary favorite.)

Mr. Ray's Bread Stuffing

Amounts are approximate, because he has no written recipe!

3-4 loaves of white bread (inexpensive is fine)

one package of celery (with lots of leafy tops), diced

1-2 large onions, diced

5-6 sprigs of fresh sage, its leaves broken into small pieces

Water (to be sprinkled in moderation)

Dash of Italian spice seasoning or thyme and rosemary, optional

Butter, optional

Lay the bread out in single layers overnight, flipping it halfway through the drying process so both sides dry out. To speed it up, you can put it in a low-heat oven to dry it out. This will keep the dressing from being too wet.

In a huge container (sometimes Mr. Ray uses large aluminum roasting pans to mix his), break up the bread into pieces about one-inch in size. You don't have to be meticulous. Mix in the celery, onion, sage and other seasonings you wish to include.

Add water in small amounts, continuing to mix it all together. You want it to get moist from the turkey drippings inside the bird, not from the water, but you need to sprinkle some on beforehand. I asked Mr. Ray for more exact instructions, but he just goes by look and feel now.

His mother put butter in hers, but he rarely does. It will be flavored by the herbs and seasonings and the fat from the turkey.

Stuff as much as you can cram into the bird—including the neck end. If you have leftover, put it in a covered casserole to pop in the oven later. Cover that with drippings from the roasted turkey pan and bake it until hot. Everyone will want the stuffing from the bird first, but when that's gone, this will be a good backup.

German Coleslaw

1 bag of shredded cabbage (or shred your own)

Carrots, onions, and green peppers (optional)

Oil (olive oil is best, or use safflower)

Tarragon vinegar

Sugar

Put shredded cabbage into a large bowl. Add oil, vinegar, and sugar to taste. Let sit for at least an hour. Toss the ingredients before serving.

NOTE: This is my mom's recipe, inspired by one her German grandmother made.

Potato Salad

(amounts are approximate—adjust them to your liking)

5 pounds red potatoes

5-6 hard-boiled eggs, shelled and cut

1/2 cup celery, chopped

1/4 cup onions, diced

1 tablespoon dill (fresh or dried)

1/2 tablespoon celery seeds OR 1/4 cup Henri's Tas-Tee Dressing

1 tablespoon dried tarragon leaves, crushed

1 cup sweet pickle relish (or more, if needed)

Mayonnaise, just enough to coat potatoes lightly

Salt and white pepper, to taste

Boil potatoes whole, with peels on, until cooked through. Boil eggs. Cool, then peel. Using a large mixing bowl, cut potatoes into one-inch pieces. Add onions, celery, and dill, celery seeds (or Henri's), and tarragon. Add about 2 tablespoons mayonnaise/Miracle Whip, then sweet relish. Keep adding more of each until salad reaches the consistency you want. Add salt and pepper, to taste.

Chill and serve.

NOTES: Mom made it with Henri's Tas-tee dressing, but when I couldn't find that, I use celery seeds and herbs. I also don't like mayonnaise, so I use it very sparingly. You might want to use more.

Rosemary-Lemon Chicken

3-4 chicken breasts, boneless (skin optional)

2 teaspoons minced garlic

4 tablespoons fresh lemon juice

1 Lemon, quartered (can use the one you juiced)

1 teaspoons fresh rosemary leaves, chopped

1/2 cup low-fat chicken broth

3 tablespoons extra virgin olive oil

Cooking spray

Rosemary sprigs, for garnish

Lemon slices, for garnish

In a gallon-sized storage bag, add chicken, lemon juice, rosemary, and garlic. Zip and toss well. Place in refrigerator for about 30 minutes to marinade. (Don't do much longer or the poultry will dry out.)

Preheat oven to 400 degrees Fahrenheit (adjusting as necessary for altitudes) and lightly spray a baking sheet or large casserole dish.

Heat to medium-high a skillet with olive oil. Remove chicken breasts from marinade bag. Place the lemons, seasoning, and lemon juice in the sprayed baking dish. Add chicken broth.

Sear chicken in skillet two minutes on each side. Transfer chicken to baking dish.

Bake 20-30 minutes (20 for smaller breasts), basting chicken with baking pan juices every`5-10 minutes.

Garnish with fresh rosemary and lemon slices, if desired, and serve hot.

Amelia Foster's Oatmeal-Raisin Cookies

2 cups quick-cooking rolled oats (not instant)

1-1/2 cups all-purpose flour

1 cup raisins

1 cup coarsely ground almonds

1-1/2 teaspoons Chinese five-spice powder

1 teaspoon baking powder

1 teaspoon ground cinnamon

1/2 teaspoon salt

1 cup unsalted butter

1 cup granulated sugar

1 cup brown sugar, packed

2 large eggs

2-1/2 teaspoons real vanilla extract

Preheat oven to 350 degrees Fahrenheit.

In a large bowl, mix together the oats, flour, raisins, ground almonds, Chinese five-spice powder, cinnamon, baking powder, and salt.

In another bowl, using an electric mixer, cream the butter and both sugars until light and smooth. Add eggs and vanilla to the butter mixture and beat well.

Add flour mixture to the butter mixture and beat until blended.

Drop by mounded tablespoonsful onto lightly greased cookie sheets, leaving about 1 1/2" gap between each mound of batter.

Bake at 350 degrees for 12-15 minutes or until done to your liking. Cool on wire racks.

Makes about 3 dozen cookies.

Kentucky Bourbon Fruitcake

Yield: three loaf-sized cakes

4 cups sifted all-purpose flour

1 teaspoon baking powder

1 tablespoon ground nutmeg

1 cup (2 sticks) unsalted butter, softened

2 cups granulated sugar

6 large whole eggs

1/2 cup bourbon (for the cake batter)

4 cups pecan pieces, soaked in bourbon overnight

8 ounces Craisins (soaked in bourbon overnight; can substitute raisins)

1 pound candied cherries (I use 8 ounces each of the red and green)

8 ounces candied pineapple

1/2 cup orange marmalade (much tastier than citron)

A fifth (or more) of bourbon, for soaking

6 yards of cheesecloth (one package will work for three loaf-sized cakes—cut into three 2-yard strips)

The night before baking the cake (and even several days or a week before is okay), soak Craisins and pecans in bourbon. (A quart jar for the pecans and a pint for the Craisins will be perfect.) Cover and refrigerate until ready for them. They will plump up with the bourbon, so don't overfill the jars.

Position top rack in the lower third of the oven and the lower rack at the very bottom, with enough room between the two to place a shallow pan of water. (The steam will help keep the cake moist while baking.)

Preheat oven to 325 degrees F.

Heavily butter three loaf pans. Set aside.

Sift flour, baking powder, and nutmeg into a medium bowl.

In a separate, large bowl, cream butter and sugar, beating with a mixer until light and fluffy, about 2 minutes. Add the eggs, one at a time, blending completely after each addition.

Drain the bourbon from the raisins and nuts and set aside 1/2 cup of bourbon for the batter. Pour the remaining liquid into a small bowl and add the strips of cheesecloth to soak up the bourbon. Set aside.

Add the flour mixture to the eggs in two additions, alternating with the 1/2 cup bourbon. Stir in pecans, marmalade, Craisins, pineapple, and cherries.

Place a shallow pan filled with water in the center of the lowest rack in the oven.

Transfer the batter to the prepared pans. The cake won't rise much, so fill as high as you like or evenly spread the batter between the three pans.

Bake until a toothpick inserted into the center of the cake comes out clean—about 1-3/4 hours in my oven. Adjust for altitudes. If the top of the cake begins to brown substantially before the cake is done, cover loosely with aluminum foil.

Remove the cake from the oven and let cool 15-30 minutes on a wire rack. Run a knife down the sides of the pans to loosen the cakes. Turn them onto the rack to cool further.

When completely cool, wrap each section in a strip of bourbon-soaked cheesecloth (about two yards per cake). Slowly pour additional bourbon from the bottle over each cake until well soaked. Place cakes into an airtight, leak-free container and store out of direct sunlight in a cool location. (I use large Rubbermaid or Tupperware containers.)

Over the next several days, turn the cakes and add a little more bourbon, if needed. Usually, there's enough on the bottom of the container when you flip them that it takes a while to evaporate all of it. Gravity will work at pulling the bourbon through the cakes, but in the beginning, you might need to add more but you don't want them swimming in bourbon. If much has pooled on the bottom, pour it off and use it to add to the tops of the cakes. Most of the liquid should be soaked into the cakes within about three weeks if you keep flipping the cakes over.

When you don't see any liquid dripping from the bottom of the container any longer, you can quit turning it. Allow a couple more weeks for the cakes to mellow before serving. (They will keep for months, even a year, if you keep them in an airtight container and out of the sun—and don't eat too much.)

NOTE: This is my mom's basic recipe but has been updated over the years when I started making them myself. It was her idea to switch to Craisins and orange marmalade, for instance.

Pumpkin-Chess Pie

1 cup sugar

1 heaping tablespoon flour

1/2 teaspoon cinnamon

1/2 teaspoon nutmeg

1/2 teaspoon ginger

2 tablespoons pumpkin

2 egg yolks

1-1/4 cups cream (can use Half & Half, or mix the two)

Pie crust for one-crust pie (Do NOT use deep-dish pie crust.)

Preheat oven to 350-375 degrees.

Mix dry ingredients together. Then, in a separate bowl, beat the egg yolks and pumpkin by hand. Mix both dry and wet ingredients together. Pour into pie shell.

Bake for 1 hour.

* You can double recipe and make two pies.

NOTE: This recipe came from a cousin of mine in a family-reunion cookbook published more than a decade ago. She called it B's Delicious Pumpkin Pie, but since there was so little pumpkin and it reminded me more of chess, I've always called it this.

Jam Cake

1 cup butter
2 cups sugar
4 eggs
4-1/2 cups flour
1/4 cup cocoa
1 teaspoon cinnamon
1 teaspoon allspice
1 teaspoon cloves
1/2 teaspoon nutmeg
2 cups buttermilk
2 teaspoons baking soda, dissolved in buttermilk
2 cups jam (I prefer blackberry, but you can use your favorite)
1 cup apple butter or applesauce (or half of each)
2 cups raisins (Optional)
1 cup black walnuts (chopped)—but you can substitute favorite nuts

Preheat oven to 350 degrees.

Cream sugar and butter thoroughly. Add eggs and mix well. In a separate bowl, sift together flour, cocoa, and all spices. Add flour mixture alternately with buttermilk (remember to dissolve the baking soda in it first) to creamed mixture. Mix thoroughly. Next fold in jam, apple butter and/or applesauce, raisins (optional), and nuts. Mix well.

Cook in 9x13x2" pan (or four 8-inch cake pans) sprayed with cooking spray. Bake about an hour until a toothpick inserted in center comes out clean. (It may take a longer or shorter time depending on your oven, but when I made this, it took nearly 90 minutes for the center of the cake to be done.)

Remove from oven. You can frost and serve cake in the 9x13x2" pan, but if you used 8-inch cake pans, remove cakes from pan after about 10 minutes. When completely cool, ice with **Never-Fail Caramel Icing**.

NOTE: Also makes four layers, if you use 8-inch cake pans.)

Never-Fail Caramel Icing

1-1/2 cups brown sugar

1/3 cup cream (I use heavy whipping cream)

1/2 cup butter

1-1/2 cups sifted powdered sugar

Combine brown sugar, cream, and butter into heavy saucepan over medium heat. When mixture starts to boil around the edges of the pan, cook two minutes longer. Remove from heat. NOTE: If you over-boil it, the icing will turn hard, crumble, and be too hard to spread.

Add powdered sugar and beat.

Spread on **Jam Cake**.

NOTE: The Jam Cake recipe on the previous page was my Great Aunt Louise's. And this icing recipe came from my Aunt Aline.

Get your Signed Books & Merchandise in the Kally Store!

Want to own merchandise or personalized, signed paperback copies of any or all of Kallypso Masters' books? New *Bluegrass Spirits* series items will be coming soon, but there's already a line of t-shirts and other items connected to the *Rescue Me Saga* series and KallypsoCons. With each order, you'll receive a bag filled with Kally's latest FREE items, including a hand fan, *Jesse's Hideout* lip balm, Bluegrass Spirits & Rescue Me Saga pens, bookmarks, postcard, trading cards, and more. Kally ships internationally. To shop for these items and much more, go to kallypsomasters.com/kally_swag.

Bluegrass Spirits series

Kate's Secret

(Second in the *Bluegrass Spirits* Supernatural Contemporary Romance series)

Grab Your Copy Today!

Kate's Secret

Single mother Kate Michaels wants nothing more than to continue providing a happy, stable life for her daughter, Chelsea. Then, after thirteen years, the return of her college sweetheart tilts Kate's world on its axis. The thought of seeing Travis Cooper again sets her pulse racing—and not only because he reignites the flames that once burned too hot for them. What will happen when he discovers her carefully guarded secret?

A realistic dream involving a recently deceased Army buddy sends Travis on a journey back to Kentucky looking for answers that have gnawed at him since his sweetheart, Katie, sent him packing. The military-precise confrontation he'd planned evaporates as soon as he lays eyes on her. Will he find it in his heart to forgive and understand to give them a second chance at love?

Can the spirits of his friend and her father right some wrongs and help Kate and Travis overcome the past, especially since the one truth that could make everything right is the same one that could destroy everything they hold dear?

Made in the USA
Lexington, KY
02 October 2017